EDITIONS
DU SAMURAI

By Arturo ~~~~~~~~~z

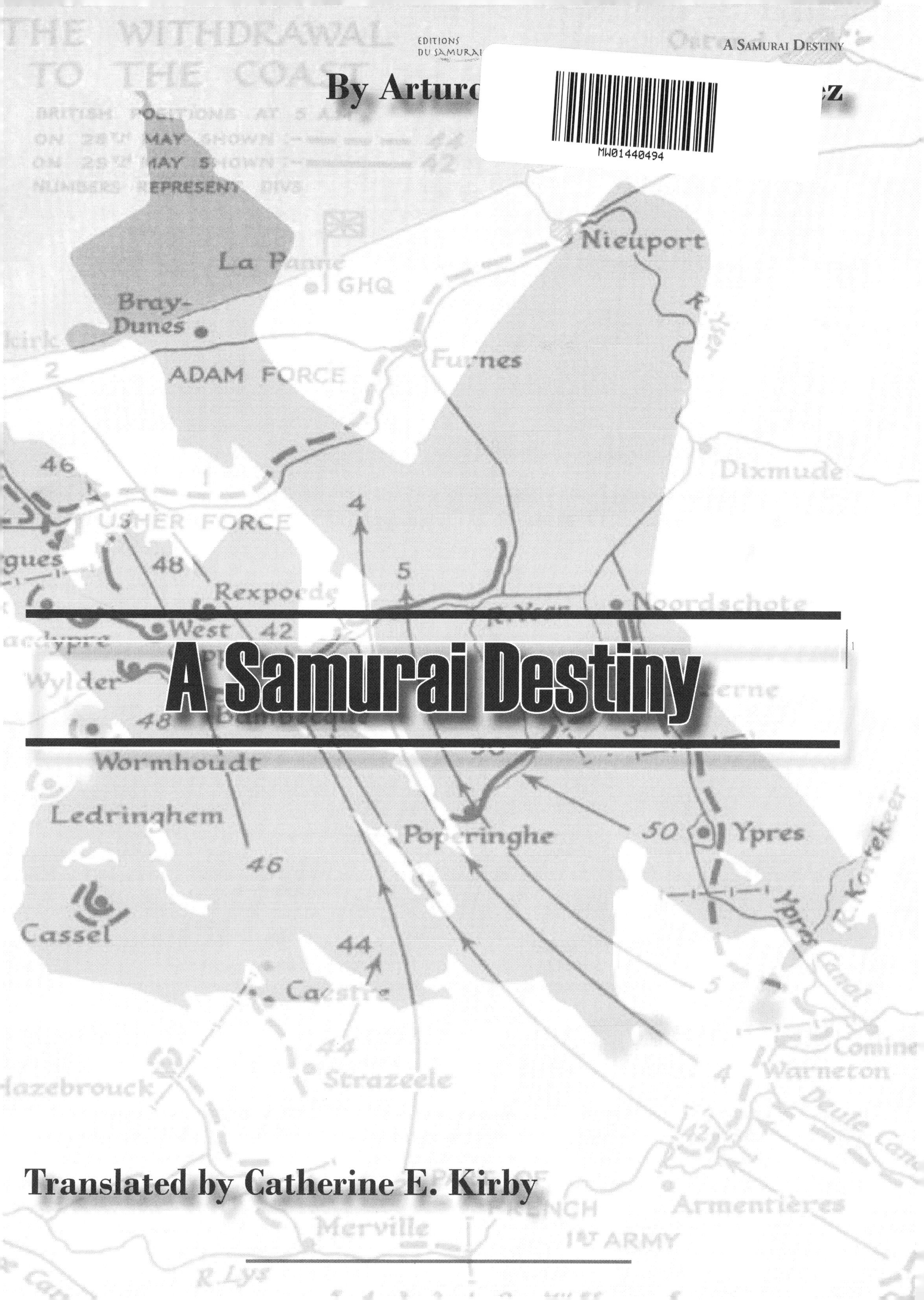

A Samurai Destiny

Translated by Catherine E. Kirby

©2021 First English Edition, Editions Du Samurai
©(2014-2018) First Spanish Edition Arturo Emilio García Méndez - Oublibion
©(2018) Second Edition, Spanish Argentine edition, Editorial Grupo Argentinidad
©(2022) International Spanish Edition, Editions Du Samurai
Editions Du Samurai; Alberto Ghiraldo 1950, 1848 Pcia Buenos Aires, Argentina. editions.du.samurai@gmail.com
Graphics of Editions Du Samurai by ©Carolina Foster
Cover Art, Design and Ilustration by A.E.G.M.
Other images published under CC ©Creative Commons

Author's Image ©Esteban Ezcurra
TRANSLATED FROM SPANISH BY CATHERINE E. KIRBY

All rights reserved, including reproduction of any sort, kind or format or media, analogic as well as digital, in whole or in part in any form, electronic, photocopying, recording or otherwise, without the clear and prior written permission of the author.

This novel is a work of fiction, although it takes place in a rigorously truthful historic context. References to real historic people and localities are used fictitiously. Some of the names belong to real people who have given their consent to appear as such. None of the specific narrated circumstances are real, and any resemblance to actual events is entirely coincidental.
editions.du.samurai@gmail.com
digiterati@protonmail.com

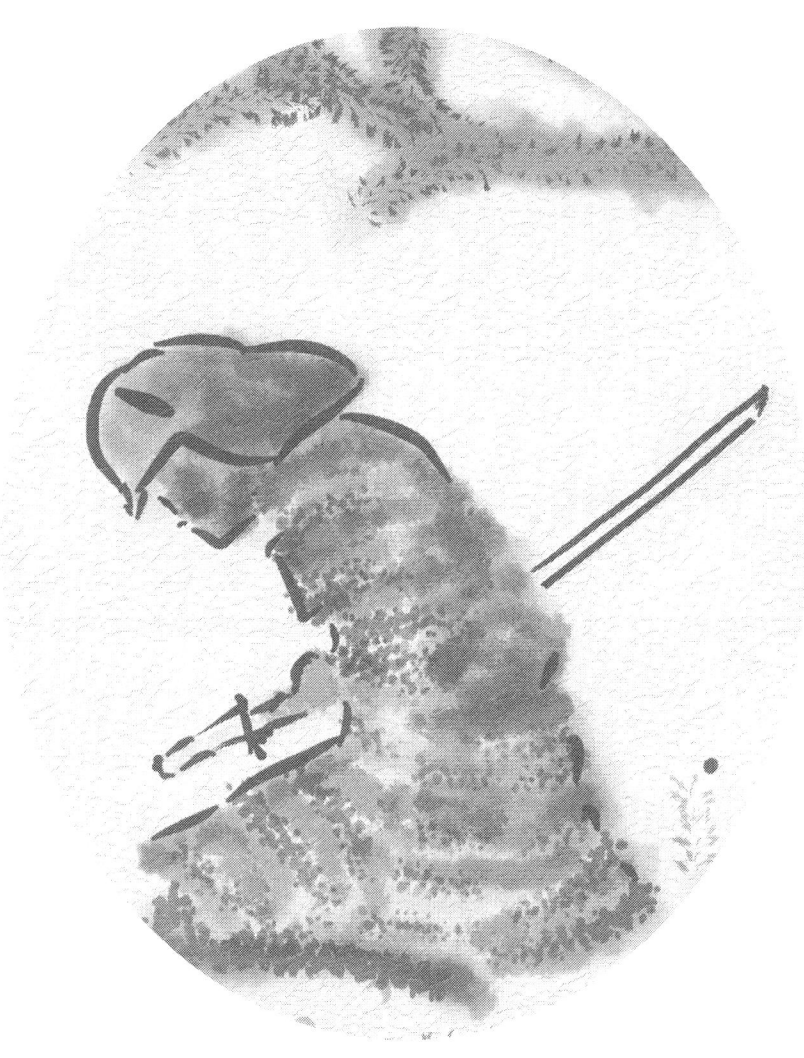
Shadow of Seppuku

ACKNOWLEDGEMENTS

To the Malvinas (Falklands) War veterans, who must never be forgotten. To those who returned alive, and those who could not endure; to those who fell, in the hope that their sacrifice was not in vain.

To my friends Gustavo Moran and his brother Germán Chamorro, to Pablo Macharovsky - I know all three and in a way, they inspired me to write this story.

To Julio Aro, for his humanitarian work.

To my brother Oscar Ledesma, born a poet and whose destiny was to be a warrior.

To Juan José Fumez and his wonderful common sense

To Nelson Unzeta and his silent and brave quest for truth.

To Colonel Lamadrid, whose human greatness honoured the country's uniform - he wore it humbly and with nobility.

To the Argentine veterans who fought in World War II, memories of whom must be recovered: they battled for the values of democracy and freedom, and were unjustly forgotten by their country and to Claudio Meunier and his tireless effort to honor them.

To my father, who taught me that honour exists.

To all my family, my clan and the families that form part of it: the Fosters, Sosas, Tedeschis, Malmiercas, García Méndez.

To my mother, whose encouragement and sincere criticism helped me to this point.

To my cousin Emilio, whose intellectual accuracy is never clouded by his affection.

To my sisters, whose love overcame my defects; and my nephews and nieces, who honour me with their appreciation and friendship.

To my daughter, because she always makes me want to be a better person.

To my old friends who always accompanied me, and those who no longer do, for whatever reason. Although friendships may be interrupted, this doesn't erase all our past together.

To Juan Andrés Videla, whose words of encouragement were always at hand.

To my friend of many years Dra. Alejandra Abalo, whose professional skills has saved me more than once.

To my therapist Lic. Graciela Marzullo, without whose intervention I would never have finished this book.

To the Sandazas clan, because loyalty forms a family; particularly Bernardo Jr. and his wife, Verónica, whose moral and economic suport was key for the first edition; and to his sister Mercedes and her husband Stuart Howser whose support was essential for the English version to come into being.

To Catherine Kirby, whose infinite patience and talent allowed my Samurai to finally speak Shakespeare's language; and who corrected the Spanish version with unflinching detail.

To the British veterans of the South Atlantic War, to those who returned and those who could not endure; to those who fell defending what they believed was just.

To Geoffrey Cardozo, for his humanitarian work.

To Lou Armour, because his experience transcends him.

To Nicholas Lutwyche, Mike Weatherley, Ricky Strange and Andy Smith.

To all Falklanders, but in particulary to Terry Peck and his galantry facing a 10.000-times bigger army; and his son, James, a fine artist.

To peace, justice and democracy, and all those who fight to defend these values.

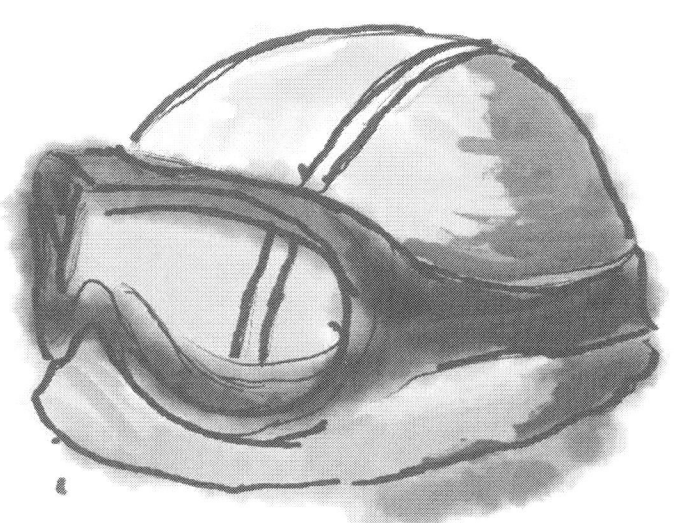

Argentine Helmet

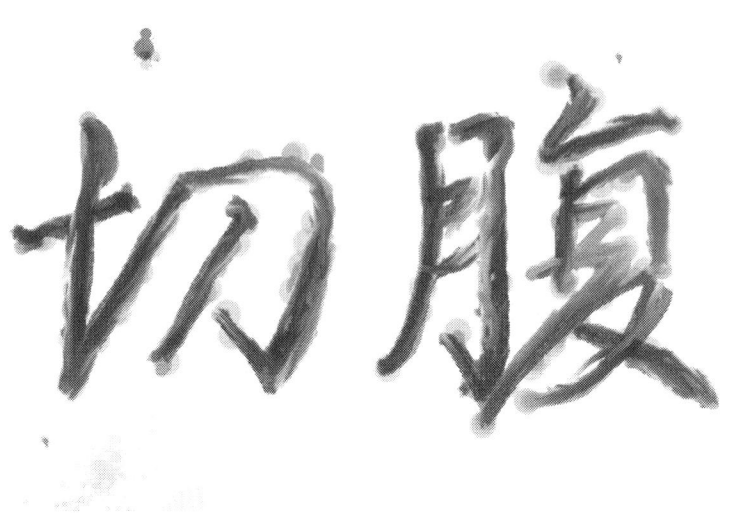

I) SEPPUKU

Seppuku

In Medieval Japan when a Samurai was confronted with dishonour, a ritual suicide was an acceptable end.

They might have been friends, but they only saw each other once, face-to-face, somewhere on those too-famous islands, and each of them was Cain, each Abel.

Juan López y John Ward
Jorge Luis Borges, poem
August 1982

I open my eyes and I don't know where I am.

I open my eyes and I don't know who I am.

I open my eyes, and I don't know what time it is or what day or what month or what year, whether it's night or day.

I blink and see the sky through my tears.

Is it the sky?

Yes, it's the sky, a grey, lead-coloured, overcast sky.

So gloomy, and I see it's rough and uneven, a spectre of different shades of grey. Cold, but gloriously grey.

There's a buzz in my ears. I can't hear anything beyond this consistent, terrible buzz.

I recognize this sound, and I remember it beyond any other sound, like a very loud and sudden peal of a bell in a closed space. At the same time it's like the sound of a low and high tuning fork in my head.

But I'm not in a closed space. And there's no tuning fork in my head.

And although I'm out in the open, suddenly my nose picks up a strong, spicy, undefinable and indescribable smell.

I also remember that smell… Yes. I remember that acrid smell, so hot it almost burns. I think of the summer and the sun burning overhead, above the entire universe around me.

But I feel very cold.

As memories return –distinguished only by my senses- I realize I'm on my back on the ground and I can only see the sky.

How long have I been here, lying on the ground?

Another something I don't know.

Is God still or does He move?

Is He movement or is He stillness?

Or both at once?

He's destruction and salvation, love and hate, He's absolutely insane and sane.

All at the same time.

At the same time!!!!

And my fellow human beings, most of them, talk to Him in the silence, build temples that He doesn't need because He has Himself, all the Universe and all it contains, from cosmic dust to the most formidable celestial body as His only temple.

He doesn't need me, my embrace or my glance - nor my home. He is all embraces, all glances, all homes.

They ask me to be brave because He needs me.

Ridiculous!!!

Absurd!!!

He doesn't need my courage, because He is courage and cowardice all at the same time, in all places.

I've heard those who say they are His messengers, representatives, prophets.

That's ridiculous.

It's what is here and everywhere, in all places, at all times, simultaneously, He doesn't need messengers, or representatives, or symbols or signs.

He doesn't need me because I'm already His.

When you see Him you know it's Him, the truth revealed.

I could try to lie because it doesn't matter, I could say the truth, it doesn't matter either.

I can be fair or not.

Good or not; bad or not; chaste or a libertine, pure or not pure. None of that matters. The judgement, the prize, the punishment – they're all things we've invented, they're lies, schemes created by a few to take advantage of the many.

Chosen people? A dividing up of the Promised Land? Interpreters of the Divine?

For all of that which is all at the same time, why would He choose one people, one person, one land? What is the sense behind an entity like that, the natural owner of all things, giving to some and leaving out others? Why would such a phenomenon have the need to write a book?

Something that has created Itself, That Is and has never been born, That which is the past, the present and the future all at the same time, as well as what is full and empty, the stars and darkness between. That Which Is… Does it need to write a book?

Time.

I can only blink very slowly. One. Two. Three, four times and that cruel sky is still there above me, unmoving, lying in wait.

Am I asleep?

I've had dreams like this. Now and again, yes. You dream you're awake but you can't move anything except your eyes, imprisoned within a body that all it can do is see.

It has happened to me.

But in dreams, although you don't know who you are, you do know, and I don't. I don't remember anything beyond the strange tolling in my head, nothing beyond this penetrating smell that fills my nose.

I try to get up.

That's when an unknown and fierce wave of intense, astounding pain tears my brain apart, invades and possesses my entire being.

Almost at the same time I open my mouth to shout, and my voice disappears and is devoured by that buzzing, that low and high tuning fork tone - it echoes all through my body.

My body.

My body?

At exactly that moment I realize I can't move without feeling ripped apart by an unbearable pain; I can hardly breathe, it's almost impossible.

I pant. I try to force the air through my nose or my mouth so that somehow it can fill my lungs.

It's not that I can't move my body, my arms, my legs or any of my ten fingers, I can't move my head from one side to the other either.

I can only move my eyes.

I look downwards and all I can make out is my chest panting unevenly…

My mouth fills with saliva and I spit upwards as if it were a sprinkler; a delicate and weak reddish spray bathes my face and my eyes.

It's not saliva, it's blood.

I don't know where I am, or who I am. I don't know the time or what day of the week of what month it is. But I know I can't move, I understand in a unique, tragically beautiful way that I am dying, if there were something beautiful in it.

What's happened?

I can't move, I'm lying face up, it's very difficult to breath but I only feel pain when I try to move.

I'm bleeding from my mouth.

I don't know who I am, or where I am, but I know I'm inexorably dying.

I can't move, I don't think I can hear.

But I can feel how the earth is trembling around me, as if an earthquake was bent on damaging me.

§

It's clear that hardly anyone pays attention, we're an unconscious species that takes pleasure in its own ignorance. How else can you explain the thousands of millions of people, all at the same time and everywhere, expecting to see, hear and feel what can't be seen, heard or felt? What human being can hear silence and sound at the same time?

They invoke and give names to that which, seemingly, can't be given a name. They wave books around which they uphold were written by that which doesn't need to write a single line to demonstrate its greatness nor its existence.

Even worse, they say they have been given orders, when it's quite plain when seeing every proof of His existence and power that He doesn't need anyone to fulfil his orders because there isn't anything that eludes that which knows it all. If it needs to do anything, it's done with a single thought!

What is even more serious, terrible and tragic, is that those thousands of millions who say they are His followers have different versions of a same book which they anoint with fearful sacredness, they place their hands on that little mountain of paper and say, "it's His Will".

His Will!!! They claim to interpret in human terms —will, desire, choice- That Which Is completely beyond our understanding.

I ask myself - with no expectation of an answer - do those who give Him a name, make Him write books, have Him give orders or take fearsome and furious attacks of revenge, understand the true essence of what we call reality?

If one thinks even a little, it's obvious how the efforts of so many of my fellow human beings is ridiculous, pathetic and presumptuous. They're convinced that to grind up a forest, dissolve it with chemical products for days and days, to then dry it in the sun and later tarnish the resultant product with ground up stones until it is dust, is a Divine order…

Yes I would laugh. But I can't, because the forest and the stone and all the substances to make paper, the book, the ink and instruments to fix those words to the paper, the writing and the hand that writes, all that has been or will be conceived, are included in that which is here.

It's presumptuous to name the unnameable, define the undefinable, destroy His work to supposedly, celebrate it.

That which is here, which is and isn't at the same time, is also simple and complex.

What we touch and can't touch, what we see and can't see; everything that touches into your senses but also everything that doesn't, everything that surrounds us and appears real and concrete, everything has a something beyond, a unique dimension of its own that pure reason can't explain.

What is there in a grain of sand? On the tip of my tongue? In each atom of the sun?

Universes in each and every one!

The universe has another universe within. Each particle of reality we believe we dominate also has an underside, a reverse, an infinite space that connected to other universes knits the intricate net of existence.

There are very few who understand the true dimension of this fold within itself, of this universe within the universes. Happy is he who understands it because then they will understand the delicate construction of reality, the delicate filigree that undoubtedly is the signature of creation.

I'm not avoiding the truth by saying this, because who can refute me? Who can deny that below the bark of a tree there is much more than that rough surface? In each corner of the universe everything is the same, that which is seen and that which isn't. Even the tiniest particle has a reverse side, a fold, a hidden face, a secret curl.

This cannot be denied except by those who brag about their ignorance. And if this can't be denied with an acceptable degree of certainty… to all appearances, wouldn't this be true?

I think of my fellow human beings and their temples and books and their merciless screams to the sky. I would like to laugh at their scandalous ignorance.

But I can't laugh.

Because it is not enough, for my fellow human beings, to say that the book was written by That Which keeps everything together.

It's not enough to transform pieces of it in the most brutal way —trees, rocks, water— to profit from them, nor to name that which cannot be named.

No.

They even have to fly flags, sing hymns, carry arms and run through fields to burn the harvest, to kill every living being with no respect for age or sex, to destroy houses… block water holes… and all in His name…

I would truly like to laugh…

But I think of my widow my mother my sisters my orphans and their tears stained with my blood because I was part of the other side – we are always part of the other side – so I can't.

Yes, then they will carry my temple to the public park and burn my wrecked body and paint their faces with my ashes in a sign of grief.

And it will all have been for nothing.

Because that which is always there, will unfailingly remain in its place.

§

I could have sworn that I'm completely deaf beyond that persistent noise, but another sound comes into my mind, in a way it's very familiar.

I don't know who I am, nor where I am, but I remember the buzz, the smell, and now this muffled drumming sound, regular and even.

I know, without understanding how, that these are steps, sloshing through a lake, a water edge or maybe a ditch. The sound is too short for my memory to capture or retain it.

I roll my eyes 360 degrees, slowly, trying to see my surroundings.

It's the only movement I can make without the most unbearable, unimaginable pain wracking my body.

Two, three, four times…

Suddenly, before I can turn my eyes again, just when I'm looking away from my feet, the most impressive face I've ever seen or dreamt of comes into view, with a fierce, wolfish expression.

The face is painted grey, white, green and black, and becomes confusing against the sky. I can't see it clearly, but his blue eyes, glinting evilly, are strikingly clear.

"Freeze or die, Argie!" He shouts at me, and I hear him clearly in spite of still hearing that far-off, echoing sound.

A very clear idea suddenly appears in my fevered mind.

I don't know who I am, nor where I am, but I know that this menacing man, dressed like a phantom with a painted face, is wearing a red beret like my father used to wear.

My father!

Like an old relic of a film, for a fraction of a second I see the clear image of a thin man, with reddish hair, light blue eyes and a large smile which barely covers a mouth full of twisted teeth.

If I don't know who I am… How do I know it's my father?

I don't know anything, I'm ignorant about everything, but I know that that red beret and those blue eyes are like my father's.

I'm suddenly aware that this man is talking in another language to the one I'm thinking in. I also know that he's talking like my father used to sometimes, and I understand everything he says.

"Lieutenant Farrington! Here sir! Here! The damn Argie is still breathing!"

I look around and now there's a crowd of identical faces, they all look the same, sombre and fearful.

Am I hallucinating?

I hear more steps. There are more people than I can see gathered around me, in spite of the tremor that now and again shakes the ground and in spite of the buzzing inside my ears; even so, I can hear them arguing while one kicks my legs again and again; another kicks my right side, another steps on my left hand.

If they have wanted to inflict pain, they've failed, because I feel nothing beyond the back and forth movement of my flaccid legs.

I don't feel any pain, just a vague notion that my body is there.

They shout.

They howl.

They insult.

"All of you over there, just stop!" Somebody I can't see is shouting. "It's an order, sirs!"

The noise around me does not stop but they have stopped kicking me.

"Lieutenant Farrington! An enemy down on the ground, sir!" Someone shouts.

"Enough! I gave a direct order! Step back now!!! Now I said!" The voice is strong, forceful, but not a shout. He talks loudly, but he doesn't shout.

"Sarge!" Strongly.

"Sir, yes sir!" Someone answers.

"Put all these gentlemen to work, right away, now!"

"Right, sir!"

Without another word, I hear the steps and voices moving off into the distance. It's clear that this voice is of someone who gives orders.

Orders!

I also used to give orders...

Did I give orders or receive orders?

I can't remember anything beyond my father's red beret, nothing beyond his open smile, his blue eyes.

The man places a knee down on the ground beside my head.

He looks at me. As the others, his face has strange paint on it, he has green eyes and I clearly see that the whites of his eyes are very red.

"Why did you do this?" He asks me, without expecting an answer.

He revises my pockets carefully.

"Medic!!!... Ronnie, over here, hurry up."

"Corporal! Check his pockets" He gives orders. He is firm, he doesn't shout.

He looks into my eyes.

"You're seriously wounded, mate...What you did was stupid, this war is almost over..."

While he talks to me, he reads something he's pulled from around my neck, while the other man checks my pockets.

"Carr..los Evans," he reads. "Evans is a Welsh name!!!"

I try to speak but can't, I have a coughing fit, spitting up blood.

"Don't speak... do you understand me?" I move my head just slightly.

Then I realize that this stranger knows more about me than I do myself.

I still don't know who I am, or where I am, or what day it is, nor the time nor the month; yet this man talks to me in a language which isn't mine and he knows more about me than I do.

"Did they called you Charly at home? That's what I'll call you, old chap." He pauses and talks to someone out of my range. Meanwhile, another man identical to my father carefully revises each of my pockets.

Now, thanks to this man who speaks a language which is not mine, I know my name is Carlos Evans, that at home they called me Charly and that I'm Welsh... No. No! NO! A terrible, tormented inner voice shouts.

I'm not Welsh. Besides my name, I also know now that I'm Argentine.

The man on one of his knees beside me talks to someone I can't see.

"So, Doc? Can we help him?"

I hear but can't see the man who answers.

"No, sir, one lung is collapsed and the other will be soon, his backbone is broken. If we put him on his side he will last 15, 25 minutes and will eventually bleed to death, with no pain... otherwise he will drown from his own blood in 3, 4 minutes..."

"Sarge, help me!"

"Sir... he's an Argie..."

"Do you refuse to obey a direct order?"

"Sir, we have injured men because of his action!"

They argue above me while they pull on my clothes, they place me on my side and air comes into my body again. I pant, I breathe anxiously even if they're my last breaths.

I see my red, hot blood dripping onto the green, damp, cold ground.

"He got what he deserved, Lieutenant Farrington…" says the Sergeant, at my feet.

Now I know much more than just one minute ago.

I know I can't move because my backbone is broken and I will bleed out until I die.

Lieutenant Farrington is still kneeling on the ground beside me. I can see his perfect waterproof laced boots. He places his hand on my shoulder. He talks calmly.

"Sorry old chap, we can't help you… Why did you attack us??? There were 30 of us and you were only 3… It was stupid and brave…"

He says he's sorry and I don't know why –perhaps because I'm dying- I believe him. Another voice interrupts.

"Lieutenant… You should see this, sir!!! This was in his pockets… An old English book… a museum piece, sir!!! Shakespeare's Henry V in Spanish… and a sort of… it looks like a code book… it has a small magnifying glass… It's written in very tiny letters!! But you should see this, sir… It has your name in it…"

Farrington has placed something beneath my ear, so my head isn't lying on the cold ground. I'm dying and some foreign men have killed me and now they are sharing out the little I have in my pockets.

"Let me see!"

In his right hand, leaning on the knee which is very much higher than my face, I can see the covers of the minuscule book with red covers. It suddenly looks very familiar.

He glances through the book, turning the small pages with his fingers –he's taken off his thick gloves- and he uses the magnifying glass to read the details.

Then Farrington shouts. Yes, he shouts.

"A thermal blanket to cover this man, now!!"

The voices around me get rougher, louder. Several of them talk together, with unconcealed fury.

"I've a plastic bag for that scum!" Shouts one.

"Pity he can't dig his own hole!" Shouts another.

"Kelly!!! Put these men to work right now..! Ronnie, here with me, now!!!"

All I can see are the laced boots and even then I can feel the tension in the air. The men obey unwillingly, I don't hear them leaving.

I try to follow everything looking upwards, I try to see the man who has the little book with red covers which is so familiar to me… but all I can actually see is a piece of that grey sky.

"Ronnie, can we help him?"

"What's up Tony? I told you he's done for!! I have people on the ground, all of them wounded, he's the enemy..."

"You should see this, Ronnie, look at this...."

I can see how he stretches out his arm above me, and I can't see who takes it...

"A code book??? It looks very old!!!"

"It's not a code book. They're English abbreviations... and it has a 1933/39 calendar... But look at this page I'm showing you...!"

"Holy shit! Your name is in it!"

"It's not me, it's my father's..."

The man kneels down beside me again and leans over to look straight into my eyes.

"You're Gordon Evans' son?"

They've just covered my body with a thermal blanket and I realize my body still has some life in it; the heat seems to submerge me into a bath full of warm water, it pours through me and takes with it the cold which I no longer noticed.

Gordon Evans' son.

In the same way that just a few seconds ago my body was hit by a spasm of pain, I'm now hit by a certainty.

I know who I am.

I know what I'm doing here.

My mind begins to shoot information as if it were a machine -after being stuck for a while it suddenly comes alive.

-Teniente primero Carlos Antonio Evans... Infantería de montaña, Ejercito Argentino!!

I try to move, I want to talk, speak out, explain. But another unbearable wave of pain shatters in my brain.

The Lieutenant who is placing his hand on my shoulder is an enemy officer.

I'm in the South Atlantic Theatre of Operations, in the Falkland (Malvinas) Islands, on the West Falkland isle (Gran Malvina), some 25 Kms. north of Stanley (Puerto Argentino). I'm a prisoner of war.

I know who I am!

I know where I am!

I try to speak and all I can do is cough and spit up blood.

I'm an Argentine officer wounded in battle, it's June 14th, 1982 and we opened fire on an enemy column around 08:40 hrs.

The man kneeling on the ground beside me is an English officer, a lieutenant, and I'm his prisoner.

"Don't talk, old chap, I know what you want to say... I have your dog tag in my hand. Don't talk."

The medical assistant behind me talks in a friendly, kind voice.

"What's up, Tony?? This man's an enemy fallen on the battlefield."

It's obvious my enemy is also tired. It's also obvious he has no empathy for my luck. That's reasonable, we're enemies.

"He has a deadly wound, even if we can evacuate him he won't make it... I told you, I can do nothing for him... What's wrong, Tony?"

Farrington, the lieutenant, Tony... my enemy, is holding the shabby little book with the red covers. Actually, it's a 1936 diary in which for 12 years my father inscribed his time at war, with very small, tight letters, always written with abundant English abbreviations and which can only be read with the tiny magnifying glass tied to it.

"This is his father's diary, Ron..."

Something in my enemy's voice distracts me from what he's saying.

"Tony, it's okay, you're tired, we've been under fire the last 15 days, we haven't had a decent sleep... Please, don't crack down on the boys... It's another dead Argie..."

I can see the head covered by the red beret silhouetted against the terribly grey sky. I see how he shakes it, gently, vaguely denying.

"You don't understand... I hardly do... I know this man... his father was Sergeant Major Gordon Evans and my father's name is in almost all of these pages because they fought all World War II together, from Dunkirk to Berlin in '45... And in Malaysia in '41, and Tobruk in '43, and so on and so forth... a war hero..."

A few seconds' silence after his words, and then the incessant shooting continues routinely.

I'm trying to understand what I just heard.

In my father's diary, that little shabby book with red leather covers there is only one name which is repeated over and over, and that is his father, my enemy kneeling on the ground by my side.

Lieutenant Anthony John Farrington.

Our fathers fought, back to back, in almost every single World War II battle.

If I could, I'd laugh at this macabre joke played on me by destiny… but I'm finding it harder and harder to breathe…

"Ron, his Dad and mine where among the first SAS members… chests full of medals… an old British Hero…"

"Sorry, Tony, there's nothing I can do. He's on the wrong side of the street, the wrong day…"

I'm lying on the ground, slowly bleeding to death, surrounded by my enemies, and among them I just had to meet up with the son of my father's best friend.

Then I have a thought. All this is bad, but for whom?

The man who is kneeling on the ground by me, the British officer who is my enemy and whose military manoeuvre has killed me, leans on the thermal blanket. He bends down to speak into my forcibly helpless ear.

"I'm sorry, Charly, I would like to fix this but it's impossible… I'll stay with you… I'll manage to get your things to your loved ones… I don't know how yet, but trust me I will."

The man who was my enemy before is now talking to me like my father did, in a low, clear voice. I feel his emotion but I can see, through my almost closed eyes, how his face reflects the enormous effort to control himself, and I'm grateful.

He restrains his feelings, not letting them show –for himself, his men, his friend and for me.

The voice of the medical assistant, who I can't see, also sounds distressed.

"I'm really sorry, Tony…"

Tony slips his hand without any glove underneath the thermal blanket keeping me warm and takes my hand. I know he's done this, although I can't feel it.

I no longer have any arms.

Or legs.

I have no body beyond my eyes. All that is left of me, who I once was, is a pair of eyes that hardly see beyond the boots of this man who until a minute ago was my enemy.

The man who is holding my dead hand and who was my enemy, looks into my eyes. I clearly see his green eyes, the reddened whites of his eyes and an undefinable wetness that make them deeply human. He looks straight at me and smiles, with a smile I'd never seen before.

It's a compassionate, kind smile.

"I'll stay with you… I don't speak Spanish, so sorry…"

I shake my eyes, I'm trying to say that it's OK, that for me, it's fine.

I can clearly feel that he's moved at being able to accompany me right to the end, to death's door.

I think of my father.

And how do I feel?

I don't know.

I close my eyes.

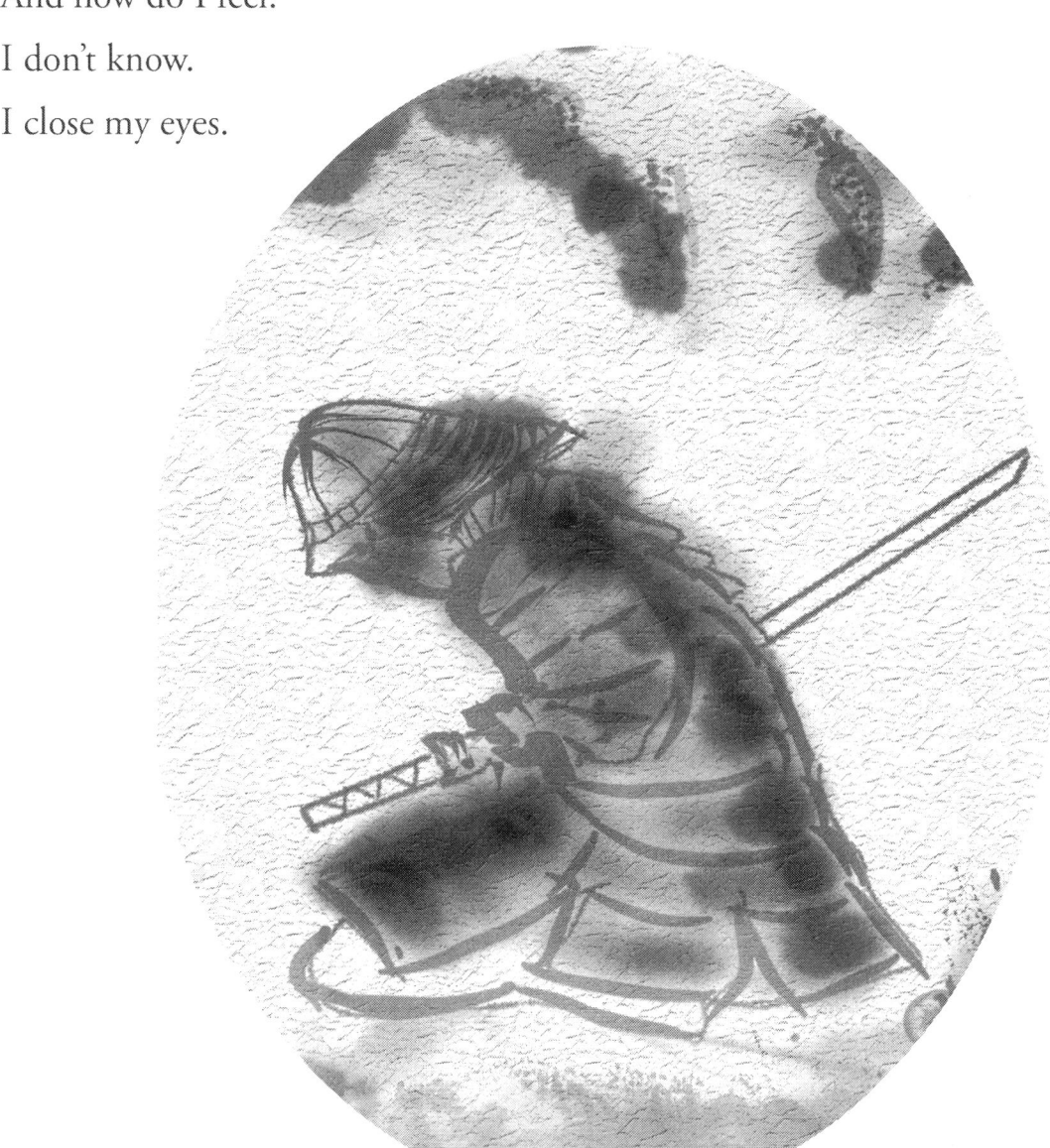

Seppuku II

II) BUSHIDO

Bushido:

Literally, the Warrior's path. Strict code that regulated all the aspects of the Japanese Samurai caste.

How many mistakes can one make in a lifetime?

Is it possible to live in error and when one dies, correct the mistakes?

It's impossible to explain about myself if I don't explain about my father and his father, my grandfather.

Meredith Evans was born in Tredegar, a village in southern Wales near Merthyr Tydifil, the United Kingdom, in the crude winter of 1894, son of Cefin Evans and Gwyn Lewis.

As almost all the poorer Welsh at that time, he was born into a numerous family. He had three older brothers, Iefan, Macsen, Parry; and three younger sisters, Betan, Siwan, Eira. Sixteen children had been born into this family, but only these seven survived.

I didn't know my grandfather except through my father's stories.

Several Evans' generations in that village – which I imagine was very poor and wretched – had been miners.

It appears that my grandfather's father, when very young, had seen a group of Welsh colonists leave on a journey to join the pioneers in the Argentine Patagonia, and he had spent all his life dreaming of joining them; he had followed all the chronicles of the time that used to give a rather epic account of the Patagonian experiment.

In my great-grandfather's rather meagre bookcase –an actual luxury and rarity in a poor family's home at the end of the 19th century- lay the memories of John Daniel Evans, read so many times that the paper was worn thin. Although it was impossible to prove, Dad said that Meredith would always claim that there was a common ancestor, a great-great grandfather or something like that, a family link anyway, with the heroic colonist who had escaped from the rebellious natives, galloping away from them on a chestnut horse and after launching his horse over a chasm, had survived. Who knows how much truth there was in all of this.

When the Labour Party appeared in the U.K., the Evans embraced the cause as others did the church. They once attended a meeting in a nearby town, a little larger than their hometown, where the main speaker was Robert B. Cunninghame Graham, a Scottish noble who oddly enough had spent his youth in Argentina, a country he always considered his second home.

Meredith and his family embraced the cause with the ardour of those who understood they finally had the possibility of ending the exploitive bonds that had submerged their Celtic ancestors into poverty ever since the arrival of the Romans, Saxons and

Roberto Bontine Cunninghame Graham in his 30s'

Normans, and which had crystallized since the 16th century when the frontiers with England had been set up.

My grandfather was born into a poor family, but they were contained by and had the virtuosity of the nineteenth century Socialists: alcohol was not abused, and they had every possible book.

He probably had three or four years of schooling during which he learnt some English. At home they spoke in Welsh, but when he had a son later in life, he only spoke to him in English.

He started to work in 1906 when he was 12 years old, together with his father and brothers, and from then on his life was dark and sad; the only islands of happiness were the Christmas parties.

They worked from dawn till dusk; they'd leave home at sunrise and return at sunset, six days a week. Any sick day was knocked off their salary, and there was no right to strike, no unemployment benefits, medical services or holidays.

At fifty they were already old men. They married young and those who could, would emigrate from Wales, generally to places where they stopped being Welsh and became British subjects.

My grandfather took over his father's dream, thinking that perhaps, one day, he would emigrate to Patagonia.

In the second half of the nineteenth century, for many of the Welsh the south of Argentina – or better said, the Welsh colony in Chubut- had become the symbol of hope to preserve their language, traditions, ways and customs- as by that time these were threatened by the growing British changes forced on and suffered by the Welsh nation.

My grandfather was still to live through worse times.

The very year he was twenty, in a small town in the Balkans a Yugoslavian nationalist discharged all his cartridges into an Austrian-Hungarian prince, and thereby dramatically brought a whole era to a halt. A few months later World War I was declared and another era began: a massacre on an industrial scale.

If I hadn't seen what I've seen, or didn't know what I do know about Europeans, I wouldn't understand how in one fell swoop, the European nations mobilized their citizens to the extent that they massively became volunteers to fight their neighbouring countries.

My grandfather, his older brothers, two of his father's brothers and all his mother's brothers joined the British Army. At that time, family members were usually incorporated into

Welsh Dragon

the same units – so the Evans and the Lewis's were all in the same battalion.

I know my grandfather always said –as did my father- that war is the only show in which the poor are seen in the front row.

Meredith fought in the Ardennes Range between France, Belgium and Germany, and as in all the European war's front lines, it was carnage.

wales

He saw how one by one, in attack after attack, every member of his numerous family fell - and all just to gain a couple of hundred metres of terrain, to hold or to fall back, and at the same time attempt to bring down as many of the enemy as possible.

My grandfather Meredith never uttered a word about the subject; everything that my father told us later he had been told by my grandmother Pepa – my father's mother- who over the years had added small but valuable tales regarding her husband's terrible experiences, having heard them during their closer moments together.

My Welsh grandfather had been lucky, in spite of having been wounded three or four times. He emerged alive and was demobilized almost immediately in mid-1919 –the armistice had been signed in November 1918- and with a uniform decorated with medals he returned to his hometown, kissed his mother and his younger sisters and all the other widows in the village, packed a few clothes in a cardboard suitcase and that same week he travelled to the port of Cardiff, to embark on his journey to Argentina.

His father, too old to go to war, had died a few weeks before the armistice, a victim of the classic pneumonia suffered by miners of the coal deposits. He was 58 years old.

Meredith didn't know a word of Spanish, although he took with him several books or magazines to help a traveller: an illustrated guide which had a text in English above each illustration and below the Spanish phonetic pronounciation; the Evans' memories; and some magazines that talked of the land of beef and grain.

Grandfather crossed the Atlantic with a third class ticket and a handful of pounds, his savings. He discovered later that they wouldn't be of much use.

I knew this "*Viejo*", as my father called him, by five or six photos he kept among his most precious memories which, among other objects, were put away in a wooden box with the profile of Argentina carved on its cover.

Among all these photos – one of the *Viejo*'s friends in Buenos Aires; another at work; another with my father, his sister and my grandfather; one of his civil wedding- there was one which had always impressed me.

The picture was, of course, black and white, but it had an amazing quality regarding its focus and tones compared to the others. It had obviously been taken by a professional, or at least a very experienced photographer.

On the back was a date: 1916, with neither day nor month, although after a few years and multiple revisions we speculated that it must have been taken at the beginning of autumn, somewhere in France.

In the background was a stable or barn surrounded by trees. At the forefront, wearing his beret and dress uniform with all its straps, stands a young Meredith holding a cigarette, with an undeniable sad smile on his face.

There was something in that look, frozen over the years, which ever since I can remember has deeply moved me.

This uniform -which in the photo looked clean and ironed- and something in his posture –a classic of soldiers at ease, one foot slightly in front of the other, the knee barely bent and his body relaxed- made me vaguely want something, which years later I identified as a military career.

Henry James Foster, 1916

Meredith was a slim man, of medium height, his face was thin and he always looked serious in the other photographs.

According to my father, he was a taciturn man on whom the war had left its mark beyond his body wounds: shrapnel in his right arm, a long scrape all along his left arm – a bullet had journeyed through the inside of his uniform sleeve and had come out of his elbow- a shard in his right leg which now and again shed some lead powder, and a scar on his right shoulder, which many years after his death we learnt was a bayonet wound.

My father could recall no more than four war tales, and none of them were related to battles, or to dates or moments. They contained just precise, useful information, almost without any blood, stench or screams; little more than a map, a topological map of Meredith's journey through hell, of his personal descent into Dante's delirium.

All of this, as my Dad learnt during his own life, was implicit in the few memories that good old Meredith had left us; it was enough to hear the silences to smell and hear the aftermath of a battlefield.

Meredith knew he was going to "*lock horns*", as he used to say when they were going into battle, because they used to give the soldiers an extra ration of brandy, which he actually preferred to keep for after the battle.

One of his Christmases had ended with him playing a game of soccer with the Germans… and twelve hours later they went back to massacring each other.

Meredith didn't ever eat brains or entrails, because even if they were cooked they still reminded him of the battlefields.

He was afraid of rats, in fact, he hated them: he had seen how, en masse, they attacked the dying men in some of those battles which represented endless days of fighting.

"It's not surprising my *Viejo* was a pacifist, right Charly?" my Dad said to me once.

Meredith arrived in Argentina like many other immigrants, in practically just the clothes he was wearing, and without knowing anyone or having any known contacts in the country.

According to my father, the money he had –his life savings- would only last him for one or two weeks after paying for a bed in a seedy and very badly reputed boarding-house near the port of Buenos Aires. The idea of making his way down to Patagonia seemed almost impossible when he was made aware that the distance from Buenos Aires to Trevelin was almost the same as travelling from London to Moscow.

In his hurry to leave Great Britain he had not realized that, by delaying his departure a few weeks or changing his embarkation port –the nearest would have been Bristol, or the equally distant Liverpool or Southampton - he could have embarked on a cargo ship going directly to Madryn or Bahía Blanca, as they regularly plied between Britain and Argentina's southern ports.

The fact is that my grandfather Meredith Evans arrived at the port of Buenos Aires in January 1920 after sailing for 25 days. He did not speak a word of Spanish; and after wandering the largest city he'd ever been in and aware it was even larger than what he ever imagined –he hardly even knew Cardiff and had only visited London when he was being given his military instruction- he started to think he had made the biggest mistake of his life -after the first mistake of becoming a volunteer in the Army.

But chance, or whatever it is that modifies people's lives beyond their actions played a radical role in my grandfather's life.

As he wandered lost in thought -or perhaps quite concerned- along the Avenida de Mayo among the multitude of Saturday afternoon strollers, he heard an impeccable English voice calling out his name and surname from a table on the pavement: to his absolute surprise there sat Harry Foster, a very pleasant, younger man than himself, whom he had met in an army hospital not far from the battle front.

Although Foster was British –he had actually been born in Madagascar- he had enrolled in the Canadian army and for who knows what reason, they had ended up in beds next to each other in that sad French hospital.

Foster had arrived in Buenos Aires two days before, and had just met up with two of his battalion comrades, Erick Meeck and Jack Fuller. The four of them celebrated that fortuitous meeting which would have great consequences in my grandfather's life.

I can well imagine those four survivors of Hell greeting each other with firm handshakes and huge smiles.

Although the other two men didn't know my grandfather, they invited him for a drink – all they had to notice was how my grandfather was dressed to realize he was broke- and that afternoon they all talked together as if they had known each other all their lives.

My father told me once that he perfectly understood those four young men: they were brothers, in fact members of a brotherhood, bastards of the same brutalized god of war.

Those three men were Meredith's friends till the end of his days.

Fuller, Meeck and Foster also gave him some information that would radically change the course of our history: the Buenos Aires Great Southern Railway (later Ferrocarril del Sur), British-owned, was preferentially hiring all war veterans who requested a job.

These men also helped my grandfather find a room in a boarding-house near Temperley station, which cost exactly half of what he had been paying.

I'm sure grandfather Meredith at that moment must have felt that the Evans' age-old bad luck had begun to change.

Not only did they find him a less expensive boarding-house near his future work, they also lent him clothes —one of his friends lent him a coat, another a waistcoat and the other a pair of trousers. Just by hearing these men talk it was obvious they belonged to different social classes, but their mutual experiences in the trenches had taught them that friendship went beyond distinctions of any kind.

Three days later they presented themselves at the personnel offices in Constitución station, and by the following Monday my grandfather was working at the Remedios de Escalada railway workshops; only two weeks had gone by since his arrival in Argentina.

His friends were given administrative jobs. These men didn't make any social distinctions, but British capitals did.

Every day grandfather Meredith travelled from Temperley to Escalada; he bought a newspaper and with the help of a dictionary, at lunchtime he tried —with a variety of results- to understand the meaning of each word.

In my Welsh grandfather's stubborn head, as firm as a rock, he still entertained the idea of saving up enough money to travel and settle in the Welsh Patagonia about which his dear departed ancestors had dreamed so much.

But it's clear that destiny had another idea in store for us.

We don't know how or who, but the fact remains that someone sent him to a Socialist meeting in Banfield —one of the two intermediate stations between Temperley and Escalada. The premises were very discreet, in this building there had recently been some repressive violence connected to the events around the Vasena workshop strike, today known as "*La semana trágica* - The tragic week". Among other activities, Spanish was taught in these premises to foreigners who were arriving by the thousands at the port.

If my grandfather thought that his life was changing when his path crossed with a former war hospital companion in the middle of the crowd down Avda. de Mayo, I wonder what he thought when he arrived at the establishment on Molina Arrotea street.

An energetic and kind schoolteacher led the Club; in his youth he had joined Leandro N. Alem's "Unión Cívica" party, but when he heard Juan B. Justo's fiery prose he had embraced the Socialist cause, guided by his admiration of that generous medical doctor as well as founder of the Socialist party in Argentina.

Ferrocarril del Sur, Temperley, 1924

For my grandfather it was like a rebirth. He was no stranger to the cause and he immediately understood that the deep, humanistic dogma of Argentine Socialism held a place for him.

The skills that its leaders practiced – battling alcohol abuse, pacifism, internationalism and a deep love of culture – acted upon him like a magnet, and as from that day on he'd spend each free moment there.

Cheekily, my father used to say that beyond all the notable virtues of the Socialists of that period, his father had found a pair of dark eyes that had dazzled him.

Maestro Porrá, the teacher who guided the club —he was the owner of the establishment as well- came from a very old South American family whose roots went as far back as the second foundation of the city of Buenos Aires in 1580, when Juan de Garay and other Asunción citizens settled in what was left of the fort abandoned by Pedro de Mendoza forty years before.

His daughter taught the classes jointly with him - she was a young woman who had just graduated as a teacher. Josefa —to me, grandmother Pepa- was not pretty. But she was so intelligent and had such a strong character that these made her intense and attractive.

She had graduated the year before from a prestigious teachers' school, and after teaching in the mornings and afternoons at different state schools in the poorer districts of Banfield, she dedicated two hours more to teaching foreign adults.

In the few photos I saw of her as a young woman it's impossible to avoid noticing the strength of her gaze; although I remember her already bent by the passage of years and all her problems, I can well understand what my grandfather Meredith saw in her.

Until the day her heart stopped, she possessed a bright determination and intelligence combined with gentleness and compassion.

Great-grandfather Porrá had become a widower when Josefa Zambonini died in 1913, and since then he had cared over-protectively and lovingly for his daughter.

My father didn't know many details about the courtship, grandmother Pepa was very skimpy with her stories and there were no more witnesses alive; over the years we later learnt that *maestro* Porrá at first had voiced his objections regarding the Welsh workman, and this did not include the difference in ages –it was usual in those times- although at that time it was more noticeable because grandfather Meredith looked at least ten years older than his actual age.

My great-grandfather was afraid that the Welshman had another family in Europe, another matter that was quite frequent in those days.

It's obvious that all doubts were soon set aside because my grandparents were married October 30th, 1920; my grandfather had been less than a year in the country.

That marriage divided grandmother Pepa's family in two. On one side, my grandparents and Porrá. On the other, Pepa's four older sisters, married to an eclectic group of gentlemen –liberal professionals, businessmen, small farm owners- and, due to the family conflict, they never showed up as uncles to my Dad.

Grandmother Pepa never saw her sisters again, not even after my grandfather had died.

Just as Pepa's father had initially mistrusted the Welshman, when he learnt the details of the tragic life my grandfather had led up till then, Porrá adopted him like a son and they were family until the last day of their lives, even at the expense of Porrá having to face the split in his own family.

With the passing years we understood that the rift in the Porrá family had more to do with ideology than anything else; the *Maestro* had educated his daughters with the values of democracy and freedom of expression and beliefs, and it was obvious they did not share Socialist ideals with him and with grandmother Pepa, but it is also likely their husbands' interests were also involved in this conflict.

My great-grandfather had not made a fortune as a teacher, although he had inherited some small properties that gave him a modest rent; he was an austere man in his personal life as well as surprisingly generous with those who were going through a needy period.

So he would often excuse rents, pay for people moving, and distribute bags of food and clothes wherever necessary; the only condition he requested was that if the home receiving his help had school-age children, that they attend school.

His family lineage was a mix going back to the times of the Spanish conquest; his father had been in the Federal party opposing Gen. Rosas, and his maternal grandfather had fallen in the Unitarian Party uprising commanded by Gen. Lavalle in 1840, we're not exactly sure of the location.

His wife also had roots in a family with history in these lands, and they were also linked to education: she was Mariano Zambonini's daughter, he had been a teacher in the town of Carmen de Patagones in southern Buenos Aires province during and after Gen. Rosas' time in the Buenos Aires government.

The library Porrá had inherited was more valuable than the few properties holding the books gathered by three or four generations, to which he had also contributed more than three or four hundred books on an infinite variety of subjects throughout his fruitful and productive life.

He had encouraged all his daughters to attend secondary schooling and the university; one of them had studied medicine following Cecilia Grierson's example, then she had married a doctor and they had become established in the city of Córdoba, doing very well for themselves. Another of the daughters was a pharmaceutist. Porrá believed that men and women should have equal rights.

According to my father, the family boycott to his parents had produced an intense and manifested desire in my great-grandfather to help them get ahead. Although he never stopped seeing the rest of his family, the important dates and celebrations he spent with his youngest daughter and his Welsh son-in-law.

Also, his influence on my Dad's education was absolutely significant.

They hadn't had any party for this wedding nor, of course, was there a church ceremony —which was another affront to the family because in spite of the *Maestro*'s deep anti-clerical beliefs the family had become quite conservative. But grandmother Pepa did have a small photo in which Meredith, she, her father, Foster and Meeck —these two were the witnesses- and one other person whose name was lost, are all smiling at the door of the Lomas de Zamora civil registry.

That summer they moved to the railway neighbourhood behind the Remedios de Escalada workshops, an orderly checkerboard of almost identical chalets, with rectangular-tiled roofs, and a chimney and walls of red brick so typically English that they could have been in any London, Manchester or Brighton suburb.

The railway company had built them for their employees, and to my father's surprise, when he was an adult he had seen similar neighbourhoods in some parts of Asia.

For my grandfather, who had been brought up in a shack with stone walls and a straw roof, who later had not known any other home than the trenches, military barracks and very poor boarding houses, that house was almost a palace.

My father's first memories are clearly anchored in that house, in that neighbourhood, allowing my grandfather Meredith to walk to and back from his work - he could return at midday and be near his family.

My father was born there on July 9th, 1921. The only baby photo of him is dated November 3rd, 1921, on the back.

When my father was a little more than three years old, in November 1924 his only sister, Cristina, was born. What initially was a happy event celebrated by the couple and *maestro* Porrá, with the passing of the months became fate's stab in the back.

The birth had been long and difficult for both mother and child, and something had gone wrong; they soon realized that Cristina could not see, and that the baby's growth and maturity was not within normal levels.

As the months went by they found that Cristina could not talk except for some babbling sounds, nor could she hear; she did not walk either.

Sheltered by *maestro* Porrá's extensive network of contacts, they had been to see many doctors, until they finally reached "Casa Cuna", the children's hospital near Constitución station, where the couple's hopes were dashed to pieces. The healthcare of those days had nothing to offer her: Cristina would be bedridden till the end of her life. In fact, she lived longer than my grandparents and my father.

Meredith suffered that blow and became more taciturn - he turned to reading books as a solace. My father could well remember sitting on my grandfather's lap while he read – in English or in Spanish- always with a dictionary at hand. My grandfather became quieter, but also more affectionate with his firstborn.

Pepa's father's support was decisive for the couple.

Maestro Porrá discovered that his son-in-law, although he had never had more than the minimum instruction or education, had a superior intelligence, plus a great desire to learn which was almost childlike; and this led him to take refuge in reading and learning.

My father remembered perfectly that after lunch on Sundays, both men, after having cleared the table –grandmother Pepa was almost exclusively occupied with my aunt Cristina- *maestro* Porrá would dedicate hours at a time to explain or to further develop what Meredith was reading.

Maestro Porrá had told my father –when he was about 12 or 13- that he had been very surprised when he saw Meredith's ability to concentrate and his willpower to follow any subject. He believed that if Meredith hadn't been just a humble member of the working class, he would have shone in any profession he chose.

My father would never forget the picture of his father reading, sitting in an old rocking chair beside the red hot wood-burning stove that heated almost the whole house, following the words, moving his lips slightly –but in complete silence- and beside him a cup of tea which he rarely finished, and which ended up evaporating on the stove.

In summer the scene was different but almost identical, this time he'd sit in the small porch at the front of the house – identical in all the houses. grandfather Meredith would take two or three sips of his tea until it grew cold. Now and again, my grandmother would replace it with a cup of hot tea.

This routine, either winter or summer, was repeated several times.

According to my father, his mother was able to attend to them all and at the same time was focused on her daughter night and day.

The old teacher realized quickly that his daughter had fallen in love with an extraordinary man, and it's clear that he did all that was in his power for my father not to repeat the family history, that his ability and intelligence find a productive direction, away from poverty.

My great-grandfather also helped my grandfather: he started to choose his son-in-law's reading matter, mixing history, geography and literature with a clear didactic goal.

My father kept the letters he had received from Meredith in the years he lived abroad and what stood out was his *Viejo*'s neat handwriting, the words very separate and carefully accented, as well as the variety of subjects he addressed.

It's clear that my father grew up in a home that in spite of a tight economic situation and my aunt's illness, its environment was truly stimulating.

Meredith was no easy or expressive talker, but he made a great effort for his son to develop his innate skills and potential.

To this was added the dedication and determination of the old teacher, which would mark him forever.

The Welsh workman of few words and the creole teacher with an encyclopaedic culture launched themselves to educate my father with the faith and conviction that they were preparing the new man.

The time came when *maestro* Porrá, wanting to give my father a higher education, gave in -or at least postponed- his mythical defense of a state education, when an old friend, John Vibart, the owner of St. Alban's College, offered my father a full scholarship in the school's primary section.

According to the story told by a member of my mother's family, the discussion between the two men –they both had very energetic and vehement characters- was as much polite as memorable, and that old Vibart had won the argument by pointing out the advantage of a bilingual education for the boy.

My father began primary school in 1926 in that prestigious school in Lomas de Zamora, which he attended Monday through Friday, and on Saturdays until midday. During the week he had lunch in the school's dining room.

In the morning he had classes according to the official Argentine plan for primary schools, and in the afternoon under the official plan for English primary schools.

Although two or three times a week they had gym classes, on Saturdays they also practiced team sports like rugby, cricket and other athletic sports. Dad began to stand out as a rugby forward not exactly because of his height but because of his speed and determination to get the ball out; I think there's an interschool cup at St. Alban's -1927 or 28- which has the name "*Gordon Evans*" engraved along with some twenty more names.

Grandfather Porrá –to everybody, *maestro* Porrá- used to take him and bring him back from school every day. My father left the house together with my grandfather –he went to work at 7 a.m. - and they walked to the Escalada workshops; then, on his own, my father walked to the train station where the teacher was waiting for him.

My father found railways fascinating, and he thought his father had a heroic job, taking apart and repairing the rolling stock which carried thousands and thousands of people. Just as other people know brands of cars or motorbikes, he knew about steam engines, which had fascinated him since childhood.

The route he had to take each morning, passing through the huge, huffing workshop so full of life, walking between big wheels and grey steam clouds he always remembered as a magical and energetic moment that inspired him his whole life.

Everybody in the workshop knew who he was and would greet him, and as my father was quite serious and also very polite, he was treated with respectful deference. He liked that and it made him feel adult, mature.

Travelling with his grandfather Porrá, on the other hand, was a great adventure, an entertaining lesson in whatever my father was interested in, because his grandfather's wide range of knowledge allowed him to always have some ready answer for my father's insatiable thirst to know.

The word "boring" never figured in his lexicon, *maestro* Porrá erased it from his dictionary.

That old man –according to my father and other people who knew him as my maternal grandfather- was an extraordinary man in every way.

When he walked down the street he took with him a walking stick made of whalebone with a bronze end and a silver handle. It was a top quality stick he had inherited from his father; some time back, playing with the walking stick, my father and I discovered that inside it also carried a sharp and rigid steel plate in the form of a rapier.

Maestro Porrá knew everybody, and the whole world knew him.

When they travelled by train, passengers and inspectors, porters and station chiefs, all of them greeted my father and his grandfather with great kindness and respect.

When they walked along Meeks Ave. to and fro from the station, the taxi and cart drivers, the delivery boys on bicycle, the bar waiters or the street sweepers, the pharmacist dressed in white, the porters with rolled-up shirtsleeves and *alpargatas*, the doctor or the lawyer wearing leggings and three-piece suits, every single one greeted him either by nodding their head or touching their hat and saying some kind word in greeting.

The old *maestro* invariably returned their greeting by saying their name or surname and my father always saw them smile, flattered that the old teacher remembered them so well.

On some occasions he'd shake the passerby's hand, always touching the brim of the obligatory hat; other times he'd stop to talk about some public interest matter, whether cultural, political or social.

Less times the conversation might be about personal matters - he was particularly shy about these because he hated gossip and deeply rejected it.

There was no disturbance or any shrillness around the old teacher, there was an aura of respect and appreciation which accompanied them wherever they went.

Ever since those trips started, grandfather Porrá had encouraged my father –a child still- to greet people in the same way and even to participate in the eventual conversations.

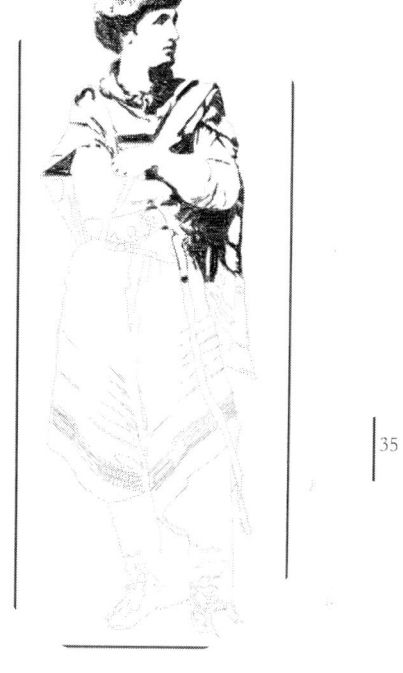

Don Roberto, The Gaucho, 1864

On Saturdays at midday *maestro* Porrá would go into St. Alban's and walk out with my father, always talking in a lively way; they would then head in the opposite direction to Lomas and walk to Temperley station.

That ritual was repeated every school day until my father finished primary school.

On Saturdays my father went to an informal "school" that the old teacher had thought up for his grandson.

In Temperley station they took a train that went through Monte Grande, leaving them in Turdera, the following station. They got into the second class carriage – the *maestro* always took the same kind of transport as the poorer classes – and in a few minutes the noisy engine left them at the station, which is quite a few metres below ground so passengers had to climb the stairs to reach the surface.

Every Saturday was the same: a cold winter day or a hot summer one, through rain, a storm, drought or hail.

Those Saturdays – as well as other free times spent together with his grandfather- were part of what made my father the man he was.

When they reached the street beside Turdera station, a rather large and fierce-looking man was waiting for them; he walked them to a *sulky* cart with very large iron wheels and wood rays, pulled by a large, very dark creole horse with a single white star on its forehead.

Don Iberra owned -together with his brother- a grocery shop, staging post, bakery and boarding house all in one about half a league from the station along the old road used for cattle herding. The Iberra's property stood on the corner of this so-called Royal Road from as far back as the colonial times, and which led south in a line following the towns of Ministro Rivadavia, Fortín Ranchos and Chascomús –today this road crosses Antártida Argentina Ave, joining Lomas de Zamora with the towns of Lavallol and Monte Grande.

The big, strong fellow, always wearing Argentine *campo* clothes –broad-rimmed hat, shirt, waistcoat, *bombachas*, *alpargatas* and a *poncho*- would help my great-grandfather into the *sulky,* and when they first started these visits he'd tell my father to get into the back –where the bags usually went- but as time went by he allowed my father to take the reins.

The trip was short and pretty comfortable; for my father it was like entering a magical spot, a dreamland, where life and the world were understandable and simple.

That corner where the building stood was already part of our history –if not of Argentina, at least of the province of Buenos Aires. The Iberra brothers had inherited the grocery shop cum bakery and boarding house from their father, who had bought it after the *Batalla de Pavón* (battle of Pavón), which marked the definitive birth of the Argentine Republic as we know it today.

The story was told that the *viejo* Iberra had paid for the building with the spoils of war which he'd picked up off the battlefield, and somehow carried off from both camps.

Only to those they trusted, the Iberra brothers showed some of the booty they still owned - there were several saddles stamped with "*GOBCFA*", *Gobierno de la Confederación Argentina* (Government of the Argentine Confederation) and two or three sabres marked "*PCIABSAS*", *Provincia de Buenos Aires* (Province of Buenos Aires).

The building was not chamfered, and was located on a flat rise that ran along what is now Antártida Argentina Ave. - it must have easily measured some fifty metres in length. It was built with baked clay bricks stuck together with mud, with no plaster or facing whatsoever, and the pavement was made of the same material. The building had a corrugated tin sheet roof that also covered a gallery, and a large number of doors and windows.

In a not too distant past it had been a staging post, a hotel for passengers –of the dozen or so rooms, only one or two were used for guests then- and when my father started going there, the building still housed a fruit & vegetable shop, a bakery, a general convenience store, and a *pulpería*, a tavern with a bar for the locals.

At the back —with access to the road for herding cattle - there were also several corrals still in use where the brothers kept the cattle; they regularly organized auctions which gathered a large crowds.

After the auction the animals were herded along the road to Lavallol station - it wasn't the nearest station but was the only one with a chute to load the cattle into the train cars, which then carried them to the Liniers cattle market.

That general store was the last bastion in the countryside before reaching the city. There were some similar places in the towns of Lanús and Valentín Alsina, but none were as well-known or visited as much as the Iberra's.

I must have been eleven or twelve years old when Dad drove us in our lovely Studebaker 59 to visit the place where he had probably spent the most important part of his childhood.

By then the building was almost in ruins; the strong walls were still there but most of the roof over the rooms had fallen because the wooden beams were gone and the corrugated tin sheets were missing. At the corner where the grocer's shop and tavern had been there was a bakery with the sign reading, "Iberra's", but there was nobody there who had ever known them or *maestro* Porrá.

Only the corrals' main posts remained standing at the back, everything else had disappeared who knows when, and the weeds and underbush were everywhere.

"Do you see, Charly?" He said to me then, in his beautiful baritone voice, while he pointed to the room in ruins. "That's where I dressed on my own for the first time… I wasn't seven yet… I put on some checkered *bombachas*, a white shirt and *alpargatas* which miraculously were my size."

Maestro Porrá had decided, undoubtedly with my grandparents' support, that besides an excellent formal education, my father would have the best possible informal education, among the cattle, dogs and *gauchos*.

While we strolled through the ruins of that building, my father's voice, which usually was quite contained and in a certain way circumspect, had become full of feeling and nuances.

My father had spent seven years there, every Saturday of the school year and many days of the summer holidays among rough but good men who taught him, little by little, some aspects of work in the Argentine *campo* and all the "*gaucho*" virtues.

He had learnt to ride always on horses for "adults" —never on ponies or miniature horses- as well as to herd cattle, and while on horseback, how to separate a cow or a steer from the herd, how to use a lasso.

He also learnt to fix fences, to sew a *recado*, to fix reins, to braid rawhide straps, to make all sorts of knots and of course, to light a fire to heat water for *mate* or to cook an *asado*.

Saturday after Saturday Dad spent among adults and young men who hardly knew how to read and write, but who were rich in the knowledge they had gained through risking their own bodies.

He was taken care of, of course. But he enjoyed a freedom that few city children learn. When he was just over 9 years old he had taken part in a brief herding –to Lavallol station, a little more than half a league- and he had felt in Heaven.

"It's a shame to see this building like this, isn't it Charly?" he said to me that time, remarkably moved. It's that my *Viejo*, due to the circumstances in his own life, was not someone who could be easily moved, he had seen and lived through terrible things which had that had hardened him in some way.

But it was clear that what he was seeing had deeply affected him.

"This is where I learnt the local creole things, thanks to my grandfather and a large number of *gauchos*, some like *Don* Junco, others a little wilder… they were all peons… simple people and they taught me so many things…"

It's funny, because I can't remember exactly when we paid that visit, it must have been during a holiday, but my memory fails me when I try to evoke the context; however, as if it were branded by fire, I recall every inflexion, every nuance in the sound of my father's voice when he was talking.

Often when he told me stories about his life, his voice became so much more expressive; I don't know this for certain, but I suspect that as he recalled his own constructive process in some way he was trying to help me with my own.

"It's a shame what's happened here, isn't it Charly?" He'd say in a quiet voice, while we strolled through those ruins and he turned over all the memories in his mind.

I know it must sound strange but among my own memories I also have recorded my father's clear experiences, which he has transmitted to me in his beautiful voice as if they were stories, tales like those in the many books in our huge library.

My father was an extraordinary storyteller, his careful and remarkable descriptions in a mysterious way would become intense and colourful films in my child's mind. That walk through the ruins of the Iberra grocery shop allowed me, in time, to understand the deep influence that my great-grandfather still had on our lives.

Horse Dance

Throughout his primary schooling my father received a very good education in two languages and he always had outstanding marks, but he had also received that *"gaucho"* blessing; my father never lived his multi-culture as something which had been planned but as something that had simply happened.

I've seen my father riding together with Junco and the other peons and I'm surprised how present *maestro* Porrá still is, dead for more than thirty years. My Argentine great-grandfather had resolved and succeeded in doing his part for my father to become a great synthesis of various cultures.

My *Viejo*, red-headed, pink-skinned and freckly had lived away from his home country since his twelfth birthday till he was twenty-seven or twenty-eight years old, and he talked with an undefinable accent - he had a way of chewing his words which was very personal and singularly his own; he did this with such propriety in the use of the language and with such a wide vocabulary that he always surprised new people he had just met; he never showed off, he was actually rather humble.

But he had studied Greek and Latin, he knew French, Catalan, some Welsh, quite a bit of German and even more Farsi; he was also very knowledgeable regarding creole horses' coats and colours, and he had a good eye for *gaucho* silverware: he knew a great deal about native and regional designs.

And behind almost all that was the clear and friendly figure of *maestro* Porrá.

Besides the Saturdays in the *campo*, Dad had received another very valuable inheritance from *maestro* Porrá; during the school winter holidays as well as the summer ones, my father was taken on a trip – sometimes five or six days, others for the whole summer- the destination was always to the interior of a province, and always related to the past.

It's clear that *maestro* Porrá did not choose journeying to those destinations by chance, he had a deliberate plan to imprint on my father's soul -a clear, defined sense of mutual belonging with the always magnificent Argentine landscapes.

When he turned seven, they travelled for several days, first in winter and then in summer, journeying along the sea coast of Buenos Aires province.

The smell of salt, the whistling of the *pampero* wind dragging everything out to sea, the *sudestada*'s disturbing strength, the colour of the sand, winter's damp cold and summer's overwhelming heat –an excuse to refresh themselves at a little distance from the breaking waves- my father recorded the memories of it all.

When he was eight, in the winter he visited Balcarce, to understand what hills meant… and that summer they also made a trip through the provinces of Córdoba, San Luis, San Juan and Mendoza – and this way he registered the whole spectrum from hills to the imposing Andes chain.

When he was nine, during the winter they visited the cities of Rosario and Santa Fe, and in summer they travelled up to the province of Jujuy, going through Tucumán and Salta provinces.

The following year they spent the winter holidays on an *estancia* in the province of Entre Rios, and almost two summer months in the Welsh region in Chubut province.

For my father that became an essential visit because he was able to incorporate the purest Welsh which at the same time was deeply integrated with the country; he learnt to sing two or three typical songs in Welsh –which he never forgot- in his beautiful baritone voice highlighting the both sharp but soft Celtic language, and which he also learnt to speak a little.

At the end of the welcoming supper when they returned, my grandfather Meredith had an emotionally moving surprise that made him so proud of his son and grateful to his father-in-law when my father sang a popular Welsh song for him.

"You know, Charly… I believe the best thing that happened in my life was to see my *Viejo* -who was not at all expressive… in fact so sparing of his feelings- and seeing him smile, his eyes full of tears that first time he heard me singing in Welsh."

So by the end of primary school Dad had received a surprising multi-cultural education; as a *gauchito*, as an Argentine citizen, as a British as well as a Welsh citizen.

I wonder what Meredith would have wanted for my father. I suspect it's the same as what my father wants for me, it can't be very different. I'm sure he was so proud when he saw his son growing and shaping his abilities, developing his skills, promising for him and his descendants a prosperity grandfather Meredith may have dreamt about in vain, for who knows how many ancestral generations.

Doctor of Medicine? Engineer? University Professor? Writer? Lawyer? Teacher? Chemist? Archaeologist? Oceanographer?

When he was eleven, they returned to Córdoba in winter –they spent almost two weeks there- and nearly the whole summer was spent at an *estancia* very close to La Pampa, where my father had worked as a "peon apprentice". With what he earned he had bought a cigar box for his father –engraved with his father's initials- and a bottle of perfume for his mother.

Those were perhaps the best holidays in his life.

Grandfather Porrá, the factotum of all those trips, was not a wealthy man; but he had a large network of relations throughout the country, through which he had travelled countless times from east to west and north to south in all imaginable forms of transport, although mainly on the vast railways network, which he had used tirelessly as it expanded over the years.

When I was young I used to think that *maestro* Porrá was a rich man. In my grandmother Pepa's house there was a photo which had been delicately touched up by hand –dated 1889- about 20 x 40 cms., in which my great-grandfather could be seen from head to toe.

Very well dressed – a dress shirt, a three-piece suit, leggings, walking stick and a hat- dark skin and eyes with a lively look, but a serious and severe expression.

No, he was not wealthy, he had travelled extensively with my father because throughout his lifetime he had knitted a wide network of friendships and loyalties that crossed over all social classes. His proverbial solidarity had left traces throughout the country and wherever he went he was welcomed with open arms.

Regardless of how much he insisted, nobody —not even the poorest of those who welcomed him- would ever accept a single *peso* in payment; so my great-grandfather used to distribute legendary gifts, not so much for their material value but because they were so appropriate for each person.

Maestro Porrá had been born in the city of Buenos Aires in the same year as the battle of Caseros, his primary schooling took place in the shadow of the conflict during the federalization of the city of Buenos Aires, when the province was not part of the Confederación Argentina (Argentine Confederation). He had worked against the war with Paraguay —in which he had lost his eldest brother- and he quietly celebrated its end, horrified by the result.

He finished his secondary schooling during the presidency of D.F. Sarmiento. The President's energetic preaching in favour of a state education and the convincing educational policy of his Minister, Nicolás Avellaneda, had awoken Porrá's teaching vocation.

He immediately stood out from among his colleagues; he used to write and publish brainy essays on different educational aspects and he frequently published articles on the subject in La Prensa newspaper. During Roca's presidency he competed for a position and was given a post as a school inspector, and from then on his career was long and very rich in events.

Through this post and backed by his intellectual skills and his austere personal style, he had cooperated in the growth of talented and able people, he had helped many individuals to find their own path and he had given very valuable and prudent advice to people from all social classes.

Over the years he had put together a wide network of contacts based on his public virtues that clearly showed up his human qualities; he had backed many people throughout his long career and he had done it in such a transparent and altruistic way that he surprised even the most cynical. Each trip with him had been a sober, didactic and happy party.

My father's grandfather had started to be called "*maestro* Porrá" during Roca's presidency and his fame was established during Juárez Celman's regime, after Porrá was jailed for reporting a fraud during the building of several schools in the country's poorest areas.

Once restated in his post, he had taken advantage of the fleeting spark the scandal had provoked to position himself as an incorrigeable founder of schools, a creator of pedagogic projects and the drive behind training teachers.

He had wanted to leave his post at the Ministry of Education during Irigoyen's presidency in 1919, but President Alvear's personal request kept him in his post until 1926. He was seventy three years old.

Maestro Porrá's wealth wasn't based on cash, yet it allowed my father to have a childhood that certainly was privileged, in a country that was in itself rich; I can perfectly understand my father coming back because that other extraordinary man had tatooed his soul with the country's soul.

Unlike other children of British citizens born in homes with mixed parents and languages, my father had learnt there was no opposition between his Welsh roots and his Argentine essence.

Every Saturday at supper-time, or the first Sunday after a trip, Meredith and my father would sit and chat after the meal and my father would then tell him –it evidently was one of his talents- about the journey and would show his souvenirs to Meredith: perhaps a coin, stones, pieces of trees, animal claws, and postcards which began to appear more frequently.

"You know, Charly, I think my father really wanted me to be a Welshman like those in Patagonia: loyal to our Argentine fatherland and respectful towards our inherited roots."

The wisdom of that formidable old man was imprinted in an indelible way on my father's personality.

When my father started his seventh grade something extraordinary happened. The Prince of Wales –heir to the British throne at that time- had visited Argentina and had distributed a quantity of scholarships for Argentine students to attend different schools in London. My father sat for the exam -25 pages in English grammar, basic algebra, English history, geometry and Latin- and because of his marks, he was granted a scholarship to one of the most prestigious schools: King George's College.

My great-grandfather was the first one to come out of the shock from this news -it arrived at the end of winter 1932- and he immediately got to work in order for his grandson to experience an education that was reserved only for the world's elite.

The family was deeply shaken.

Grandmother Pepa swung between happiness, pride and the fear of losing her son. Meredith went through a similar process but in silence as usual, in addition to a much hidden resentment against the British Empire, which wanted to take his son away.

He was a worker in a British company, almost all his friends were from the British community –Welsh, Irish, Scots, English, Canadian, Australian- and some of them married to "native women". But in his deepest being, he hated what he thought of as the oppressive empire, and he joyfully celebrated his son's creole schooling.

But his reasoning was stronger, otherwise my father would never have been able to embark for Great Britain just after his twelfth birthday.

Dad finished seventh grade in 1933, to enrole in King George's College latest Janaury 25th, 1934.

A feverish activity took place in the Evans' family home during the last months before my father's journey. Buying clothes, financial cautions. *Maestro* Porrá was preparing a farewell that would match my father's parallel education.

It's clear his grandfather Porrá knew they would not see each other again.

He went with my father by train to the next station after Junín, Buenos Aires province, where they were met by Archdeacon Luna, a friend of *Don* Iberra's and one of his countryside teachers, together with a tall and gentle blue roan saddled with a complete *recado* ready to ride.

From that very station stop they were going to be herding over 500 head of cattle; the 1930 economic crisis had forced the price per head to such a low level that even with the loss of herding cattle for 300 Kms, it would still be more profitable than sending them by train.

For those first eleven or twelve December days, my father acted as the "trusted peon" on that herding trip.

It's clear that that journey is directly related to our own life —my father's and mine- in the Argentine *pampas*. Once when we were riding together near the Paraná River, he recalled that trip to explain how much he owed it for his survival in three different wars.

Calmness when confronted with anything unexpected; paying attention to prevent risks; a good sense of humour when faced with stress, exhaustion, thirst, sudden fear when confronted with a perturbing or risky event; a clear understanding of danger. He had experienced all of this, in one way or another, on that last trip across the *pampas*.

"You know, Charly… the afternoon we herded the cattle into the Iberra corrals… we were very dirty, we'd been washing in the animals' water troughs for ten days… and all of those waiting for the herd treated me differently… Those who knew me and those who didn't… And my grandfather's serious expression, but his burning eyes… They all shook my hand and patted me gently on the back with their big hands… On the counter there were some glasses of *grapa*… I looked at my grandfather, and he nodded… Then everybody there toasted my health, a long and productive life… I felt myself a man then, and it wasn't because of the *grapa*, believe me…"

Christmas Eve was noisy, Christmas Day, melancholic. The project was that my father was to spend five long years at the boarding school, as the family budget would not allow for a yearly return trip. Everybody was hiding their deep sadness, trying to inject an epic note comparable to his herding that cattle and which had already become his own life legend.

I don't know what they would have done if they had had any inkling that my father would spend fifteen years away, and live through three hellish wars.

Each of them had made important contributions for my father to turn into a young man with benefits, and those last ten days were invested in practical things, such as careful home-made clothes that could be easily enlarged - warm, strong and light all at the same time, with the best fabric of those times. Grandmother Pepa, who had already been sewing for clients outside the family for several years, made his overcoat as well as his pyjamas, all with a discreet monogram and a label with his name embroidered by hand - his underclothes as well. My father returned to Argentina with some of those articles as his only civilian clothes.

At home and in his friends' homes everybody talked to him in English so he would get used to it. Even grandfather Porrá, with an unmistakeable Argentine accent, talked to him in an English which was strict regarding grammar as well as a very wide vocabulary.

In the port of Buenos Aires the fresh morning of December 26, 1933 was the last time my father saw his *Viejo* and his grandfather.

Today it may surprise people that a twelve-year-old boy was allowed to travel alone on a transatlantic ship for a trip lasting twenty to twenty-five days, but in those days it was common for boys of that age to work at all sorts of trades, as well as emigrate. A boy of 15, slightly older than Dad, was part of the ship's crew.

The scholarship paid for a third class ticket, and parents could pay the difference for the student to be upgraded to his own cabin in first class.

My grandparents decided that, after all, Dad came from a working-class home and the difference in value was better invested in the fabric of his clothes and in books which were going to be absolutely necessary.

Maestro Porrá had added his distinctive stamp to the trunk, an unforgettable, fine gift. A wooden box with a carry-handle, and a top that could be locked; on the cover, a delicately engraved profile of Argentina in relief. Inside the box, a tin full of *yerba mate*; a *mate* gourd with an alpaca stand and its metal tube with a gold-tipped mouthpiece; a compact kerosene heater; a quality enamelled kettle; an Argentine cockade for the Argentine holidays of July 9th and May 25th; and a letter written with the old teacher's fine and clear handwriting.

"I know you won't forget us, neither your country nor your family because I know your soul, what you're made of. I'm giving you these useful souvenirs so that when some days get rough, you can hold on to something; you rode amongst gauchos, you are ALREADY a man. It's now time to become a man of substance. The future is yours, use it well. I love you…"

Grandfather Meredith brought home a special gift, which a typographer friend had prepared especially for him.

It was a diary which fitted perfectly in the palm of a hand; however, it had a large amount of pages, nearly 300, and its covers and spine were carefully made of leather, dyed red. From each end of the spine, hung two leather strings delicately worked: from one hung a very small magnifying glass which could be tucked into one of the flaps; and from the other hung an ink-pencil —one of those which when licked writes with an almost indelible stroke- with a sharp point and which could be tucked into the other flap.

The first six pages were annual calendars from 1934 to 1939.

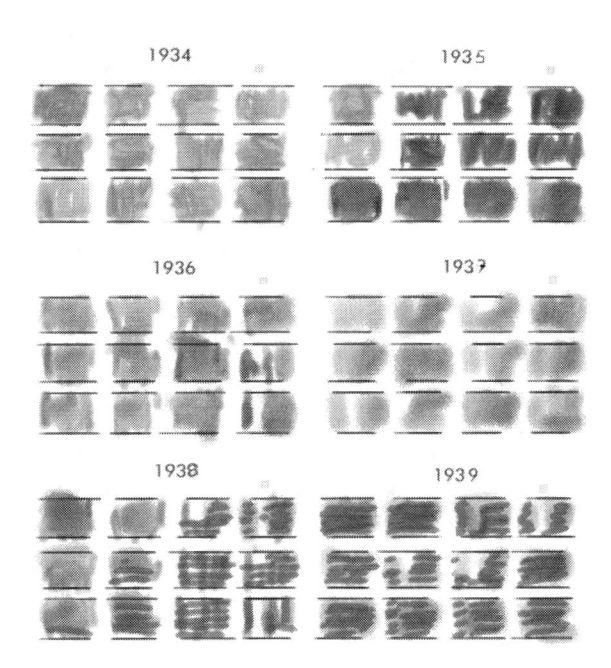

III) Hagakure

Literally, "*hidden under the leaves*".

A 17th century revision of the Bushido code

to face the Western cultural invasion.

"You know, Charly… of all those people, the only person I saw again was the one I missed when she didn't come that morning to the port…" he told me once.

I loved my father to tell me the story of his life because he was an extraordinary narrator and his stories always moved me.

He didn't tell them very often. When he did, these moments were intimate, clear and very deep, during which he offered me fragments of his life so that I could learn from them; or perhaps as he told them, he made better sense of the events that destiny had forced upon him. So I imagine those scenes very clearly, as if on a television screen in my head; I see the faces and imagine the places I've never been, remember things I haven't seen.

Other things he didn't tell me I've simply imagined.

For example, he never told me about his mother's and his sister's farewells, but I understand he would keep shyly quiet about such intense feelings.

I can envision in his words the faces, feel the silences, the austere gestures, the tears held back until the end, caresses and hugs that were stifled.

Copenhagen

I, who have never travelled much further than a few kilometres.

At dawn that day they travelled to the port in a hired car - although the ship was leaving a little after midday, they preferred to arrive good and early in order to say goodbye calmly, or perhaps they might even have been driven by the fear of arriving late due to this extraordinary event.

The driver and Dad's father helped him to carry up the heavy trunk – from grandfather Porrá's deposit, one of those with drawers and a place to hang one's clothes – it would accompany him for many years - and they all tried to hide their sorrow as best they could.

They were all dressed in their best clothes, almost as if they were going to a party.

Meredith was wearing a blue suit and a matching tie with grey stripes, and Porrá had dressed in a brown linen suit with a waistcoat, and a Panama straw hat.

My father was wearing one of his everyday outfits for the first time, a white, light-linen shirt with epaulettes, front pockets and grey short pants down to his knees. Although the two men had advised him to wear *alpargatas* during the trip, grandmother Pepa had insisted he at least wear leather laced-up shoes for the parting.

The *maestro* that day was affectionate, but silent and serious; he knew the slim chances of seeing his grandson again, he was close to eighty years old. I wonder what our good

Meredith thought? He knew very little about farewells, but the both times he had done this his life had changed radically and irreversibly.

Once my father was installed in his cabin – shared with five other people- the two most important men in his life, with very few words and very strong handshakes, began to leave the ship, very loath to do so. When they arrived at the gangway leading them down to the ground, first Meredith and then *maestro* Porrá hugged him for an eternal second each, and to whisper to him their best wishes for his trip.

"Farewells in ports have a certain ceremony to them, Charly… Everything is a ritual which is repeated each time a ship leaves… Perhaps when there were sails and no steam it was different… I don't know, perhaps they had to wait for the wind… On the other hand, in my childhood years it was different… The steam ship had a departure time… in the port, which is noisy, suddenly there's a silence and then whistles and bells ring, orders are shouted, the steam motors and the tug-boats' horns sound… and when they cut loose the moorings, people shout out their goodbyes to their loved ones who they might not see again… They wave handkerchiefs or hats or simply whatever is at hand… so that the person on board can see them as the ship moves away… now with planes this happens in a few minutes… but before, everything was slow, there were pauses… manoeuvres…"

That trip was another fascinating adventure for that twelve-year-old boy who would later be my father.

Although he was not allowed to disembark in the layover ports -*Rio, Santos, Fuerteventura, Vigo, Southampton*- just with seeing the city silhouettes and sense them from the port made him feel a true traveller.

His cabin companions were a good part of that intense journey, which was almost as adventurous as that last cattle herding.

In the Third Class cabin #344 C – the last on an open-air deck- on the Danish ship "Copenhagen", travelled an old Frenchman, an airplane mechanic who after living in Argentina for over 24 years – his story was that he had put together the first plane that entered the country, many years before the European war- he was on this return journey because he was now unemployed: he had been fired "unjustly" from the "*Aeropostal*" company, as he repeated often during the times he told tales of his feats; a Catalan typographer from Barcelona who was returning home, driven by the political unrest which was sweeping through Spain; two Englishmen who the others discovered halfway through the trip were followers of Sir Mosley; and a young Argentine architectural student who was planning to spend a year or two studying European cities and living from whatever work he could find, like a Bohemian.

This eclectic group of travellers, confined in a small cabin, miraculously were able to make my father's trip bearable, even a fun one.

It's clear today they knew perfectly well it would be a long time before he'd see his family again, and in a tacit way they all cooperated so that those twenty-odd days would be if not pleasant, at least comfortable.

Nearly all of them had spent time in exile, some of them more than once, and they knew it would not be easy for my father. In those times poor people did not travel for pleasure, they were emigrating and that meant they would not see their loved ones again.

My father was mature for his age and he had been educated to relate to people coming from different environments and above all, to actively confront his own fears; his travel companions really admired him and his serene behaviour during the brief but very intense storm that blew up by surprise as they left Uruguayan waters.

His kind and respectful manner, his appropriate and pertinent conversation, his self-confident nature – all the virtues which I knew about him in my life as his son – all these too helped them in treating him like a young and respectable adult.

It was on that trip that my father already began to show some of what he had learnt in his "Argentine *campo* school": he played the "*truco*" card game with surprising dexterity. This most popular card game in Argentina, similar to other European card games –such as the Catalan *truc*- took root on that ship like an epidemic; very soon the duo -my father and the architectural student, the youngest of all the adult passengers- had organized a tournament in which some ship officers, passengers in First Class as well as an almost unbeatable couple of Uruguayan engine operators, all participated.

That *truco* tournament soon became an almost daily activity, in which they didn't play for money but for prizes the players themselves donated; generally it was food and drinks that they shared, celebrating the day's winners.

My father hadn't any proof about the following, but at some point he thought there were people from First Class who were placing bets on the winning teams. There was an unconfirmed rumour that two young *estancieros* had lost more than a thousand head of cattle against a North American diplomat.

As all ships at that time, it was a perfect example of a wide world inhabited by different social classes and in which several languages were spoken – Danish, English, German, French, Galician, Catalan, Italian, Spanish, Portuguese – and in which, naturally, the intense conflicts being experienced in that period were also represented.

"You know, Charly… the whole world was trembling around us… Mussolini was already successful in Italy and there were Fascist movements all around the planet… A year before Hitler had won the elections in Germany at the beginning of 1933, and immediately was revealed as a dictator; but the socialists and the communists were observing the Soviet Union and there were thousands of anarchists in Spain… In all the large cities around the world there was fighting going on in the streets, with cudgels or guns… Throughout all countries, from Chicago to Shanghai, many people had lost their jobs due to the 1930s depression, so there was a great deal of discontent, hunger and abuses… but on the "Copenhagen" we were like the "League of Nations", in appearance indifferent to all; we played *truco* in pairs, and there was a German paired with a Turk, a Catalan with a Frenchman, a Basque with an Italian… We drank *mate* and played cards… There were many shouts of *retruco* and some chewed off verses in *gringo* languages…"

Driven by the world crisis, quite a few foreigners who had lived for many years in Argentina were returning to their own country, taking with them their creole habits; politics used those immigrants. Mussolini gave away land in Libya, Spain was a cauldron with Machado and Primo de Rivera, and Argentina was shaking with the patriotic fraud installed after Gen. Uriburu's coup against President Yrigoyen.

The laughter, jokes and arguments about points, the lying and friendly tricks, all the fun of a game which is sometimes played for money were all very much remembered by my father.

He was always impressed by the fact that only a few years later, many of those pacific players in the *truco* tournaments would end up killing each other in savage battles.

It's true that there had been arguments among the passengers, not so much because of the cards but because of politics.

The unstoppable rise of Hitler in Germany encouraged the fascists, who had the support of many economic sectors, and interested in stopping what they called "the Red danger": communists, socialists and the most feared, the anarchists; but the ship's crew —almost all Danish- were very quick and efficient in halting any attempt at violence, and the most aggressive men were immediately confined to some specially prepared cabins.

My father's education had a political stance, he had almost been "indoctrinated". He knew he was engaged in the conflict around him and was conscious he must pay a great deal of attention to what he said and to whom. At home they believed in an idealistic and profoundly humanistic socialism such as defined by Juan B. Justo and J.B. Alberdi.

But confrontations between the Nazi-Fascists and all that was progressive - from the Christian Socialists who were lesser reformists up to the most unappealable anarchists– was already clear, and they used the most open violence as a reason, there was no stopping or controlling them.

In my father's cabin, except for the two English syndicate members, fortunately all his travel companions belonged to one or other of the rival "bands": the old Frenchman was quietly communist, the Catalan typographer was also discreetly an anarchist, and the young architectural student, without actually having a defined ideology, was clearly against the "Blackshirts".

It's likely that the great social success that father enjoyed among the Third Class passengers was directly related to the seriousness with which he read books, every morning after the breakfast *mates*, sometimes after lunch or after dinner. It was never more than an hour or two at a time, but it was surprising how focused he was, and even more so when they realized the speed with which he finished the books, in one or two days.

Although for my *Viejo* it was a pleasant way to kill time on board, all the families would look at him respectfully, pointing out to their children that this was the attitude to pull themselves out of poverty.

I myself, who ever since I can remember saw him read and devour books at an amazing speed, have been impressed. I know that when he was twelve years old he could read books in English and in Spanish – always with a dictionary at hand- in only a few hours, and as an adult I've seen him read French and German the same way.

Only when I was able to read did I understand the extraordinary nature of my Dad's skills. Although he read at that speed, he retained up to the smallest detail, and for more complex concepts all he needed was to re-read them once and then he could quote entire paragraphs of what he'd read.

Later when I was just over 8 years old, he taught me the technique of reading in blocks –which he had learnt from his grandfather Porrá – and I learnt to read almost as fast as he did. Although my school marks were always good, I was never outstanding, perhaps because I didn't inherit his perseverance in studying; or perhaps because I had nothing to prove.

The truth is that his travelling companions, privately convinced of the connection between his intellectual ability, reading, studying and prosperity, felt even more sympathy when they saw him put so much energy into books.

I've often imagined my father when he was twelve, sitting in an old chair on the lowest stern deck – Third Class – reading books from the small library in which there were no more than about 60 books, mostly for studying; the rest were a selection of adventure stories by the best known authors of that time. Some of them were in English, others in Spanish.

Julio Verne; Emilio Salgari; Mark Twain; Horacio Quiroga; Domingo F. Sarmiento; Echeverría; Lucio V. Mansilla; Alberto J. Payró; both Dumas', father and son; Álvaro Yunque; R.L. Stevenson; H.G. Wells; Joseph Konrad; Jack London, travelled with him.

After the invariable *truco* game after a meal, there was always someone who asked my father what he was reading then and he used to give them an outline.

My father would always remember with pleasure those moments when his companions listened to him very attentively as he made a careful summary, full of details, on black arrows, lost children, time machines or submarines, loose cannons, Arctic seals or journeys among the native *ranqueles*.

"You know, Charly? People don't choose to be ignorant… I think if one can choose, most of us prefer to know… but if it's almost a privilege today to have a good education, at that time… well… I saw it in my *Viejo* who hardly had any schooling, and as soon as he had *maestro* Porrá in his life he took advantage of every second with him… I went to the best schools at that time… and my grandfather and my mother, both teachers, right? At 12 years old I knew more than some of my fellow travellers, at least about some things anyway…" he said to me once, while we were rowing along a stream heading for the Paraná River.

What is most likely is that they saw in him the future that they would have wanted, not for themselves but for their children or their grandchildren. The fact is that all those good people used to do everything possible to make him feel comfortable, and the transition from the protected safety of his family home and his hometown to being alone and estranged in the British boarding school be as least difficult as possible.

Not everything was wine and roses. Two terrible summer storms distressed them – the one between Brazil and Uruguay, the other as they arrived at the Canary Islands – which allowed my father to show his manly self-confidence and his calmness when faced with danger.

I learnt myself, over the years, how valuable it is in an extremely risky situation to be surrounded by serene people, so I understand perfectly.

In his brief but very rich experience among the *gaucho*s doing tasks that always implied some degree of risk, my father had quickly learnt the value of calmness and level-headedness and he applied it his whole life; and if this is quite remarkable in an adult, it is surprising in a boy of twelve.

He recalled with real delight all the programmed evacuation drills; he used to wait anxiously for them and after they were over, he was always congratulated by one or another officer.

They entrusted him with organizing the smaller children of several families travelling in the ship's Third Class and he did it so well that all the parents were most grateful for his work.

Whenever the ship came across dolphins or whales in pursuit of the abundant shoals of fish, the sailors would shout "dolphins port side!" or "dolphins at the prow!" according to where they were seen; and all the children would run towards the side which had been shouted out, led by my father -who never dropped the book he happened to be reading.

One night, nearing the Equator, an officer invited him to see the blue globe in which it's possible to see the constellations of both hemispheres, and for the effect to be even more dramatic, the bridge lights were turned off.

During his abundant nights under the open skies of Europe, Asia and Africa, he again saw those skies furiously illuminated by millions of stars, but he never forgot the deep feeling of his small size he had been aware of that night in the middle of the Atlantic Ocean.

The party for crossing the Equator – with its ridiculous initiatory rites- made him laugh as much as the Carnival festivities in Lomas de Zamora. They named him Poseidon's beloved son.

Another night they took him to the prow where they surprised him with the stunning brilliance of the glowing microorganisms' trail through which the ship was sailing.

He was astounded by the sight of the Teide volcano's snowed peak showing on the horizon, visible as a cloud from a great distance; and when they sailed in the colder waters of the northern hemisphere, he had been anxiously waiting to see the St. Elmo's Fires playing on the cables surrounding the ship's funnels, a phenomenon he had read about in Salgari, Verne or Konrad's stories.

A few kilometres from the first European port of the trip – Vigo – they witnessed the running aground and sinking of a ship with a British flag, and how they rescued the survivors. There were no victims except for the old steamship, and my father watched the whole rescue manoeuvre of bringing the survivors aboard the lifeboats.

He remembered even the smallest details of that event, when some of the "Copenhagen" crew members -directed by an officer- had boarded the lifeboats fitted with an outboard motor launched from the Third Class deck, and coordinating the rescue with the crew of the sinking ship; above all, he recalled the expressions of panic of the passengers when they were helped into the lifeboats.

Once they arrived in Vigo, the ship emptied noticeably. In my father's cabin only the two Englishmen were left. Only then did those two characters – syndicate members as I've said, followers of Sir Oswald Mosley – approach him. They knew his destination was King George's College and they were eager to attract him to their cause; it's clear their efforts were not successful.

That trip was his last breath of freedom before entering the British world. Up till then he had lived a kind and generous life. Argentina was, almost like today, a land where social mobility was possible. Today, too, it's likely there are social barriers but they're permeable, and at that time they were also lax and permissive.

The son of a Welsh worker had shared hours of play and study with a judge's son, the sons of a public servant or a farmer; they played rugby at school and soccer in an empty lot and they mixed without much protocol. My father himself was a clear example of this: his father was an immigrant worker and his mother had an American ancestral lineage.

He was invited to his friends' birthdays and they came to his; sometimes he visited their homes and sometimes they came to his, although the social centre of his life had been primary school.

As today, Argentina was then a republic.

Now all that had been left behind.

His arrival in Southampton had been a shock. All the ports he had seen up till then had appeared small due to the steamship traffic, including some clippers he saw at this wide entrance to the British Empire. It would not be the last time he saw the English coast, but never again with so much concern as to his future.

Two people were waiting for him at the port – a preceptor and a manservant to carry the luggage- and their serious and stiff attitudes were like a clear premonition of what was to come.

Once the necessary introductions had been made and before disembarking, with great ceremony the preceptor had expounded on the rigorous behaviour code – social and academic – and the protocol rules among peers, professors, workers and administrative staff that would rule his life over the next five or six years.

Although at his same age I chose a boarding school of which I have some of the best memories of my life, I do understand how Dad hated that school. It's true that when I announced my intention of wanting to attend the Liceo Militar (Military College) for my secondary schooling, he was against it; it was then that he told me, in a very detailed account, his ill-fated days as a boarder, I suppose in the hope I would give up my idea; but on the contrary, it's very likely his stories full of sad and lonely times helped me to overcome my far less terrible fate as a military college student.

"You know, Charly? I find it incredible that a boy of twelve or thirteen is sent fifteen thousand kilometres away from home, placed in the hands of complete strangers… Some of my companions had even spent all their primary schooling in the same conditions… Just imagine, they came from the extreme four corners within the Empire… Boys of six or seven, away from their parents, their siblings… Those who were luckiest were visited once a year by their parents or they had family in England who took them out on the weekends… A terrible British Empire system… so many people far from their home… People who grew up unhappy! Their first steps had been in another land, where they had heard other languages and had smelt other odours… Those people grew up yearning for the far off lands which in some way was their fatherland… Isn't it said that one's country is the land of our infancy? If their first steps were in Burma, that's their land, it doesn't matter where their parents came from… I was born here, I'm an Argentine…"

He told me this when he was recalling his trip by train from Southampton South to Waterloo Station in London, where they changed to a hired car to take them to the terminal of the railway line going to Enfield.

The change between what he was leaving behind and what was coming couldn't have been more different. The port and its incredible amount of movement had had an impact on the view of this twelve-year old boy, but the city's hustle and bustle, the railway trains and the difference in the train carriages filled him with wonder. In just a few minutes he was able to see some of the most famous train engines of that time.

The noise of the crowd, after twenty five days on the water, left him stunned, so much so that throughout his life, when he was worried about something, he invariably dreamt with those memorable images.

It caused no lesser impact when they crossed London.

Great Britain was attempting to get out of the 1929 crisis, unemployment was still very high, and even so, my father remembered that the hustle and bustle on the streets was truly worrying. There was an extense variety of vehicles – carriages pulled by horses or people, motorcars with two, three, four or six wheels moving from one side to another.

Never had the south of Greater Buenos Aires seemed so far away.

It was Tuesday, January 23rd, 1934; winter was launching its usual curse over London and the warm clothing specially sewn by my grandmother and worn for the first time demonstrated her skills as a seamstress. My father remembered with gratitude the quality, warmth and comfort of his underclothing. The family precautions had been more than adequate.

He had not liked those two men who had picked him up. There was something subtly disagreeable about them, a kind of conceited air about the preceptor, while the manservant seemed dumb, he ignored my father with such an intensity that he made him feel invisible, he practically did not look at my father during the whole journey.

Mr. Swaness, the preceptor, was unpleasant, a pedant and a bully. On the ship, when my father had put out his hand openly to shake this man's hand, he immediately felt a disagreeable touch. And the manservant just left my father's hand hanging in the air, without a word.

After he heard the preceptor recite all the school rules and regulations, he felt the man hadn't liked him. For the rest of the journey to the school a real dislike grew in Dad for this man, and it was clear the feeling was mutual.

Arrogant and contemptuous, superficial, for most of that over three-hour journey Swaness reviled against anything that wasn't British and more precisely, English. Of course, he discharged all his ignorance about South America and its licentious customs that ruined the *race*; and as he said to my father, at least he was white…

The monologue regarding the superiority of the British culture and its civilizing performance on the world only stopped when that dreadful man stood up for a moment, and my father took advantage of pretending he was asleep, which of course then actually happened.

The boring speech did not stop my *Viejo* from feeling surprised at the train compartments and the cold but educated indifference with which he saw how the passengers treated each other, and he could not help recalling how *maestro* Porrá would greet everybody equally with courtesy.

At the end of the afternoon, he was greeted in the old school with the same stiff English courtesy as had taken place at the port. He was received by the Deputy Headmaster, Professor Cabot Cuttler, who also had a long speech about British superiority and the excellence of the British educational system in general and particularly in that institution, and how the Crown cooperated with its subjects' education. In that school, founded by order of King George II so the sons of the colonial civil servants may be educated in a civilized land, the best future administrators of the Empire were formed, according to Cuttler.

Why did the highest-ranking civil servants in the colonies send their sons to that school? Because of its strictness and discipline, its precise protocol and observance of the rules.

They told him they would be watching him closely: a scholarship granted by the Prince of Wales was an honour that not everyone deserved, he must always be equal to these circumstances; his social class – his father a worker- and being the son of a native of a country which did not belong to the Empire were conditions that placed him in a school where he didn't really belong; he must prove by his social behaviour and his academic performance that the above was untrue.

After that terrible speech he was led to the dining room, where he had his supper together with other boarders. Once he had finished his supper – during which he could feel eyes on him throughout the meal- he was taken to a bedroom which he would share with three other boys of his same age.

Although he was exhausted by the trip as well as this radical change in his life, he could not sleep that night. He also realized that this was not going to be the only night under these conditions.

The truth is that my father's family – my grandparents and my great-grandfather- believed that this school was the epitome of world education, and from the academic perspective this was probably true, as a student there he had received an elite education. But as far as the emotional and human side, taking into consideration his previous experiences, the school was a prison, an undeserved punishment.

He did the only thing he knew how to do. Study, and more studying and reading all day. He found out very quickly that the school was like a jungle or an ocean, where the predators hunt the weak, where a small fish is devoured by large fish.

In contrast to his travelling companions, who just a few days before had treated him with deference and affection, his room companions ignored him, paying him no attention at all.

That same week he joined the rugby team and his natural flair for sports gave him the advantage of avoiding being picked on; also, a couple of months later he started boxing lessons and his speed in hitting accurate blows did the rest. Swimming lessons – with the novelty of a covered pool – made him not a very quick swimmer but an incredibly tenacious one.

Shortly before the summer recess he was confronted by a boy in the highest form and quite much larger than himself, but despite his size he was not able to beat my father. So he was left alone.

On the other hand his academic performance, which before had been brilliant, was almost mediocre. He studied for hours on end and his marks were just enough to get a pass. They demanded more and he responded by studying even more.

It didn't matter how much he studied, how much determination and willingness he showed, his marks were only just enough for him to pass the courses, they never reflected his efforts. He would learn, over time, that there was a more or less tacit agreement between the teachers -covered up by Professor Cabot Cuttler- for him not to stand out in any way.

For a part of the world's ideology at that time, my father was an anomaly in the system, an unforgivable error which should become invisible.

That was how it was handled from the beginning and it lasted till his last summer there.

During those days and not without tears, he buried his childhood. He was very conscious that those he had left behind fifteen thousand kilometres to the south considered that this school was the best life being offered to him, an opportunity to be taken advantage of, so he just gritted his teeth and became a library mouse… which he only left to train for his rugby, swimming and boxing practices.

He only cried at night, in silence, once the dorm lights had been turned off.

King George's College was a few kilometres from Enfield, on Ferny Hill Street, an ancient road. It was very close to Barnet, a small town that had grown around the school and later, after the railway lines had reached Enfield and a bus ran to and fro from London, Barnet had become a refuge for the growing middle class, and the school had become more like a military college.

The school had been founded by the order of King George II of Hannover, the last English king to be born abroad, on a 64 hectare – 128 acres – property expropriated from a Jacobite in the 1645 rebellion, with the intention of educating an elite group of administrators for the Crown's properties. The school was surrounded by a very thick live berry-type hedge with long thorns and on which grew large, unsavoury fruit. The thick hedge – it was about 6 or 7 mts. wide and perhaps four mts. high, had a sort of gallery on the inside all the way along, leading to secret exits from all four corners of the property.

Within the perimeter there was another wall, made of large Dover stone granite about four metres high, in the shape of a star with battlement towers at each end. Within those walls there were some 16 hectares – 32 acres – of carefully distributed buildings.

A few metres from the formidable entrance (which was four metres higher than the wall) was the main two-storied building. The entrance had a double-leaf gate made of African wood -even harder than *quebracho*- measuring some six mts. wide and three mts high, and behind this a portcullis.

The main building held the library, the administrative offices and the 8 or 9 classrooms. Behind this, over 80 metres away and joined by a stone path along which grew beech and oak trees for shade, were the kitchen, the dining-room and a small dispensary and infirmary.

Towards the south was another building, in the same style as the main one, also on two floors and distributed in two wings: on the north side were the students' dorms – the younger boys on the top floor, the older ones below- and on the south side, the teachers' bedrooms. All the buildings were some 40 or 50 mts. from each other, joined by solid stone paths and surrounded by a large quantity of leafy ash, oak, chestnut and acacia trees. The paths crossed a green, well-cut English lawn, on which it was forbidden to set foot.

On each side of the entrance gate on Ferny Hill St, inside the property, were two solid buildings which on the outside appeared to form part of the wall; these held the maintenance workshops and the head of maintenance's room.

"Near the wall on the northern side -more than 100 mts. from the main group of buildings- stood a covered gymnasium that included a pool, with changing rooms, showers and bathrooms; a cricket field; a rugby field; several places for Olympic disciplines and surrounding them, an athletics track. In those years the sport jousts with Eaton – another more socially eminent royal school and King George College's greatest competitor – took place four times a year and the results were published in the Times.

Getting in or out of the school was practically impossible.

That winter slid by together with secret and silent tears which the spring hardly softened, to finally stop definitely once they were well into summer. That first British semester nothing was easy for him.

When the English summer arrived the school began to empty slowly as it did every year. Many pupils' families lived in different parts of Great Britain; other boys were collected by their parents, who travelled thousands of kilometres to spend a few weeks with their sons; those who remained, such as my father, generally were the worst off financially, as their parents invested all their money in the dreamed-of education for their son and couldn't afford a single penny from such far off places as Rangoon, Shanghai or Sydney.

And last of all were those scholarship holders like my father, those who barely paid for their clothes and food, and much less for trips, holidays or pleasure cruises.

Besides the pupils, a small group of teachers and preceptors lived at King George's College to control the boys as much as to give a few extra courses on their subject. Young or old, they were generally boring scholars on their subject, and my father took as much advantage of them as possible.

It was a man's world, beyond the three or four plump women who managed the kitchen and cleaned the bathrooms.

Shortly after his thirteenth birthday and thanks to Derek Jones' disloyalty, he got to find a peaceful place. Derek Jones was a year older than Dad, he had grown up near the Arctic –his father was the manager of a Crown property in northern Canada- and Derek was a fighter and a bully.

Derek dared my father to a fight, just the two of them alone -with no witnesses or third parties- in a secret place he had found.

Derek had very skillfully disabled the inner latch of a window in the changing room bathroom in the gymnasium, and he used this place whenever he wished; all he had to do was slip in unnoticed into the room and stay out of sight and hearing of the few people left in the school.

Derek bet that he had the right to that place and that he would knock out my father quickly – but he made a big mistake.

Both boys practiced boxing under an instructor who made sure the fights were covered by boxing rules, avoiding any knock-out or hurt to either fighter, but Jones wanted to fight with his fists, no gloves or guardians or custodians.

My father didn't beat him to a pulp because he was still small and wasn't heavy enough to hit very hard; even so, his knuckles hurt him for weeks. On the other hand, he fought so intensely and fiercely that Derek was totally exhausted and had to give in, while my father kept on dancing around him, hitting, and until Derek let himself be hit three times in the face in order to finish the hours-long fight.

It took about a week for feeling to come back to my father's arms, hands and head from all the blows he had received and given; some of the bruises took weeks to disappear.

After that Derek passed as something similar to a friend among all the pupils. Now and again they exchanged some kind or respectful words. It's probably this fight that made the bigger boys keep from bullying him.

Derek kept to his word and never used that place again as a ringside without asking for permission, and they shared that secret until father's last day at the College; their paths would cross again, in more dramatic circumstances, in 1940.

Dad had discovered during his sleepless nights that if he mentally sang in Welsh his anguish didn't disappear completely but at least it diminished.

When he won *"the right to use"* the large gymnasium bathroom –actually, the disabled window latch allowing him to secretly use that place – he had no idea what he could do there, as he did not drink, or smoke or masturbate yet; but to celebrate the costly victory he'd spend his nap time, and just from boredom, and playing with the acoustics of that spacious tiled room, full of partitions, he began to sing.

My father's voice had inherited grandmother Pepa's musical qualities - in the house in their railway neighbourhood there had always been an Italian upright piano, a gift from grandfather Porrá – as well as the voices of the traditional Welsh choirs: he had a beautiful, colourful baritone which he didn't even have to make louder to be heard. At thirteen it still didn't have its current colour, but his special tone was already there.

He found that when he sang the four or five Welsh songs he had learnt in Patagonia, what took place in his head at night was exponentially multiplied. Singing those harmonious, colourful songs had healing effects on his spirit.

His schedule became split into rather strange parts that summer. He went from boring Greek and Latin, or maths and calculus classes to a joyful moment almost the whole afternoon, day after day, waiting for the beginning of classes almost as if he were condemned to death.

Shortly before, something took place that would have a definite impact on his life.

He sang with his eyes closed, focused as only he knew how, listening to his own voice, attempting to correct what he was hearing in the song, when suddenly behind him he heard a throat being cleared and a voice in English.

"You sing well… that's Welsh… I don't think… you came from Argentina, I was there when… Where did you learn? Who…?

Dad almost had a heart-attack.

Behind him, holding a toolbox was the head of maintenance, the same worker who had carried his luggage off the ship and who had ignored him that fateful morning in Southampton.

He was a heavy man, with inexpressive eyes and austere gestures, dark but with early greying hair. He was hardly beyond fifty years old, but clearly he was soon going to be an old man.

Eurwen Glynn, "*Don*" Eurwen to my father, was a good man who had been mistreated badly in his life, a person that destiny had dealt with cruelly, and who had got used to hiding any thought or feeling behind an inexpressive face and a very subtle disdainful attitude.

My father was extremely concerned, he felt an up-till-then unknown fear as to how this man had found him. If he fulfilled his duty he would be obliged to tell the school authorities what he'd witnessed and this filled my father with terror. He couldn't bear to think about the possibility of being expelled and sent back home.

My father didn't tell me what he had said to *Don* Eurwen, but because of what took place over the following years it's clear that whatever he said must have deeply moved this man.

A few days after this encounter my father decided to go back to his secret auditorium, once he realized there hadn't been any report. On a moonless night, warmed by the southern wind, he carefully slipped into his "private" auditorium with the same skill he would show later, on the battlefield.

When he opened the window – which had not been repaired-, he found, hidden in a way only whoever entered through the window would find, a small book with yellowed covers and rough paper pages. It was almost a magazine, with some twenty traditional songs written in English and Welsh, with instructions on how to sing them. On the last page, printed at the bottom, a line which was difficult to read: "1883 - Printed in Trevelin, Chubut, Argentina." On the back cover, pencilled in with clean and neat handwriting: "Can I listen to you again?"

My father was very doubtful about accepting the head of maintenance as his public. All his life until he arrived in England he had been surrounded by adults who had respected, protected and loved him - and then suddenly he had found himself submerged in a world of indifferent adults and peers who were almost cruel.

A letter from his grandfather Porrá played a great part in my father's decision to accept Eurwen; it's clear that although the old *maestro* didn't know what was taking place – my father used to carefully censure his letters to Argentina, avoiding any comment which would convey his unhappiness – he requested my father be careful regarding anything unsavoury anywhere around him, but not to be afraid of approaching and learning -not only from his teachers and professors- but also from the cleaners, cooks and the maintenance personnel. *"Don't forget that, just as you, all of them have a story to tell, even the clumsiest and ignorant. Pay attention to them, because wisdom also talks through them; don't let yourself be influenced by the well-heeled, who are mostly incapable of seeing the values in their fellow men regardless of their social background, and for sure in that school there must be more than one person who disdains the working class, and you're being criticized for this. Do they forbid you to talk to the workers? It's an absurd prohibition, undoubtedly you must follow the rules, but it's more important to follow your own conscience. For centuries the rule was to have slaves. You and I know that to violate that rule is an act of justice. So, obey the rules as long as they're not in conflict with your moral conscience,"* he had written.

The next time his path crossed the old man's he gave an almost imperceptible nod and the man, without looking at him, made an identical gesture back.

The first time he sang in front of *Don* Eurwen, my father felt strange and uneasy. But when he looked at that man's face -hard and weather-beaten- his thick and callused hands, and wearing a classic dark grey overall and heavy shoes -seeing him as moved as his dear Meredith, the feeling was replaced by the warm safety he thought he had lost.

In his voice, the Welsh hymn **"Mae Hen Wlad Fy Nhadau"** sounded absolutely unique to *Don* Eurwen, with its sad, melancholy words:

Mae hen wlad fy nhadau yn annwyl i mi,

Gwlad beirdd a chantorion, enwogion o fri;

Ei gwrol ryfelwyr, gwladgarwyr tra mâd,

Dros ryddid gollasant eu gwaed.

Gwlad, Gwlad, pleidiol wyf i'm gwlad,

Tra môr yn fur i'r bur hoff bau,

O bydded i'r heniaith barhau.

Hen Gymru fynddig, paradwys y bardd;

Pob dyffryn, pob clogwyn, i'm golwg sydd hardd,

Trwy deimlad gwladgarol, môr swynol yw si,

Ei nentydd afonydd, i mi.

Os trisiodd y gelyn fy ngwlad dan ei droed,

Mae hen iaith y Cymry môr fyw ag erioed,

Ni luddiwyd yr awen gan erchyll law brad,

Na thelyn berseiniol fy ngwlad.

This land of my fathers is dear to me

Land of poets and singers, and people of stature

Her brave warriors, fine patriots

Shed their blood for freedom

Chorus:

Land! Land! I am true to my land!

As long as the sea serves as a wall

For this pure, dear land

> May the language endure for ever.
>
> Old land of the mountains, paradise of the poets,
>
> Every valley, every cliff a beauty guards;
>
> Through love of my country, enchanting voices will be
>
> Her streams and rivers to me.
>
> Though the enemy have trampled my country underfoot,
>
> The old language of the Welsh knows no retreat,
>
> The spirit is not hindered by the treacherous hand
>
> Nor silenced the sweet harp of my land.

The summer of 1934 was therefore, memorable.

The second meeting my father took his *mate* set, about which the worker had discreetly inquired. And to my father's surprise – he had almost left his habit because he found it boring to drink *mate* on his own, and he had been forbidden to do this in public – the man tried and liked it. They did not meet every day, but now and again they found time to meet and have some *mates* away from any reproving looks.

Ever since my father's arrival at school, they had pointed out to him that *mate* was a "savage" habit that he should avoid, at least publicly.

When classes began again, the day hours were full of students and professors who at all hours were wandering everywhere, so the only chance to visit his "private salon" was at night time, once the lights in the students' dorms had been turned off at 8 p.m.

Over the following years my father realized that this good man had seen how alone he was at school, at a time in his life which should have been completely the opposite, and this man also knew —because of his connection with the librarian – about the tough tests to which he was unjustly being subjected, and as time went by he had felt a growing empathy towards the boy.

My father wrote to his confidant, adviser and teacher telling him about the events – knowing he was letting himself in for an epistolary scolding – and giving him some details on the treatment and working conditions of the workmen; he soon received a long as well as an apt reply.

Porrá warned him again regarding the harm that could be wrought among men, about the danger of breaking rules and of their importance in a civilized society, highlighting that the degree of civilization should be measured by their treatment of workers and the deprived. He also attached some carefully chosen cuttings from the Buenos Aires Herald, indicating pointedly that they were for *Don* Eurwen…

As well as the Herald cuttings, grandfather Porrá also always sent him past issues of the "Claridad" magazine, from which Dad chose some articles and then translated them, carefully and meticulously, to the joy of that man, who's coarse and rough aspect hid a heart and sensibility that deserved better.

This Welshman would play a fundamental role in the chain of events that made my father the man he is today.

Just as my father would leave him material to read in the secret mailbox the workman had set up in the toilet of that bathroom, Eurwen started to leave him newspaper cuttings, magazines, flyers.

The Welshman was a conscientious Labour activist who could not openly be himself in that deeply conservative school, ideologically distant from any benefit for the working class.

It was a delicate issue for both of them. If they were discovered by pupils, professors or any manager, that friendship and exchange of ideas —so in agreement with the progressive and free-thinking spirit in which my father had been educated and so opposite to the school regulations- could have serious consequences for both my father and Eurwen.

They weren't being paranoid.

For Eurwen to be fired at that age and without any letter of recommendation didn't mean him having to face a helpless, unprotected old age because he did have a reasonable income from the rental of a property in Cardiff, but it could mean serious and possible legal consequences.

For my father, on the other hand, it could mean the beginning of frightening consequences that could point to a very bleak future.

The fact is that until Dad left that school, Eurwen was his friend in the shadows, a family member, a protector.

Classes and the autumn days pushed their meetings further apart but not their communication. My father's mood changed completely, and he was cheerful and happy again. He increased his efforts at studying although his academic position among the bottom-of-the-class pupils did not improve ostensibly.

He cared very little.

A lonely Christmas, surrounded by strangers who if not hostile were basically indifferent, and the absence of *Don* Eurwen, made it the worst Christmas in his life. However, after having written a 12-page essay on boy kings and their regents, his lively and agile mind also came up with an idea that would make his life in Britain a little easier.

He sent a long -a very long, 16-page letter- to Meredith requesting a special exeat permission for the weekends, from Saturday midday till the end of Sunday eve, 8:30 p.m.

His reasons communicated strong logic, and he used such an immensely rich language and an erudite background that even Pepa, the most reticent of all, ended up supporting the request.

Meredith had begun to work when he was 12 years old and Dad was reaching his 14th birthday, a logical comparison added to the fact that he had been on his own for a whole year, without going out, almost a prisoner in a school surrounded by a very high wall; he had no idea of the world around him beyond the trip that took him there -this was one of the important points.

He also told them about his friendship with the Welshman that included songs, biscuits and *mates*, and finally, he added a summary of what he knew about his friend, his history, which undoubtedly was what most moved the family.

Eurwen Glynn had been born in Cardiff, he was older than my grandfather Meredith. He came from a family of masons. When he was 14, between the years 1898 and 1911 he had worked in Canada and the U.S.A., where he had saved some money, and in 1915 he was finishing a small two-story house with shops on the ground floor to rent. Having this advantageous position he would be able to marry his boyhood girlfriend – and then he was called up by the Army.

The war did to him what it did to all his generation: destroyed his life.

In 1917 he returned home with a very badly-wounded leg – his right leg was almost completely paralyzed- and he got married without any great celebration in 1918. Then in the Spanish flu epidemic in 1919, he lost both his wife and his newly-born baby overnight.

Just a few days after the tragedy, life's twists -the exotic scheme that weaves the silk strings of our existence- brought Eurwen a letter from an emigrant companion who was leaving again for Canada, and was looking for a replacement at his post as head of maintenance at the prestigious royal King George's College.

Eurwen rented out his Cardiff property and in less than ten days he was installed at his new job.

It was clear that the idea of the letter asking for his parents' permission was based on the principle that my father was –or at least he felt himself to be -ready and prepared to take control over his life and that he felt worthy of this independence.

Whichever the case, it was effective. Pepa and Meredith signed – before a notary public, then in the Foreign Affairs office and at the British Consulate – an extensive permit allowing him to leave and move outside the school within the days and hours allowed by the school without any other paperwork than to advise a responsible adult. Although not completely, Dad had managed to obtain a partial freedom.

The permission would be valid as from the day of his fourteenth birthday, July 9th, 1935, a date which inexorably arrived.

To his surprise, the same day and apparently from Argentina, he received another extraordinary gift. Recognisable even within the careful brown paper wrapping, waiting for him in the preceptor's office and leaning against a wall was the unmistakeable profile of a man's bicycle, complete with back and front lights and a luggage rack.

My father was almost totally happy that summer.

Although the wrappings and the careful placement of the postage stamps appeared to make it true that the gift had come from Argentina, my father knew immediately that his Argentine family had not sent the parcel.

Don Eurwen had kept all the stamps from 18 packets – letters and parcels- that my father had received over the last semester. Eurwen oversaw, among other things, the cleaning of the whole school and that's how he must have been able to keep the stamps. He was also responsible for picking up parcels and packets that were not delivered by post, which allowed him the complete bicycle masquerade.

The following Saturday my father anxiously watched when *Don* Eurwen left the school grounds on his motorbike -an old 1915 Norton 500- with a sidecar, as he did every Saturday; there was a little detail the Welshman hadn't taken into account and that my father hadn't ever communicated: he didn't know how to ride a bicycle.

It sounds strange, but it's true. He was totally confident as a horse rider, but never in his short life had he ridden a bike, as he hadn't had any need to learn.

My father wasn't someone who would back down, so he went out onto the main road distractedly pushing his bicycle and following the rough map that Eurwen had made for him. He walked by the roadside pushing his bike towards a group of large houses, surrounded by extensive gardens but empty of people.

That first time outside the school was another milestone in my father's life – he had been living for a year and a half in England and had never left the school property- so he was confronting the challenge of a new world without much awareness of the risks being run by a young boy on the road.

As always, he was lucky. It was a peaceful neighbourhood, and seemed to be solitary and have very few inhabitants. So my father launched himself down Lancaster St, perpendicular to Cockfoster Avenue, the main road cutting across the road leading to the College. He got onto the bike… and of course, fell off.

Again and again, my father tried getting onto the bike, following the techniques he had seen other cyclists applying, and the same amount of times he finished on the ground, sometimes right away, and others after having ridden not more than ten steps.

He had been trying more than an hour to achieve his goal and all he'd managed were bruises, bumps and to scrape his hands, elbows, knees and thighs. His clothes –he was wearing the "dailies", the oldest and most worn and which he had chosen purposely- were starting to show his many falls, and all my father was achieving were new ways to land on the hard cobblestone road.

His despair and discouragement were about to take over when another guardian angel crossed his path.

It was an hour in the summer in which if he were in Remedios de Escalada, Lomas de Zamora or Banfield, it would have been advisable for him not to go out: the streets were deserted because it was *siesta* time and in the heavy heat he might meet up with the bogey man, an elf or a gypsy woman who stole babies and children. But he was in Barnet, near Enfield, and nobody had warned him he might run into danger.

Every time a vehicle or person went by, my father pretended to be walking placidly, pushing his bike, trying to show indifference and that it was all very natural.

This is how Mrs Cummins appeared, out of nowhere.

She was a mature, energetic woman with strawberry-coloured hair, still far from being old, with a matronly body and features of an extraordinary beauty. Her bright blue eyes stood out against a soft, brown skin.

She was riding a green bicycle that had a straw basket at the front and a wooden box at the back, which somehow didn't fit in with that smart neighbourhood of typically British houses; although they weren't sumptuous, they did clearly speak of a considerably comfortable life.

She was wearing a simple, wide, colourful dress, which covered the plump figure of a mature woman; it had a flower design in pink tones which stood out on her apparently tanned skin. At a time when uncovered arms or ankles was considered in bad taste, this energetic and luscious woman was surprisingly indifferent to being seen as she was.

My father tried to hide his problem when the woman began asking kindly but insistently about him being there on the road at that time, when most good people were in their homes. When he said he was a pupil at King George's College, the women pointed out that if this were true he couldn't have permission to be out; so my father had to explain about his father's authorization and offered to show it to her —he always carried one copy of the permit- so she had to be satisfied.

They were both silent then, each waiting for the other to leave. My father knew he could not get on to the bicycle without falling off, so they both stayed there a long while in silence, smiling in a friendly way, when finally the woman spoke.

"I've been watching you from the window in my room for over an hour. It's obvious you don't know how to ride a bike, young man, so listen to me..."

Sitting on her bike, she then proceeded to show him every movement, with precise instructions on how to ride his own bicycle without falling off.

Evidently this women was a very good instructress, because right then and there he was able to pedal off without any problem. They both rode around the deserted neighbourhood, and when it was clear that my father could now be called a cyclist, the woman invited him in to have a glass of lemonade and a piece of strawberry cake.

The afternoon had flown by quickly and it was almost tea-time. It was clear his projected ride to Surrey was not going to happen; however, the object of the permission was to meet people and see something more than just the school…

Mrs Cummins was as far from being the prototype of a British woman as my father was to being a member of the royal family. If Eurwen Glynn was something like a father to him in those days, Sylvia Sullivan Cummins was something like a mother.

Although it took my father many months to get to know *Don* Eurwen, he was sure that in that first afternoon Sylvia must have told him her entire life, in a fun summary, full of colour and laughter. She was currently a bored and down-hearted woman who had lived a happy, entertaining life.

She had been born in India - her father was a Catholic Irishman, a Sergeant Major in the British army and her mother was the daughter of an English adventurer -he had died young- and an Indian mother. So Sylvia was not actually suntanned but brown-skinned, and she had inherited her father's blonde hair and blue eyes.

She had been orphaned at age twelve, and was sent to a convent as a boarder – her father being Catholic- with the intention of preventing her maternal family from bringing her up according to the Rajasthan customs and practices.

When she was 15 she had run away from the convent to marry Mr. Cummins, fifteen years older than herself. He had a promising career in the West India Railroad Company. They had lived in different regions of India between 1895 and 1928, when Mr. Cummins had fallen ill. They returned to England to find adequate treatment but unfortunately the good man had died at the end of 1929.

The widowed Mrs Cummins had three sons: John Daniel, Ronald Eric and Robert Stuart, who were scattered around the world. John Daniel was in India managing a transport company which worked well because it was linked to the railroad, created foresightedly by Mr. Cummins before World War I.

Ronald Eric was a ship captain in the Merchant Navy, and Robert Stuart was a First Officer in a war ship sailing between the Chinese, Sumatran and Borneo seas.

Mrs Cummins, who from the first day begged him to call her by her first name, was thus living alone, except for a Hindu servant girl who silently did all the housework. Her sons wrote her long letters and sent her photos but did not visit very often -neither they did seem close to or even willing to get married in the short term, so she did not even have grandchildren to look forward to in the near future.

After her husband died she had dressed in black and attended the local church, seeking solace for her pain – she had loved her husband and had been very happy with him.

She also sought some social life - but after four years in that direction without any real happiness she had abandoned almost all contact with the outside world, staying within the walls of her home and becoming totally involved with a dream garden.

She had a heated winter garden where she grew Oriental flowers and some exotic fruits in winter and summer. The winter garden was not much larger than my father's home in Escalada and the space it occupied was less than half the garden; here grew a variety of roses and other flower bushes. In different corners there were fruit trees — at least seven types of berries- and in the sunniest corner, a small vegetable garden –to feed two or three people- with a complete and permanent production; off to the side, four rabbits and eight hens provided the house with meat and eggs.

Mrs Cummins was charmingly vital and she was as alone in the British world as my father was, their loved ones thousands of kilometres away. An immediate and mutual liking sprang up between them.

She did not have any money problems – Mr. Cummins had invested his large amount of savings in precious metals and Oriental stones, avoiding the temptation of quick earnings on the stock exchange and real estate speculation, so that he had left her -even after the international crisis year- a good, solid fortune, easily convertible to cash.

At that time Mrs Sylvia's standard of living was very comfortable, which perhaps today is more common, but my father had never seen any of these "luxuries" even in the best-off homes he had visited in the far-off southern districts of Greater Buenos Aires.

She had a washing-machine, central heating, a dishwasher, and telephones in several rooms, a radio and a big record-player; and in the kitchen there was a large refrigerator – not like the one in the Escalada house, which was an icebox with blocks of ice- but very like the ones seen today in any shop.

Her sons were also very generous, periodically they would send her small amounts of money that she hardly spent, perhaps sometimes she'd buy some nice dresses, and plants and seeds.

My father filled an emptiness in Sylvia Sullivan Cummins' life and a genuine, lengthy friendship was born between them, which was only interrupted by her death in 1958.

After that Saturday when my father learnt to ride his bicycle, the Cummins home became his safe refuge, a warm and kind home from where he would organize his week-end excursions, firstly to *Don* Eurwen's refuge, and afterwards up to wherever his strength lasted or gave out.

Undoubtedly Mrs Sylvia was a noble and generous person, who adopted my father without much questioning or expecting too many answers. He slept there –in a comfortable, large guest room with a private bathroom – on that weekend and many more. This good woman made sure my father's clothes were in good condition, she sent his good Argentine shoes to be repaired and she gave him -always very simply and without any fuss - some practical and good quality clothes so that he wouldn't wreck his school clothes during his weekend jaunts. She'd just leave them for him on the guest-room bed.

Grandmother Pepa and Sylvia wrote regularly to each other without ever meeting, they were true pen friends over many years.

That summer of 1935 was the first my father had enjoyed since he made that formidable herding journey at the end of 1933. He started training his muscles in order to ride the many kilometres on his brand-new vehicle with one objective in mind: to visit *Don* Eurwen in South Surrey.

It was a 45-kilometre return trip that a practical cyclist could resolve in one day without any problem. After two or three weeks of pedalling daily along the secret passage that ran within the hedge around the school and looked after regularly by *Don* Eurwen, far from the eyes of the few inhabitants left in the school, my father felt ready to go out onto the road.

He slept at the Cummins home the night before, he had a good breakfast before dawn and at the first sunrays, he departed on his journey south along Cockfoster Ave., not with the simple map that Eurwen had drawn for him but with a brand new BP roadmap which Mrs Sylvia had given him.

Although nowadays it is normal for women to drive —my mother comes and goes regularly between Esperanza, Santa Fe province and Buenos Aires- in those days a woman at the wheel was still a rarity, and of course Mrs Cummins did so quite happily: she had a small Morgan convertible she used on special occasions.

She had tried to convince my father —unsuccessfully- that it would be much better if she drove him in her car, pointing out the many dangers on a road; some years later she confessed that she was afraid that Eurwen was a danger to him.

It's funny, because the two people who cared for and loved my father during those years, Mrs Sylvia and *Don* Eurwen, did not like each other. For the Welsh worker, that woman was a classic example of the colonial middle-class who had become rich by exploiting distant lands; for the woman, Eurwen was a political agitator working to overthrow the established order. Some years later, when my father had disappeared in Spain, they both left aside their differences and busily started communicating with his family in Argentina.

That day he rode for almost three hours, stopping now and again to take a look at the map and make sure of his position heading towards southern Surrey. He was carrying a thermos bottle holding deliciously cold blueberry tea and at the back on the luggage rack was a small basket in which he had an enormous turkey sandwich and a generous piece of lemon pie.

Although now and again he saw similarities between the houses of his neighbourhood with others in Temperley or Lomas de Zamora, that first journey through the London suburbs awoke in him a strange feeling of not belonging in that clean, tidy and orderly décor.

He finally reached his destination: a worker's neighbourhood, with houses which were similar to his railway neighbourhood, not only because of their classic style and finishing, but also because they were built in blocks of two houses together, and all the houses were identical; differently to his neighbourhood, these houses were two-storied.

At the end of a long street, where a group of workers' houses ended and the green English countryside began, just on the corner crossing with a Royal Road there was a building –a rather large shed but very dilapidated through lack of maintenance- with a sign reading, "O´Sean Automotive Repairs & Professional Driving". My father had finally arrived.

Don Eurwen was very happy to see him, he normally spent Sundays on his own.

Over the following months and until his journey into Spain, my father's weekends were alternately spent at the workshop and at the Cummins home, between a recently discovered comfort and the masculine refuge. In the future, the latter workshop was the building from which he left several times to fight with Mosley's blackshirts over who owned the street.

In the end my father eventually got to do that trip in just over an hour, riding through the London suburbs from north to south. On that first return trip, Eurwen carried my father's bike on his motorbike back to Mrs Sylvia's corner, and there my father bathed and changed his clothes to return to school.

It was several weeks before my father met the owner of the workshop.

Eurwen had met O'Sean during the time he was an immigrant in Canada and the U.S.A. O'Sean was quite a bit older and under other circumstances one could say that because he was over 60 he must be an old man, but the truth is that this dark and bitter Irishman possessed a prodigious physical strength and an amazing vitality.

He was not "a good man". Since his childhood he had fought the English through the Sinn Féin and once peace was declared after the 1916 rebellion –which ended most of Ireland's independence – he had not accepted Belfast's breakaway. In the fighting he had lost much more than his father, one brother, two brothers-in-law, two sons and one son-in-law.

He had lost his sense of humour, his humanism and his compassion.

Eurwen had coincidentally met up with him again when he started working at the College; he was looking for a used motorbike and O'Sean had placed an ad in a local newspaper offering a motorbike for sale.

Afterwards, while having the motor and other details needing to be fixed on this used vehicle –the Irishman did the work, insulting the vehicle and using incredibly coarse language- Eurwen found that this old, solitary and bitter man had a family: the widow of one of his sons who had died in Belfast, and a boy –his grandson, 12 or 13 years old; and in order to spend some time with them he needed someone to sleep in the shed once or twice a week.

So whenever Eurwen had a day off from his work at the school, he'd spend time in that dismal shed, where he read, slept or just rested, totally alone, surrounded by all kinds of dismantled vehicles, wrecks in different degrees.

My father began visiting the workshop regularly; but he also started visiting London and surroundings as a tourist, accompanied by and under Sylvia's tutorship. They went to different cultural activities to those in the school's curriculum, such as concerts or plays, especially to see Shakespeare, of who Mrs Cummins was a devotee.

Therefore, spread over the three worlds, the school, the Cummins house and O'Sean's shed, Dad began a new life, intense and full of nuances.

He also began to be interested in politics and to follow international news, either on Sylvia's radio or through the flyers and pamphlets that O'Sean and *Don* Eurwen handed to him.

Very probably because of the way in which Barnet's small middle-class society – definitely conservative- had treated Sylvia, she admired and was very interested in hearing all about Clement Atlee, leader of the Labour Party.

Coincidently –or not- Mrs Cummins and *Don* Eurwen were strangely in agreement regarding many things, but they expressed a mutual dislike which over the years really amused my father. If they hadn't been British, one could have said each was jealous of the other.

They were in agreement against all fascists and in envisioning Nazi German and fascist Italy as real risks in the short term. They did not agree on the way to deal with them. Eurwen was a follower of Ramsay MacDonald, Sylvia followed Attlee.

Eurwen, Sylvia and my father were very moved when they learnt in the newspapers of the death in Buenos Aires of the Scots nobleman -a friend of Argentina- Labour M.P. Robert Cunninghame Graham, and they joined the large procession at his funeral.

Autumn passed into winter; Christmas and the New Year 1936 were the beginning of my father learning about politics, and this would lead him towards the worst evil, war and destruction.

My father spent Christmas with Mrs Sylvia –she gave him a warm leather jacket for his motorbike rides with Eurwen- and he spent New Year with *Don* Eurwen and O'Sean.

This was the first time my father saw a hand-gun close up. They fired several rounds inside the shed with an FN 9mm parabellum pistol and his mouth dropped open when he saw the metal bodywork of a 1928 Rugby full of 11 or 12 bullet holes.

Don Eurwen reproached the old Irishman for encouraging my father to use such a lethal weapon, but my *Viejo* –who despite his boxing ability and knowledge was not violent- only saw it as a dangerous tool.

My father also found out that he was a remarkably good shot in any position.

O'Sean prepared different-sized targets –there were abundant empty tins of soup, peas and corned beef, bottles of spirits and tins of oil- and he placed them in different places and at different distances, playing with the sizes. The old man shouted –yes, he shouted quite often when he had been drinking, and he was always drinking- "Beer!", or "Beef!" or "Peas!" according to what he chose, and my father would shoot.

Young Franco

O'Sean started to speed up and my *Viejo* never missed. So during the cold afternoon of January 1, 1936, they used up about ten cartridge clips.

It would turn into a watershed year for all of them.

Once the Christmas holidays had passed – a generous period equal to our winter holidays – my father returned to his routine at school and alternating his weekends. English politics were mixed with international politics and many voices began to talk about the "Spanish affair" –as an influential conservative newspaper called the fighting taking place in Spain – and its possible consequences to the capitals invested in the Basque country, in the case of a possible Popular Front triumph.

Independent socialism – a minority that supported Attlee- demanded that the British government support the Popular Front and denounced the obscure network of economic interests that were attempting to influence British foreign policy, which was not acknowledging the results of the elections in Spain held in February.

My father began to accompany Eurwen who, although he was a pacifist, supported the pickets of the political activists that stood outside the exits at public events –races, boxing, soccer- in order to spread the news on what was taking place in Spain; and more than once they clashed –with sticks, chains and now and again fists- with the blackshirts who were trying to stop them, more and more frequently.

War was approaching together with spring.

The political events in Spain were speedily following each other, more serious every time, and each time more violent. Not a day went by without new and bad news regarding the coalition government – this was the Republican front which gathered the liberals and the leftists - wanting to install a full democracy, starting with the autonomy of each of the countries forming Spain.

Attacks and counter-attacks were very frequent. Nobody was surprised when the 1936 summer holidays brought with it a civil war in Spain.

Churchill and Attlee tried in every way to convince Ramsay MacDonald and Chamberlain about the need to support the Republicans, totally opposite to their idea of encouraging a "non-intervention" policy, and for which they created a special committee.

Calvo Sotelo's assassination, Primo de Rivera's imprisonment and the lawsuits covering the 1934 Repression were the reasons put forward by Franco to lead the civil-military coup in July, and in a short time it had turned into the Spanish civil war.

The subversive alliance of economic capitals, the international fascist forces and part of the Spanish Armed Forces against a legally chosen government voted in by the elections and called the Second Republic, broke out that summer and lit up Europe with gunpowder and explosives.

The Spanish war, right from the start, was fully covered by British politics and the press. Educated people and the unionized workers, and in general, every person interested in politics knew what was going on, and from the beginning of the hostilitiesthere were journalists reported from each of the opposing sides.

Also right from the beginning, there were voluntary foreigners among the Republicans, such as the athletes who participated in the Parallel Olympics in Barcelona, organized by leftist athletes as a rejection to the Olympics organized by the followers of Hitler in Munich, Germany.

It was an intense, raging summer.

My father felt the heat of adrenaline, not only once but many times. The sound of the cudgel coming at a head and wielded by a brute, the whistling of a steel blade cutting through the air.

Just as everybody with leftist leanings -from the lightest to the most extreme- supported the Republicans, the Conservatives joined British fascism to support Franco, whose emblematic flight from the Canary Islands into power was in a de Havilland DH 89 Dragon Rapide.

All over Europe – except in Hitler's Germany and Mussolini's Italy – and the rest of the world there was an massive movement to support the Republic, and my father, Mrs Cummins, *Don* Eurwen and O'Sean took part in it.

The English Communist Party, together with the Third International and the Soviet Union directed by Stalin started recruiting volunteers at the beginning of December 1936, and the liberal press followed with intense interest the vicissitudes of the creation of the International Brigade and within it, the British volunteers: the British Brigade (officially the "Saklatvala"), "Lincoln", "Washington", "Mackenzie-Papineau", the "Connolly Column" comprised by a small group of Irishmen.

That intense year also brought a novel experience to my father. In his childhood he had compensated his intellectual work at school with sports and work in the countryside;

one could say he had worked as a young peon. Since arriving at King George's College he hadn't had any other activity than sports and studies. So when O'Sean offered to teach him car mechanics, my Dad accepted gratefully.

As was always his way, he performed an extra stretch. He ordered some books on light mechanics and studied them well, taking advantage of the Christmas holidays to put theory into practice.

The old Irishman was the absolute opposite of being a good teacher: bad-tempered and peppering his talk with foul language, he gave relatively clear instructions and showed my father how to use the different tools, with no formality or courtesy; there was something in this man that made my father rather uneasy, like the slight fear of a caged beast.

As the months went by he became skilled with the tools and he learnt how to remove every vestige of grease so that he was squeaky clean, something celebrated by Mrs Sylvia.

The much announced death of several English soldiers on the Jarama road, one of the first great battles in the Spanish war – young workers, intellectuals and students- were a reason -whenever possible- for bitter discussions between Eurwen and O'Sean.

Those harsh conversations on war and peace slowly began developing a sense of responsibility in my father towards the future, which matured in the spring.

He would soon be 16-years-old, and in some way he already was responsible for living on his own account, moving in a diversified, contrasting world which made him feel like an adult and as such, he decided he would leave for the Spanish war.

The last Sunday in February 1937, in the afternoon, after a long discussion between the Welshman and the Irishman about the international intervention in Spain, about war and peace, in a silence between the two contenders, my *Viejo* simply announced that he would be leaving for the war front as soon as he could.

Both men were equally surprised and they never even managed to answer.

In the following days my father began to organize things in order to fulfil his goal.

Eurwen and O'Sean reacted differently. Again and again, Eurwen tried by every means to dissuade him from his purpose.

At the beginning, when he heard about my father's intention, the Irishman disbelieved and mocked him, but when in his most polite way my father asked him kindly if he would box with him, O'Sean realized he was no longer a child, and he supported my father in whatever way he could.

Furthermore, the old Irishman had a far from insignificant military experience in his fight against the fearsome British army: he was an irreducible member of the I.R.A., he had fought during the war of Independence and still at this age he dreamt of finding some way to throw the British out of Belfast.

Following O'Sean's advice, my father began training his body and mind to best resist the tests which he would have to pass. He had the physical condition of a sportsman, but he began to realize this was not enough – he would also have to be able to walk for many kilometres carrying a pack, and spend days without eating, drinking or sleeping.

So he began to get up one hour before breakfast to run around the athletics track carrying a backpack full of stones, and he also ate more to accumulate reserves. Mrs Sylvia was the first to point out that he had begun to put on weight – and he reduced his number of visits to the library.

Although he had spent the past years at school reading as many hours as possible, now he only went to the library to consult several military books and manuals from different periods, among which there was a translation into Latin of a Chinese book on the art of war, translated by a Jesuit; the first edition in English of Von Clausewitz's writings; a manual on the different fencing schools with careful illustrations; the internal regulations of various regiments; a guide for fighting with a bayonet containing detailed, large full-page photographs.

Soon each hour he spent on sports became a training, if not completely military, at least of resistance. He now used the passage inside the hedge where he used to train on his bicycle, to march on foot sometimes the whole night, in almost complete darkness, as he sought to improve his performance.

Eurwen lost no opportunity in trying to dissuade him from his idea, just as my *Viejo* would do with me in the future, and he began to tell him the many and bloody stories which up till then he had kept quiet about for 20 years.

My father also approached Dr. Samuelson, the Science, Hygiene and Health professor, with the excuse of learning the basic first aid theory and practice – the old doctor responded enthusiastically, thinking my father was awakening to a medical vocation. My father therefore took advantage to learn everything about the body's vital points and the different consequences of each possible wound.

The school year was winding down with the arrival of summer, and the war in Spain grew or lessened according to the sad diplomatic dancing by the English or French (and their allies) who –in fact- never completely condemned the Francoist uprising nor did they provide arms and equipment to the Second Republic army.

The presence of military advisers, a large number of pilots together with their modern German planes and several thousand Italian volunteers supporting Franco were condemned by word, but in actual fact it was only an attempt to stop Englishmen from enlisting in the Republican army, even threatening to jail anyone who tried.

Eurwen hoped that all these obstacles would make my father desist from his project, trusting that the English Communist party –in charge of recruiting volunteers, and concerned about the image of war in the face of public opinion as the evolution of the "Spanish affair" was being closely watched – would not accept just anyone as a recruit, and that my father's youth would be a reason to reject him.

O'Sean was part of the solution, and King George's College and Mrs Sylvia the other part.

Summer and holidays were approaching, in July my *Viejo* would be 16 and he couldn't find a way of getting to Spain to fulfil his purpose.

Frequently the older pupils – the group to which my father now belonged – would take short trips of five or six days to France in order to put their knowledge of French into practice.

With expenses covered by the pupils themselves and monitored by the severe Monsieur Pochard – a slender, tall man, who used a monocle particularly when he wanted to admonish one of them – would be their guide on the trip through France, from Calais to Avignon, passing through Paris and Toulouse. Since that journey had been taking place for 10 years it had become almost an institution, a custom reserved for those who could count on the professor's goodwill as well as pay the £28.

In the middle of May 1937, while they were removing a truck's gearbox and with the stealth of someone used to doing things against the law, O'Sean offered my father a set of falsified papers to cross as far as Paris, where the Communist Party office was in charge of recruiting volunteers for the Brigade.

My *Viejo* had never dealt with this sort of affair, he had never had any contact with any outlaws or fugitives, although as a theory he knew the difference between these and political dissidents, revolutionary activists, all those outlawed because they had rebelled against injustices and abuses by illegal, intrusive power.

More than once he had heard his grandfather telling stories of family members –parents, grandparents, uncles- the pursued or the pursuers depending on the period, exiled, jailed or running from the avenging justice of those in opposition to their ideas, and Eurwen, without being direct or frank, had insinuated that the Irishman wasn't "a loyal and honest subject of the British Crown", but a conscious activist of the I.R.A. (Irish Republican Army). So my father wasn't surprised by this offer, but he asked for one week to make a decision.

That same night, after a hot shower before having his dinner – as almost every Sunday with Mrs Sylvia- he was incredibly surprised when she announced she had gone to King George's College and introducing herself as a friend of the Evans family of Argentina, she had arranged the financial details of his trip to France as a gift for his 16th birthday.

That last week at the College was perhaps the most difficult of his life. Mrs Sylvia's generosity, which had smoothed his way to France, almost made my father hesitate at actually going ahead with his project of joining the Spanish Republican army, his heart feeling crushed at the possibility of ruining his friendship with that woman who had given him so much.

But he understood that if that matter stopped him -considering the pain that he would be inflicting in Buenos Aires was not doing so- he was really lying to himself and he wasn't really willing to go to war.

So the following weekend he confirmed to the Irishman that he would use those documents; he would not enrol in the Communist Party's office in Paris but would do it directly in Spain. He had seen the proximity between Avignon and Port Bou or Andorra, two of the mountain passes that were most mentioned in the press.

May ended, bringing in a warmer June which he spent with algebra exams —he worked on the theory of calculating artillery fire thanks to his considerable speed in using the calculus ruler – as well as history and English literature exams; and for the first time he openly failed them both, one because of a lengthy piece on the injustice of the colonial system in a historic context, and the other for the analysis of an obituary on John Cornford, the young English poet fallen in the Spanish war.

The date for leaving for France was set for July 10th. My father spent his last weekend in the company of his benefactor and friend Mrs Sylvia, and was almost as quiet and taciturn as Meredith. My father was aware at that time that there was a possibility they would not see each other again. An instance that would happen again, in the future.

Among his school companions he had no close or other type of friends, there was nothing in that place that tied him or that made him want to go back on his idea. He made arrangements with Eurwen so that, when the College sent back his possessions to Argentina, these be diverted and kept in some corner of the old Irishman's workshop waiting for his return.

He boarded the train a little before dawn, and when the whistle blew, he suddenly scrambled out of the train and running up to the old Welshman, he gave him a brief but very strong hug and without uttering a word, he quickly boarded the train again - it had already started moving, carrying him onwards to his absolute destiny.

This is how my father left for the war.

Republican Infantry

IV) KATANA

Katana

A type of Japanese sabre, curved and with only one cutting edge, traditionally used by the Samurais. It usually was about 1 mt. long and weighed some 2 kg.

"... for the first time I've heard the bullets whistle over my head. At last I've learnt what I am in those circumstances, much more serene than the Moors. But at the same time, I've understood what has always surprised me: why Plato (or Aristotle?) places courage a the lower end of the category of virtues.

Of course, it is not made up of very wonderful feelings: some anger, some vanity, much stubbornness and a vulgar pleasure regarding sport. Above all, the exaltation of one's own physical strength which, however, has no concern in this at all. We cross our arms over an unbuttoned shirt and we breathe deeply. When this happens at night, we have a mixed feeling of having performed an enormous stupidity. I will never again admire a man who is only courageous."

Antoine de Saint Exupery

Torino

The motor's soft vibration must have helped me doze, because when I look at my watch on my left wrist I find that over 35 minutes have gone by since we left my son at the Military School gate and we're driving along Highway No. 9.

I look at my brother-in-law, who is driving without a care, a cigarette hanging from his lips and a happy smile, just as when he's seducing a woman. He's a funny and likeable guy but this unworried attitude driving at over 180 kms. per hour is risky, reckless, disturbing.

"Where's the fire, Carlos?"

He laughs. He accelerates, and the motor's noise is felt inside the car.

Torino 380 W

"What's up, brother? I don't suppose the Welsh soldier is afraid of dying, huh?" He laughs out loud.

I should curse him, kick him, punch him on the nose.

But I can't. He's been my friend for over 20 years, he's my firstborn son's godfather, my youngest daughter's favourite uncle. He's the eldest madcap son of the Rodrigué family, a comedian turned doctor, the man who introduced me to my wife. He's family. And I know he enjoys making me mad.

"Although I did learn nobody dies the evening before… Yes, I'm afraid of dying in a stupid car accident! I'm not a soldier, I'm a farmer… perhaps a Welsh *gaucho*!" I add, smiling, "Come on, Carlos, take your foot off the accelerator, there's no hurry."

Carlitos, as friends and family call him – except myself when I don't like what he's doing. He's just bought the latest Torino, the coupé 380 model, the top line of the Argentine car design, bodywork by Pininfarina, designed by Argentine engineers for IKA-Renault Argentina. The national pride capable of racing at over 200 kms. per hour, successfully tried out on international tracks.

I met him during my brief time in the *Fuerzas Armadas Argentinas* (Argentine Armed Forces).

He was doing his military service and I was the Drill Sergeant Instructor.

He was an unbearable subordinate, a guy who liked to play jokes and of course, whose military conditions were the worst; as he was quite much older than his conscripted companions' class 1930 – he was in the postponed conscript class 1926 due to his university studies- he used to incite them to commit all kinds of violations.

They used to follow him because he was a good leader: he always accepted to take responsibility for his stupidities, regardless of the punishment due.

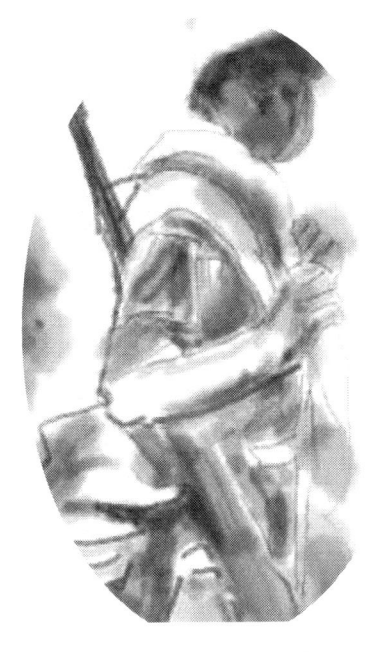

Republican Infantry

If he'd been under the orders of somebody less tolerant than myself, his atrocities —which included among others, the total destruction of an Army motorcycle; imitating the voice of an officer in order to punish a boastful, reckless second lieutenant; and manufacturing several false overnight leaves -not for himself but for his companions— they would have given him many more days of arrest than I gave him, even a court martial and very probably, clapped him into a military jail.

The truth is, after over ten years in the army, three cruel wars —fighting in two of them and as an instructor in another- I could very well understand his disregard of rules, military protocol and blind obedience.

Besides, just like now, he used to make me laugh at my own anger. And afterwards, knowing that my father had been his father patient and that my grandfather had been his grandfather's friend, one day he invited me to supper at his home – just about ten minutes away from my house in Remedios de Escalada, on the corner of the building where my parents had met- and there I met his sister, who today is my wife.

He had managed – through his father, who was the well-known Dr. Rodrigué from Banfield – to do his military service as a healthcare worker in the National Military College, but those contacts hadn't been able to help him avoid the instruction period, and this is when our paths crossed.

Besides being an incorrigible joker, he was educated, kind and a brilliant conversationalist... and a mediocre student. When I met him he had just started studying for his doctor's degree —taking twice as long as any other student; he graduated in 1962, with the whole family (including myself) having pushed him all the way.

My brother-in-law took charge of the Clínica Sur just four years ago.

It is a prestigious healthcare centre, created with patience and much effort by my father-in-law towards the end of the '30s decade until he made it into a model clinic of private healthcare; my brother-in-law has become the living heir – due to his father's weariness – and spends every penny coming from the business.

The car is beautiful, the insides covered in real leather, the dashboard made of high-quality wood; ample, comfortable seats. There is careful attention to every detail.

Very different to my old, stoic Studebaker and even more comfortable than my wife's family-size Rambler.

The road slips by beneath the headlights, cutting through the night's heart as a plough does the earth, yet at a stunning speed, while on the highway shoulders the signs and milestones, telegraph and fence poles follow one after the other hypnotically, seemingly identical but which I know are different.

I know this road by heart, every post, every coppice, every crossroads.

Carlos is a good driver; he's watchful of the traffic, which as we approach Rosario begins to slow down. But he doesn't slow down, he zigzags among the trucks taking advantage of the night to enter the city of Rosario.

If this highway were like the Ave. General Paz, the ring road around the city of Buenos Aires with two lanes in each direction, Carlos' driving wouldn't scare me so much. But this road is a narrow two-lane highway for both directions and full of traffic…

Quite some time before midnight we left Rosario's lights behind, as well as its intense traffic, unmarked crossroads and railway crossings without barriers or linesmen.

Carlos is happy: he's killing three birds with one stone. He's dropped his godson at school; he's driving me to our farm, and he's beating his own record, which he established when one or two years back he took five hours in his DKW Fizzore to cover the Buenos Aires-Esperanza trip. It's something that gives him a childish enthusiasm, which makes me laugh when I'm not sitting in the passenger seat.

He's trying for the closest time of two and a half hours, a small plane's flying time -a Cessna that a friend wanted to sell him, and which frankly I think is much safer than this craziness on four wheels.

He doesn't care that we had to load petrol three times – in San Martín, Ramallo and when leaving Rosario, a period of time which he subtracts and thus cheats on his own timing- nor that we're zigzagging between 40-ton trucks; or that we're running the risk of an alcohol-filled local driver crossing the highway in his little '29 Chevrolet truck without even an oil-lamp to light its way.

No, of course not, he wants to demonstrate that his Torino is a land airplane.

If my Studebaker's starter hadn't failed – the first time in ten years, some failure in the power system – I wouldn't have accepted to ride with him.

He likes to drive at night because he says there is less traffic. I point out to him that one also sees less. And he guffaws. He loves to tease, he knows he makes me laugh with his self-confident charm.

"You weren't afraid in Normandy and you're afraid here?" he challenges me.

"Fortunately, I'm very afraid… and you know, I wasn't in Normandy… I was in Dunkirk, and that was enough… And believe me, if I didn't shit my pants it's because I hadn't eaten anything for at least four days…"

He gets serious and looks over at me for a second, and I reproach him quickly with a "Look at the bloody road!"

I'm always amazed at people who, never having been in a war, insist on wanting to know details about it. I was a volunteer at 16 in the most brutal war imaginable –in fact, my experience is that every war is brutal- but I never felt attracted or fascinated by anything military, by war or violence. The truth is I prefer the countryside.

"Ah, well… as you were in so many battles…" he answers, while he exhales cigarette smoke.

It's strange, because when I returned to Argentina I stopped smoking and it was very hard to do; but when I saw him light up, I had a sudden and uncontrollable desire to smoke.

When Carlos sees me go through the whole rite –pull out a cigarette from his packet lying on the dashboard, tap it against my wristwatch, and while holding the cigarette push in the car's lighter, and when this jumps back, put the cigarette between my lips and take a drag…

He looks at me, astonished, "What're you doing, mate? After so many years! Is something wrong…?"

I push in the car lighter.

If we had been in the front lines, under fire, I'd have put my hand on his shoulder and say that someone has walked over my grave. But I can't.

I don't get to say anything.

Carlos shouts out something unintelligible until I look at the cone of light from the headlights and I realize he's mixed up the words "horses" and "shit".

I see three of them. I see the Torino's bonnet lowering as it brakes screeching against the asphalt. I clearly see the first horse's legs hit against the bonnet's edge and they break up noiselessly and almost immediately the explosion and jangling noise of the roof's metal sinking beneath the animal's weight over our heads.

I don't see the other two but I feel them hit against the car's body one after the other.

Just as in the war, the initial explosion finds me –surprises me, like Derek Jones- without having lit up. There is an infinite number of lesser noises, metal dragging, the sound of hot steam, of metal pieces turning and hitting other metal objects, the puff of crushed glass.

Then silence.

The same silence as when the artillery has quietened.

Am I alive? I try to breathe but I can't. Yes, I'm alive. But it's obvious I'm dying. The memory of Atisha and his last smile flood through my brain. Infinite compassion for all feeling beings, humans and non-humans…

Hispania

Scots & Irish

I haven't opened my eyes yet, although almost painfully my mouth is already open, pulling in air desperately. The horrible feeling of a final breath is still with me when I open my eyes, feeling the shaking that I first confuse with my death rattle but which my brain quickly realizes is Harry's big, strong hand shaking my shoulder.

Republican T-34

"Wake up, boy, you're having a nightmare," he says, dragging his words as only the Irish can.

"Wow... I dreamt I was dying in a car accident..."

He laughs loudly. "Seen from here that would be a really stupid way to go!" He says, spitting out the words, and I laugh as I drink down the warm tea he has handed me.

The sun hasn't come up yet but its rays are lighting up the sky already.

I don't think about the dream, not being able to breathe, or death.

I've been in Spain for six weeks and for two of them I've been at the battle front. It's forbidden to think of death here even though nobody says this, because it's right there before us, a few hundred metres in front, at the end of the fascist rifles.

Harry offers me his official flask – the one in which he tries to always carry tea, nearly always cold, not the one with alcohol- and I swallow the strong, sweet liquid which I'm convinced has energizing ability. He hands me a piece of hard bread and two hard-boiled eggs that he's stolen for me at a nearby farm, abandoned by its owners once the battle started.

Harry must be 26 or 27 years old, he has a receding hairline, almost black, untidy hair, dark green eyes and is very tall. He has the best jokes about the Scots – always referred to drunkenness and greed- and he's never completely sober or completely drunk. It's a mystery as to how he manages to get hold of Irish whisky or brandy. According to his mood, he can be aggressive or melancholic, regardless of how much he has drunk.

A supporter of the Irish Republican Army at 17, he has attached himself to me in a surprising and moving way. We liked each other as from the moment we met, and he's covered my back ever since I moved to the front lines.

Harry Moore has an amazing ability to talk and he frequently employs this –or at least he tries- to benefit himself, and if it weren't for his partner Jack Peebles –his brother-in-law and counterpart- who humorously and good-heartedly fixes up all the illegalities to obtain brandy, food, cigarettes and bullets- it's likely Harry would end up in serious

Il Ducce

trouble. From what I've seen, he's a cool shooter, a focused and efficient fighter, the duo he and the Scotsman make is lethal for the fascists.

Harry is an Irishman from Belfast, but he lived for a few years in South Africa, where to earn his living in the diamond mines he learnt how to handle explosives, which he does with great skill. Before I met him my judgment about Irishmen was based on O'Sean and truthfully, this was not very positive: the old Irishman was silent and when he did talk, he was lewd, blasphemous, nasty and full of hate. While Harry is a bright man who talks his head off, full of funny tales and with a sense of humour making everybody around him laugh.

Jack is more or less the same age, or perhaps a little younger, a Scotsman from a town to the north of Edinburgh, he's a watchmaker and an expert in setting up delay artefacts and explosive traps.

He's reserved, quiet, but when he feels more confident and is among friends, a surprising sense of humour appears, rich in irony and sarcasm. His courage and cold blood have inspired me since I arrived at the front.

He covers his red hair with a Tommy helmet which is always loose and at an angle, except when he goes into combat: he then ties it firmly under his chin.

I hope to be able to live through this like he does, serenely and calmly.

His solid, strong body —which he can launch like a rugby forward in body to body fighting- makes him a frightening and fierce fighter.

I don't think again of the dream, of not breathing, or of death.

They came over together to fight —although it sounds strange, Harry is married to Margaret, Jack's younger sister- and Jack gives back the best jokes about the Irish —ignorant, bullies and drunks- that you've ever heard, in answer to his brother-in-law's jokes.

They are what you might call my older brothers, godfathers, Guardian Angels.

I look at the sky where the sun is brightening and burning still at the beginning of September, and we prepare for another extremely hot day. Summer refuses to go, it appears in the morning and Aragon lights up and burns like a torch.

In the distance the fascist 15,5 gun roars and the Republican earth trembles; they don't know where to shoot their shrapnel, they search for our hideouts like blind men with a large stick, hitting meticulously at the Aragonese ground trying to cause the most harm possible, sweeping the whole area as they continuously fire their terrifying artillery.

I'm at war...

A little less than two months ago I was a pupil at a prestigious English school, a prison of gold from which I escaped into this hell, and which every day tests my convictions.

I'm at war...

In silence I go over the diary in which I've been writing down the last 45 days of my life, while I chew the hard bread and eggs for breakfast.

I'm at war and I know why I'm here.

This time separates me from my former self more than all the oceans which have separated me from my home; this goes through my mind like the circular file holder in the recruitment office of the International Brigade in Albacete.

I can still hear in my head the ever more agitated discussion with those two men responsible for recruiting men, two incredibly stubborn officials from the International Communist Party, an Englishman and a Frenchman.

Never before had I felt so angry in my life and even less had I dared to manifest it: in two languages, those men were rejecting my documents not because they knew them to be false, but because they had received a report from the French police on my escape from a school excursion, requesting I be detained and sent back to France.

And there we were, shouting at each other in English and in French, when we were interrupted by a formidable kick against the closed door by a solid, tall man, wearing the classical NLC uniform, the powerful central anarchist syndicate: Republican cap, a blue overall, khaki shirt, thick, laced shoes, two cartridge belts crossing his chest and on his waist an enormous holster for a Mauser 1915. His arms akimbo so his fists are resting on his waist, this man doesn't shout. He roars.

"What the hell is all this shouting?"

To my surprise, that voice brings back memories of some incredibly wonderful times. His light brown eyes pierce me with the same fierceness as at my opponents, but they suddenly brighten with joy.

"My God, if it isn't Gordon Evans! Shit! How you've grown! You're a man now!"

Standing in front of me, one of my cabin companions on my trip to England: Pep Torrens, the typographer from Barcelona. He hugs me with a strong and never-ending embrace. He pulls away without letting go of my shoulders, looking at me, his eyes shining and almost wet.

"You've come from England and that King who-know-what-the-shit school, to fight in the Spanish people's war?" And his smile is full of hardly hidden emotion.

"This is truly a lovely, agreeable surprise in this shitty war..."

Neither of the recruiters understands a word of what Pep is saying nor what is happening.

One of them picks up the French police file and says –he actually murmurs- that this is bad propaganda for the war, and what he doesn't say is that really, this is bad propaganda for the communists.

Pep speedily pulls the document out of the bureaucrat's hands –a talent which he later would tell me he had acquired when he used to pull things out from the printing press while it was running- he looks at the piece of paper, crushes it into a ball and chucks it into the wastepaper basket with a perfect aim.

"Look, I don't understand a fucking word of what you're saying. I've come from the front and I need volunteers who at least speak English and Spanish, and I've just found one who I also know has plenty of brains and balls. I couldn't give a shit for Frogs or roast beef eaters… What sort of shit communists are you sending an anti-fascist comrade back to the French police?... This boy stays, he's more useful than you two bureaucratic pen-pushing motherfuckers…!!" He says it all in one go, without even breathing.

Both men's faces are puce with anger, but I learnt later that Pep is very well known here, he's one of the hard-liner leaders of the ICP (International Communist Party) and his formidable performance at the Madrid front together with his deceased friend and comrade, the legendary Durruti Buenaventura, have given him a place in the Republican army which made his every word a strict order.

The tragic death of Durruti at the beginning of the Madrid defence had eclipsed Pep's performance, but later his leadership at Jarama coordinating the international battalion's efforts had been praised; he had not been displaced to Aragon, just sent there so that his military knowledge would oblige the fascists to slacken their siege of Madrid.

Although the region was partially occupied by the Francoists, the loyal zone was in fact governed by the anarchists, who occupy political positions everywhere.

And there and then he orders me on my first war mission: translate for the two recruiters what he had just said, particularly including the insults.

I learnt later that this was no more than one more unimportant anecdote in the confrontations between anarchists, Trotskyites and communists, who were ripping up the Republican net; it had blown up a short time before with the violent dismantling of the brigades of the Workers' Party of Marxist Unification, and later the confrontations would reach their peak when they took over the Barcelona telephone company.

After leaving instructions to one of the three men who were with him, he hugged me again with a big, warm smile.

Holding on to my recruitment documents, Pep's man Lluis Lloubet, who had been waiting for the paperwork to be finished, accompanied me to the airbase -the XV International Brigade Headquarters- and that same day I began my obligatory month of training.

Training… if you could call it that. I was given a set of one shirt, pants, heavy shoes with soles that were nailed and sewn – made by group of communist shoemakers- as well as the classic Republican cap, an Arisaka rifle – the Japanese model was an exact copy of the Russian Nagant – and this had a fixed bayonet which stood almost 50 cms. above my head, a cartridge belt and twenty five bullets, of which six were not of that arm's calibre.

Every day we were given our breakfast –tea with a hard malt biscuit, if we were lucky a tomato, or that delicious Catalan bread spread with tomatoes, and sometimes one or two slices of fresh cheese; and later we were given lessons on how to use guns and shown fighting tactics.

Clement Attlee

To my surprise – up till then I had only used a firearm once – I discovered that my success at my New Year's Day practice with O'Sean had not been random: I found that in Albacete, by some kind of a natural gift, I'm an excellent shot with any gun I'm instructed on how to use; and in addition, thanks to my knowledge of algebra, if I had not already been sent to fight under one leader, I would have been taken to be an artillery gunner: the light recoilless Schmidt cannons in my hands become precise destruction tools, taking full advantage of their design; also, thanks to my algebra learnt at King George's College, my precision with a mortar astounds me as much as my trainers.

Although I'd never been a great bowler –cricket had basically bored me- I discovered that when I threw grenades they were efficient and effective even at over 40 mts. away.

Very probably the physical training I had put myself through at the College was much more demanding than what I was given at the International Brigade headquarters, and the truth is that the discipline, military rigours and respect for hierarchy –the base for the pyramid of command as far back as the Romans – were practically non-existent. On the other hand, the political training which took place after a not very abundant lunch -vegetables and potatoes and very little meat, and generally just old chicken— had a very long and persistent communist and pro-Soviet cut; references to comrade Stalin's outstanding qualities were present in almost every single class.

Those of us who were there coincided in at least one thing. We were there to stop the fascists and if possible, make them pull back until we finally beat them.

This was where I saw Harry for the first time –he came to give us a talk on the use of industrial explosives and how to recover the pieces which had not detonated –our own and the enemy's- and he almost ended up coming to blows with a Brit who defended the rights of the Irish Protestants. And we immediately hit it off.

That afternoon we left the barracks to find the town's old bars, and the new ones which had sprung up around the military base.

It was clear that drinking to the extreme was very common among the volunteers and it was normal to come across people from all over Europe – Slavs; men from the Mediterranean; Flemish; Germans; British- many of them slightly intoxicated, but others completely drunk. Even so, fights were rare and usually it was between the English, Irish and Scots.

That night, with Harry, was the first time I drank more than the one glass of brandy which occasionally *Don* Eurwen used to give me during the Sunday lunches which we shared now and again: I got truly drunk, so much so that I fell to the floor almost unconscious, I peed my pants and threw up my meals from the last two days onto Albacete's cobblestone road, and nobody seemed to be surprised at our state.

Even drunk, I still found all of it strange.

Of course, the weird feeling was that I had yet to hear the ferocious whining of the Stukas; the mortar pops; the rattle of the machine-gun fire; the trembling of the artillery against the ground; the stench of powder and the screams of the wounded and the dying.

Three days later I received my orders –a piece of paper with the shield of the Republic and the XIV International Brigade seals, and I was sent, without passing through Madrid, burning every day beneath the Francoist bullets – to the Aragonese front, where my friend Pep was commander of a unit of three sections with two companies each, a total of six hundred men, two hundred of which belonged to the International battalion, one company spoke English and the other French, personally chosen among the most experienced Jarama survivors.

My work was far from being a gift or a prize in the traditional sense of those words, and although for many of my companions it was a kind of punishment because it placed me in the face of the enemy to be captured and tortured or simply assassinated by a sniper, my role as a letter carrier –I had to deliver communications, battle orders and orders from the commander to the chiefs of each foreign section- was a challenge, an honour that specifically compelled me.

Therefore the importance of my role and the fact that two veteran fighters were assigned to me –they were survivors of the disaster lived through by the British battalion at Jarama and heroes at the Brunete failure- made me join the war with my morals and self-esteem at a high level.

Having met Harry at Albacete, I then met Jack on the outskirts of Belchite, very close to Zaragoza in enemy hands, and where a battle had started for the control of the region in the middle of August - with them I lived through my first blood, my first battle, my first terror.

Pep had no intention of sending me to my death at all, something I'm very sure of;

he knew the merits and defects of the two English-speaking fighters he had requested and had been sent from the International Brigade leadership -not without certain arguments and a political tug-of-war- and these two men must be my protectors in the mission to be assigned.

This is what led me into the war immediately from the very first day, climbing up and down the hills and heights in the region, crawling through the trenches carrying instructions to the chiefs of the platoons —even those right at the front- confronted by the enemy and many times under intense and live fire.

Pep had himself lived through the difficulties of giving orders in Spanish or Catalan and have them understood by the English-speakers —North Americans, the English, Canadians, Scots, Irish, Welsh- the French and the Germans.

His task force was a special unit, born from the atrocious experience in Madrid, whose role was to hit violently against the enemy where it was least prepared, destabilizing the front lines, breaking them up, obliging them to divide up their forces.

Its members had been chosen personally by Pep, one by one, with absolutely no attachment to their political origin. My extensive handling of Spanish, English, French and rudimentary German were crucial to him. Therefore Harry and Jack had the priority order to accompany me and protect every one of my forays, on every single of my missions.

It was so since my first day.

Belchite and its surroundings is an area full of gorges, ravines, steep and rocky, and among every fold, small green valleys which before the war were inhabited by hard-working peasants and farmers.

I know I will never forget that day and every single detail of my first day on the battle front.

Remembering it now, only ten days later, it is simply because this blue sky from which very soon the sun will be burning, and which made this area so rich, reminds me of that other sky.

Eighteen new recruits arrived pretty scorched in the back of an old truck from Albacete, none of us having slept a wink during the whole journey.

We got out of the truck at midnight after many very uncomfortable hours —later, when we lived through all kinds of lack on the battlefield, that journey would seem funny in retrospect —and although they ordered us to sleep, the far off rumble of the artillery and the sound of the rifle fire (the battle had only just begun) made this order seem useless.

The men who had travelled with me were sent to their respective places and I finally was alone, waiting for my orders.

These arrived shortly before midday, Jack arrived together with Lloubet and Harry. The red-haired Jack, so different to his daring friend, was quiet and almost shy, he spoke very little and talked in a murmur, dragging his "r's" with that beautiful Scots accent. I also liked him right away.

Lloubet took me to Pep, and I was very surprised when he asked me to translate the orders for my two comrades, which I did with a great deal of shame: they were to protect me with their lives. They fulfilled their orders that day and many more.

He then handed me some sealed papers that I had to deliver to the three commanders located in the very centre of that insatiable fire, and he explained they were maps with instructions which I must translate for each. The orders Pep was handing to me came directly from the High Command. It was my first day at the front and I was going to be submerged in the muddy waters of the war.

After having spent the last years in the English climate, cold and unstable, I find the heat in the valleys almost unbearable, although as soon as one climbs up a few metres the climate becomes soft and agreeable.

We set off walking first along a road which enters the town from the south, then a local road towards the east, and finally towards the north along a rough stone path among the red-coloured heights of the area.

We delivered the first dispatch in a stone trench area above which one could hear a bullet whistling now and again.

In the distance —much clearer and more intense than we had heard at Pep's headquarters- we heard the terrible death symphony with the clarity of an orchestra.

I didn't know it then as I know now, but I guessed I would soon get to know -just as my beloved grandfather called it- the monster Leviathan's belly.

Which I did: I saw it, smelt and touched it.

This first company controlled the detour of the main road which led into the Aragonese mountain range.

The second position was a mortar site, which with deafening pops belched out its broadside firing over and above the hills.

The third position was separated by a short valley from the rest of the units, and this was precisely its objective: prevent the fascists from taking control of that area, which was key to control one of the accesses to the town of Belchite.

My rifle – gigantic and uncomfortable- really bothered me and I didn't know how to carry it.

Jack, who was my same height, carried a Berthier rifle with a dark butt, with the classic North African guns' decor and which hardly came up above his shoulder; he helped me to settle it on my back and showed me how to move with that iron and wood bar tied to my shoulders and crossing my back.

My mission accomplished —I also received written dispatches from the officer in charge of that position- we started on our way back, at the same time as the fascists were launching a total offensive in order to take over the valley and destroy the mortar emplacement.

We hadn't got to the end of the path leading down when the enemy firing increased, forcing us to find cover behind a short stone wall, trapped between the firing of the fascists and the furious answering fire of our own troops from the heights around the valley.

I didn't pee my pants but I heard that this has happened to many brave, courageous men, running in fear, throwing down their guns and seeking shelter.

There is nothing worse than being trapped between the firing lines, in the middle of a brutal, fierce battle in which neither band will ask for or give mercy.

The nationalist squads couldn't get into the valley, under fire from the top of the hills, and we couldn't move forward without running the double risk of being hit by our own or enemy bullets.

The obvious truth I faced that day was that firing practice is certainly not the same as firing in battle.

Jack and Harry, lying on either side of me, took turns to shoot, the former over the top of the wall which was no higher than one metre, the latter through a hole which if it hadn't been made on purpose, at least was very useful precisely at that moment.

Lying relaxed on the hard stone ground, those two crazy men joked while shooting, just as calmly as if they were having a cup of tea.

The continuous explosion of the bullets, the frightening sounds as they hit and glanced off the stones, the terrifying, industrial sound of the German machine guns provided by the Nazi government and which the nationalist army had been using intensely, all this added to the truly annoying matter of trying to manipulate my own rifle –completely the wrong scale- making me almost lose my serenity, which I'd managed to keep up to that moment before this first difficult dance.

Jack's calming hand leaned for a second on my left shoulder, and Harry's enormous hand did the same on my right ankle.

"Don't worry, lad, we're getting out of here," said one of them.

"I'll bet 10 shillings we do," said the other.

"I won't take that up, I don't bet against myself," said Jack with his typical playful laugh. This comedy act under a storm of bullets, and they never stopped firing with perfect synchronicity, each allowing the other to reload their rifle with a lethal efficiency.

I finally found how to manipulate my damned rifle, to load it and start firing above Harry's head.

I had no idea where I was shooting for my first rounds, until I understood not only where our enemy was hidden but also when to do it so my comrades had time to reload.

Minutes went by and the battle intensity did not increase but neither did it diminish.

From each height our side was firing with every arm available, and from the valley mouth the fascists responded bullet for bullet.

We spent the whole afternoon like this, beneath the fiery sun; the three of us emptied my flask and I finished my bullets on my own. Fortunately the bullets in my cartridge belt which were no use for the Arisaka worked perfectly in Harry's Enfield. When I finished my munitions all I could do was keep under cover and wait, holding my fixed bayonet at the ready, waiting for the enemy to come for us.

August was becoming a worse September, the hot summer sun over our heads, and all we could wish for was that the mountains would finally swallow it so we could try to squeeze out of that hell.

Jack's wine and water boot was emptied. Then Harry's cold tea. When the sun had finally hid behind the hills but there was still light Jack and Harry stopped firing. Neither our men above us nor our enemy below paid any attention to our ceasefire.

The sunset colours were shining in the sky when just as it had begun, the firing of the nationalist army began to ease off and at the same time we heard the orders for ceasefire in English echoing through the hills.

"Let's move!" said Jack.

"Yes, let's move!" replied Harry.

And we started running downhill, miraculously without tripping, protected by the slight sunset dusk of a dying summer day.

We were out in the open but nobody fired at us. Or they were dead or they'd left, who knows. But that wasn't our problem, we had to return with the messages without being killed or captured.

Which almost happened some fifteen minutes later.

None of us actually knew the region and although we had a map —which Jack handled very efficiently- the decreasing sunset light betrayed us because at some point we must have taken the wrong path and we ended up, unexpectedly, at a group of buildings – perhaps a larger farm than others- where it was clear there had been some fierce fighting because one of the wooden buildings was still burning and the fire was lighting up that terrible scene.

There were bodies scattered around and one could hear the moans, some voices asking for mercy, calls to mother and to the Christ, voices insulting God.

I'd never seen a dead body —except once at a wake where I'd gone with my grandfather- so moved by an almost morbid curiosity I approached a body in a Republican uniform and therefore separated from my companions.

This is when I saw them.

Some thirty or forty metres from us, walking amongst the ruins, there was a small group of some six nationalist soldiers who were revising the bodies or finishing off the wounded with bayonet thrusts or with their butts.

One of the soldiers saw me and he immediately started racing towards me at great speed, pointing his bayonet, which was reflecting the bright flames around us.

For a second I was paralyzed, but when I heard his scream, almost a howl, 'Die you fucking Red!', I instinctively got into a defensive position —my rifle parallel to my body so as to deflect a brutal blow- and hardly moved, but with this single action my amazed and furious enemy flew past, and he never got to face me again because the extraordinary length of my rifle with its bayonet allowed me to make a quick downward thrust almost to the butt into his back, below his shoulder blades.

Two things happened at the same time.

The man screamed again, not with a war cry but this time in pain, so frightening, intense and deep, something I'd never heard before.

Of course, I'd never fought in a war.

Paralyzed and surprised, I let go of my rifle which remained stuck inside the body of that poor man while he fell to the ground, howling, kicking, skewed like a fish on a lance, rolling on the ground with the rifle trembling violently in his back.

I was absolutely impotent, paralyzed and disarmed, watching as my first victim, the first man I'd assassinated, lay kicking and dying an agonising death.

At the same time his companions saw me and rushed towards me, without realizing that Harry and Jack were coming up behind.

Unmoving and unarmed I saw another man, the closest, was racing towards me also pointing his bayonet and when I began to think I was a dead man, Jack's compact, hard body crashed ferociously into him and threw him to the ground, and in one single movement he thrust his bayonet in the fallen man's side, pulled it out and almost without moving from his place he hit hard against the rifle carried by the man coming behind the fallen man, and with his incredible strength he made the man let go one of his hands, leaving his chest unprotected, and Jack quickly thrust his rifle against that chest and to my great surprise, he pulled the trigger – later I would learn that Jack always kept one last bullet for the body to body battles- and that poor wretch was blown out of the way.

Meanwhile Harry had pulled out from his uniform a small Browning 7.65 pistol, a gun that was not popular among the fighters because it was dangerous and ineffective –it's difficult to determine if it's loaded and its impact is not great- but in the hands of that blessed Irish demon it became our salvation that terrifying and unforgettable afternoon.

Almost without looking he finished off the fallen man who was still kicking, and with deadly aim, speed and impressive coolness he stood next to Jack and one after another, he shot dead with a single shot to the heads of each of the three remaining men running towards us – starting with the one nearest and ending with the one at the back. This man had begun to slow down but had not dropped his rifle.

It's clear they too had run out of ammunition and that's why they were going through the bodies of our comrades.

When the shouts and the shots had ceased, my whole body began to tremble, it was terrifying and uncontrollable. All the tension accumulated on that day exploded and I began crying and cursing King George's school, Great Britain, Franco, the fascists and the damn war.

Harry then embraced me, holding me in a brotherly way while he whispered in my ear.

"It's alright, lad, it's OK… don't worry, it's fine… crying is good, it helps… you're alive…" It was then I got to know Daisy, Harry's unofficial flask that was, as always, full of alcohol (which no matter the origin, he called brandy) which the three of us drank hugging each other until there was not a single drop left, illuminated by the last embers that hardly hid that terrible scene with all the scattered bodies.

We couldn't sleep, we kept our backs against the ruins and stayed very alert, scared that at any moment another enemy patrol would come upon us and our luck change.

It was during that sleepless night that I learnt Shakespeare was not in error when he wrote of the happy few, of the brotherhood of men of arms, of the survivors of horror and death.

Not many days have gone by since that one and nevertheless, I have changed.

I no longer tremble when I kill, I take aim and know that on the other side there is a fascist who has passed over to a better life. I no longer cry after a battle, my war is just, my cause is good.

In the inside pocket of my jacket -which I use as a cover during the cool Aragonese nights- is my grandfather's letter that arrived yesterday, and which I read whenever I find the chance.

Jack asks me what am I reading and I translate the main parts of this private declaration the best I can, a legacy from that good man.

When I'd finished, I looked at my comrade and saw tears in his eyes.

He then said, nodding and whispering, "You are a lucky man, lad, you have a guiding light to help come out healthy from this craziness… Don't worry, you won't lose your way."

The sun rises from behind the mountains. Harry puts out the fire which kept us warm during the night, there is the sense of the first coolness of autumn which has yet to arrive, but which is tenuously insinuating and imperceptible, the starry sky dominating the world. A while later Jack comes up. We're being called by the commanders. Belchite has not fallen into our hands yet, Pep needs us.

The war continues and now and again, I think of my home, my mother and my sister, my father and my dead grandfather. Will I ever return to my dear Argentina some day?

I don't think about it anymore. The Republic needs us to survive.

On the Outskirts of Teruel

Time passes, the war continues, proud and victorious we leave Belchite; somebody is arrested for suggesting we've spent energy which was indispensable, that this was like the Pirro battle.

The political commissioners always bring us good news, encouraging news. Haven't we won in Quinto? Have they been able to take over Madrid? The sharifs are unchallengeable, they are always correct, one step ahead of the fascist rabble.

Fuentes del Ebro is halfway between Zaragoza and Belchite, in a manner of speaking. Being the capital of the province, it's still in Francoist hands.

We regroup and prepare for our attack on the fascist trenches some days later, while the autumn coolness, already with us, brings with it the slow cyclical agony turning the trees yellow. Just a few days before, there was a contrast between the trees' thousand greens and the ochre-red tones of the Aragonese hillsides and valleys.

The Ebro can be seen in the distance. The vital strength of the potent river hypnotizes me and I think of life.

Sitting on the ground, now and again I glance up and look at the distant meandering river, writing in the small diary with red covers that my father gave me when I left Argentina.

I write down the facts, the battles, skirmishes and anecdotes. I use English abbreviations, a practical system with a cryptographic aspect allowing me to register a great deal of information in a very small space.

I register everything there, as from when I left Enfield, each anecdote, detail and incident from Minute One, when I boarded the train to France, when I gave *Don* Eurwen the last hug.

The pass over the Pyrenees, and the smuggler with the name of a poet, Marcial Lafuente; the Albacete airport and the communists who are attached to the rules; Pep and his anger; Belchite and the skirmishes; our commander Wintringham wounded in the Quinto streets; all this has been carefully written in with its corresponding date. I use a magnifying glass and an ink pencil – when I wet the point with my tongue the strokes become indelible- so as to make the writing as small as possible.

I don't know why exactly, but I feel better thinking that if I die in battle someone will take the trouble to get this book to my parents; definitely it's an almost vain hope, but maybe there is someone respectable among my enemies over there on the battlefield.

We are under fire in a beautiful landscape.

Belchite is in our hands, so is Quinto, but at what a price… and now Fuentes, between Zaragoza and us.

The Republican artillery thunders and the rebels hit back.

The earth trembles.

The air above fills with the fearsome Messerschmitt ME109, with the Junker-88, with the Heinkel 111 provided by Hitler's Germany, with Mussolini's Capronis and Fiats which confront Stalin's Poliakovs. Sometimes we witness fierce aeroplane battles, sometimes they bomb us without mercy.

If before I liked train engines, now I love planes. Yes, they're frightening, but they're also beautiful when they fight each other making impossible manoeuvres, continuously challenging gravity's laws.

And when they attack us on the ground, the seconds appear eternal and deadly.

They regroup us to advance towards Fuentes del Ebro.

This time we're going to take part in a big battle, we'll move forward like infantry in the Soviet style, our vanguard covered by the powerful and fearsome Russian army tanks, the T26 which have already demonstrated their deadly efficiency in Madrid.

We move forward, but the tanks go too fast or we're too slow, so the result is that we lose their protection and in only a few hours, on October 11, we're meticulously shot to pieces; it's a miracle that my two friends and I don't fall in the battlefield. That's when I feel the bitter and painful taste of defeat.

It hurts the body, the soul, one cries and implores for survival.

Jack and Harry fight like lions at my side, their rifles on fire, picking up ammunition from those who have fallen, encouraging the survivors. But it's clear that all our courage isn't enough. We're denied Fuentes, and together with it, Zaragoza.

With this, we move back and the Republican army reorganizes itself…

Reorganizations are a constant throughout the Republican army, and very noticeable in the International Brigades; the battalions are moved from one place to another, where the Dimitrovs were before now the Papienau-Mackenzie are placed, today you're with the 30th Brigade, tomorrow with the 129th.

This is simply the exterior manifestation of the continued anxiety that affects the whole government. The fighting, the palace plots are an open secret: Dr. Negrin is governing, but the Spanish Communist Party and the Soviet advisers have the power, the communists repeat blindly.

The defeat at Fuentes del Ebro is a hard blow that makes the political commissioners' task very difficult, and they try to convince us in every way possible that this means nothing.

We spent ten long days on the firing line, firing at each other from trench to trench, smelling of excrement and urine, of death and powder, praying no longer to defeat the enemy but simply to avoid it moving forward. Praying that the enemy artillery not get as far as our positions, dominating our fear as if it were an untamed horse, and possessed by a hunger that made our insides painful.

Many go crazy, sunken in clouds of flies and fearful of the hordes of rats that devour the putrid bodies of those who have fallen; the nauseating smell is constant and unbearable.

Morale is at its lowest level and more than one of us thinks about the impossible, of returning home.

We are volunteers but we can't resign.

We hear of some desertions, which is quickly and severely punished with prison. Executions are talked of, but the only direct case I know of is Second Lieutenant Winston Smith, who went to Barcelona for four days to visit a woman, he was publically degraded and that's all. Finally they move us away from the front, our unit is sent to Modejar, waiting for orders.

The days are all the same; we smoke, we drink, we sing to kill time after our very meagre supper; the rancid tobacco goes the rounds and we dream it is Turkish, that the cheap moonshine is brandy; we sing war songs, songs about women who are far away and who wait for us; songs about workmen victories.

We are veterans already and know that tomorrow the Grim Reaper can come by and collect his due.

Teruel Last Day

Time passes, autumn fades and leaves in its place a winter that moves on us with a harshness that is unknown to me; the strange British climate, its Atlantic dampness and its cold rainy days and occasional snow are nothing beside the Aragonese cold on its flat fields.

We wait, with soldierly patience, to be given some destination; at the beginning of

September they move us to the rear guard of what -according to what everybody is saying- will be the battle in which we'll define this war.

Although no-one is saying it openly -the political commissioners have ears everywhere and the punishment for spreading despondency is severe, including death- the Republic has failed.

The advance of the rebels to the north and above all Madrid's luck seems to have entered a disturbing plateau –which in the long run benefits the Francoists because they receive support from the Nazis and fascists, so this does not help to lift morale.

Very few of them believe in victory any more.

Neither Harry nor Jack are worried. There are cigarettes –I took to this vice after the Fuentes del Ebro battle and I can vouch for the fact that it calms a soldier's anxiety- there are warm clothes and alcohol, which although of a doubtful quality, intoxicates the senses.

Joseph Stalin

Rumours abound and run from man to man, company to company, battalion to battalion, and there is one, specifically, which has us on the alert.

We are to march but no-one knows when.

Troops are concentrated around the town of Teruel in Aragón, but the International Brigades have yet to be invited to the party.

Meanwhile, from reorganization to reorganization, what is left of the British battalion is now called Battalion 57 as part of the Republican Army.

Clement Attlee, the Labour leader who has attempted to convince the Brits regarding the importance of saving the Republic, visits the troops. In an unusual gesture, this man who I admire so much runs the risk of visiting the volunteers, as a very clear and conclusive show of support to what we're doing, to what Spain's Second Republic means.

It's just a gesture which the British government ignores, while they put pressure on the French Popular Union government to halt the flow of indispensable weapons to balance the impressive support that Franco has received from Hitler and Mussolini.

We hear that deposited in some place and held at the frontier by the French Customs, there are 10,000 machine guns, tanks, planes, all for the Republic...

Unanimously and as a retribution, the troops themselves baptize the first company in Attlee's honour.

At the beginning of December a dispatch arrives from General Lister to General Walter, saying that Harry, Jack and I should report to headquarters around Teruel, which we do beneath a fine and constant snow storm which will end up covering everything with a layer of several centimetres of powdery snow.

This benefits us as it halts any plane flights. It's very clear that the fascists are infinitely superior in the air battles.

Pep, in spite of the political storm that consumes the Republic and which confronts anarchists, socialists and Stalinists, still keeps his warrior's prestige.

Unlike those who have lost their honour and life because of their political stance, the commanders overlook his militiaman's background without any formal military training: his efficiency in the front lines has made even Ramón Lister place him under the command of the farmer Indalecio González, to head a small group of veterans —including some Madrid survivors, witnesses of Durruti's death- in order to harass the Francoists.

My knowledge of languages is no longer required, they trust us as their report carriers.

The cold is ever more intense and becomes our ally: the Teruel garrison, inside the city and also in control of the "Muela" – the plateau around the city- don't have enough warm clothing, food or fuel: they will end up burning church pews, furniture in the houses, doors, books, libraries. On the other hand, the Republicans, who possess the most important textile plants in Spain in the hands of the workers cooperatives, have provided us with good winter clothes with gloves, socks and caps which keep us a little warmer.

The war is bad enough without having to add cold to our lives…

It's funny because as Christmas draws near —a date which in our group means practically nothing because we're under firm anti-religious, anti-clerical and anti-Catholic convictions- people around me become kinder and smile more often.

Two or three days before, at the city gates and in view of the famous "Muela" —covered now in barbed wire, fortified strongholds and machine guns- we take refuge in a half-destroyed building a few metres from the highway, which in fact leads straight to the enemy's position- we've met up with a group of quite a few Spaniards who are sitting around a fire trying to lessen their intense cold from the snow.

A large pot is put onto the fire and each man throws in anything they have: a piece of bacon; a fistful of the famous Dr. Negrín pills, also known as Republican lentils, which are the same as the normal lentils but very much tinier; others have chickpeas; some potatoes and finely chopped sausages; a little rice; a little corn flour; a very thin chicken; the remains of an old rooster; some pieces of a mule who died in combat; many pieces of hard bread —there's an abundance of the latter, which is not nutritious but at least fills the belly.

This is the famous "bayonet soup".

In spite of the imminent battle, two guitars appear. For the first time since arriving in Spain, I sing the Welsh hymn without music, alone, in one of those silences which sometimes take place, and Jack recognizes it immediately. He gives me a hug and whispers into my ear —*I'd kill for some bagpipes.*

A young, blue-eyed blond man plays the guitar and he's clearly a master musician of this instrument, he brings out some wonderful sounds from the guitar with great feeling.

The snow falls through the hole where once there was a roof, and now and again we hear the whistle of a bullet; the Francoists are exhausted and without any ammunition, the city will be falling in a few hours, maybe even last up to a day or two; we have supreme confidence in a victory, something I haven't seen before. Belchite was a victory, yes, but its strategic importance was quite relative.

On the other hand, Teruel is key to controlling the region and opens up roads to central and western Spain.

If we win perhaps the adverse luck we've had in the war –Madrid is still in the minds and hearts of those of us here- will change and will allow us to defeat the fascists.

We sing, drink and eat around the campfire which hardly heats our hands, but the hot food and alcohol heat our soul and temple our spirit. When the coals die down, the pot is empty and liqueurs are finished, the guitars become melancholic. The blond boy is German and he sings something that I recognize is Bach.

Later the guitars become Andalucian.

Afterwards the young German and I get to talking, we tell each other our life stories safe from the enemy's bullets and beside the dying heat of the campfire.

He tells me about his passion for Mudejar art, the importance of Teruel and its architectural monuments which are being destroyed in this hellish war.

And also his deep loathing for our enemies, who have taken everything from him: his home, fatherland, family, profession, love.

He's Jewish, a Socialist, an artist. Everything Hitler has prohibited, everything that Nazi Germany has persecuted until death.

His tale reminds me of why I am here.

The day has not yet begun –it is winter and the sun rises late- when from position to position trench to trench, an order is given electrifying us like a galvanic current.

The Francoists' German machine guns begin their devastating pulverizing work from the "Muela" plateau and we three go in and out again and again between their rounds, carrying reports and news.

Finally the Muela plateau falls and on Christmas Eve 1937, the Spanish Second Republic's army enters the main old quarters of the Mozarab city.

The grey sky and the terrible snow which covers everything protects us from the fascist army in the sky, of which little by little they have begun to take possession.

But let's pay attention to the wounded, those who become careless, because the general who defeated Napoleon is ruthless and doesn't distinguish between Republicans and Francoists. Everywhere there are frozen bodies, those mutilated by gangrene and trench foot.

Imprisoned in the garrison –the municipal hall, church, police headquarters- and completely surrounded by our superior forces, the fascists –led by d'Harcourt- stick to their position following to the letter that damned Franco's orders to resist to the last bullet, to the last man.

The battle takes place within a radius of four or five blocks… but my God, what a battle. They have hardly any water -they have to drink the filthy snow- no food or fuel, they are literally dying of cold, almost as much as from our bullets, even so they refuse to surrender.

The fight takes place within the very buildings, firing from holes in the floors, defenders from the higher floors, the attackers from the lower ones.

I'm not the only one who feels a certain admiration for such intense enemies, but we are careful not to say it out loud.

We spend the end of the year under fire and it's not until January 8th that finally, the last survivors surrender.

I don't feel proud of our victory: one after another, the rebel chiefs are executed and everywhere there is retaliation against the defeated. Jack, Harry and I shield ourselves behind our function that gives us a certain freedom of movement, to keep away from the massacre and not find ourselves involved in it.

We three think the same: if we execute the defeated, if we kill off the wounded… in what way are we unlike them?

"The snow, the cold, the wind, the enemy have cut intensely into these December days and on these harsh hills, ready to devour ears, crystallise the breath, take away these soldiers' warmth.

The snow, the cold, the wind, the enemy have fought the stone spirit which holds them, but they have not managed to soften nor allowed this red, furious and warm stone to give in, in spite of the cold, the wind, the enemy's efforts to leave her white, frozen, in pieces…"

Miguel Hernández

Goodbye Spain

I look at the calm and deep blue of the Mediterranean Sea and I understand why it awakens poets' hearts, with its light grey clouds and gentle waves, soft, fragrant wind, the quiet noise of its deceptive docile waters against the white bellies of the ships and small sailboats anchored here and there.

Slender and at the same time beautifully formed, her slightly untidy black curly hair frames her sharp-featured and exotically attractive face.

Large mouth, red lips, a square chin and thick eyebrows frame her large coffee-coloured eyes, and a long neck emerges from the softest, slimmest body you can ever imagine, the lightest-brown skin tanned from the days spent outdoors.

Everything about her moves me to the core. Her harmonious voice and her vehemence. Her political coherence and her vision of the war which we both consider lost.

We sit on the edge of the esplanade, our feet hanging down towards the sea.

We stare out at the horizon, just because we like to, but also to see if we can spy the *Caproni* planes which sometimes fly from Genoa over the sea to discharge their hateful machine-gun fire and flames on old, kind Barcelona. There are signs everywhere —despite the careful work of the volunteer cleaning brigades- of the air raids.

We have been talking since dawn, walking, smoking and now the silence between us takes me slowly into the recent past, thinking how this woman —my saviour in the sad days of the Teruel defeat- came into my life.

Teruel… a terrible name in my memory.

The freezing cold and death, the hardly-celebrated victory which then slipped from our hands.

Death…

I observe her beautiful face, her forehead slightly frowning in a serious, unmoving, silent gesture, her eyes lost on the distant horizon above which the dark night is slowly disappearing.

She must be remembering her beloved island, down south across from Africa, held by the fascists from the very first day.

We have spent a great part of this year as comrades-in-arms and we have been friends since she helped me survive the days after Teruel…

Teruel… that cursed place…

I am overwhelmed by contradictory feelings, ever since I stepped onto Spanish land. She's the most beautiful woman on earth and not because I was told but because I have seen her, brave as a battalion of men.

Is this what war is like, this war, all wars?

Absurd contrasts, contradictory feelings every step of the way. Teruel took away the best friends a man could ever have and placed María in my path.

To think I thought I knew what defeat meant at Quinto.

But no.

I survived Teruel, yes.

But a part of me —two parts really- stayed behind, rotting among the rubble of the Aragonese city that for sure one day will be known as the tomb of the Second Republic… and for me, where my friends met their death.

If I close my eyes, I return to those fateful, freezing February days. If I open them, I see María and the blue and maroon colours of the sky, the Mediterranean and sun emerging from the Francoist land.

Taking Teruel drained so much brave and good men's blood -and we were only able to hold it for little more than a month.

Keeping us there meant draining men and machines from the Madrid front, we were told.

And we clung to the old rocks as cats cling to tree branches.

We endured the non-stop firing from the German 15,5 cannons and the snow and cold and wind, and when it grew lighter, we also endured the discharges of cannons marked with a Swastika - they'd laid to waste the Soviet fighter aircraft known as "*moscas*" and "*chatos*" marked with a red cross.

We endured attack after ferocious attack of the RIF infantry and cavalry from the Morrocan plains until, once we were drained of reinforcements and artillery, they began to break up our defences. Break up means that they moved over piles of bodies of men who had fought until they were exhausted.

That's how we all felt, Harry, Jack and myself.

Exhausted, lack of sleep, hungry and cold – they all lead to one losing track of space, time, hour of the day and the day itself.

Where were we?

In a city in ruins, covered by snow red with blood.

It was no longer about victory, messages or orders.

It was about survival. We ran, not like rabbits, but like bighorn goats – the Pyrenees wild goat- jumping over rocks, bodies, ditches, walls.

Our fate was sealed at a crossroads where the four corners were in ruins but one of the walls was higher than the rest –two walls at an angle as well as part of the tiled roof were left.

The three of us stopped to take a breather and rest under cover.

Along a perpendicular street we saw two lines of our own men moving, keeping very close to what was left of the walls, and when they passed by our hideout they would be absolutely exposed.

From each end of the crossroad the nationalists were already closing in, and none of us hesitated.

Harry and I shot from above, while Jack chose an open doorway, and we covered for our comrades so that they could continue to retreat, not without some of them falling.

The nationalists brought in a German machine gun which I blew up with a grenade. They brought another with the same result. The Scotsman did not let them settle and the Irishman covered my every throw. And our men kept passing by.

Then they brought along one of those damned little Schneider 7,5s whose armoured plate made me waste my last grenade, it bounced and only wounded one of their artillerymen, and ended our luck in a battle which was inevitably lost.

The first cannon shot blows away part of our wall and most of the wreckage falls on Jack.

Like an agile cat Harry jumps down from a considerable height and pulls his brother-in-law out from among the debris and continues to fire from that spot.

The nationalists do not even show themselves out in the open but the cannon, hidden behind the next corner a block away, waits patiently to tear us apart at the next move.

It wasn't necessary.

From above, firing deadly shots at the damned fascists, I saw when Harry pulled out the last packets of dynamite that Jack kept in his backpack and placed them among the stones.

He was setting up a trap. It was clear we were retreating, leaving a little gift for the enemy.

"Let's get moving!" Harry shouts at me.

And I jump down as a bullet furiously hits against the spot I had just moved from a second before.

As I move I see, to my horror, Jack's two feet –in spite of his thick shoes- and his right knee totally in pieces. The Scotsman hasn't uttered a word, or a moan.

I pick up one of his arms and look at Harry to help me.

"No," says Jack, with his usual mischievous expression but with a sad smile.

Harry's face is transformed. He's white as a sheet and in his hand is the detonator –a dynamo that generates a small power discharge to start the explosion, and a handful of cables that run to the different points in the ruins which up till then have been our cover.

"Go, I'm done for… otherwise, they'll kill us all," Jack sighs and smiles, "I'll cover for you."

"No!" I shout.

Jack looks at me, and Harry first glares at me, then speaks in a sweet, quiet voice. "Come on, Gordon…" He sighs… "He's right, we can't drag him and get out of here." He swallows.

"Harry…" I try to speak, to think.

"Quickly," says Jack. "They've stopped shooting,…" And as he finishes speaking another discharge of the 7,5 cannon demolishes the place where I had stood only one minute before.

Harry throws the detonator into the hands of his brother-in-law, who has curled himself up on the ground.

I know what he's planned to do and I can't stop him.

Harry grabs me by the thick cloak and pushes me towards what is left of a wall on the opposite side of the street, where there may have been a garden or inside patio.

I have still to cross through the opening which at some time must have held a door, and looking back I see Harry, carefully and lovingly, covering Jack up with a piece of a door.

I clearly here one speak to the other.

"I love you brother."

"I love you too… take care of Gordon… kiss Maggie and the children…"

"I promise…"

Harry pushes me and we start running and jumping again among the rubble.

One wall, two walls, three walls, another street and from behind, a deafening and unmistakable explosion, heard among others.

My blood boils, I cease hearing, thinking, seeing.

Harry drags me, pushes me, pulls me. He doesn't shout or I don't hear him. I don't know if he feels like I do, ethereal and weightless.

I see red and blurry, just a small dot in front seems to look something like I've seen before. I'm moving like an automat, no consciousness, pushed by my instinct, no thought. We run, we jump. We run again, we climb. We run, we jump.

We end up walking along the road heading southeast without knowing what to do, as so many others.

We're a disbanded army - the men get rid of their useless guns without ammunition, and the riders have disappeared; there are no officers or NCOs, just a mass of men —many with wounded bodies, all with wounded souls- trying to find a refuge after the defeat.

I have scratches on my face, on my hands.

Harry has emptied his Daisy without looking at me. We walk beside each other, in silence, united by the burden of our friend's death.

We walk all night, to keep as much distance as possible from that city which at some point we thought we'd protect with our lives; but we also walk not to die from the cold.

The road we've taken is marked by the dead and the dying.

Dawn and the world turns a grey-white. A dense, hard mist like sugar foam in the park…

I open my eyes, and my endlessly-turning thoughts quieten.

"What are you thinking about, young man?" She speaks with her sweet, deep voice.

"And you?" I answer in order to escape from my memories.

"I asked first… but what does it matter… the sea reminds me of my Fuerteventura… and for sure you're thinking of yesterday… stop, stop struggling with the past… leave the dead in peace," he says, while he lights up a cigarette for each of us by placing them in her sweet mouth.

I don't answer, I don't want to lie.

She hands me the cigarette. I inhale the smoke, keep it in my lungs, and exhale it in small breaths, enjoying the tobacco's spicy taste, the soft drunkenness of the first drags.

I close my eyes.

I see again the headlights of the truck that breaks open the white veil, cutting off our retreat that dawn. Without any guns, we face our own men, Republicans, freedom.

But we quickly understand, without any trial or ceremony, this is a disciplinary squad especially sent to squash those abandoning positions in Teruel; and they will be handing out exemplary punishment to the cowards who turned their backs on the fascist enemy.

A team of executioners and we, their victims. They herd us into the truck with their bayonets.

Harry looks at me and speaks only once on that brief, last journey. He whispers.

"When I say "run" you run like a rabbit being pursued by the devil, you don't look back, not even once… you run until you can run no more, then you run more… understood?

He doesn't even move his lips, I nod very slightly.

We don't go very far. The truck stops, they make us get down, pushing and insulting us, they aren't many more than us; they're armed, we have either lost our rifles or we have no more ammunition. Among us there is more incredulity than protests.

I can't believe it either.

Is this how everything is going to end? Executed for cowardice? What is the sense?

They push us up against a stone wall. The mist has dissipated. The sun has still to come up.

Harry pushes me to the end of the line and then stands in front of all the condemned men. He doesn't shout, he hardly looks at me and says, "Run Gordon!"

Then with surprising speed he pulls out his pistol from his pocket and first shoots the political commissioner, who falls back without uttering a single word. Then he fires at the nearest man holding a rifle.

Now he does shout, he roars like a lion.

"RUN GORDON!"

I obey him as he continues shooting bullet after bullet.

I clearly hear the bronze cartridge shells as they hit the ground.

Other condemned men rush the executioners; I hear the commotion of the fight, then three or four rifle shots sound at the same time, then others, and again some more.

In the dawn, all that can be heard is the noise of the soles of my shoes hitting the stones.

"Are you a fool, boy? Leave the dead in peace."

I open my eyes and María is looking at me, her forehead furrowed.

"Have you decided? Stop thinking about 'what if… Listen, you'll get nowhere going along that road… That's what took place, that's enough." Her voice is spirited and decisive.

Negrín's government will be dismissing the international brigades today, they are sending them back as a gesture to appease Franco. The defeat has been negotiated in Munich. We are being expelled with the intention of the international fascist volunteers having to also abandon the war.

A.Hiteler

The truth is I have nowhere to go.

In England I must face the consequences of abandoning school; I have no other documents except those provided by the Republic; my father in Argentina has not written to me since he learnt of my destination, my grandfather is now dead… I'm here, I'm a Republican soldier and I will suffer the Republic's luck.

María is kind and inflexible.

"Listen, the best thing for you is to go to England, complete your studies in a free school and then you return to Argentina, if you like it so much…" And she sighs as she exhales the cigarette smoke… "Because here, nothin' will be left… if they catch you alive, they'll execute you as a mercenary."

"And what about you?" I answer.

"Nothin' at all goin' for me…" she sighs… "I can't go back to my island… and I won't let them catch me alive…"

She looks at me with those bright, brown, intense eyes. She smiles sadly and strokes my face with the back of her hand.

I also look at her and can't avoid the chill up my spine.

Thinking of that soft, brown skin torn to pieces, that wide and intelligent forehead mashed to bits by rifle butts, of her tender eyes completely out of their sockets… the terrible things I've seen time and again among my battle comrades fill me with horror, a cold, clinging horror which sticks to my spine.

Before my reactive feelings can show in my eyes or come out of my mouth, María Camejo stands up and takes my hand.

"Come on, pretty boy, the parade is about to start… be good, do what I say, I'm older than you and I'm more experienced, I know what's best… take advantage of this and go back."

I shake my head.

"You're stubborn, my pretty flower…" She laughs and shakes her head. The dark-brown, curly hair hardly moves and she quickly grabs it up with one hand and with the other rolls it into an untidy bun, which she fixes to her head with a stick which I carved for her.

We walk along holding hands as if we're a couple; we join other people who're walking, all in the direction of the parade with which the Republic will say farewell to the international volunteers.

But we're not a couple.

We're comrades-in-arms.

That day she came out of the blue, from a hardly-discernible path covered in dirty snow. She ordered me, "Follow me, quick… there're execution squads everywhere… it's a miracle you're alive."

So we went further into the hills surrounding that cursed city.

She was with a squad of Partisans, an eclectic group of armed civilians who had a particular relationship with the Republican army, who did not want them but needed them: their guerrilla tactics distracted people, they seized material, they captured everything they needed from the enemy.

The majority are anarchists, some surviving Trotskyists from the POUM (Marxist Unification Labour Party) purge and in a lesser number, those like María, with no definitive political stand although with a clear sympathy for the PSOE (Spanish Socialist Labour Party).

That freezing night seems so distant in time… and the days that followed so terrible. Pep and the Joint Chiefs-of-Staff fell with many thousands more in the retreat from Teruel; the executions of chiefs and officers became almost a habit that filled the whole army with hate and discouragement. We retreated as far as Belchite, the army attempting to keep organized.

María and her people took care of me firstly as another survivor of the purges and the Stalinist brutalities – they were the government's only support- and afterwards, almost immediately, they became aware they had no other among them who was such a good shot. So I remained as in a limbo of those disappeared, among the regular army turned guerrilla.

And all we had conquered bravely we lost in the same way.

We retreated for three months… leaving behind a great number of dead bodies, the bravest and self-sacrificing men.

It had taken us so long to conquer Belchite, yet they took it back in a day. And this was not because the Republicans had not fought – piles of cadavers remained as silent witnesses of this battle.

The owners of the sky, the fascists, shot down at us untiringly. The fresh infantry – Italians, Germans, Moroccans, pushed us back metre by metre, our Republican territory shrinking to the point that it was finally divided into two.

This was not an easy victory for the Francoists. They stopped advancing at the Ebro and we regrouped in Barcelona.

Today the international troops' are on parade; the Republic bids them farewell triumphantly and my eyes fill with tears when I hear the warm clamour of the multitude inflamed by the *Pasionaria*'s magic words.

Just as the Roman legions were in their time, my comrades-in-arms are celebrated and cheered loudly by the Barcelona citizens, today the capital of the Republic.

They return, I am staying. I'll be joining the final battle together with what is left of the Republican army.

The Ebro Army

A column of men and a few women walk along the narrow road which winds among the Pyrenees and from that height, now and again, one can see the Mediterranean's intense blue waters. Sometimes a truck drives by carrying loads of people; thousands of people are dragging luggage as they walk; sometimes somebody pushes a trolley; a cart pulled by horses and loaded with belongings, pieces of a life which will never return -they all pass by me. There are more and more people as we approach the frontier. It is heart-breaking to see that they have to leave things behind because they can't carry them, anything that exhaustion obliges them to abandon; they leave the little they have left, parts of a life that will no longer be Spanish.

The excessive luggage remains behind on the edge of the highway, marking the retreat of not just an army but part of a Republic which a few hours ago has ceased to exist.

I am one of them, just one more. Dressed in rags, hungry, in pain…

A dream, an ideal, my friends… a pain which doesn't allow me to breathe.

Nothing behind: death, destruction, reprisals. A few kilometres in front, Port Bou and after that, Cerbere, France.

We are so many, too many, and it's likely we won't be welcomed.

As we approach the frontier the silence grows and takes over; we slow down. The frontier! Life, but also defeat.

The exile the ancient Greeks used to compare to death awaits us on the other side. I buried my friends here… and my future. My family is thousands of kilometres away on the other side of the earth, as far away as China.

Where to go? North, seeking Calais, try to reach England.

How will I cross the sea? I don't know, I don't have a plan or an escape project; I arrived here as a boy with no other plan than to fight the fascists, and today I'm a defeated man, a member of a defeated army, a citizen of a defeated republic with no papers.

It's of little comfort to think I'm not alone, that this crowd walking on these cold February days is in the same condition as myself; but when I see families carrying small children, I can't help thinking that at least I'm not dragging anyone else to my fate.

What will become of us? Nobody knows, but as at other times, rumours abound everywhere.

Daladier's government classifies us, separates us, places us into groups, decides who will continue -if there is plenty of money, if there is family, relations- who will remain in concentration camps, a word which conjures up the worst image. I have no family, friends or relations in France, I have no money, jewels or belongings, I have no documents to prove I'm British and if I'm lucky, the school is still looking for me because of my escape… I'm a perfect candidate for a "classification" camp, surrounded by barbed wire…

As we approach Port Bou, our marching slows down; all about us are improvised camps, army tents made out of canvas or blankets, bonfires to keep the cold out during this terrible 1939 winter.

To my right, now and again I glimpse the Mediterranean; yesterday it seemed so beautiful, today it seems dark, grey and stormy. At my back Girona, further back Barcelona and even further, Ebro.

Nothing ties me to the Republic anymore, the Republic that has consumed the lives of so many valuable and good people and which now, in its death pains, throws us out.

Exhausted and frozen stiff, I stop to rest; while the endless column, murmuring like a procession, and from which emerges the silence of the men, the women and children crying, passing by me like a human river; all the faces show the same sadness and despair.

I sit on the side of the highway.

I start to re-read my diary, but I don't need it to remember… Everything is so fresh, so fixed in my memory…

The summer and the Ebro battle, in which the Republic played and lost its last game, a battle I'm sure will figure in history books as one of the longest and greatest in Europe, with thousands of infantry and hundreds of tanks on both sides; not in the air -the German and Italian fascists had devastated all of ours.

The parade, the farewell to the international brigades…

And the return to the front and once again the hell of a battle in winter. Then the retreat, the breaking up of some of the fronts, the orderly retreat in others.

The squad which had protected me acted with a certain independence, just on the edge of confronting our own side; the more the nationalists advanced, the more obvious were the differences with the communists.

Bleu, Blanc Rouge

By Christmas 1938 defeat was already in everybody's mind. And the tales coming out of each area fallen into the hands of the Francoists -whether true or not- passed from mouth to mouth.

We'll all be executed, said some.

Only the officers, said others; the political commissioners, the…

Despair and defeat had already settled amongst us even before the enemy had taken up any position. The orderly retreat from Aragon after the Ebro defeat, however, made a few think about resisting, or launching ourselves again, of counterattacking and resisting; war in Europe is inevitable, and then those who have turned their backs on us will quickly provide all those things that have been denied us up till then: weapons, ammunition, fuel, medicine…

Rumours about those who up till today were directing us. The government has abandoned Spain definitely and will not be returning. The noise in the street says then that they're distributing passports among the communists, and all the chiefs… and then arguments continue amongst us.

Half of Barcelona says that Madrid resists, and this is true. Let Miaja govern, Negrin and the communists have abandoned us… Rojo has a plan… January flies by hidden among the hunger and cold, and February arrives…

Every day we heard from someone who knew someone who knew…

England is preparing a supporting force, France will deliver tanks, Mexico will be sending planes -one day we heard that the Russians were preparing an airlift…

The next, that 1,500 had been executed… First they execute children… The North Africans rape every single woman no matter their age…

So the first days of this year have passed.

Ever more reserved, every day María simply repeats, "Go back, pretty boy, you must return… Your parents are waiting for you, your friends in England will receive you with open arms…"

My answer didn't change.

"If you come with me… I have failed my parents by abandoning school; I've failed my friends by using their money to come here… I'm like you, alone in the world, wherever you go, I'll go."

She didn't get angry, just shook her head, annoyed.

"You're so stubborn, pretty boy…"

We slept in each other's arms against the cold and once I kissed her on the lips; she allowed it for a second and then pushed me away softly but firmly, stroked my hair and spoke in a deep voice, "No, boy, it's not the place or the time… It's not enough that you're a brave soldier."

Sir Winston Churchill

Still holding me, her cheeks wet with tears, she spoke again.

"Haven't you said how much you miss your country, there on the other side of the sea? I've felt this since that cursed summer of 1936… A whole lifetime of that? I can't, I don't even want to imagine so much pain… Not even all your love could save me… What will we live off in France, in England, in Argentina? You and I, neither of us completed our studies, we've been fighting for years… What can soldiers work as? Anyway, there is going to be another war, everybody is saying so, then we can defeat Franco…"

"So I'll stay here until that day comes…"

The eternal and calm argument, between two stubborn people, consumed our days. She never said she loved me, and I, out of shyness, never said it and now, on the French border, I regret this from the depth of my heart.

The human river doesn't stop, but some, just as I, step away, gazing out at who knows what kind of secret dream.

I know mine, I know what I've seen and what I've been through; I'm sorry for none of it, only for not having spoken up, for not having told María that nothing else mattered to me, that for me the war had lost all sense since Teruel and losing Harry and Jack -and that when I had met her everything had changed.

We fought on together ceaselessly then, until a few days ago, until this craziness called war in which we had served -without stopping or doubting- bit back at us, at our hands and our heart.

I didn't fight on for the Republic, for socialism, for democracy, I fought for her.

Then everything fell apart.

At the beginning of March everybody knew that the Republic was dying, even though our information was very poor and came in bits and pieces, and many times from very doubtful sources: the fifth column here was just as active as in Madrid.

From France, Negrin made changes in the cabinet and in the Armed Forces, surrendering all the power to the communists, while more and more people started going into exile in a climate of fear, discouragement and despair.

C-47

In what was left of the Second Republic, everything went into shock.

Casado, a name which is pronounced like a prayer, races through the remains of the Republic.

When a group of military men arrive at the building we used as a refuge, we had already heard of General Casado's coup against Negrín and the communists; as soon as we saw the half a dozen of uniformed soldiers, someone said, "We must resist!"

But María, with her usual cold calm, said in a clear voice, "More resistance? Haven't you had enough? Come, let's give up our rifles and end this…"

Having said this, she opens the door and greets the officer –an NCO with a prematurely aged face- who without much explanation, tells us we must hand over our guns and any explosives, whether they belong to the Republic or the National Army.

We no longer talk of the enemy, fascists, rebels…

We are complying with this order when someone – I don't know who and couldn't care either- throws down his rifle into the pile and a shot and smell of powder is released, surprising us all in spite of its familiarity.

The *casadistas* put up their rifles but they never get to aim at anyone because everyone –including my comrades- are horrified as they look at the same point to which my eyes have turned as to a magnet.

María has fallen on her back onto the floor, a pool of blood gathering around her. She has gone quite pale. I don't know how I get to her -I kneel by her side and pick up her hand, speaking absolute gibberish, out of control.

I look at her and she looks back into my eyes, alive as ever and she whispers, "I'm cold…" As she speaks I scream out for a blanket and cover her, but there's nothing I can do. The blood seeps into her hair lying on the ground, she gives one shake and she's gone, growing cold as I hold her.

Of all the stupid ways to die in a war, María had been trapped in the most stupid way of all, a stray bullet fired by no-one, when everything was over…

The officer wrote a report, we were all questioned, we signed a document and next morning we were sent out onto the street. Nobody was able to tell me what they had done with María, but I was assured she would be buried with her name.

I don't know what happened after that; I slept during the day and walked at night. Someone said we had to go to France, that foreigners were executed. I walked out of Barcelona and joined the caravan of penitents.

The Spanish civil war had ended.

Brittania Rules

Home Sweet Home

I look at myself in the hall mirror of the small Odeon Theatre and I'm still astounded by the reflection: my hair is combed back with brilliantine, my face is clean and below my nose grows a thin, soft moustache.

My body, slimmed down by the travails of the last two years is now, however, covered by a well-cut, made-to-measure suit.

A gift from Mrs Sylvia, who has not ceased to spoil me since the moment I crossed her doorstep, dirty and ragged.

It's a few weeks since I arrived, and I still haven't got used to four meals a day, or having hot baths and clean, new clothes to put on every morning.

I carry the weight of my friends' deaths, of my comrades, of María, the bitter taste of a defeat, and those days wandering around the south of France, avoiding the police like a fugitive, living off the charity of many good souls, who knowing where we came from -there were so many unfortunate comrades roaming around with no direction- shared their bread, cheese, some vegetables, perhaps some cold cuts, and gave us news about where we could get food or shelter, where the authorities wouldn't find us.

I only looked at my image in the mirror about one minute –the time it took Mrs Sylvia to powder her nose- but I could not avoid feeling upset when I saw myself, among other members of the audience, having come to enjoy the play by the late García Lorca.

The magic of the Andalucian elf has not walked amongst us; I must be honest, I didn't like the play; the Andalucian poet's beautiful intensity has been sterilized by an inefficient translation into English, converting it into high-sounding speeches and with none of the Spanish verve.

Mrs Sylvia, intelligent, intuitive and with her maternal wisdom respects my silences, but when I manage to open up my heart and allow the pain under my shell and my distressed soul some freedom and air, she listens with a devoted attention.

She is a mother, a friend, an invaluable companion.

We walk out onto the street into the fresh air of a London Spring; a taxi awaits us, reserved previously, to take us to Barnet. Mrs Sylvia prefers not to drive her car at night.

I've offered to be her driver, but with her usual good humour she pointed out that she preferred to pay and so be able to talk to me without worry.

I open the door of the black car, identical to almost all the other cars circulating around us. Mrs Cummins gets in and while she gets comfortable, my attention is caught by a beggar who is shamefacedly asking for help from the passers-by.

She's already inside the car, ready to leave.

My heart is beating hard and I hesitate to get in. From this distance, I think I've recognised a familiar face.

"What's the matter, dearest? Why are you not getting in?" She talks very delicately, smiling kindly.

I ask her permission to take a moment or two, and she nods, still smiling.

I cross the street and as I approach the thin, gaunt man, dressed in carefully mended rags, my heart starts beating with an almost painful intensity.

I stop in front of this man, who reflects what I was only a few weeks back, and before looking at his face, I notice that he's trying to hide the end of his right arm: his right hand is missing from above the wrist.

It takes me only a second to recognise Robbi Brecher, the young German I met during the Teruel battle days. We had drunk and sung the whole night long, accompanied by his wonderful guitar-playing.

At that time we still believed in the possibility of victory, the fascists were enclosed in the beautiful medieval city and all the Republican Army forces were preparing to push them out. The winter was upon us but we were well wrapped up against the cold then.

He was born in Dresden, and between 1929 and 1932 he had studied to become a professional musician, he had to abandon Germany after the Nuremberg laws were passed.

The Nazi law had simultaneously left him without his girlfriend –a gentile; without a job in the Municipal orchestra; and without a house because he was Jewish as well as a socialist.

Exiled in Spain towards the end of 1935, at the time of the July coup he had been working as a music teacher in Barcelona; he joined the Republican army during the first days of the war, acting later –just as myself- as a liaison with the German-speaking Thalerman battalion.

It takes him a few seconds to recognise me and when he does, his blue, transparent eyes fill with tears.

We embrace, and in very few words in his stiff English, he tells me about his capture and the pleasure his captors had in smashing his arm with the butt of their rifles, while another kicked his guitar into little pieces. With the same economy of words, he tells me the details of his escape from the prison camp, the way in which luck in the form of a German doctor, an old family friend, had saved his life twice over: one by amputating his hand and the other by helping him to escape from the prison camp in which he was surely destined to die.

He sleeps in train stations, in parks, in doorways, always afraid of being arrested.

He entered England illegally, thanks to the help of a French Basque smuggler who sympathised with the cause. He has no documents, he could end up in jail or even worse, be deported back to his home country. Old Nevil's government is very capable of doing this to cool down the aggressive Nazi foreign affairs policies.

I have a great deal of money on me, although I have no way of earning it; Mrs Sylvia insists on filling my wallet with one pound notes until I have ten or fifteen –a large amount- and which I don't hesitate to give to him as I say goodbye.

When I return to get into the car, Mrs Sylvia with her usual self-confidence in questioning, asks me without hesitation, "Who is that young man, Gordon?"

I explain to her as the car starts off and almost without interrupting my tale, this wondrous woman orders the driver to turn back and to stop in front of the beggar; then speaking to me without any possibility of a reply, "Please, invite your comrade, I would like to hear first-hand about life in Nazi Germany…"

During the trip Mrs Sylvia shows once again the incredible size of her generous heart, as she invites –with her characteristic kindness, impossible to refuse- my companion-at-arms to have dinner with us at her home.

And with her usual humour, she points out, "I don't suppose your hotel will miss you if you don't go back for a few days, will they? I have an extra room although you will have to share the bathroom with Gordon. I hope this won't be a bother…"

I have to make a great effort not to break down; when I see the tears pouring down Robbi's cheeks, I force myself to look out of the window of the car, which is slowly driving us home.

With the tact and maternal kindness which Sylvia has shown me so many times, she reaches over and hands our guest a white handkerchief, and says in a soft, kind voice, "Don't worry, my young friend. I was born, raised and lived all my adult life in India. I live far away from my sons and I don't have many friends in London. I know very well what it feels like to be uprooted, just as Gordon knows it. You will have better days," she says, and with a deep sigh, continues, "That at least is what I hope for you and for all of us."

Although we haven't talked about it since my return, nobody doubts the shadow of war is over Europe.

Mrs Sylvia's care shows in every one of her gestures, in her every word. She doesn't question, she converses kindly, and now and again she lets slip a question, always to the point, always appropriate. The trip from London is brief.

We arrive at Barnet.

We dine in silence. My companion-in-arms eats without lifting his eyes from his plate, and Mrs Sylvia excuses herself and leaves the table. As I did a few weeks before, he devours his dinner with a prisoner's hunger.

Mrs Cummins has had the kindness of seeing that the meat and potatoes –a large quantity- are cut in such a way that Robbi will not have to feel uncomfortable by only being able to use one hand.

I show him his room –across from mine- and I can't help noticing that the bed is already made, pyjamas and perfumed towels are carefully doubled and placed at the end of the bed.

Mrs Sylvia herself, while we were dining, has been busy with my comrade's wellbeing.

At breakfast next morning, Robbi is dressed as I am, with clean, well ironed clothes.

Matahji, the woman who has been housekeeper of Mrs Sylvia's home for many years, attends to our needs in silence.

Among my papers I pick out the card that my last saviour had given me, the man who smilingly and kindly paid for the four dishes of *tripes a la mode* in Cahen, the one who brought me all the way back to Mrs Sylvia's house.

I read: Lt. Anthony J. Farrington, and a single telephone number which I immediately dial.

The dialogue is brief and friendly.

"Good morning, I'd like to speak to 2nd Lt Farrington…"

"Speaking… Who's this?"

"You may remember me, we met a few weeks ago, in France…"

"Oh, yes, how are you!? Have you decided to accept my proposal?"

"No, really I'm grateful but no… Actually, I'm calling about someone else, a comrade-in-arms… but he's not English, he was born…"

"Please, say no more... I'll give you an address, tell your friend I'll see him there... Be so good as to describe me to him so he can recognise me... we may be able to help each other... What about you?"

"I hope to be able to return to my country as soon as possible... I hope you understand..."

"Of course. Tell your friend I'll meet him at Trafalgar Square at 12:30 pm. I hope you and I meet again, sir, thank you for calling, it's been good to talk to you again."

"Thank you so much."

That day Robbi had lunch with Farrington; he returned to Barnet, spent three or four days with us, said goodbye and I didn't hear any more from him until many years later.

Dunkirk: Bring the Boys Back Home

Either it's a small world or fate is conspiring with my destiny. Standing in front of me, with his likeable, cheeky smile is the man who took me back to England in April 1939. Little more than one year later here we are again, face to face, and despite the uniforms and his insignias, he puts out his hand.

"Corporal? This army is done for if an experienced soldier such as yourself is a corporal... and as a battalion mechanic!"

I salute him as I should due to his Second Lieutenant rank, and still feeling amazed, I shake his hand.

I explain briefly, summarising.

"Eurwen Glynn & Gordon Evans Mechanical Repairs and Truck Transport" painted on the old sign on O'Sean's barn.

The Battle of the River Plate and Mrs Sylvia's losses. My incorporation as a volunteer and my current occupation.

I don't go into the fierceness of the Nazi attack, the surprise due to the speed with which they appear, men who die without even getting out of the trucks, the columns of vehicles attacked by flights of Stukas from above, the M109's machine-gunning the roads, the Heinkels dominating the sky.

He asks me how I got here and smiles when I point to my workshop truck. In theory we are a rear-guard unit, but in the confusion of these last days we ended up on the outskirts of Dunkirk almost at the same time as Lord Gorth's vanguard forces.

Although yesterday the Nazis have mysteriously suspended their flights and we haven't seen their infantry, we know by experience that in a few minutes their trucks, their armoured cars, their self-propelled cannons and modern planes may appear.

Second Lt. Anthony (Tony) Farrington is as kind as a shirt salesman; the first time I saw him, in the south of France, I was a ragged and smelly beggar, and yet he invited me to lunch knowing that I hadn't eaten for days, and ordered —always kind and smiling- that I be served four consecutive dishes of a tripe, potatoes and rice stew.

That day he made me get into his Morris 6 and we crossed the ferry from Calais to Dover, and he used his influence at the Ministry of War in order not to complicate my entering the country without any papers, which I had lost during the retreat from Aragon.

And here, once again in hell, this kind and smiling man insists that I accompany him, he needs me on a mission for the Ministry of War.

"Come on, Corporal, I'm sure you know everything we need in order for me to comply with this task…"

I place myself at his service.

"Destroy your truck and instruct your men to do the same with all the vehicles that aren't indispensable. Nothing that is useful should fall into German hands… And clear the roads!" he orders.

Smiling, he says, "Can you drive a motorbike? Get one, we'll need it," and then he offers me a cigarette.

I get moving as I smoke; I give my orders and make my preparations; as I finish the cigarette I've managed to find a Norton bike with a sidecar, and a mounted Bren machine gun with it.

The abandoned vehicles are everywhere; the ever-increasing number of troops are filling the streets near the port and beaches.

The quiet around us is somewhat scary, if one can say that only solitary shots from the 15,5 cannons mean it's quiet… but this is different to the thousand flaming furies from the sky, and on the plains the never-ending firing from rifles and machine-guns, against the sporadic but terrible cannon shots…

Farrington doesn't explain to me why, when all the British Forces are retreating, he wants to approach as close as possible to the enemy; but I'm a corporal and he's an officer, he gives the orders and I obey, it's that simple.

The first thing we do in the middle of the chaos is look for headquarters; one after another, we pass the checkpoints where Farrington, without ever losing his politeness, his smile and friendliness, presents his papers; we finally reach Lord Gorth's quarters. Because of Farrington's lower rank we have to go through many filters, but each time he presents his papers he goes up one step more, he's sent to talk to someone higher up in the chain of command.

I'm not comfortable with this task; I'm a mechanic and corporal and around me there are only high-ranking officers now.

Finally they let him in to see the old man.

While I wait, I look at all the faces around me and see the same worried expressions I saw at the Ebro offensive; nobody trusts there will be a victory.

The meeting is brief; Gorth is preparing to return to Great Britain. He has disobeyed orders and instead of confronting the Nazis on the French Belgian plains he has retreated to our current position. According to Farrington, he will be rewarded by Churchill's new government; there's no way the British Forces can triumph over Hitler's war machinery.

We leave the city behind and search for the front line, but the line doesn't exist, it moves with the forces concentrated at Dunkirk, and the rear-guard has become the vanguard line.

The farms along the main and neighbouring roads of the French-Belgian plains are being evacuated, and the focus of halting the Germans is being established in the empty buildings.

Trenches are being dug everywhere; there are no more regiments or battalions, only officers, NCOs and soldiers who are organizing themselves almost miraculously; the previous encounters with the Nazis have decimated the tableaus, there are entire units of soldiers in which the highest rank is a corporal.

They have grouped and organized themselves because the order from London has been clear: stop the Nazis wherever possible so that the troops can be evacuated by the Royal Navy.

One day has passed since that order and a line is beginning to form, with Holland in the north, Belgium in the west, France in the south and in the east is the saving Atlantic Ocean.

The stillness all along that diffuse frontier is deceptive, I know this - I've lived it many times in Spain. The Nazi infantry is hidden somewhere out there.

The warm spring air transmits the birds' songs but we can't hear or see any plane, which is incomprehensible; they have what it takes to finish us off, why don't they do it?

I have the feeling that we're in that cruel cat and miserable mouse game and we the British army are the mouse.

We cover the line, from north to south; Farrington takes notes and now and again they stop us to question us; from the 2nd Lt's bag he takes out the documents and showing them provokes some anxiety in those who are controlling us.

At each stop the same thing takes place: they look for an officer to guarantee the authenticity of those papers. Again and again the same scene: they return making the same classic English military salute.

We spend the whole day doing this. In the evening we approach Esquelbecq Castle, near the village of Wormhoudt, where a communications truck is established and a field hospital is being set up. Farrington demands making the call himself and once again the same sequence - as usual, he gets his own way.

Night falls; we return to the city which is no more than 25 kms. away, but the road is literally strewn with trucks and military cars, columns of soldiers, carts pulled by horses and groups of families fleeing from whatever will be taking place.

That night Dunkirk is chaotic; although the blackout order has been given, in several places there are bonfires and soldiers gathered around them, unsure of what to do.

Everything is very disorderly and the amount of soldiers without anyone in charge is huge, it's worse than disorganized. Farrington orders me to take him to the port, where very slowly troops are being taken on board. I don't think that in the Spanish War there was ever so much of a mess as there is here; there is hardly any water, or food.

Without any officers, the soldiers raid the shops; there is fighting and the Military Police have to intervene, they are crucial but there are not enough of them; so they begin forced conscription: an MP patrol looks for the biggest soldiers amongst the crowd, the sober ones, those who are still calm.

Farrington's papers save us from being taken on.

We leave the city once again, the arrival of soldiers and vehicles overwhelm any attempt at organization.

We leave the road and try to sleep by the side of our vehicle; the noise, the movement and the tense waiting for the Nazi attack keep me in a state which is not totally vigilant, but neither is it sleep; on the other hand, Farrington has thrown himself on the ground, covered himself with his coat and is sleeping peacefully, even snoring.

With the first sunrays, we get onto our bike and again take to the road for our drive along the front. The amount of people heading towards the town had diminished during the night, but with the first light, everything has returned to the previous rhythm.

Then the deafening noise of the motors of Hitler's planes breaks in upon the dawn; they pass furiously over our heads and before our eyes discharge all their ammunition onto the town at our back.

The evil forces have woken up from their lethargy and are vomiting fire on Dunkirk.

We see the columns of black smoke that in seconds can be seen covering the horizon.

They will not disappear again.

We halt our journey, astounded as we watch the dreadful spectacle in the distance; and this is only the beginning. Impotent, from our side road we watch the Nazi planes emptying their bombs on an almost unarmed city; then they return, passing very low over our heads and again opening fire onto the columns of soldiers and civilians who are fleeing towards the sea.

I had seen this before, I had lived this before; but one can never get used to this terrifying idea of being absolutely defenceless in this type of attack.

Panic and chaos take hold of those on the road.

The attack is brief but the effect on the victims is devastating. Civilians and soldiers try to get back into some order and continue moving, but the spectacle before them of a city in flames is very disturbing. Where to head… There is no safe place.

Farrington changes his mind; we don't return to Dunkirk. We'll look for the southern limit, the line of contact with our French allies.

The network of roads and lanes that join villages and small towns is very intricate and complex, crisscrossed by the regional web of roads and lanes.

A truck is stopped almost in the middle of the road, and a corporal signals us to stop. They are lost. They know that the French are in the south, and that somewhere in the east lies the Nazi army.

The worse thing is that their truck's motor won't start, and it's not for lack of petrol.

Second Lieutenant Farrington waits, sitting in the sidecar, and as I'm about to look into the motor, from inside the cabin a head pokes out and I hear a very familiar voice.

"Who the hell gave you permission to touch my truck?"

It's the sleepy voice of Derek Jones.

When I look at him, he blinks a couple of times and rubs his eyes —it's obvious he's been sleeping- he looks at me and shouts.

"Gordon Evans! This is incredible..!... I heard you'd died in Spain!"

He gets down from the truck and shakes my hand, an great smile on his face.

"Corporal..?... Shit, Gordon… Just because I went to King George's they gave me these stripes…" And he shows me his sleeve with the 2nd Lt insignias.

"A mechanic…?... Man, when I finished school you used to spend your day in the library… Oh, that's right, you didn't finish school, did you..?... I heard that you'd gone to the war in Spain but also that you'd died there. You were really stupid, pal… But you were the bloke with most balls in the whole damned school…"

Derek smiles as he talks.

What does fate have in store for me? Coincidences are pursuing me…

It's not the first time; the day before yesterday it was Pep in Spain, yesterday Farrington in Dunkirk, today Derek on the French-Belgian plains…

Farrington gets off the bike and stands in front of us. He smiles only slightly, but rigorously salutes Derek. The Canadian looks at me.

"Is this ass your boss?"

"Derek… We're at war with the Nazis… the 2nd Lieutenant has to…"

"This ass has the same stripes as me… What the hell d'you need? D'you wanna fight? I'm talking to my friend, not to the corporal…"

Farrington smile has dropped. He ignores the provocation.

"Corporal, can you get this truck to start?"

"Look, asshole, he'll touch my truck if I allow him… My orders are to wait for a truck for my men…"

It's clear that Derek hasn't changed at all, he's still the same bully. The physical difference between him and Farrington are very clear: Derek is broad and full of muscle, and he must be at least a head taller than Farrington.

Farrington doesn't blink an eye.

"Second Lt, I have orders to follow, I don't have time to argue with you or anybody. If you're looking for a fight, a few miles on there are enough Germans for you…"

He looks at me. "Corporal, do you think you can do something, or not?"

I stick my head under the hood and the burnt alternator is in plain view. Without a spare part, the truck won't move. I give this information to both officers.

"So, Corporal, there's nothing to be done… Say goodbye to your friend… And Lt, burn your truck and take your men to the city… You can't get lost, it's over there where you see the columns of smoke… If you march, you can be there by the evening, we're about 18 to 20 miles…

"Burn my truck… Are you joking or what, you ass? The British Crown placed it in my charge and you, a mere desk 2nd Lieutenant is going to tell me what to do with it… Listen to me, you shit… I don't know what they taught you in that school for queers… but I don't intend to burn anything… Unless you can get me on the ground in a fair fight…"

Farrington's face looks as if it's made of wax.

"Listen 2nd Lt, there's no time to waste on stupidities and much less with an ass like yourself… I'm giving you orders from the British Army's Chiefs of Staff, signed by Mr. Churchill… It's clear that your monkey brain can't understand the seriousness of this situation… we must destroy all material we can't ship back to England… and that includes your truck. Have you understood, you fool?"

Derek smiles and tenses up. He's got what he wanted, made my new boss lose his temper. He gets into a boxing position.

"Come here, you ass… If you can manage to hit me once in the face, just once, I'll burn the damned truck myself."

I stand in front of Derek.

Dunkirk

"No, old chap… It doesn't work that way… We've come from an interview with the old man… 2nd Lt Farrington was given his papers… The 2nd Lt, just like you and me, is obeying orders…"

"This has nothing to do with you, Gordon… I know how much you're worth… I don't want to fight with you… I want to fight with this Sandhurst asshole who thinks himself so superior that he can give me orders… Come here, you fairy… Let's see what you've learnt at the Academy…"

Farrington turns and gets back into the sidecar.

"Come on, corporal, we have things to do…"

"Derek, listen, you have to burn the truck and lead your men to the beach… The Royal Navy will take us back home…"

"You're not going anywhere with that queer…" He relaxes, abandons his tough stance, smiles at me.

"D'you have a cigarette, Gordon? I finished mine last night…"

I search in my pockets and find a packet with one cigarette, my last one… I throw it to him.

"I mean it, old chap… Don't leave with that fairy… D'you have a light?"

I shake my head and look at Farrington, who shows me his lighter.

I smile. It's clear that Farrington hasn't let himself be impressed by Derek's foolish talk.

I walk up to the bike and just as I reach Farrington I hear the terrifying howl of the attack sirens the J-88 plane designers have placed beneath its wings. I don't have to look up to know what's happening.

The argument between Derek and Farrington distracted us, otherwise if we had been paying attention we would have heard the distant murmur of the plane, even if it was very high up.

I shout.

"Get out of that truck, now!"

Derek, the cigarette in his mouth, looks at me. Farrington does as well, and at the same time, they both look up. Time stops. I take Farrington's arm and literally pull him out of the sidecar to the side of the road. I don't have time to cover myself. Right in front of me, not more than 20 mts away, there is an explosion and its blast throws me backwards.

The bomb has fallen exactly where Derek was standing – he literally disappears before my eyes, devoured by the deafening explosion. I feel the wind blast from the machine-gun but miraculously, I'm unhurt.

The whole front of the truck has disappeared along with Derek. The motorbike was hit by one shot, which destroys the carburettor. Farrington still hasn't quite understood what has happened.

Partially lying across the road, the back part of the Leyland is a desolate picture: some bodies, badly wounded and bloody, are strewn around the ground, and from inside the truck the painful groans I've heard before, in which the cries of the wounded are heard along with the moans of the dying men.

I try to stand, dizzy and deafened by the explosion. I instinctively turn to look back and see the plane not in a nosedive but close to the ground, firing its guns at what is left of the vehicle, to kill off any survivors. I throw myself to the ground again, but for now I'm not their target.

When it has finished its pass, shooting at the smoking truck, the plane climbs up almost vertically, leaving us in the sights of the gunman at the back, who discharges bursts of shots onto our spot while the plane climbs, making a long turn and roll above us, getting into a position to make a second pass.

Farrington is kneeling to my right, clearly shaken, he can't quite grasp what's happening. I stand in spite of having lost my sense of balance with the explosion. I manage to get to the bike and I'm surprised at my ease of pulling out the Bren machine-gun from its mount.

It's a heavy gun – nearly 13 kgs when loaded – but I don't feel it. I half-turn and see the Stuka flying over the tops of some birch trees which have no leaves yet, and some five hundred metres away its machine guns open fire in short bursts, leaving furrows in the ground, and it flies in a zigzag motion trying to hit us.

When it's only one hundred metres away I open fire, also in short bursts, aiming carefully at the cabin and then at the grey belly of the air beast, which flies over us with a terrifying noise.

The plane performs the same manoeuvre, it climbs almost 60 degrees and speedily accelerates, so as to place us once again in the sights of the rear gunman, who opens fire and impacts Derek's smoking truck, but when it has climbed perhaps two or three hundred metres the plane rolls over on itself and the nose points straight at the ground at full speed.

Farrington has managed to sit up and we both watch in amazement as the Junker-88 ploughs into the ground, becoming deformed like a cigar being put out in an ashtray, and at the same time it explodes in a ball of fire and black smoke; a figure which we recognise immediately as the rear gunman flies out into the air in his seat, first it climbs high and makes an ellipse which projects it forwards, then it lands onto the road some five or six hundred metres away from us.

Derek's truck is burning as if it were paper, releasing a nauseating smell of a mix of the truck's rubber tires and burning flesh.

"My God…" says Farrington, brushing off his uniform.

"Do you always fire like that, Corporal?"

It's clear he's still much shaken, but his character has taken over. He lights up a cigarette with shaking hands, he passes it to me and when I look at his hand, it no longer shakes.

"Poor bastard… poor boys…" He then adjusts his cap, straightens his jacket, picks up his backpack full of his documents, looks at me and says, "The motorbike doesn't work, right?"

I don't need to look at it closely to know that a shard from the bomb has blown the carburettor right off.

I fire a short burst against the fuel tank and at the motor, which starts leaking oil. Farrington puts his lighter close up –it had never reached Derek's hands- and the fuel starts burning at the same time as deflagrating with a deafening, dry pop which shakes us.

We walk along the road, I carry the Bren on my shoulder; the lieutenant, not pulling any rank, carries the heavy backpack with several magazines.

We walk by the dead Nazi still tied to his seat, black with smoke and oil, hardly recognisable and stained blood red. Neither of us looks at the defeated man. What for?

After an exhausting two-hour march beneath May's pale sun, we met up with a French Colonial Army company. To our surprise, before us are half-a-dozen Africans, black as coal, dressed in blue uniforms, wearing the classic helmet with its crest and with a white officer in charge. They stop us, surprised by our uniforms and the considerable distance from our lines, insinuating that we could be infiltrated Nazi spies.

Then the company chief appears, impeccable and martial, cool but friendly. Although he's a small man –his height (just as Farrington and I) is at the limit of what is "acceptable" for the regular army- he has a particular way of walking, of moving and observing, an energy and authority that I've only seen in great chiefs; the blacks and the whites all look at their chief with equal devoted admiration: it's clear that he's adored as Caesar.

"Lt François Ragon, French Colonial Army, your papers please."

Farrington answers in bad French, and as soon as he's introduced us, the atmosphere changes.

Second Lt Farrrington's French, which I'd already heard in Calais, gives us away.

"*Vous avez pas besoin des papiers… rien d'autre que un anglais peut macher les mots comme ça!*" [You don't need papers, nobody except an Englishman could chew up words like that!] he exclaims, and his men burst out laughing. I can't help smiling, and I lower my eyes.

"You too, Corporal?" he says, with an angry gesture.

And he again repeats the badly pronounced French, asking his men why they're laughing. Then I see a mischievous brightness in his glance and realize his anger is only faked, he's showing his charming wit, and he returns our papers to us.

The French lieutenant turns to me.

"*Et vous caporal, parlez vous français?*" [And you, Corporal, do you speak French?]

I look at my chief, who gives me permission to talk with a slight gesture.

"*Un peu, mon lieutenant...*" [A little, Lieutenant].

The French lieutenant smiles slightly.

"*Ah! Me... Voyons... Vous parles mieux que votre sublieutenant!*" [Ah! But I see you talk better French than your 2nd Lieutenant!]

He makes a sign and the soldiers around us move discreetly away. Farrington isn't frightened by our host and ally's taunting, and with studied politeness and protocol he explains our situation, not daunted in the least by the Frenchman's mocking smile, and now and again, the latter asks him to repeat a word or a phrase.

It's clear that the Frenchman is amused by Farrington's efforts to speak his language and the poor results, but soon Farrington's charm and his efforts achieve a better end and the Frenchman invites us to share his breakfast.

Although in the north and east the fighting has started, the entire south in Nazi hands has still not joined the firing.

We gobble down the cheese, bread and cold cuts he offers us. In exchange, we tell him about our encounter with the Stuka.

Ragon shakes his head, concerned.

Unlike my 2nd Lt, he just like myself, has seen how they attack, quick as lightening and fierce as rabid wolves. It's obvious it'll be difficult to return to Dunkirk… And even more difficult to return home.

Operation Overlord Über Berlin

I feel the freezing wind hitting me like a smack in the face; the soft hissing made by the parachute's strings from which I'm dangling doesn't distract me; on the other hand, the landscape, barely illuminated by the first night of a crescent moon…

In the distance we hear the deaf roar of the Dakota's motors starting up, the airplane in which the North American pilot has brought us to this place in an impossible, crazy and risky manoeuvre; we flew almost touching the tree tops from Italy, flying over the French-Italian border and the Alps' lower mountains to avoid the Nazi mobile radars, and for two hours we continued very close to the ground until the very edge of the French-German frontier.

Then, ten minutes before the jumping off zone, he climbed to the highest point a DC3 can reach to then –in a combined display of craziness and skill- he launched his plane into a descent with both motors cut off as if it were a simple glider and not a truck with wings.

Two minutes from the zone he levelled to around 150 mts – always descending due to gravity- in order for us to jump, while the plane made a 360° turn leaning on its right wing in the smallest radius possible: we were twelve, and we had to accomplish this every 20 seconds, making a total of 2 minutes.

Then another 3 minutes–if he's lucky and skilled- to start up his noisy motors at a considerable distance, between 8 and 10 kms on… and keeping at no more than 30 or 40 mts. from the ground. One error, a little garbage in the carburettors, a church spire not diagrammed into the navigation maps, and he and his crew would never return to his Floyd County in Virginia.

The plane commander is a young, smiling, calm captain, with an intense and penetrating look in his eyes, and he told us all those flight details in a briefing we had half an hour before boarding.

The object of that crazy flight: that we may land, as silently as possible, in the heart of Nazi-occupied France.

My drop lasts just over a total of one minute.

Drop onto the ground, pull up one's legs, roll the least times possible, place one's arms in a position of combat and at the same time get rid of the parachute; fold it up carefully, paying attention to any sign of the enemy, dig a hole, carefully bury the delicate silk material.

We've rehearsed it over and over, two weeks ago we had to confirm our parachuting skills which we learnt at the "assassination school" in which we were trained after Dunkirk.

We're the best, they told us.

They didn't tell us we were being held up at Monte Cassino. We knew it actually, because we were at the front line and saw the obstinate resistance of the Panzer Grenadiers brought from Russia.

At some point we'll soon be invading Nazi Europe, therefore we must help the Résistance in occupied France… In silence, I seek my companions in the grey light. If we dropped where we were supposed to, we should be on an ally's farm… it's a large property, some 10 or 12 hectares surrounded by several lines of trees which don't allow a good vision but at the same time could be a great hiding place for a machine gun.

With my skin and hair standing on end, I trot along the snowy ground trying to be as quiet as possible, but signaled by the ridiculous sound of a cricket in winter, which clicks twice and is then silent.

Again, twice. Now I can identify its direction.

Tony Farrington has one knee on the ground and makes the small metal device click again, it's far less obvious than military whistles.

In just a few minutes and in absolute silence our unit gathers around our chief. Everything goes as planned –up to this point we are exactly within the plan's instructions- we must move some 200 yards to 220° north-east and stop to listen to our ground contact's signal.

For two weeks we've practiced, gone over and revised the operation, again and again; we're in Berlin's back garden and if we're trapped, our end can be guaranteed.

Clearly and briefly, from among the trees we see a dim light that comes on and is immediately turned off. Everything must be quick and silent, far from the sight and ears of the enemy and its many minions.

Tony signals to me with a nod. I move forward on my belly, relaxed as a tiger ready to kill or die.

"*Le porc est toujours dans l'avatoir…*" [The pig is always in the slaughterhouse…] I say, pronouncing each word carefully, careful not to shout…

"*Mais le bourreau est toujours dans ça chambre.*"[But the executioner is always in his room.] They whisper from among the bushes. I click my device.

In silence we gather with our hosts, as tense as we are. We follow them into a very large stable.

The intense smell of dung and straw from the animals and in the environment pulls me away for a second and triggers my childhood in the *pampas*, but I control my feelings and come present.

The cows are moved away and a hidden trapdoor is opened in the floor, which swallows us all up.

They turn on a light and we can finally look at each other's faces.

"We can talk while the light is on but if it's turned off, we must be silent… is that clear?" says one voice, which seems vaguely familiar.

Tony beats me to it.

"Captain Rasputin!" He says with surprise. "You're our contact?"

"Brumel?" He says with a laugh. "Can't the English send someone who speaks French?"

He then looks at me and smiles when he recognises my night disguise.

"Corporal Spain, I suppose?" He approaches me to shake my hand. Still smiling, I show him the sleeve of my uniform without any stripes.

"Sergeant now, Captain, I was promoted after Dunkirk…"

A brief current short as a blink but intense as lightning runs up my spine.

Captain Ragón, our companion in the most unfortunate adventure of the whole history of wars, the evacuation from Dunkirk's port and beaches… is our contact.

Our *nom de plume*, as in any partisan army, hides our identities.

Brumel, Rasputin, Spain, Machinegun, Grumpy, Stoner.

Our refuge, which we had entered by a very small door, is an almost ridiculously enormous building that is not only a stable but also a milking shed. We're in the milking shed area - among the cows, beneath the straw filthy with cow dung there is this trap door which separates us from a world controlled by Nazis.

The underground room is small for the twenty people who are hidden there, but it has two or three connected rooms: it's the FFI base, the free French Forces of the Interior or French Resistance.

As in no other place, here war is to the death.

The Nazis consider this area is their own territory.

Alsace and Lorraine have been the traditional focus of conflicts between the French and Germans.

Verdun is a few kilometres away, that terrible battlefield in which millions of men lived and died in WWI.

Metz is also in the area and its NCO military school quarters, which has provided so many chiefs to the Wehrmacht (Armed Forces) and to Germany in general.

The region also has one of Europe's main railway nodes, with access to Austria, Yugoslavia, Switzerland, Italy…

Since 1940, the French here have been the object of all kinds of persecutions, unless they form part of the French Nazi party, cooperating fully and faithfully with the Vichy and the Gestapo[1] regime; repression is fierce in the hands of the French, strictly supervised by German Nazis, who keep the best cases for themselves.

The Resistance is bitter and active, in spite of the brutal and merciless reprisals; scientific and meticulous torture to keep a person alive in an ocean of pain; executions without any trial, and unappealable, summary trials are all current and daily.

An important part of our mission is to collect information on the Nazi forces' movements and where possible, attack military objectives. The other is to coordinate the FFI military actions, delivery of equipment, sending and receiving messengers.

Connection with London is hazardous, depending on luck with the messengers, who

---

[1] The abbreviated form for Geheime Staatspolize or Secret State Police.

make a trip according to need; radio messages are reduced to emergencies, as the Nazi system detecting any broadcast is very efficient.

It's not Berlin, but if we're not in the heart, at least it's the innards of the Nazi world.

Minutes of terror, hours of fear, tedious days; weeks of waiting and months of uneasiness passed as from our landing in February until June 1944.

There were numerous losses. Brave, good, generous people who fell into the hands of an implacable enemy.

Dawn of June 5, the Toul FFI network fell in an unexpected raid and held in an abandoned farm; eight Frenchmen and two Brits fought for two hours, resisting a force which was six times the size in number and weapons.

Corporal Anderson, both arms broken by a fallen lintel, was the only man captured and that same dawn he was locked up in the Gestapo's quarters at Nancy, and savagely tortured.

If the Nazis learnt of our location they would launch a massive offensive in all the region, which would place the whole organization of the important, extensive local network around Nancy at a direct risk; we all knew this, and it was clear that our mission included the possibility of death and torture as an alternative. But what the corporal did went beyond any duty.

Anderson -Grumpy- realized that sooner or later he would betray us, and physically unable to kill himself, he bit his tongue until he cut it right off.

He was executed the night of June 7, when the Nazi defeat in Normandy was already confirmed; he was shot in the back of the head in his cell after he had been tortured for 28 hours non-stop.

The Allied landing —we had received the announcement in code through the BBC on the night of the 5th- found us shut into our refuge, knowing that Anderson was in Nazi hands.

Although our refuge was relatively protected by the owner of the establishment Gaspar L'Asperge and his business negotiations -he dealt in cold cuts, milk and dairy products jointly with the Gauleiter[2] and other local Nazi authorities- we knew it was all provisional.

L´Asperge ran serious risks playing a two-ended game: the Nazis trusted him and his commitment to the cause; once a month he'd go out riding with an SS colonel who was guarded by a full company as protection.

Any vague reference of Anderson's regarding cows, and all of us, including the property owner, would follow his same fate.

Until the arrival of the North American tanks we lived by night, and also died by night, beneath that dark, mortal fire.

We finally emerged from our underground world, cooperating with our Allies to free that part of Europe.

---

[2] Gauleiter were the Nazi authorities for every zone, a political party position established by Hitler.

It wasn't easy.

We accompanied the slow Allied advance towards the Saar River and we remained on this side of the Rhine until the Russians entered Berlin.

If only everything had ended there.

The Peace of Saints

I look at the ocean before me and close my eyes. I sink into the warm embrace of meditation to free myself from the images that keep returning.

Being in the now dissolves my memory.

For a while, my ghosts, the newsreels I have closed up in my head go to sleep, they turn off.

The sound of the waves, the soft breeze, the intense salty smell, the birds' calls, go through and beyond me, I let them go.

I arrived yesterday and I slept on the beach. I wander through Visakhapatnam without fear. I was told so many things and they were so wrong.

Don't go to India! You'll be murdered… Nearly everybody told me they hate us. When I was here the first time in 1942, I was warned it could be dangerous to leave the supposedly safe neighbourhoods.

India is fascinating and complex, it's impossible to classify or define; its thousands-of-years- old cultures coexist sometimes in peace and others in conflict.

What are two or three hundred years against three thousand? As China, India resisted the colonial assault in many ways, but it also devoured the settlers, absorbing and transforming them, as it did with Mrs Sylvia, as it is doing with me.

My comrades-in-arms —the few of us left in the British Islamabad legate, in current Pakistan- tried to dissuade me time and again from my project of crossing both countries down to the Bengal Gulf, by train, walking or by whatever other means.

I was sick of the Army.

We beat the Nazis in Europe at a tremendous cost.

On May 22, 1945 I was given 12 weeks' leave, at the end of which I knew I wouldn't be discharged, I wouldn't be able to return to my country.

Instead, at the end of that summer we were sent by plane to India, not to fight against the Japs —who had been defeated by the North Americans thanks to their use of a novel and terrible weapon, the atomic bomb- but because of the possibility of a local armed rising seeking independence.

Ghandi had been detained, but they weren't sure up to what point the little man with the spinning wheel and loincloth was not only going to revolutionise the Empire, but even the world, in which peace became a subversive weapon, a revolutionary instrument.

They couldn't know - they were so confident in their military power, in the force of our machine guns… They weren't prepared for what actually took place.

Great Britain would not have been able to face another war, even a colonial war: the war against Hitler had been –in spite of the victory- a catastrophe, devastating to the economy and the whole Empire was shaking from the post-war crisis.

But the real menace of the National Hindu Army, which had been led by the now deceased Chandra Bose, armed by Germans and Japanese and which we had defeated in Burma in 1942, made us return to the "Pearl of the Empire".

Those who thought that the British occupation of the Hindu sub-continent would end in another war were favoured by history; almost no-one among the British believed that the "satyagraha"[3] that Gandhi preached could have any possibility of success.

Punctuated by blood and powder, the Hindu colonial past was rich in battles and fierce repressions.

How could a gaunt little man, voluntarily identical to the poorest masses of the low classes be able to declare and obtain Swaraj[4]?

From the bottom of my heart I'm grateful that the Indian National Congress party had him among their leaders, because it's probable that my fate would have been similar to those executioners at the Amritsar massacre during the Sikh Baisakhi festival. I wasn't born to be an executioner.

I think many preferred Bose's blood and fire to Gandhi's civil disobedience.

But although independence was achieved by peaceful means, it was clear that once the objective had been reached, the delayed effect of the Imperial forces' Lahore resolution attempted to sterilise the powerful magic of the civil disobedience movement.

On August 15, 1947 I shouted,"Jai Hind!"[5] along with the troops, and I felt happy and celebrated jointly with my corporals –whom I'd met again on our second trip to India- when the Labour government finally agreed to the formidable country's independence.

Some days later, Senghor, without any goodbye, announcements or bureaucratic procedures, disappeared without anyone knowing what direction he'd taken.

On the other hand, Korrum went –with no in-between levels- from a corporal in the British Army to Colonel, in charge of setting up special units in the army of recently-born Pakistan; his first official act was to ask the high command that they request the British

---

3   Holding onto truth, which translated into civil disobedience, a non-violent resistance
4   Independence
5   Long Live India!

government for the loan of a contingent of military advisors, among which he specifically requested Tony and myself.

Both governments agreed.

At the time I couldn't –nor can I now- define what I felt. Korrum was a good man and in a certain way, we were friends.

His rise was well deserved. And continuing under Tony's orders was not inconvenient; we had gone through too many oceans of fire together and had survived so much, suffering both fear and death; more than comrades, we were undoubtedly brothers-in-arms.

But on the other hand, every day my feelings of missing my country, my house, my family were ever stronger. The urgency had burnt out, Nazism had succumbed before the joint action of an extensive coalition of nations; but Great Britain would not free me from its services: for these His Majesty paid me crumbs and denied giving me back my life.

Of course, my full-dress uniform had three lines of medals on the jacket that deceived one regarding my condition as a slave.

But one day, I called it quits.

All because of a film.

Every now and again they'd show us a film as entertainment and sometimes just for information.

That's how my life in service to His Majesty ended.

A news reel was reporting on the situation in some part of China, recently invaded by the Red Chinese Army forces, and while we smoked and talked and waited for another trivial film, the voice of the announcer, in a dramatic tone, began describing how officials of Communist China were preparing to eradicate Buddhism, violently.

The screen showed a line of kneeling monks and behind them, a Chinese officer shooting them in the back of the head.

Very impressive, of course.

But all of us there had gone through the most terrible war and had seen and done terrible things.

Yet an intense and fiercely cold feeling went through my chest when in the foreground I saw -his eyes closed and a saintly smile as he was shot in the back of the head- the man who had brought peace to my soul.

Atisha, sitting in a meditation position, was the first one in the close up, the last one in the line of monks –young and old- and he was being brutally executed before a quiet camera filming him as he left this life.

I shouted. I howled like a wounded wolf and it was difficult for me to come back to the room, to breathe, to think or to feel anything like peace.

Tony, my friend and my chief, helped me.

No-one, either in the Pakistan army or any of the few Englishmen who were with us, said a word about my reaction. Everybody, at some point, had broken down when faced with the violence we had experienced.

For me, that had been too much.

Three days later I left, after my friend Tony's hug, with my release papers in my bag and a handful of pounds –just a few, because since 1940 I had been dividing and sending most of my salary to my mother in Argentina and to Harry's widow, Maggie Peebles Moore. I had so many pieces of advice against doing this trip, but I left to cross India in search of the sea, to cross the Pacific and return home.

And here I am, on this infinite, solitary beach, with the jungle at my back and the port in sight, sitting in the lotus position as my teacher Atisha sat in front of the bullet that killed him, trying to live according to his teachings.

My hair has reached my shoulders and a sparse beard covers my face. I live in shorts and Hindu shirts; I cover my head with a ragged Australian hat which Wes Mosteland gave me at my farewell, one he had worn throughout the war.

I've been wandering through India for four months and my eyes are full of its contradictions, its incredible landscapes, extreme poverty and extreme wealth, deserts in the north and jungle in the south.

I've heard every language, I've seen every face. India is more than one could see in one lifetime.

It's clear why the Brits invaded it and dominated it for so many years: there is not one India, but many. Each province is a country, has a different language, customs and traditions to the others. Clothing, food, music…

Now I'm at the other end, at a port, looking for a ship to cross the Pacific and get to South America.

I want to travel, live in peace, quieten the pain I carry, extinguish the volcano that is consuming me, I want to love, live, learn, leave a legacy.

I get up, walk to the sea and for a long time I play in the waves of the Bengala gulf, while close by, fishing boats are at their work.

They're good people, they allow me aboard with them, I help bring in the nets and they want to pay me for my work with a few rupees – I reject them, smiling.

It's enough to have some fish which I cook near the line of trees around the beach.

The city and the port are in view.

Every two or three days I walk to the port along the docks to see if any ship will accept me as crew to South America. I don't mind washing the decks or peeling potatoes, I want to return home in this way, with the hope that the landscapes and sea air will clean my soul.

I walk along the shoulder of the road that joins the village to the port and sometimes there's a cart, sometimes a truck which shortens my trip.

I spent the day walking along the docks, but with no luck again.

At sundown, the noise from a bar like any other opens up my appetite for a beer. I don't have much money, enough to eat and sleep on the beach; I drag my backpack with my few belongings: three changes of clothes, one which has travelled with me since Argentina; one full-dress uniform from which I've removed every military insignia… very few things.

I would actually like to be like Atisha yet I don't dare leave behind all my belongings and affections to become a beggar monk.

I put together my own cigarettes with Hindu tobacco, which is what the poorest people smoke; I live like an untouchable, like the poorest of the Hindus and I'm happy, for the first time in many years.

I drink a beer of doubtful quality and smoke a cigarette at the counter of the bar in which no-one pays me any attention.

Time goes by, I have another beer, then someone approaches me and stands next to me; he looks at me, smiles and speaks to me in German.

"Englander?"

"*Ja, ich bin Engländer, aber ich spreche kaum Deutsch, um nach einem Bier zu fragen.*" [Yes, I'm English, but I hardly speak German to ask for a beer.]

He smiles.

"A little English I do speak! Drink would you with an old enemy one beer?"

Now I smile.

Why not?

That man is not very different to me, he might even be myself…

"A little German you speak, a little English I speak, beer we drink both! I invite!" He says it enthusiastically, and introduces himself: Hans Hooften, Corporal of the XIV battalion of the Panzer Grenadiers.

There at my side, inviting me to drink beer, is one of the men I confronted at Monte Cassino.

How strange is destiny, how strange a warrior's destiny, obliged to kill and be killed by the men with whom he'd drink a beer.

We talked.

We talked some more.

We talked a great deal.

We talked all day into the night, all night into the dawn, mixing cheap whisky and beer.

We smoked Borneo tobacco with hashish which he carried in his bag, and we walked along the docks waiting for dawn; we were drunk but lucid.

He told me his story and he listened to mine.

A family of peasants, five boys and one girl, the youngest. Shameful poverty and no work for anybody. He, just as his father, had begun looking for work when he was 12 years old – until Hitler and his people got busy giving every good German a job.

And every good German went to school.

And every good German had medical attention.

He had left his child's job to go to school. His eldest brother had died as a volunteer in Teruel… The next brother down had unhesitatingly entered the SS Forces in 1938.

He himself had been called up just before the invasion of Poland. His family had emigrated to Dresden to work for the victory of the war industry; the two youngest brothers had entered as volunteers in the Kriegsmarine (Nazi Navy), one of them in the submarine corps.

I told him about Argentina and the *gauchos*; about my grandfather and my parents; about the sacrifice of my Welsh ancestors on the altar of the other war.

About my lonely days at King George's college; about *Don* Eurwen and Mrs Sylvia; about the Spanish war and my comrades and Teruel; Maria; defeat and Barcelona.

He told me with tears in his eyes how he had participated in a gang rape in Poland, in which the whole platoon had abused a young girl the same age as his sister, and this memory haunted him night and day.

I told him how I had executed the Japanese officer in the Burman jungle and of my meeting my liberator Atisha, and how I had seen him die with a saintly smile on his face.

He told me how all his family had died during the bombing of Dresden; and he showed me a photo of his parents and his sister, a girl with tender eyes and blonde plaits.

He had been a Nazi up till 1942. On the Russian front he had begun to lose faith because he saw the SS members' brutality against their own and the enemy; their demanding results without the means ended up convincing him of the craziness of that regime.

He had fought simply for survival at Stalingrad and Monte Cassino, and afterwards at each place where he found himself; until hungry and without any ammunition, the only survivor of his platoon, he had surrendered to the North Americans near Kassel. I told him about Corporal Anderson and others like him who had died from Nazi brutality, and of my fear of dying during those last days of the war.

I reminded him of the extermination camps, and all he said was he had never met a

Jew.

We forgave and absolved each other, we became human. When the sun had come up and filled the sky with red and purple, he talked to me of his destination.

He was travelling with other compatriots on a ship with an Australian flag, captained by a Chinaman and with a crew from all over Asia, to reach French Indochina; our allies and his former enemies had recruited them to suppress the Communist uprising intended to finish off the French Empire in that part of the world.

They did not have a Gandhi, and France —broke and poverty-stricken- needed the products of its colonies to re-launch its economy.

There was a surfeit of soldiers: Europe was full of men who didn't know how to do anything except fight, and just like Hans, had simply lived their youth between horror, mud, dirt and pain. They could not imagine a long life, they had lost everything in the warring maelstrom, including dreams and hopes.

He invited me to share this journey which he knew would be his last.

I boarded that ship, and across from Vietnam— as the natives called their country- I understood that I did have dreams and above all, a home to return to.

It was a long journey – the ship sailed from port to port seeking cargo and without any definite destination more than trafficking what it carried, until it sailed towards South America in search of Chilean salt for a New Zealand company.

I disembarked in Valparaiso and one day, I arrived home.

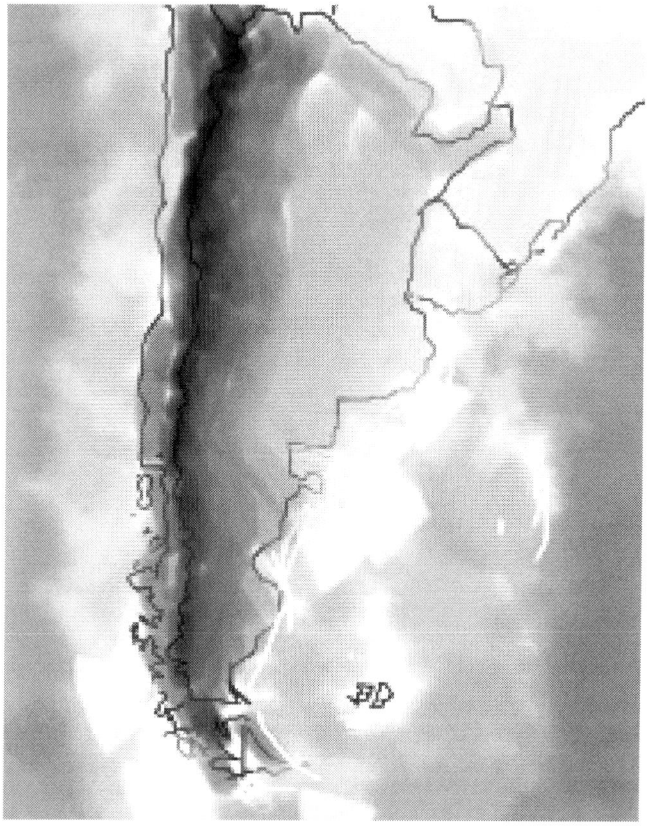

A Samurai Destiny ÉDITIONS DU SAMURAI

V) GEISHA

(Extracts from Mariana Rodrigué Evans' Diaries)

On Small Things

April 20, 1947

Dear Diary,

For my fifteenth birthday yesterday, Carlos gave me this diary which is the perfect gift!!! Sometimes I hate my brother, and other times I love him so much…

My party was at the Banfield Country Club, we were more than one hundred people, adults and children, friends and family. All my aunts and uncles, cousins and also all my school friends from Barker College and the girls from my hockey team from Lomas Club, all the girls from the Banfield Club tennis team, some of the boys from Lomas Club's rugby team and other boys from St. Alban's College.

My Dance Card was as follows:

John Melgbaugh

My cousin Aníbal Duero Rodrigué

Carlos Gramajo

Darío Escudé

Damián Gramajo

Armando Rodríguez Roda

Manuel Cash

Andy McCall

My cousin Andrés Duero Rodrigué

My cousin Cecilio Duero Rodrigué

Blight Simpson

Roberto Gramajo

Mariano Silles

Ramón Cash

Diego Marlow

Emilio Mesa

I was given two pairs of high-heeled shoes (one is blue velvet!!!), a complete collection of books (all Louise M. Alcott's, several by Jules Verne, Romeo & Juliet, Othello and Hamlet, A Thousand and One Nights, etc.), a handbag, a new bicycle, a powder compact and lipstick, 4 tickets for the Colón Theatre, three silk blouses, one skirt, two imported Wilson tennis rackets and about five tennis ball cans, a book on music, a film projector and a camera; and the Lanzani-Mora band playing at the party… They played until 4 in the morning, fox trots, big bands jazz style – how I love "Stardust"!!!!! – beep boop and *tangos*.

All the food was served by Gallardón. I'm still Absolutely Happy!!!

November 30, 1949

Finally!!! I've finished secondary school, I was an escort to the flag bearer: I cried when I saw the proud expression on Papá's face. Carlos can't stop teasing me and says I mustn't study medicine… He knows I'd finish before he does!

Mamá doesn't want me to study at the University, we argued about this. She says the University isn't a proper place for a "girl from a good family". She failed with Neneca and Inés, but insists with me. How can a man as progressive-minded as Papá be married to such an old-fashioned woman like her?

March 1, 1950

The Year of Libertador Gen. San Martín!!! There are reminders on all the walls, images of Perón and Evita everywhere!!! Perón and Perona up to my ears… In the end I registered at the Mentruyt Teachers College, I'm first going to study to be a Geography Teacher, then History. It'll be three years before I can start working and be independent. Mamá is already looking for a boyfriend for me. And it so happens that the ones she likes, I don't.

This summer was terrific, the best one ever; I played tennis and won two club tournaments and they want me to join the federation, because in the club I can only play against the boys, no girl can beat me. Of course Mamá is against this, she says sport at this level is not feminine, she says the same about hockey… All I can say is that the powerful feeling when facing my rivals is unbeatable!!!

I begin classes in 12 days. My mother's comment: "Women who work end up being spinsters, like your sisters…" What can I say?

November 22, 1951

Whenever something important happens I write; today I'm writing and also re-reading some of the 50 pages written in each of the 4 diaries over the last four years, and I can hardly believe the things I've written… I should really burn them!!! If anyone should read them… I don't think I'd like that…

What's happened is that Carlitos invited home his Drill Sergeant Instructor from his military service. About two months ago he told Papá about this man's attitude during the September uprising when he protected his subordinates (he locked the conscripts and cadets into their bedrooms) and my doctor father remembered the surname right away, it seems that this man's grandfather and my father had been friends and what's more, his father had been his patient.

I think he's the handsomest man in the world! He looks like a film actor! He's not very tall, maybe medium height, he has reddish hair or sort of brown-reddish… his hair is very short, he came dressed as a civilian, blue linen pants, a light-coloured shirt –light-blue almost white- and a short military style jacket, khaki colour with a collar and epaulettes, no insignias and a red beret, everything beautifully ironed, and no tie! According to Carlitos, it's partly an English uniform. This way of dressing is a little strange! He's quiet, he has intense blue eyes and a moustache which doesn't help to hide his age - he's 30 years old…

He talked a lot with Papá in spite of Carlitos' constant need to joke; Carlitos tries to make him talk about the war, it seems he knows a great deal about it.

According to my older brother, in the Military School they said he fought in the Spanish civil war, in the European war and in India!!!

He looks so calm…

I think Papá liked him as much as I did…

His name is Gordon Evans and I'd like to know him better.

December 12, 1951

Gordon has asked Papá if he can come by to 'visit' me!!! Papá asked Mamá, she asked me and I said I'd need two days to think about it… just to bluff a little, of course, because I'd already made up my mind the first day I saw him.

December 14

At last, Mr. Evans invited us to the cinema!! Tomorrow Saturday we'll all go to the matinee in the Gran Lomas cinema: Carlos, Inesita, Neneca, mother (as chaperone), Mr. Evans and myself. Afterwards we'll go for hot chocolate and milk at the Gallardón. I'm so nervous!!!

December 17

In-cred-ible! The best afternoon in all my life. Mr. Evans is an old-fashioned gentleman, he's been educated to observe without it being uncomfortable, he has the most appropriate and right words, he pays attention to me and to all the women around him, and his conversation!!! And I was so distrustful of his military background… He has such an interesting conversation, he's travelled in the East, and his knowledge is so impressive; and he never took up on Carlitos' verbal games when my brother was trying to make him react! Those childish things my brother does makes him look so ridiculous next to this Man in capital letters.

December 31

This afternoon Mr. Evans came by and when we were alone maybe for one minute on the porch bench –drinking cold lemonade on such a hot day- he asked my permission to court me officially, and of course I asked him for a couple of days to think it over. He smiled and said he'd wait until eternity if it were necessary. He's so poetic!!!

January 2, 1952

On the 1st I talked with Papá and Mamá and they accepted, although with all the protocol rules, he will have to ask their permission.

I'm happy, he's a wonderful man.

January 5

Gordon came to dinner yesterday. He brought wine for Papá and a Gallardón cake for Carlitos, and a bouquet of roses "for the ladies". He was like one of the Three Kings with all those presents in a basket!!

Eva Peron

At dessert time he officially asked to court me.

Papá had already agreed to give him permission, which they talked over together in a private meeting in Papá's office, behind closed doors.

Papá came out quite charmed – although he didn't say much – I think that between him and Mr. Evans there's a gentlemen's understanding- and he says that Gordon is an extraordinary man.

February 15

Gordon came to the Club as our family guest. He's a good swimmer and he has a slender and muscular body. Very discreetly –and not so discreetly- all the girls watched him dive from the highest diving board. I think he likes Carlitos, otherwise I would have killed my brother!!! His jokes are so… inappropriate! Gordon is calm and quiet, but when he talks… all the girls are jealous. He likes reading and he doesn't have extreme opinions about anything. It's very obvious he doesn't like discussions and arguments.

Macacha Basualdo's brother, Tomás, one of Mamá's favourites – once he finishes two more subjects at the University he'll graduate as a lawyer – made a scathing and insulting comment about Perón, and very calmly Gordon said that as he was in the national army and Perón was the president elected by the Nation's citizens, he therefore couldn't listen to insults against his Commander-in-Chief. Tomás smiled, turned around and left. Could they have been arguing about politics or about me?

Later he took the trouble to explain to me about his position.

He knows very well that in my family we're not Peronists; that Carlitos is frankly and openly very much an anti-Peronist and that Papá approves of some things –especially regarding public health- but he sees too many things that he doesn't like.

When Gordon returned to Argentina in 1949, he had been away for 16 years. He came in through Chile, and for a few months he worked on the railway route being built to bring salt from the Chilean Atacama region, and while he worked up north, he saw people – he says people, not "blackies" or "darkies" as Carlitos and his friends call them- who were happy and hopeful.

When he arrived in Buenos Aires, after working in the mountains for 5 months, he met up again with his mother, and saw that his sister's wheelchair –she's been a cripple since she was born- had been delivered free because his mother was a widow and she didn't receive any pension.

And his Mum, who has always been a seamstress, had been given a sewing machine, and both things came through Peron's wife's foundation. He wouldn't be a grateful person if he didn't acknowledge these facts… (He said it like that, calmly and firmly… and with such bright eyes that make him so handsome!!!) And he added, always very calmly and without getting excited –not like the brute of my brother- that should Perón close the Congress and burn it like Hitler did, should he have the labour leaders executed like Franco did, or should he jail and kill the opposition like Stalin did, only then will he oppose him, and with weapons!!!! And he made it clear he was not a Peronist, but that he agreed with the reforms that were taking place in the labour world and that his Mum was, for good reasons, a Peronist.

He explains things so well… He doesn't seem to be a military man.

March 8

GORDON ASKED ME TO MARRY HIM!!!!! I must write all this down before I forget any detail! He arrived home after midday, wearing his dress uniform, he invited me to walk around our garden… and he asked my permission to ask for my hand in marriage!!! He looked so handsome, he looked like Alan Ladd with those sad eyes and his enchanting smile!!!

Talking in his deep, sweet voice, he said, "I'm going to share something very important to me… Many years ago I left Argentina and destiny took me all around the world… I now feel I'm home again… and I only need one thing to make this real to me… Will you marry me?"

I said yes, of course.

Mamá and Carlitos were the last ones to know. Papá arrived back from the Clinic at tea time, he and Gordon shut themselves into his office and they talked for exactly 15 minutes, and when they came out Papá was very excited, he called Inés and Neneca – Carlitos was at the farm in Santa Fe and he should be arriving tonight or tomorrow, Mamá was at mass- and Papá announced that Gordon had asked for my hand in marriage and that he had said yes.

They fixed August 16 as the date for our engagement, and the wedding on Saturday January 17 of next year!!!!

When Mamá arrived back from mass she found us all celebrating; I don't think she liked that Papá had accepted without consulting her.

Juan D. Peron

When Gordon left, Mamá began with her "buts". Where are they going to live? What are they going to live on if an Army NCO doesn't earn enough to live decently?

Mamá doesn't want me to marry Gordon, that's clear enough.

March 22

Gordon just left. He came for supper, invited by Papá.

He brought some news. On April 1st he's leaving the army, he applied for his discharge today and he has eight days to return some things, and after that he's free. On April 2nd he starts working at Anglo, an English meat-packaging company, as a cattle buyer. He's very enthused, even as a learner he will be earning almost double what he earned in the army.

Mamá made a remark regarding the importance of having a professional title, and Papá stopped her by talking of a medical doctor who had just graduated and was working for him and was earning less than Gordon's salary.

Gordon's happy, he has to be out riding, checking the herds. It seems when he was young his grandfather taught him a great deal about working on a farm and he likes it. If we both work we'll be able to earn enough to live on and also save for when we have children.

I'm even happier that he's leaving the army. I think Gordon needs work which takes him away from war, weapons and violence.

Sunday, April 12

Gordon had lunch with us, and at tea-time we went to his house "officially". Because of his younger sister's condition —she can't move, she's been a cripple since she was born— Mrs Evans seldom leaves her home; they do have a wheelchair with which they move around the neighbourhood.

Mrs Evans had cooked a sponge cake with a home-made *dulce de leche* filling, which made Papá very politely ask for a second helping. Mamá hardly said a word. She can be so disagreeable and annoying, on purpose!

Mrs Evans -as Gordon calls her in that clear English that he speaks now and again- is very sweet and polite, with very bright brown eyes. She doesn't smile much but she never shows any sadness or a bad mood. I like my future mother-in-law and Papá —who already knew her- really likes her.

It was very nice to see Papá hugging her when we said goodbye. Mamá complained of a headache because of the smell of disinfectant.

"My favourite smell. A smell of hospital, and cleanliness…" said the doctor. And Mamá couldn't say anything further!!!!

April 27

Gordon invited Papá, Mamá and I to have tea at Gallardón. Papá is so happy with our engagement, Mamá says nothing but she's clearly against it. Gordon is very happy at his work; he finds it easy, he feels efficient and he knows that he'll soon be earning a good salary and that makes him even happier.

May 1st

As it's a holiday —there's nothing open, not even the kiosks- and Perón and Evita will be giving a speech on the 9 de Julio Ave, Papá invited Gordon to lunch —they both like the same meals: this time it's "puchero" – and at dessert, Papá remarked that it's likely Evita will not be a candidate, he had heard the rumour -from a trustworthy source- that she was seriously ill.

We talked politics —this is unusual. Gordon includes me in the conversations about politics and it's clear that Papá approves of this while Mamá doesn't -and about the tension that will be generated when Eva retires from politics. At home she's severely criticized, but the truth is that it's thanks to her that we women can vote.

May 3rd

For the first time they let us go out on our own. It was siesta time, we went to have a cup of coffee at Gallardón's. That's it, we walked along in silence, just holding hands. It was very cold and a bothersome drizzle hardly wet our clothes. When we arrived home, at the front door he said to me in his beautiful voice, "I love you, Mariana." He looked at me with that deep look that makes me tremble and for the first time in my life I felt myself blush from head to toe, such intense goose bumps… with all my might I had to keep my whole body from trembling. We hardly gave each other a peck on the lips and I know I'm his for ever.

May 25th

Against my mother's wishes, I got up at 5:30 a.m. to meet Gordon. At 6 a.m. they were serving hot chocolate to the soldiers that were taking part in the parade at the new Lomas de Zamora Municipality's square, on Perón Ave in front of the Eva Perón square… what can I say.

Gordon likes to present his respects to our homeland's symbols, sing the National Anthem with the crowd, wear the cockade on his chest. From the bottom of his heart he's convinced that having fought against the Nazis, he was also defending his country.

I really like to see him quiet but excited, saluting when the troops go by with their martial steps to the sound of trumpets and drums. In order not to get into an argument with Mamá, I promised Papá that I would go to 11 o'clock mass with her.

To my surprise —Gordon had confessed privately to me that he was no longer a Christian since 1942, but in order not to offend anyone (he didn't say, but I thought of my mother) he said he preferred not to make this public- he not only accompanied me to the Lomas Cathedral, he also went in and accompanied me throughout the mass, except to confession and communion.

I know he did it for me and Mamá had to fully accept his attitude.

July 26

Eva Perón has died!! Papá, Mamá, Gordon and I were at the cinema and just before 8:30 p.m. they cancelled the film showing at the Gran Lomas cinema (we were watching "*La bestia debe morir*" (The Beast Must Die) with Narciso Ibáñez Menta). Many people started crying. I was sad when I saw an older couple hugging and crying together as if one of their children had died.

Dad's information was correct.

Gordon was distressed. He accompanied us home and immediately wanted to leave to see about his mother and sister. Papá offered to give him a ride. I wanted to go as well, Mamá didn't want me to go but Papá agreed. Of course, Mamá then came with us.

I got into the Oldsmobile at the back on the right-hand side and Gordon on the left. Mamá sat in the front and didn't say a word.

Mrs Evans was calm but much moved. She's a person full of gratitude and the truth is she was very favoured by the many positive changes the Foundation did for her. "Alms," says Carlitos; Mamá says, "They take advantage of the poorer people's needs."

Papá doesn't protest about that, and he defends many of the improvements in the hospital system –in spite of the defects he sees. He's concerned about how they put both their names on everything – avenues, buildings, vehicles- photos everywhere, the spying –the porter at the Clinic openly works for the government- censorship and mistreatment and persecution of the opposition – my father has signed every single petition for each case – all this does bother him.

I think it's reasonable if my future mother-in-law suffers because of Evita's death. It's not reasonable to celebrate it, as I heard several at the club do.

August 10

The mourning for Eva and her funeral is all that is happening. The day before yesterday the name of La Plata city was changed to "Eva Perón". There are already two provinces, one with his name, one with hers, and a large number of streets, avenues, squares… The time of her death, 8:25 p.m. is recalled by the radio stations every day in a serious tone of voice, "At this time, Eva Perón, Argentines' spiritual leader, entered immortality."

The funeral has gathered thousands and thousands of people. On the 6th Gordon took his mother and his sister, and against my mother's opinion –of course!!- I went with them. We went to the Labour Ministry, where they've set up a funeral chapel, all covered in wreaths. Gordon's mother requested he dress in his British army uniform with all his medals, and a black mourning ribbon on his right arm, like everybody is wearing.

I was a little afraid –people get so excited and England is considered almost like an enemy- but nobody paid us any attention. Gordon gave his military salute to the country's symbols and to every officer who crossed our path –there were military men everywhere- but nobody questioned us.

It's all very impressive, it seemed like a queen's funeral, the walls on the streets are covered in posters, all the flags are half-mast, black crepes on everyone's arms –they're obligatory for the public servants- lines of wreaths…

The crowd's anguish somehow reached me because I felt like crying while we were in the line –it wasn't long, they let us go in front because of Cristina's wheelchair – and the truth is I didn't feel very different to all the others who were there. I understand what Gordon means when he says "people" and I understand it more and more why he's so upset –although he hardly ever says so- when people talk of "blackies", "natives", "niggers".

It was just a second, Gordon's Mum left a small posy of violets on the coffin, Gordon gave his military salute and I made the sign of the cross, and when I saw her white profile in the shroud's lace I realized how young she was.

How many shattered dreams must have remained in that little body? Is this the person we hated so much?

A small body in a too large coffin, the scent of flowers together with that indescribable smell of all wakes increased one hundred fold –it's already been two weeks- the permanent weeping breaking the silence, among the deafening noise of a voluntarily quiet multitude bent on dragging their shoes…

What can I say? Now I know that Gordon is very moved and affected by other people's pain.

In a certain way, he's like my Papá, concerned about his poorest patients until he's exhausted.

I see him tighten his jaw to hold back his feelings, his eyes are sadder than ever, and I love him more than yesterday, and surely less than tomorrow.

Carlitos, to fight, bother and provoke, left a small piece of paper stuck to my bedroom door: "Yay for cancer". It doesn't even make me angry. It makes me sad.

Because of the mourning imposed throughout the country, Gordon and I decided to postpone our engagement party till September.

August 30

Like every Friday, Gordon came for supper yesterday. He brought the mille-feuille cake from Gallardón –Papá's weak point- and they set September 13th as the engagement date, without any party.

Gordon left at 10:30 p.m. and at 10:33 p.m. the third world war broke out.

Mamá finally confronted Papá and myself.

She didn't miss out a thing: she believes that Gordon is not the appropriate man for me. He's poor, he doesn't have any other career than as a soldier, he's seeking to better himself socially and economically, and –this is a total slur- that he's a Peronist and is going to ruin us socially. That it would be better to stop the engagement now, and they should send me on a cruise up to New York... she even had some brochures!!

I've discovered today that I'd never seen Papá so angry.

He didn't shout. But he hit the table with his fist and said, "I haven't heard so much foolishness in a long time", and he broke the brochures into little pieces.

He didn't raise his voice, but he used such a tone... He reminded my mother that his parents had been immigrants, just as Gordon's father was, and her parents had never accepted them. He'd studied medicine while working at a grocer's. The house where we lived was bought with what Grandfather Manuel had left him, while Grandfather Carro Córdoba had been an irresponsible pleasure-seeker and Carlitos had taken after him... And if this wasn't enough, Gordon's maternal grandfather came from a generations-old family in Argentina; while the Carro Córdoba family members were stealing cattle, the Porrás were already an honest and cultured people...

Mamá was struck dumb, and I stopped crying to hear him say all this without shouting, but emphasizing each item... the air could have been cut with a knife.

Mamá took advantage of a silence, rang the bell for Ramona to come and clear the table, and I excused myself saying I had a headache, and I shut myself into my room.

They went on arguing for a long time.

Afterwards Mamá came and knocked on my door but I pretended to be asleep.

We'll never talk about this subject again.

September 14

Gordon and I are finally engaged. It was a very small gathering, the family and some close friends. Two of Gordon's friends from work, Derek Foster –he's also the son of an old friend of Gordon's Dad- and Charly Dodds; Papá's best friend, Dr. Rosemberg; three of Mamá's cousins and Aunt Herminia (Grandmother Perica Azulay de Carro Córdoba's younger sister). Mamá took advantage of the national mourning period and didn't invite anyone from the club. The Urien twins came, some of my friends from school and two of my colleagues from the Teacher's College, Liliana Herrera and Diana Ballestra. Carlos grilled an enormous rack – Gordon brought it from the Liniers cattle market- and at dessert time (it was a home-made caramel mousse made by my fiancé's mother), Papá announced our engagement and our wedding date on February 14th.

We're going out into the country for our honeymoon.

November 12

We spent the whole weekend looking for a house; Papá offered us his car but Gordon rejected his offer, always charming and kind, but for a reason which convinced my Dad because it was so sensible: we have to find a house which we can get to without a car... Mamá didn't say anything, but gave one of her sighs which my father calls "a Regina Passini sigh".

But finally and thanks to one of Gordon's colleagues from the plant, we found the perfect house: five blocks from Mármol station, it's at the back of the owner's property and her own house, a very friendly German widow, her surname is Schumacher.

It's a moderate rent, it won't be difficult to pay. I graduate at the end of this year and I already have an assured job at Barker College, so next year we'll be even better off.

Gordon has rejected all Papá's offers of a loan and it hasn't been out of pride or anything like it. He feels more comfortable just depending on himself; since he left for the war in Spain until he returned home he always depended on others for his living: his parents, the Republic, the British Crown, the Pakistani Army, the Argentine State, and in exchange, they could do what they wanted with him, as if there was a right of life or death over him.

Now he depends entirely on his work and nobody can say anything if tomorrow he decides to work for Swift or Cap, he's paid well for a job in which he feels competent, he has no vices on which he spends his salary, he gives me half for me to keep. The other half he divides into two, one half for his mother and the other for his own daily expenses.

I'm so used to seeing Carlos spending money he doesn't produce, I'm very impressed with Gordon's austerity; it's impossible not to progress by the side of a man like this.

December 26

Mother again! On the 24th Gordon arrived on his new bike, with a basket full of gifts for everyone; ten minutes after midnight he gave everybody a present from under the tree, and then left 15 minutes before 1 a.m. On the 25th, Carlos and I took the Oldsmobile to pick up the three Evans, as they were coming to lunch at home. Mamá went up to her room saying she was unwell.

Papá went up to see what was wrong, and when I saw his expression I realized she wasn't ill at all.

We had a peaceful lunch, we toasted Christmas, we opened the gifts Gordon had given us last night —simple things but very tasteful: Papá received some handkerchiefs very beautifully embroidered with his initials; Carlos a very large Cuban cigar; Neneca, Inés and myself some lovely head scarves which can be seen in pictures in European magazines and are so fashionable. Papá went up to take Mamá hers and he came down almost immediately.

Gordon's sister is like a large baby. She has to be spoon-fed, wiped and washed when she moves her bowels; she has to be lifted into and helped out of her chair. But she doesn't react to her name, and is always, always smiling. If you touch her hand she returns the touch but if you talk to her she doesn't reply, because apparently she's deaf as well as blind.

Mamá got up from the table the minute she saw us arrive with Gordon's sister in her wheelchair, she "felt unwell" when seeing my future sister-in-law's disabilities; Neneca, Inés and I sat around her and with Mrs Evans' permission, we did what we could for her.

Neneca, with her usual tact, offered help with her physiotherapy techniques to help Cristina's muscle tone. Inés asked and offered, with the same tact, to take care of her dental work – next year she graduates as a dentist; Papá and Mrs Evans talked at length, they've known each other a long time. Christmas lunch was really marvellous.

At siesta time we let them have Inés' bedroom so mother and daughter could have a rest; Papá, Carlitos and Gordon went into the living room to smoke, and we three got together, like when we were children, to secretly protest against Mamá's proverbial prudishness, as from today we've baptized mother "la Vieja".

La Vieja came down when she heard the Oldsmobile leave with the guests. Papá is very angry; he went to have supper with the people who were on duty at the Clinic; my sisters and I said we'd already eaten too much and we left her to have supper on her own.

December 27

Today we finally agreed on our rent with Mrs Schumacher; we paid three months in advance. On January 1st we'll start getting the house ready and we'll move in at the end of February after our honeymoon.

January 2, 1953

My two sisters and I have spent the last two days painting the little house on Thorne Street. It's quite small: one bedroom, a bathroom, a living-dining room the same size as the bedroom and a kitchen which is smaller than the bathroom. I think that the whole house, with the little garden at the back, can fit into the Banfield house living room!

These two days were also used for confessions, some of them quite impressive.

Neneca has an Uruguayan boyfriend who she still doesn't dare bring home, and Inés... is seeing a man who is separated and has children!!!! And Mamá is concerned about Gordon and his sister with her disabilities...

We laughed a lot when we thought about Mamá's reaction when they finally find the courage to tell her!

February 10, 1953

I've just come back from my "hen party"! I write this and I still can't believe it. Tomorrow is the ceremony at the Lomas de Zamora civil registry; and on Saturday, at this time, I'm going to be a complete woman, joined to the man I love for the rest of my life. My sisters, the girls from the Teachers College, the Urien twins and the girls from the Club organized the gathering at the Basualdos.

We laughed so much!!! They couldn't believe I'm still a virgin, with such a handsome man as my future husband; but the truth is that in spite of my most intimate desires, he has taken more care of me than I have myself!!! He wants to have the traditional, true wedding night… And I so love the way he kisses me!!! I can't wait to sleep beside him.

He's so sweet, so loving… Sometimes when we are alone, sadness shines out of his glance, he stares off into the distance; I know that sometimes –very few times since our relationship started- he remembers the past, but different to other Lomas boys – such as Miki Kowalic- who have also been to war, he doesn't drink, or smoke, he doesn't get into fights.

There's a serenity in my man which is not free of pain, an inner strength and a spiritual purity that moves and charms me. He's beautiful, on the inside and the outside.

We're having the party at the Club, and from there we're taking the train to Santa Fe, we'll put our bicycles in the goods carriage and then we'll bike to the estancia… really, my husband is truly exotic- Mamá said he was crazy, that it was dangerous, "the blacks" could attack us!!!! Gordon didn't laugh; very seriously he said that he thought he was capable of handling any dangerous situation… Papá was going to tell my mother off for sticking her nose in what was none of her business, but Gordon was so self-assured that Papá didn't say anything in the end.

Another thing that amazes me about my man is the care in the way he treats my mother, who tries to hide her dislike but is not very successful; he's kind, polite, he never responds to the horrible things la Vieja may say, and he always has some little attention towards her, once he brought her some liqueur chocolates –the Corso brand- another time some tea from China for her and her friends' 5 o'clock tea; tickets to the Colón Theatre… When I protest or complain, he listens carefully and then he says, "My love, you must be forbearing, I come from nowhere, I've spent half of my life fighting wars… I wouldn't like me either if I were her!!" Or, "You must understand, you're her youngest daughter…" Always in favour of family, of understanding, of harmony. He's so good…

My wedding dress is something else: *doña* Pepa his mother made it; Mamá wanted Jamandreu, that's Evita's couturier!!!! But Papá explained to her the inconvenience of spending the equivalent of two years of Gordon's (good) salary on a dress… and besides, Mrs Evans could give it something that no dressmaker could… So then Mamá brought a French magazine lent to her by Nenina Basualdo –Tomás' mother- with horrible designs, enormous, long trains, until finally Neneca brought a last year's "Para Ti" and there we found what I wanted: modern, simple and very elegant. And my mother-in-law was masterful in making it. Papá, Gordon and Carlos are going to wear morning suits rented in Casa Martínez.

Carlitos organized Gordon's party. I think it was the most negotiated stag party in the world!!!

Knowing Carlos, Gordon gave him a long list of "no's". And I didn't hear this from Carlos but through Nenina Basualdo. Tomás, Carlos' friend –and his guest- said that

Gordon had been very clear: no heavy jokes –he told them that because of his war traumas he could possibly have a "bad reaction"; no prostitutes… They went to a canteen in the Boca neighbourhood, they drank copiously and they were truly surprised because my man drinks very little, maybe one or two glasses of wine with his meals and sometimes a brandy with Papá… But it was really clear that he can drink like a Welshman!!!

Carlos got up after lunch, he was literally green and although he didn't say anything, he didn't look well at all. On the other hand, Gordon came for lunch and he looked as if he'd slept all night!!!

I've never been happier.

March 2, 1953

Gordon has just left for work, I don't start classes until next Monday, so I have one week of *"dolce far niente"*… well, this isn't really true because I have to see about things here at home… but our house is so small that in two hours everything shines!!! It's so funny…

The truth is we were given lovely presents: all the furniture, two sets of china, a gas stove, an ice chest!!!! A combined radio record-player, sheets, a set of pots and pans… we don't need anything.

Wow, I have so much to tell… Where to begin?

Let's start with the civil wedding ceremony.

The witnesses were Neneca and Charly Dodds. It was a simple ceremony in which the justice of the peace –an old friend of Papá's and Gordon's grandfather- warned us about the risks faced by married couples in the modern world, the mutual duties and women's new rights. When we gave our consent and signed the marriage registry –first Papá signed giving his consent, I'm still a minor- and when we three looked at each other we saw that all of us had tears in our eyes and we began laughing… It's clear that Papá and Gordon understand each other very well. When we walked out, rice!!!

That was Friday. Then we each slept in our own home, because for Mamá it was "very important that a woman be pure when she reaches the church ceremony, because the only one who can guarantee the sacrament of marriage is a priest…"

I hardly slept and neither did Gordon.

Papá said that the Saturday was his and he wouldn't listen to anyone or anything against it. The lunch was brought from Gallardón, Papá put a chauffeured car at Gordon and his family's service, a nurse for Cristina and he sent the same lunch to them as we had. At 2 p.m. the hairdresser arrived, at 5 p.m. the manicurist and at 6 p.m. the make-up girl.

At 7 p.m. I got into the bath and at 7:45 p.m. Neneca, Inés and Mamá helped me to dress so I wouldn't mess up my hair; at 8:15 p.m. they brought me my bouquet and at 8:30 p.m. I sat in the car… with my heart beating a thousand miles a minute and at my request, we spent a little slow time going through Lomas de Zamora, we went by Barker's College and the Mentruyt Institute.

At 8:45 p.m. we arrived at the Lomas Cathedral, and its entire front was completely decorated with natural flowers.

Carlos was waiting for me at the door... he looked so handsome! It's time he found a girlfriend and stops being such a loose cannon... he accompanied me up to the door where Papá was waiting for me, Papá was serious at first because he didn't want his feelings to betray him, but as we started to walk down the aisle –very slowly, looking at every detail, each vitraux, each flower, every face of friend or family- with Mendelssohn's nuptial march playing and me trying so hard not to cry, my legs stopped trembling and my whole body turned very firm.

At the front, to the side of the altar, was Gordon, his best man Alec Thompson and Mrs Evans.

The ceremony was beautiful.

The priest was a surprise, because he was the son of one of Papá's friends and he gave us this lovely sermon about peace in our hearts, and love in all its forms – loving friends and comrades, brothers and sisters, parents, children and finally the love between a woman and a man; Gordon was truly affected by this sermon and it was obvious by his expression that he was very moved.

I don't think I'll ever forget that expression.

Then Father Guillermo blessed the rings, "you may kiss the bride" and Gordon kissed me and I was trembling like a leaf...

When we left, I very purposely threw my bouquet for Inés!!!

The party was another surprise: Papá is an amazing organizer!!! It was at the Banfield Country Club again, only for 90 people because the mourning period for Evita is still in place; again the Lanzani Mora orchestra!!! At 12:30 a.m. and once we'd changed, we went for our wedding night at the Alvear Palace Hotel.

And the wedding night...

There are no words in the human language to describe what I felt at that moment. Gordon picked me up in his arms –his strength is amazing- he carefully placed me on the bed, turned off the light, he closed the blinds only slightly so that the light from the street would surround the room, he undressed me with exquisite care and if he was nervous I didn't notice because his fingers were unbuttoning buttons and unhooking hooks while he kissed me with passionate tenderness.

At the beginning I just let him do what he wanted, I was trembling with fear and desire, but as his kisses –first on the mouth, but then on my face, my ears, my neck and when I no longer had any clothes on, my breasts, my belly, my belly-button – my body, and as if my hands had a life of their own, they launched into pulling off his clothes...

I didn't know being a woman could be so intense; I had been told I would feel a sharp pain, and my father, who had overcome his natural shyness, had given me a long talk in his study at home, full of scientific terms, explaining what would happen to me; he did not talk of or warn me about the volcano that would light up inside, about the raging hurricane on fire that would possess me.

I did not feel a single pain, on the other hand I slid down an interminable toboggan on which I slid up and down with no effort at all. One time I had read the term "we were one body", and that's when I understood what that meant.

I was filled with such an extreme happiness that I couldn't help crying just like when I was a little girl, so then he hugged me tenderly, kissed my forehead and when I opened my eyes I saw his eyes shining with an incredible emotion.

When we slept, totally exhausted, the sun had come up a long time ago… but it's summer, so sunrise is real early.

The honeymoon…

Gordon is a very special being; he's gone through hell, he's lived in it, he's been submerged in everything that's most brutal and abject since he was very young, almost a child; yet there is something very pure, very vital in him… and our honeymoon was magical, directly related to that pure and playful little boy which he has inside him.

Everything that took place was marvellous and full of surprises.

We left by train on Sunday at 8:30 p.m. My husband had carefully prepared the bicycles for the trip, and Carlitos had had them loaded on the train. Instead of taking the traditional suitcases to the hotel, we took bags which fitted over our arms and onto our backs, which soldiers use and although I had heard their name, "rucksacks", I had never seen one -or maybe I had during some parade- but I hadn't really paid any attention.

Although I had left my bride's dress with my mother and sisters, the clothes which I had on –party clothes, a white dress with a petticoat which my mother-in-law had also made- would not survive in those rucksacks for 10 minutes… To say nothing of Gordon's suit, an impeccable blue material cut in such a way that his beautiful and perfectly proportioned body looked outstanding… so we left everything at the hotel, and they promised to have them sent to my father. We dressed in light summer clothes and with our rucksacks on our backs, walked along Alvear Ave up to Retiro station.

We must have looked, not like two foreigners, but two travellers from the Moon, walking along holding hands! And our heavy rucksacks on our backs…

The first surprise was that when we got onto the train, I realized my husband had bought tickets for tourist class, and I had an unstoppable laughing attack just thinking of my mother's expression should she get to know.

The second surprise was on the trip itself; it's not so bad to travel in tourist class, people play cards, drink *mate* – there was one complete family, about twelve people, who heated water on a kerosene heater which they hid when an inspector came through; in another group of seats there were several men playing guitars –they sang a chorus of the Peronist march four times… And they were amazed at Gordon's voice; that was the third surprise of that unforgettable trip: my husband has a beautiful voice, he knows quite a lot of folklore songs and he even dared to sing a tango; and he deeply moved a Spanish couple –she was from Madrid, he from Zaragoza, they escaped from the war in '39- when he sang a Republican song a cappella that says something like, "there comes the Ebro army…"

And when they learnt we were on our honeymoon!!! Laughing, they clapped, they gave us religious stamps, they congratulated us and shared their drinks and food, they invited us to their homes, to their towns… I felt rather ashamed of so much attention from these humble people.

On the other hand, Gordon was happy as a boy with new shoes, smiling and joyful to receive the blessings from all these dark-skinned people with such generous hearts.

The trip turned out to be very short for us… Because the passengers in that carriage sang and toasted us until dawn… so we had two wedding parties!!!

The train arrived in Santa Fe at dawn and a friend of Papá was waiting for us there, Tín Sandaza and his nephew, an elegant and serious young man whose age was the subject of long discussions with my husband: he said he was no more than 15 and I said he was closer to 20.

Don Sandaza offered to take us in his Ford T but Gordon, firmly but kindly, rejected the offer. That good man, distressed when he saw us with our rucksacks and bicycles, said simply, "Listen, *Don* Evans, the Santa Fe sun is not like the sun in Buenos Aires… your wife will end up with sunstroke… it's more than an hour by car… You'll be travelling all day if you go on your bikes!!" And he shook his head at my new husband's smiling negative; he then handed him the keys of the estancia which had belonged to my mother's family, and which Carlitos had practically ruined after he was discharged from his military service…

We didn't pedal all day long. Close to 11 a.m. we stopped by the roadside, under a grove of trees beside a stream, and for the first time in my life, I camped.

I then saw another side to my husband. Gordon can move about in Nature as if he's part of it.

He put up a very simple campaign tent, just a thick canvas top beneath the bridge, he cut some weeds beside the stream and made a thick mattress on which he placed a blanket, thin and soft as a sheet, so I could lie down –I was really exhausted, we had hardly slept during the whole journey- while he, displaying that energy which totally captivates me, gathered firewood, fished in the stream and cooked a lunch which we accompanied with the wine which *Don* Sandaza had added to our meagre luggage.

We didn't make love till after our siesta. We slept beneath the bridge; a light, agreeable wind blew under it and made bearable the fiery Santa Fe heat and the unendurable chorus of cicadas.

But when we did make love, it was for hours. Then at dusk we bathed naked in that stream of dark, fresh water.

We bathed completely naked!

Now that I'm writing it I wonder what la Vieja would have thought if she knew… But at that time I didn't even think of her…

We slept with our arms around each other, with no clothes on like savages, our bodies locked together in spite of the heat, paying no attention to the noise from any vehicle –car, cart, truck, bus, motorbike…- which eventually must have driven over the bridge, smelling of smoke and sweat…

We got up just after sunrise… He prepared some home-made bread in a tin!!! We had some mate and then we biked for two hours until we arrived at the gate into Estancia Puerta del Chaco.

The truth is it was worse than I'd imagined. The padlock on the gate was just a formality, because there were two rows of wire missing from the fence. One of the casuarina trees at the entrance had fallen over onto the road. The garden around the house had weeds as high as one's waist, and half of the hedge dividing the garden from the other buildings had fallen over… and the corrals, the barns…

Don Saturnino, the caretaker hired by Carlitos, was plainly very drunk at 11 a.m., surrounded by a pack of very thin dogs, and when we arrived he showed his displeasure; but Gordon just stared fixedly at him and he disappeared… and we didn't see him again.

There are bones scattered all over the place; so what was very clear is that the "caretaker" hired by my irresponsible brother gets his behind-hand salary payments by selling the cowskins; he and his dogs eat the meat and whatever is left over is eaten by the vermin…

We inspected the house, which was absolutely uninhabitable; so we decided to camp beside the river. We were alone for ten days, like Robinson Crusoes, and my man demonstrated his amazing qualifications.

He fixed up a canoe whose bottom had fallen out, and we took the canoe out onto the river and fished every afternoon; we ate what we trapped and fished – Gordon taught me how to set up traps to catch hares, he improvised a sling with a leather strap and he surprised me with a dusky-legged guan quite much bigger than a chicken- and we used rice, flour and some tins of beans, peas and tomatoes which he had packed for our trip.

For ten days we were Adam and Eve in Eden. Very sadly, we had to return…

1953

Ufff… With work and the house and Gordon, I don't have or don't find time to write, but the following is worth writing down.

The day before yesterday, when we both returned from work, underneath the door there was a note from the post-office saying they were holding a certified letter in Gordon's name. In the morning, something very unlike him, he told his boss he would be leaving early so he could go and pick up the letter at the post-office.

He came to pick me up at school because he wanted to share the letter with me. His friend and protector of his time at school in England, *Don* Eurwen, is seriously ill but also, has willed him a small fortune which is at his disposal already.

Today we had supper with Papá and Mamá because Gordon has an idea of what to do with this money and I can do no less than celebrate it: he's going to make Papá an offer for "Puerta del Chaco".

Two days later.

Papá not only consented to sell us what is left of the estancia, but he also set a lower price than the one offered by Gordon, taking into account the property's very poor condition.

Papá's idea is that with what we save, we invest the money in tools and improvements to the land for it to be productive once again, something it hasn't been for a long time.

Gordon resigned his job, although he'll only leave when they find his replacement; next week he'll go and stay on the property for two or three days to make a list of the work and all the indispensable needs.

I'm going to resign my job as well… I'm going to miss my classes, but I'm very enthused with the project.

1954

It's been almost a year since we've been living on the estancia… Never in all my life have I been as happy as this year we've spent together, working side by side, from dawn till dusk, with no Sundays or Mondays.

We've had faithful friends who have helped us enormously.

Starting with *Don* Sandaza and his nephew Bernardo, who in spite of his youth is a fine, honest man; our neighbours as well, who little by little have approached us shyly, lending us tools, helping us and giving us advice.

Again and again Gordon has demonstrated his abilities, both to get work done plus his ingenuity.

As soon as we arrived, in three weeks he made the house inhabitable, and I seconded his work. I learnt to paint, scrape, place tin sheets, glass; and I helped him fix fences, gates, hedges and corrals.

We bought a small tractor —an offer from the government, as they had received a load of Czechoslovakian tools as part payment for the sale of cereals- and we sowed some pasture for the animals —we've bought 100 cows and half a dozen bulls- and cereal seeds.

Prices are low, but we don't expect any great profit. We've also planted a large vegetable garden and have about 50 chickens.

Most of our food comes from our work, all we have to buy is salt, oil, sugar and *yerba mate*.

Papá has come twice to visit us, Mamá always makes an excuse, she says that to see us living like "natives" depresses her. Carlitos comes at least once a month. We took the train to spend Christmas with them and to visit friends.

I don't miss my other life at all, I'm incredibly happy.

June 19, 1955

So, all that we thought could happen has finally taken place and it has ended badly. The atmosphere of confrontation that had begun with the Corpus Christi incidents – in which Carlos and all the young men from the "Lomas de Zamora Sagrado Corazón" parish took part- and all the things that took place afterwards came to a head both brutally and logically: a sector of the Navy and the Air Force rose against Perón, they bombed Government House and Plaza de Mayo.

We heard about this disaster almost directly, over the radio. Gordon is very worried, he doesn't like the sound of these events. The day before yesterday Carlitos and several friends appeared here in order to lie low.

The burning of the churches in Buenos Aires will be a milestone in the confrontation between Argentines.

Gordon and Carlitos got into an argument, Carlos demanded that Gordon join the rebellion, that they need someone with his experience. Gordon has refused.

I understand his logic completely. In 1937 he joined the Spanish civil war to fight against those who shaped the July 1936 coup d'etat.

Why would he radically change his position now and become someone who rebels against the constitutional government?

He does believe that Perón has lost his way a long time back, but that there will soon be elections, and that this is the only way that authorities should be changed.

Carlos has been very rude, he's shouted at Gordon and forgotten he's in our home.

Gordon could have told them they must leave, and instead, he got up and went to fix our pier…

I was about to ask them to leave myself, but when I went to take Gordon his meal and consulted him about it, once again he showed me he's the appropriate man for me. "No, my love… They'll be safe here, and if we send them away they might be at risk and I'm not willing to have that on my conscience… It doesn't matter what he said to me, he's my brother…"

I love him.

September 24, 1955

Well, finally the revolution has overthrown Perón, who has sought refuge in Paraguay. General Lonardi gave a speech to the country calling for national unity and said there are neither victorious nor vanquished.

Yesterday Gordon travelled to Buenos Aires to see his mother, who is probably upset and sad. He himself is not happy, he doesn't like breaks in the constitutional order; he's convinced that if Perón had been left in power until the next elections —next year- he would have lost them.

I doubt this, as I have before.

There's no doubt the regime was intolerable. But I don't know if the true solution is this one. I don't believe that breaking the law is the way to impose another law. I hope this is the end to our problems and the beginning of an Argentina in which we deserve to live.

I didn't go to Buenos Aires, I don't feel like having to tolerate Mamá and Carlitos who must be happy because of Perón's downfall, it's all too sad to celebrate.

There're so many things to do here on the estancia.

May 20, 1956

I'm not unwell… I've had morning sickness for a whole week, so on Friday we got into the Jeep and after an 8-hour long trip (I vomited the whole way), we arrived in Banfield at Papá's clinic, and they tested me right then and there. I'M PREGNANT!!!!

On Sunday we gave the news to both families and on Monday, in spite of Mamá's protests —I must say Papá was almost in agreement, he was thinking of the dangers of the trip- we returned home in our Jeep, which is slow and uncomfortable but it's ours. The doctors who believe in natural childbirth say that a pregnancy is not an illness…

If it's a boy it will be called Carlos, if it's a girl, Bethan, a Welsh name, one of Gordon's paternal aunts' names.

January 25, 1957

Uff. At last, back home. Carlos was born on January 17… Natural childbirth, no anaesthetic in spite of Papá's opposition. We had studied, read and we did it. It was… How shall I put it… an intense experience? A strange mix of pain and pleasure and anguish and serenity and fear and courage… All together, at the same time. I was at the clinic and I didn't let Papá participate at all.

The obstetrician, Donald Boyle, a shy and agreeable young man, from an English family, knew quite a lot about natural, painless childbirth and he managed to bear with Papá's and other doctors' pressure at the clinic, saying we should do things the "traditional" way.

Gordon was dying to come into the delivery room and his arguments were pretty convincing: he had lived a good part of his life at war and he was used to blood and hearing screams.

Boyle didn't dare go so far and he obeyed Papá, he said he was sorry, and that it wasn't possible.

Charly is such a good baby, and my pregnancy was very pleasant, full of lovely feelings. He weighed 3.8 kgs. He breastfeeds voraciously and sleeps most of the time.

Both families are overjoyed with their first grandchild. Grandmother Pepa knitted and sewed a marvellous layette in white and light blue with his initials on every single garment —even his nappies have a monogram!!! Mamá and Papá gave him two cribs —one for our house, one for theirs…- and Carlos already made him a member of the Country Club (my brother is a member of the Board now that he's a "doctor", even though he finally graduated less than six months ago… ten years to complete a career that takes six…!!!); my sisters have given Charly enough toys for every single year. I don't think he's going to need any more toys for the rest of his life with all he's been given.

Gordon is absolutely absorbed by the little boy. He picks him up, he rocks him, he hugs me while I'm feeding the baby, he attends to my every need… he even washes my underwear!!! At first I was very embarrassed, but then I understood this was such an intense and deep gesture of love that I accepted it just as it was.

Since September, Gordon has hired people to help us on the farm, as I won't be able to help him with the chores. Recommended by our good friend, *Don* Bernardo Sandaza, *doña* Herminia came into our home, joining Junco, Gordon's peon, foreman and friend, a young, short and very strong creole, horse-tamer and cattle drover. She will help me with the house chores.

(Mariana Evans never continued writing in her diaries; after the accident, she read them several times. After Carlos died, she burnt them and deposited them on Gordon's grave).

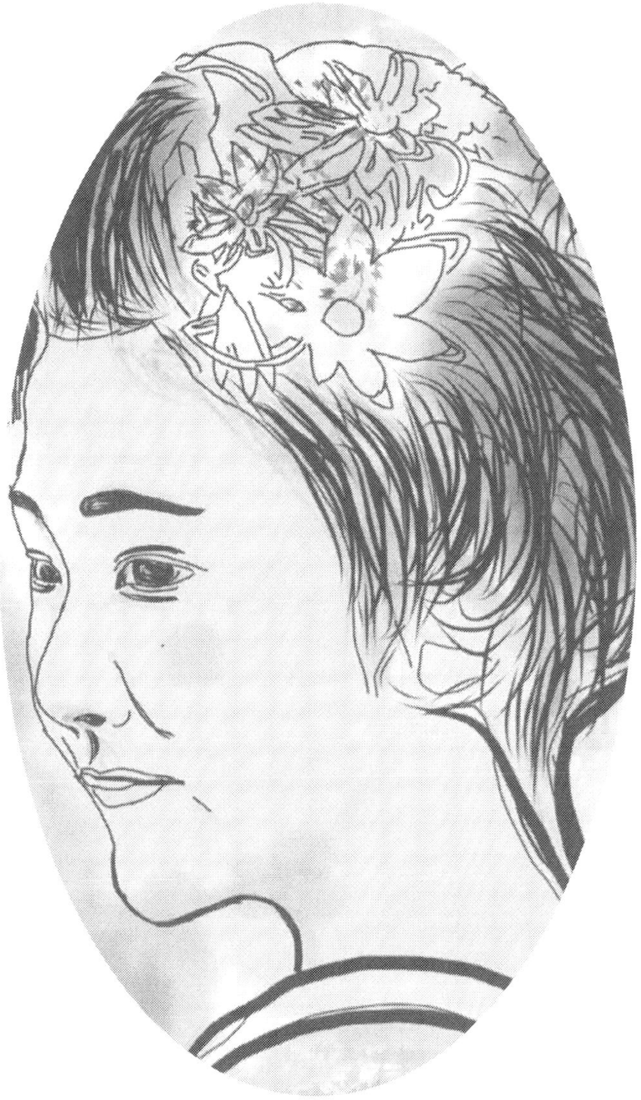

VI) HAIKU

Haiku:

A Japanese poem form. It is a very brief poem, generally formed by three lines of verse with few syllables – the first line has five, the second seven and the third line is again five syllables. It usually refers to a poet's amazement and bliss when contemplating nature.

Andorra, July 11, 1937

Dear Papá, Mamá and grandfather Julio,

I hope one day you'll be able to forgive me for the pain and anguish I know you undoubtedly went through when you received the news that reached you before this letter.

I'm now at the frontier between Spain and Andorra; in a few hours I'll be leaving with somebody who will help me to cross the border, as I mean to join the Republican Army.

I'm not sure where to begin… You read the news just as I do, and you know what is happening in Europe -Germany is now under the brutal, iron rule of the dictator Hitler- and glorious Italy -whose opera you love so much, grandfather- governed by fascists almost since I was born.

It's essential to stop them and now is the time, Spain is the place; otherwise a racist and brutal poison, the plebiscite-simulating authoritarian and fascist dictatorships will be merciless in Europe.

I want, need, wish you to understand me; over the last four years I've lived at a distance, and if it hadn't been for your letters I don't know what I would have done. There have been marvellous, good people everywhere –thanks to your timely and generous written permission I've travelled quite a bit around Great Britain- and I can also say that save one or two boys, I met the worst and most evil of my peers at King George's College.

grandfather, it's true that the academic level is impressive. My French is good; my English is fluid and I have a rich vocabulary; I've read Greeks and Romans in their original language –Latin is truly marvellous- and my last year's German course at least allows me to listen and understand almost everything, even though I can't speak it fluently as I do French, English or the American-Spanish as you like to call it; and believe me, you'd be amazed at my command of algebra and geometry. Did you know that the Biology teacher is a medical doctor? He was a doctor during the Great War and he suffered mentally to the point that he never again wanted to attend to anyone who was seriously wounded.

But it's also true that the person who I could say was the closest to being a friend left this year; and to come to the point of greeting each other kindly and with respect we had a punching fight for almost 3 hours!!!! I know that King George's College is one of the most important in Great Britain and probably, in the world; but I also know that they don't want me there.

If grandfather had heard the speech spoken to my face the day I arrived, already over four years ago, it's likely he would have moved Heaven and Earth to stop Cabot Cuttler from ever again being head of any other school with so much prestige and historical past. Among other things, he said that my "blood was not pure" because my mother is not British. The same statements as the Nüremberg 1935 laws!

All these past years I've kept silent about how they've treated me out of respect for the enormous effort you made in order for me to be here. I can't help thinking how much you must have sacrificed for my stay to be more comfortable and bearable. I know perfectly well that the scholarship didn't cover lesser details such as food and clothes washing. Here £120 is a large amount –you could have bought a modern car with the three years' fee you have sent- and I can perfectly well imagine that in Buenos Aires this amount stretches even further.

As you must know from other letters, the librarian Mr. Moresby was a companion-in-arms of *Don* Eurwen, so he has been an accomplice in our healthy friendship being kept hidden from any pupils, teachers or school authorities' indiscreet or critical view.

It's absolutely forbidden for pupils to talk to "inferior" people, i.e. the workers. If I worked in this school, I wouldn't be able to even give him an appreciative glance, Papá; I would be sanctioned. If they knew I'd travelled to Edinburgh and Cardiff with him, they would legally process him for attempted corruption.

All the effort I'd put into my studies has never been reflected in my marks; it was Mr. Moresby who confessed the following -and he was very embarrassed about it: there's a more or less tacit agreement among the teachers and Mr. Cabot Cuttler for "the son of a Welsh workman and a South American woman" not be allowed to excel in any way. Not even good people – but undoubtedly weak such as Dr Samuelson (the doctor I told you about before) - have been able to ignore this wickedness.

This is why my academic reports have never reflected all I learnt. grandfather, I followed your advice, and I absorbed everything I could from my teachers. The library has been my refuge and books nearly my whole world over these past years.

This is not the reason I've left the school. If I'd stayed there, by July 1939 I would undoubtedly be returning to Buenos Aires, having graduated with a management degree which would allow me to enrol without any problem in any university. It's clear that if I put up with it for four years, I can do it for two more.

But if I'm here on a journey to who knows where, it's because I firmly believe, with all my heart, that the Spanish Republic II cause is worth defending. Just as grandfather and Papá, I felt very indignant when before Christmas 1936 we heard of García Lorca's martyrdom; here a few newspapers reported it and the Communist party has used it as an example of fascist barbarianism; Mrs Cummins cried when she read a beautiful summary of his life published by a poetry magazine.

Just imagine, he's practically unknown as an author –he has not been translated yet- and even so his death has moved many people.

If they can shoot a poet, what will they do to the workmen? What was done in Germany and Italy is now being done in Spain.

I'm going to defend you, Papá, who work in a railroad workshop; I'm going to defend you, grandfather, a poet and a teacher. I'm going to defend you and my sister, Mamá, who are the very image of all that the fascists despise: tenderness and fragility.

And I must do it now, because if we don't stop them, sooner or later the fascists will take over all Europe and from there will remain forever in power together with those who are already in Argentina.

Please, remember that *Don* Eurwen had nothing to do with the decision and planning behind my project; he tried by all reasonable means to convince me to let it go and his only "fault" is that he has been too loyal to report me –if all he'd done was only insinuate that I had this idea, you would have taken measures to prevent me doing this- with the risk of hearing claims from you.

Believe me Papá, *Don* Eurwen, who did not come out unscathed from Belgium in 1917, believes like you that peace must prevail at any cost –to the point of even voting for Mr. McDonald in spite of working for and admiring Mr. Attlee- and he didn't want me to participate here in the fight against fascism, but he respects me as a person and believes I can take charge of my own life.

I believe just as Mr. Attlee and Sir Churchill that concrete actions must be taken to avoid the illness spreading to other countries.

Something must be happening if two men who are such opposites to have come to an agreement. The policy of "appeasement" is a total failure, it makes Hitler grow; a Republican defeat will mean France will be surrounded.

I perfectly understand your position, Papá; it's the same as *Don* Eurwen's and up till now at least, also the majority of English people who support pacifist and conciliatory policies with that terrible Hitler; but the Anglo-German Naval Agreement of 1935 made the Versailles Treaty disappear, become confetti, and it's clear that the Stresa pact – my God, an agreement with Mussolini!!!- created some months before through MacDonald's behest did not lead anywhere.

While Spain was beginning to bleed and burn, Hitler followers' *anti-kominterpakt*, together with the fascists and the Japanese Empire, was not announcing anything good. From one extreme of the world to another those in power are seeking allies and chiefs of state to crush the workmen's just claims. Should I just sit back and do nothing, knowing that if we don't stop them the world will burn like Europe burnt before? If the rebel Franco is not defeated, there will be an even worse war than the European war, you know that. Each man counts.

I am no longer a boy: I buried my childhood in hours of loneliness and pain, with all I ever loved fifteen thousand kilometres away.

More than once, when I took part in independent Labour acts, I've been in fist fights with the black shirts, so I know what violence feels like already.

I consciously chose to stay in this school because I respect you, my most beloved family. Today, respecting myself, I've taken the road to arms to defend your same ideas.

I beg of you to understand my decision. If anything should happen to me, I want you to know that my last thoughts will be of you four, the best family a man could ever have.

With all my love, respect and gratitude,

Gordon Evans.

King George's School, Enfield, July 6, 1937

Dear Mrs Cummins,

I'm writing a few hours after leaving for France, full of grateful thoughts not only because of this gift, but also because of the years of friendship which made my days in Britain so much better, and easing the distance from my loved ones.

Yet I must confess that we won't be seeing each other for a long time, if we ever do again. I hid my project from you so as to avoid any disagreement until such time you may end up being in agreement.

Once this letter has arrived –I've made arrangements for it to be posted on the date I leave- I will be abandoning France in order to join the Spanish Republican Army as soon as possible.

I will be fulfilling my duty according to the ideas we shared regarding how a progressive world should be, nothing more. I hope one day you will forgive this shameful lie that I'll carry on my conscience for the rest of my days.

I give you my word of honour and promise that I'll find a way to give back the expenses for this trip. If anything definitive should happen to me on the battlefield, please don't have bad thoughts about me and forgive my soul.

In gratitude and affectionately,

Gordon Evans.

Buenos Aires, August 16, 1937

Dear son,

I'm writing these words, the first ones since those ill-fated days of last July, in very deep sorrow, without any idea regarding your destination or how you are. My anguish began the day we received the cable from King George's College on July 14th and the airmail letter from Prof. Cabot Cuttler on July 21st; and the death of your grandfather, my father. Yesterday afternoon, our loyal Anita, who has been with us for 30 years, found him lying dead in his bed when she took him his breakfast; on his desk was the letter without an envelope which I'm sending you together with this one.

I've lost my father, my teacher and my spiritual and political guide. Your father is devastated; you know well that he found in my father all that he wished for and needed: a family, knowledge, respect and affection. I took the liberty of reading your grandfather's last letter and I must say, even with my heart still tightly full of pain, that it is full of light and truth.

Just a few hours ago we left his body lying in his last resting place, the family's mausoleum in the Recoleta cemetery.

The arrival of your letter on August 2nd, which your grandfather read until he knew it by heart, and the letter from Mrs Sylvia on the 6th have lessened, at least a little, our terrifying uncertainty. If possible of course, please let her know your destination in a cable, so we can write to you and send you whatever may be necessary and is in our power to do so.

I'm not going to ask you to return, even though my heart is screaming for me to do this. Your father had thought of demanding that the British Embassy have you sent back home, but your grandfather convinced him not to do this. Today, after reading your grandfather's letter, we both cried, terrified at the possible consequences of not having done it.

You will have to forgive your father, he's not going to write. He's angry, sad and more silent than ever. He's terrified, like I am, that you will lose your life. But he's also deeply sorry that you have left your schooling.

Prof. Cabot Cuttler's letter has left us, also, with a very bitter taste. You have been expelled from the school in the worst of terms. They have lodged a legal complaint in France and in England due to your disappearance and they've committed to do the same in Spain, although they cannot guarantee that authorities will respond.

Within the next few days we'll be sending a cable to the school authorities to request that they withdraw all these complaints. It certainly would not be good if you were detained and held to be sent back to Argentina. Your condition as a British citizen places you under the protection of the Crown, but also under their laws. I beg you to always keep this in mind.

Your sister fills the silent days with all kinds of sounds and gurgles. We bought a radio and we have definitely proved that although she doesn't hear, she's very sensitive to vibrations. I place her hands on the wood cabinet and she smiles when there is someone talking, but she laughs when music is played. Maybe someday we will find a way to teach her to talk.

I'm not in a mood to write further, I'm full of fear and sorrow, which will only cease when I see you come through our front door. One last request: write to your father; as your grandfather pointed out, give him time and he'll write to you again.

Please take care of yourself. I love you with all my heart,

Your Mamá

August 18, 1937

Dear Gordon,

I'm writing to you after several week of not doing so, still under the devastating impression left by the news which arrived from England a few days back, and having deeply thought through the ideas I want to write down for you, having weighed each word I'll be using with love and care.

I'm now 83 years old, and for several weeks I've been sensing an almost imperceptible conviction that my days in this world are coming to an end, and that one of these nights I will fall asleep only to awaken —not in the arms but at least in the clear company- of my ancestors. In their presence I'm your direct spokesperson; so it's imperative to remind you of things I have tried —I believe successfully- to teach you with the intention of keeping the spark of knowledge and human progress alive, such as was passed on to me.

I'm not going to reproach you for your untimely escape and above all, for the risk in your destination. I have seen the surprise, pain and fear reflected in my children, your parents, and I understand them perfectly; a part of me participates with them. We shipped you off to follow our dream of a better life for you without thinking that we could be sending you to a worse life, a bitter loneliness, an undeserved exile.

But at the same time I can't set aside considering the situation of the world in which you are moving and growing. The cause you are going to defend is just, yet I can't say whether the path you've chosen is the correct one. Many years ago I witnessed my older brother leaving to follow the happy, patriotic song of a crazy Mitre, only to die as a hero in the infamy which was Curupayti; and I myself participated —in one way or another- in three revolutions. I believed – as my brother did, as you do, that the cause was just, that they were worthy of spilt blood, our own or the enemy's.

Who can know? Today with the dice rolling inside a dice cup, nobody does. My mother, who was a warrior's orphan, knew that the sacred monster -the brutal and evil god of war that gives birth to innumerable countries as it does to injustices, spilling the blood of the just and the sinners like magma on the world's battlefields -a human history of which we are all sons and daughters- she could have begged for her own flesh and blood; yet, like a Spartan, she celebrated my brother leaving. She regretted this her whole life.

Don't ask that of your mother, and much less of your father. She has witnessed the suffering and hurt he withheld after all those years spent in the European hell, and they writhe in pain thinking about what could happen to you. Your letter has not convinced them as did the one sent at the beginning of 1935, but I don't believe there's a God in the world that can convince them there's a good enough cause to allow them to sacrifice their first born.

I myself, now at the doorway to life, knowing that one of these mornings I'll finally know all the answers, definitely know I'll not see you again, at least on this level, so I'll not utter any reproach, claim or cry foolish tears when faced now with what is inevitable.

I have given you elements in your education that undoubtedly are directly related to your departure, I know this and accept it. I did it consciously, knowing that this was a possible result.

I would have preferred that you finish your secondary education, go to the University, become a doctor, a professor, writer, lawyer, scientist, engineer or artist - complete your education rather than lose your life on a battlefield. But I'm absolutely certain regarding the purity of your impulse, the intellectual sovereignty of the ideas which nurture you and are leading you to savagery and cruelty. I believe your thirst for justice was planted here, in this far-off, peripheral country and I'm not surprised, because it was built by just and noble men and you were educated in their traditions.

But I'll be giving you some advice, perhaps in the form of a testament, my last will. I'm not going to pretend I don't know about or don't agree with your father and mother's claim, I add my own enthusiastically and with hope. Be very careful, don't risk your life, just do what is necessary, expected and just enough. Always try to return whole, regardless of the war's result.

You will find within the heart of Hobbes' Leviathan more than one supreme truth that will enlighten you for the rest of your days. Treasure this knowledge for the coming generations. Your father's pacifism was not born in the ecclesiastical halls but in the mud and horror of the battlefields; I hope that as he has, you can tell your story.

Live each day and enjoy the most common and tiniest pleasures around you, from clear sunshine on a fragile spider's web –a transparent metaphor on life- to a simple dish of chickpeas.

Never be tempted by evil or unnecessary damage; the violent cruelty of impunity or simple revenge dressed as brutal justice. Always be aware that wars end on the battlefield but continue forever in the fighter's heart and conscience.

Be unsparing in combat, and just and merciful after death and ambush. Always keep in mind how magnanimous and noble Gen. San Martin was with the defeated; as well as Gen. Lavalle, wild and brave and so fearfully crazy when faced with the enemy's fire, yet he avoided the useless slaughter of a mass execution; and above all, never forget Gen. Dorrego's nonsensical sacrifice, which he paid for with dishonour as well as his life.

And this example is very valid, because in that ill-fated civil war you are less a foreigner there in Spain than any other European: we Latin Americans are favourite sons of that deep, tough yet kind land, and this compels you more than other men regarding your enemies. They too are Spaniards and in a way therefore, distant relations.

Don't do anything you may later regret. Be just and generous.

I understand, just as you, that fascism is the cruelest side of capitalism and it must be stopped, and I agree with your analysis -Spain is the place, this is the moment. I believe your political opinion is unobjectionable: Hitler, Mussolini and the world's fascists' course must be altered and I agree that they will not stop unless defeated.

Be understanding with my good Meredith. Your father is angry because his own experience has made him into a convinced pacifist and I hope that, like me, you understand the deep and very reasonable roots of his thoughts.

Survive, because he will forgive you. If you die it is likely that in a life beyond, your mother will punish you… I won't get mixed up in that. I saw my mother – who had eight other children- broken and eternally in pain for the son brutally torn from her breast by a decision equally independent as yours.

We men cannot understand women because the experience they go through in the flow of life separates us like the emptiness in space to the nearest planet. How could they ever accept as something natural that he whom she carried in her womb would be blown to bits? Impossible!

Don't take part in any acts of revenge, looting or ignoble actions, and don't be afraid of seeming less courageous or masculine because you refuse to hurt the weak and defenceless, the helpless, the elderly, women and children, in all of them always see your mother and your invalid sister. Mercy, kindness and honour are virtues that truly shine wherever they are absent.

War is synonymous with impunity as measured by the lowest instincts in a human being; keep alert, don't allow evil -which truly exists- to make you blind to virtue, nobility, generosity and love of life; I know what sort of person you are, what you are made of, I remind you of this so you'll focus on your values, on what we have willed to you, in order for you not to get lost on this difficult road you have chosen.

Avoid hate, be compassionate and always think twice before leaving your trench, try not to be always the first or the last when you enter the battle. Learn to differentiate cowardice as a permanent state from a momentary weakness, a bad moment, a treacherous instinct; keep away from those who want to be first, and support those who are in the second line, because you are no different and therefore are not immune to a moment of weakness.

When the time comes to obey don't do so without thinking first, and above all, remember you must not accept immoral orders; don't forget either that you have become part of a terrible form of Armed Forces in which your life may be taken without reprisals or punishment.

When you meet a good leader follow him wherever he goes, and be his nearest friend, his most faithful guardian, his most loyal swordsman. Believe me, you will never regret this.

When you must lead, never forget that your subordinates are beloved sons of fathers and mothers who will suffer as much as yours if you fall in battle. Don't ask for anything you are not willing to give.

When you find a good subordinate, let him know this. They're not your friends, but it's essential that you trust each other. You'll never need to boast about your courage, I know you have what it takes, I've seen you ride bravely and nobly, earning the respect of adult, brave men. Keep away from the reckless as well as the cowards, he who disregards his own life will also disregard yours.

When everything is over, when the thunderous roar of cannons is silenced and the machine-guns grow cold, I beg of you to find a good woman and populate this land, this rich, fertile Argentina that will await all the time that's needed to make of you a good, happy and prosperous man.

I will be ending my writing on this paper but not in my soul, which beats every second awaiting news of you; I'm tired, I accept I'm already an old man whose strength has lessened. I have been blessed with 19 grandchildren, who I've seen grow and prosper. I love them all.

But my relationship with you is different: you are the youngest, the last one and I won't deny I feel much closer to you. If I could transcend death it would only be to accompany you and your risky destiny.

I won't ask you to remember me, I know we are permanently united; one day you will tell your children about me and they will do the same with theirs, a far-off day, and in this way I will remain alive, in some way present.

I love you sincerely, your grandfather

Julio Porrá

November 1, 1937

Dear Gordon,

Don't think you can escape from me so easily. What you have done is bad and cruel, but you are not. It's the time in which we live that has practically forced you to do what you did; and I believe intensely that in the long run nothing else is possible.

I know perfectly well you are doing what many good people think must be done, but I would have wished you didn't have to run such a great risk.

You're right, if I had known your plans I would have done everything possible to stop you and I wish I had had the opportunity of doing so. But destiny showed up and as the saying goes, God knows why.

Once again all the people I love are far away, and some of them in certain danger. I'm strong because I must be, but Heaven knows I am fearful when facing destiny's windmills.

I know you are in contact with your parents in Argentina, please do not forget them, they need you alive and in one piece, write to your mother as often as you can; I know through my own experience what kind of dark terrors awaken in a mother's heart, such as kilometres and ignorance.

Please, whenever you can write to me, count on me and within my possibilities, I will help you.

Your sincere friend,
Sylvia S. Cummins

November 23, 1937

Dear Mrs Sylvia,

It's difficult for me to express how thankful I am for your forgiveness.

I can't describe more than Aragonese landscapes, which in some way remind me of Northern Argentina, as much as I recall.

I have some brothers around me who take care of me. The food is as good as it can be, sometimes rather too little, but the spirit of solidarity with which we live makes this unimportant.

To talk about God when one is faced with human evil is not worth spending your time; try instead to convince English politicians, public opinion, your neighbours to help us. Fascism is our mortal enemy and everything possible must be done to defeat it.

I think of you and send you a kiss, you're part of my family.

Affectionately,

Gordon Evans

November 18, 1937

Dear Mamá,

I can't set down any written details because for obvious reasons there's always the risk that one is giving information to the enemy, as I can't know a posted letter's destiny.

Incredibly, despite the continuous help that Franco receives from Germany and Italy, we are resisting. The world, its arms crossed, observes how legality is brutally crushed in fifty percent of Spain, and does nothing more than talk. I am referring to governments. Because people, such as yourself, such as *Don* Eurwen or Mrs Sylvia are decidedly supporting our battle.

The world's democratic governments are denying us rifles and bullets while tanks, planes, soldiers, arms and ammunition daily leave Hitler and Mussolini's hands, obviously into rebel hands.

Among us there are fighters from all over the world, all of Europe, the three Americas, some Asians and most likely some Africans, but we don't have enough ammunition and supplies because other than the Soviet Union, all the rest of the "free nations" -with Great Britain as the leader- have neutrally taken Franco's side.

What will happen to our country? The very little news that we receive here is not encouraging. President Justo will be succeeded by Ortiz. Don't ask me how because I've no idea, but I received a printed document in which Ortiz recalls that he formed part of President Yrigoyen's government. How badly things must be going over there if we must be happy that Justo is being succeeded by another like him and not by the fascist Uriburu (may God keep him and not let him out of Heaven…) or any of his minions. Ah, what a terrible mistake was made by those who allowed the September revolution!

Meanwhile, we've been resting in a beautiful little village here. People are very kind to us and invite us to eat and drink whenever they can. The truth is that the only thing war brings is hunger and a lack of everything.

Please, give my father my most loving regards and my deepest and heartfelt feelings for you and my sister.

Your son,

Gordon Evans

NOVEMBER 1937

Dear Father,

I understand perfectly the reasons for your anger. Perhaps if I'd known what I know now, I would not be here. There's the Spanish saying that experience is like a comb given to you when you have turned bald…

In these few months since I arrived here I've gone through enough to understand you thoroughly. I don't expect your leniency, because I know that the reason behind your anger is a just one, I know how important it is in this world in which I live to count on a good, complete education.

You must know that among the international Republican volunteers here, I gained my position as Commander Torrents' courier thanks to my knowledge of languages learnt at King George's College. I can even make myself understood with my German comrades!

Yes, Father, everything bad about war is partly balanced out by the extraordinary solidarity among the world's people: there are representatives from nearly every single corner of the planet, I hear a multitude of languages and see every facial features imaginable, all united to stop a fascist triumph.

I'm still hurting from my grandfather's death, and I think I'll be in pain my whole life; I know you share this pain, it's something else that unites us, as well as our love for my mother and sister.

In the here and now I understand perfectly why you're a pacifist, from the bottom of my heart I believe it's the best possible idea in a world of equality, but that day has yet to come… Deep in your heart you know - even if you don't approve of what I've done- that I'm right, my cause is just and I'm fulfilling my duty as a man.

Once again I ask for your indulgence; a word of forgiveness from you would be enough for my days to be easier.

Affectionately, your son,

Gordon Evans

November 1937

Dear *Don* Eurwen,

Since my last letter from Albacete, I have been through very long and daily war experiences. I'm not the same boy you said goodbye to at Enfield station, but I suppose you already know this, because you warned me so many times… I can't say I'm sorry, it would be childish.

Now the events and things in my current and future life are out of my hands. If I survive –I promise I will do my best- yet it will always be by staying true to my ideals.

Among my comrades-in-arms I have glimpses of what humanity's future brotherhood could be like. It's so far off… But we don't fight without hope, despite the fascists attacking us with their abundant ammunition and supplies, even if the rest of the world has been deaf to our suffering and pain.

I'm not going to waste your time by moaning, it wouldn't be fair on those who fell in the mud-filled trenches. But neither am I going to be tricked by hate. No, I don't hate those who are mistakenly pointing their guns at me. Even if I survive this and my hand is callused from holding my weapon pointing at them, I'll not hate them. I'll consider this the price for being a better human being.

I've never done this so I must do it now: thank you for all you did for me. When I found it impossible to fit in to that horrible place, your silent support helped me to move forward and not give up. Our friendship as men has made me into the man I am today. I have a father who is very sad and angry because of the steps I've taken; just as I consider him the father of my childhood, if you allow me I will consider you the father in my adulthood.

It will be some time before I can write again, as we're going forward to some place where we'll be crossing the fascists. When our task is done, if I survive, I'll contact you.

Sincerely yours,

Your comrade

Gordon Evans

July 1938

Dear Gordon,

News from Spain is not good. All newspapers are in agreement on only one point: that this is a dead-end road; nobody believes that the Republic's situation will end well. As do all the people who love you, I read every single word that's published and listen to every single radio report on the Spanish war.

I feel bad because I don't understand a word of Spanish, when now and again I can tune in to some of the shortwave broadcasts from Spain.

Yes, I've bought a new radio on which I can even listen to Moscow Radio, which broadcasts news in English. But there's a difference in the Moscow reports' optimistic slant to the opinion of the majority of British newspapers, which is extremely pessimistic.

What is very clear is that the Republican politicians cannot agree with each other. I think it was Napoleon who said that victory has many fathers, but that defeat is an orphan... that's not verified here - when you see a continuous change in a government's cabinets you will notice that the Republican weakness has many fathers…

The situation here is actually not much better. At least the war is not over our heads, and if old Neville is right, it might never be.

The rumours of an agreement to remove the International Brigades abound; this is a step that will promote peace agreements between the parties. The Times is not my favourite newspaper, but what has been published is that if the Republicans remove their international followers, the Italians and Germans will do the same. I hope so, for your own sake and for all those caught in the suffering of war.

In the hope of seeing you soon,

Your friend and comrade

Eurwen Glynn

Gordon Evans, for his mother, Josefa Porrá de Evans

(Never sent, it was sealed in an envelope reading "By the hand of British Army First Sergeant Evans, G. Last Will for Mrs Josefa Porrá Evans).

Dear Mamá,

If you receive this letter it's because life has left me before I can even live it.

I want you to know that in all these long and painful years away from home, the only thing that has kept me away from melancholy at missing everything, has been you. Every morning my eyes remember your tender smile and your kind eyes.

I think of your look, your hands, your voice, of the memory in my mind of your lap when I was small, and I'm infinitely grateful to life having placed me in your hands. This means that I know what peace and safety are because I've never felt them as I did under your care.

I think of my father and I'm really sorry I hurt him with my departure to this place, but to this day I've been faithful to his lessons. His memory kept me healthy and alive when all around me there was only horror and hopelessness.

Ever since I received my grandfather's letter, it has been my light in this gloom, my guidance on the mountain, my compass in the ocean. It clarified things again and again every time I read it, and believe me, this was many times. It's obvious that if you are reading this, they weren't enough.

I ask you for my sister's forgiveness, I won't be able to take care of her as I should have and there is no real forgiveness. Poor man who took my life, his conscience will carry more than just my soul.

I, like all those around me, alive or dead, we're where we have to be, we're doing what we have to do, we'll carry our blame forever and our same destiny will be the proof of our innocence.

Yes. I'm to blame for many things but I'm also innocent of all of them.

Mother, my life has been short, but you have given me so much light that it has made it all worthwhile.

Loving you, your son,

Gordon Evans

Barnet, May 16, 1939

Dear Papá and Mamá,

These last weeks since I left Spain all I can think of is about returning home. Ever since that day, *Don* Eurwen and Mrs Sylvia have shown even more generosity than they had before. When they learnt of my wish to return home, they both offered to pay my return ticket.

Just as I rejected you paying for my return ticket, I've done the same regarding these good friends. Everything that has taken place is my responsibility and I don't believe it reasonable that others pay for it.

Don Eurwen has therefore offered me more than work: to be his partner in a business he started after leaving his job at King George's College. "Glynn & Evans Mechanical Repairs, Local Trips and Transport", in which he invested a good amount of capital in renting the workshop occupied before by Irishman O'Sean; he also bought a lorry. My part in the partnership will be my work: I will soon have my license to drive heavy vehicles. When I'm not driving, I'll help *Don* Eurwen with repairing the cars and motorbikes brought to the shop. I really like working with motors.

We'll take advantage of the clients left by the Irishman, we're even completing the work which hadn't been finished, and we've made some trips to Liverpool and Southampton. Recently I picked up some goods from an Argentine ship and very generously they gave me several kilogrammes of *yerba mate* (they wouldn't sell it to me), so I'm able to drink *mate* again.

As things are turning out, it will take me some two years to save up the money to return to Argentina. In a good work week I earn £ 6-16, on a bad week £ 0-15-10.

From Monday through Saturdays I sleep in the workshop and on the weekends I go to Surrey, to Barnet on *Don* Eurwen's motorbike, because Mrs Sylvia always has something to fix in her house. She also has some activity, some event to go to. She's so kind!!! The cinema, theatre, dinners… At first I was ashamed to accept so much undeserved generosity, but she confessed to me two or three days ago that my company had made her life very happy.

Spring and its drizzle is coming to an end, Mrs Sylvia's vegetable garden looks very impressive and I'd love you to see her flowers in the greenhouse —orchids- because they're extraordinarily beautiful.

Please kiss my sister from me and be patient, with a little effort the day will come when we'll be able to hug each other again.

Loving you,

Gordon.

June 3, 1939

Dear son,

Mrs Sylvia's cable of April 15th greatly relieved this home, which has been on tenderhooks since last October, when we learnt you did not figure among the British volunteers that had returned home. The letters we sent were not returned, so all our news of the year has remained in the Spanish post.

Your father has brought your grandfather's library home. It has taken him every single weekend over nearly a year to take it down and pack everything up. Your bedroom and the living room have books from floor to ceiling. He is usually silent, he misses your grandfather, he misses you, and as always, his habit is to read and be silent, he looks for the oldest books, those that have been marked by his dear teacher.

Your sister has grown but she has not put on weight, or at least it doesn't seem more difficult to lift her. Every afternoon before supper I turn on the radio for her —I lean her hand on the speaker's fabric- and she laughs happily at the music, especially when foxtrots are played. In spite of her condition, she smiles often and she lets us know when she likes something or when she doesn't.

Your father agrees with your decision to work to pay your return ticket, and considers that mechanics is a very good profession, and England a good place to develop this. I'm very happy knowing you are surrounded by good people such as Mr Glynn and Mrs Cummins, whose letters too have been our solace in the uneasy months we lived after your departure for Spain.

I'll update you on last year's news of Argentina, as I'm supposing that during those terrible days you could not have heard much about your own country. This is only a summary, your father has put away the newspaper cuttings which he's keeping for when you return.

In February one of your grandfather's friends committed suicide, the writer he supped with one or twice a month until this man showed his support for the September 6th coup; it's likely Leopoldo Lugones could not bear the quantity of blunders carried out by those criminals which he helped and praised. Almost at the same time Ortiz took office, Justo's candidate. As the Vanguardia newspaper wrote, "a change for nothing to change".

We socialists, in spite of the fraud by the Conservatives, have managed to get men such as Palacios and Dickman into Congress. The "progressive" congressmen have other guides such as Ghioldi, and of course all of them are continually criticized by La Nación newspaper and Criterio magazine.

Your father and I believe you should return as soon as possible. The risk of a war since the Germans annexed Czechoslovakia is huge, and you're in Great Britain as a British citizen. If a war should come you might find it difficult, if not impossible, to return…

Your father listens to the BBC every afternoon when he comes home from work, and afterwards he tells me about what he's heard. I don't share his faith in Mr Chamberlain's appeasement policy, I think that to give in again and again ends up encouraging the delirious demands of the Nazi dictator.

I would like to have my sisters' faith to pray to an all-powerful god to prevent another war! But the truth is I'm not very optimistic in this regard.

Sending you all a mother and a father's love for their son.

Mamá

PS. On July 9th this year we'll be having a double celebration: Independence Day's anniversary and your eighteenth birthday!!!!

September 6, 1939

Dear Papá and Mamá,

Our worst fears have been fulfilled. These last days in Poland are nothing but the announcement of what is coming. What I saw the Francoists doing over and over again will now be practiced on a never-before-seen scale. The Nazis' technical superiority will devastate Europe.

Mrs Sylvia is deeply affected by Helena Swanwick's suicide – she's the pacifist whose book Mrs Sylvia sent you last year; it's terrible, but very logical considering the horror that will be taking place.

Poland will be followed by France and of course, then Great Britain, and there's nothing I can do to avoid the call to arms. My desire to return to Argentina is obviously out of my hands now, it's completely up to fate. And based on what I saw in Spain this won't be a brief war, it'll be so cruel it'll horrify future generations.

It would have been so easy to prevent! It would have been enough to support the Spanish Republic… They'll have time for regrets, in the end.

Don Eurwen and Mrs Sylvia are saddened, and besides, Mrs Cummins has every reason to be worried, as her two younger sons are in the East, one of them on a Royal Navy ship. Both of them are already at the battle front, even though the war has yet to begin.

And what will Argentina do? What does President Ortiz say? And people? What do my fellow citizens think?

The truth is I don't want to return to war, but if I'm called up I won't do anything to avoid it.

Please kiss my sister for me, as it's obvious it will be a long time before I'll be able to do it.

All my love,
Gordon

October 3, 1939

Dear Gordon,

We're following the news closely, and some of it with horror. The little news that comes from a devastated Poland really makes our blood run cold.

The Nazis have some support here, even in the government. Last year we felt worried when they flew their flags in the Luna Park stadium, marched in their uniforms and sung their hymns. Afterwards they smashed shop windows saying those shops belonged to Jews. La Nación newspaper, which is not read daily in this house, covered the event and published the personal, signed greeting from the German dictator.

In *Don* López's grocery store and in Vergara's bakery I hear many people speaking against the war, nobody in favour of Hitler.

The British community gathered a few days ago and your father took part when invited by his friends Foster and Meek. You know well that he's not in agreement with Great

Britain but he's much more horrified by the Nazis. He's very worried about your future, your sister's, and the world's…

Your very worried, but loving

Mother

December 27, 1939

Dear Papá and Mamá,

I'm sorry to have to write to you to let you know that this morning I enlisted in the British Army and by tomorrow morning I'll be in their ranks.

I wasn't going to do this, I was going to wait till they called me up, but something terrible has happened in the last few days.

In the Battle of the River Plate, which ended in a British victory, Mrs Sylvia's son died – he was serving on the Achilles as commanding officer of the battery and they were all killed when the Graf Spee fired on them.

To make it even worse, in the Graf Spee's raid in the South Pacific, between November 12 and 14 it sunk the SSM Karthum, a cargo ship that was on its way to India, and Mrs Sylvia's youngest son was working on this ship. Although we have no details –there were no survivors- it's very likely that the captain of the Karthum tried to avoid the Nazi ship from seizing it, as it was carrying military material from Australia to India.

So Mrs Cummins has lost two of her three sons in the war at sea.

Because of this tragedy all I can do is enlist as a volunteer. The week before I reported to the Royal Air Force, but the medical exam showed I was colour-blind –it's a chronic eye condition that makes one confuse colours – and therefore I'm not apt for piloting planes.

I followed *Don* Eurwen's advice and reported to the Royal Army as a mechanic and thanks to my driving license enabling me to drive trucks – a gift from Mr Glynn, who said, "it was an investment because he couldn't drive…" – once I pass my instruction period I'll be made a corporal.

I said nothing about my Spanish experience. I don't want to end up at the battle front, not if I can avoid it.

I imagine you will understand my situation.

Please give my sister a fond kiss and all my love to you.

Your

Gordon.

June 14, 1940

Dear Papá and Mamá,

Although I know Mrs Sylvia has sent you a cable, I've wanted to write a letter myself to tell you I'm all in one piece, with some bruises and physically exhausted, but whole and living.

These have been the most difficult days in my short existence, and since this war began they've definitely been the worst, even more so than all those final days in Spain.

I've seen unthinkable things, prodigiously horrific, all together in a brief lapse of only a few days.

The way the whole British Army Expeditionary Forces' campaign developed was a failure, that was clear in Sudan, but what took place over these last few days I believe will end up changing –not without great effort and blood- how future events evolve.

What I went through between May 25th –which I celebrated on my own, sitting in my truck singing the anthem, watched in astonishment by private Purvis – and June 4th have been the most intense and terrible days I've had to live through.

A very large army being persecuted like a beaten dog by all kinds of ground and air machines, and by a compact army armed to the teeth and hitting at us again and again. None of the English soldiers were remotely prepared to face these superior forces; they weren't able to show, until these last few days, their astounding courage; they simply never had time to get out of their trucks… Fortunately Lord Gort demonstrated his wisdom and level-headedness and instead of launching us into a useless battle in which we would have been destroyed, he preferred an honourable and organized retreat. In the future you will know how much you owe to this old man.

What they should have learnt in Spain they're learning now at a high cost. My comrades who died beneath Franco's bullets and artillery died for nothing.

The fact is that this time luck was on our side; in spite of the human losses, our leaders have found a way to release us from a definite defeat. More than half a million British men and Frenchmen rescued under the falling bombs and bullets. Almost a miracle, if I could believe in them. I was a witness and part of it.

Seeing the courage of my British and French companions, and the nobility and sacrifice around me, leads me to trust that the victory day over the Nazi-Fascists will come. From the air, the latter attacked the columns of civilians who were escaping from the fierce combined attacks of the infantry and tanks, I saw it all. I can't think of all this without recalling my fear and horror.

It's essential to fight them.

As has happened before, chance once again placed somebody I knew in my path.

When the Nazis had already surrounded us at Dunkirk, I again met up with Second Lieutenant Farrington, the young man who helped me return from France to England.

It's a long explanation but I'll sum it up like this: I was assigned to work for him and in that mess we ended up involved in the fighting in the south, east and northeast of the French port, and this helped to stop the Nazis long enough to evacuate most of the BEF.

I believe Farrington is a new friend, a respectable comrade, a fighter worthy of being obeyed. We were probably the last to be evacuated, in Captain W. Tenant's boat —this is how he introduced himself- and when we were lifted aboard there were bagpipers on the bridge making music with a sound stronger than the wind, waves and bombs.

When we arrived at Dover we were handed meat sandwiches, hot soup, coffee or tea to whoever wanted them, cigarettes and many cheers.

And the faces… my dear ones, I'll never forget the faces of that multitude of comrades… all of them looking the same, smiling their relief and hope in brotherhood. My smile was no different than anybody else's, united with all those around me in the certainty that we had been saved from one big battle.

But I also know that as from that day on we are one, we are united by a destiny and we won't be defeated, possibly with some crazy sacrifices.

I can't think in political terms, I only dozed a little on the boat; I spent the whole day with Mrs Sylvia whose tears of relief are, I'm sure, the same as yours.

All I can say is that Mr Churchill's speech in Parliament yesterday afternoon sums up everything I feel, what we all feel. And I subscribe to his warning of wanting to give "this miracle of liberation the attributes of a victory"; history will eventually tell us why they weren't able to destroy us when they had us trapped.

We'll fight even if we're left on our own, even if we're the only nation on earth to confront the Fascists; with everything we have at hand, wherever we are and whatever the conditions, we'll fight again and again, we'll never give in.

Please write to me, I'm not sure what destiny has in store for me, I'm still a corporal in the British Army and it won't be long before I'm reincorporated into active service. Second Lieutenant Farrington is going to request that I be assigned to him and it seems he has the contacts in the military bureaucracy to manage this.

A hug for you three, my family, my dearest loved ones in all the Universe.

Your son

Gordon Evan

P.S. Please give my sister a kiss and a brotherly hug from me.

June 8, 1940

Dear son,

For the second time in my life I'm obliged to write to give you bad news. The happiness I felt on receiving Mrs Sylvia's cable on the 6th was wiped away by the infinite sadness that hit me that same afternoon, when they came to pick me up, to tell me that your father had died.

Unfortunately, because he followed the news in the newspapers and on the radio –the BBC report at 7:30 pm was essential to him- this affected his health seriously, to the point that on May 29th he felt very ill before supper.

The pharmacist on Soler St. was very kind and allowed me to use the telephone to call Dr Rodrigué –who was one of your grandfather's friends- and he arrived home within the hour. This good man had your father interned in the British Hospital in Barracas district.

I can't even describe to you what these last days have been since then.

How was I to divide myself? With who could I leave your sister? Who do I not attend to? Plus the deep anguish I was feeling in not knowing what you were going through or your fate.

I'm not complaining, dear son, neither am I reproaching your absence because I know this situation we're living through is all beyond your will. But in this time of anguish and pain I miss you so…

From the beginning, the doctor's diagnosis was not good. Papá had had a complicated stroke.

This man, Dr. Rodrigué, was a saint. He brought me a nurse to take care of Cristina, he drove me in his car back and forth to Barracas and when I wanted to pay him he told me he was'nt going to take money from his dear friend Maestro Porrá's family at all. He even paid for the nurse…

On the morning of the 6th the cable arrived confirming you had survived the Dunkirk battle, and shortly after midday the doctor came to pick me up to give me the terrible news.

The doctor accompanied me and helped me on the spiritual side as well as with all the paperwork. When your grandfather died, my sister Nora's husband, Dr Danuzzio, handled all the bureaucracy, so if it hadn't been for this very Good Samaritan I would have felt even more lost.

We held the wake in the Holy Trinity Church and he's resting in the British Cemetery in Lavallol.

So, relief and sorrow on the same day.

I love you and I'm so happy to know you're alive.

Kisses from

Mamá

July 7, 1940

Dear Mamá,

I can't believe that life is being so cruel to me, to us, in this way. What did I do? What wrongs have I caused? I would like to believe in God to insult him personally.

When I left for Spain I believed —and I still believe- that I went to fight on the side of reason and justice, and in those bitter days I lost my grandfather.

I survived the miracle of Dunkirk and very happily I wrote the letter you will receive immediately before this one… when I had already posted it we received the cable with the tragic news of my father's death.

There's nothing I can do from here, more than what I've written in the cable I just sent you: I have no more tears to shed. My father was a good man who deserved to live many happy years by your side.

I can't find words to comfort you because there are none; I'm not going to tell you to be strong, Mother, because it would be asking you to be something you already are, what you have already given, but please forgive me for not being by your side at this terrible time.

Mrs Sylvia, who has already written to you, has been accompanying me as if we were family, and she has her own grief… Does history consume so much human pain? Ask for so much strength from women?

I can't guarantee I will survive what is to come but believe me I will try with every cell of my body, each second of my conscience, each gram of my will, to return to your side to hug you.

Your son who loves you,

Gordon

Bombay, March 1941

Dear Mrs Sylvia,

What can I say? Since our arrival thirty days ago I've been trying to resort to all my knowledge of languages to give you a light description of all I've experienced the last two months.

Ever since we left England we have had to travel in numerous circles to avoid the Nazi wolves and there's not much more I can tell you about this: secrecy is also a weapon. I saw actions at sea and believe me, it's so frightening as to make one crazy. Not all of us who left arrived, but we did arrive.

Seeing the view before me, it looks like Kipling was too short-sighted and ignorant, a bad translator of the scents and visuals that impact our senses; his descriptions and images hardly reach the first rung of reality: from the ports to the deposits, from the main streets to the suburbs, each small fraction of what one can see is amazing.

And you know very well how much I like old Rudyard!! I'm still looking for the words to describe the multitudes and faces, costumes and buildings, the smells and colours, noises and silences, birds and insects.

We are not free to come and go wherever we'd like with our permits: many Hindus don't like us and many directly sympathise with our enemies (the enemy of my enemy…) but I'll find a way to explore everything I can.

They promoted Tony... and me. With my new rank as a sergeant I have certain responsibilities: two corporals who are, believe me, right out of Conrad's inkwell; one is half English, blue eyes and dark skin, born in Burma, with an impressive tattoo of the Goddess Kali –the one with the many arms full of weapons, the goddess of assassins- on his back; and an agreeable and very well educated young Muslim –he must be the same age as Captain Farrington- with a very good sense of humour.

When I hear the rest of the officers… I fully understand the little love the inhabitants have for the British. This is not the case of Mr Farrington, from whom I've never heard a negative comment about anybody regarding their social or racial origin, he's a truly just man. Other officers treat the natives really badly, Mr Farrington doesn't behave like this with them. If you're good at your work he's noticeably respectful, if you're not you'll be justly punished - in general this is appreciated by those under him.

My dear Madam, I'll end this now so I can send it off this very afternoon. I'll write again soon.

Sincerely yours,

Gordon Evans

Bombay, March 1941

Dear Mamá,

After nearly six months of a training so intense that more than once I thought of resigning from the Special Corps, then a day like any other they gave us the order to embark without even giving us time to say goodbye to anyone, and even less to send off any letters or cables.

We sailed for 27 days and we crossed the path of a submarine ~~which sunk two of the ships in our convoy but we understand that this was paid in kind, the deep sea charges from the destroyers did their work.~~

We arrived at the beginning of last month and we have been going through an intense process they call "acclimatisation"; Europeans fear everything: the water, the sun, the food, the insects, the locals.

I find this place fascinating; it brings back memories of when my grandfather and I travelled to Jujuy, the people's dark skin, the colours of their clothes, the smell of the multitudes.

We are in the plains but many times when I look north, I see the mountains clearly; the air is light and full of scents, from the most marvellous (species and fragrances of essences) to the most disagreeable ones – in the native neighbourhoods the bathrooms drain out onto the street.

They haven't allowed us yet to walk freely along the streets in order to avoid any confrontations; people accept us only because they can do nothing about it.

As soon as I can, I'll try and go out without my uniform, so as not to call attention to myself.

Mamá, I want this letter to go out with the next mail so I'll say goodbye; I'll soon send you a letter with my impression of some outing.

Please give all my love to my sister,

Your son, Gordon Evans

Naples, Italy, 1943

Dear Mrs Sylvia,

So here I am, all in one piece. You must surely know this because the boys in uniform and a telegram have not called at your door.

I believe you already know how things went in Asia. India has been secured, but the rest of the possessions are still being fought over.

We flew from India to North Africa several months ago in support of the victorious and bloodied African army, and we defeated the fascists with no national distinction; but I must point out that the Italians don't show much resistance, they seem to be happy to end the fight, some of them have been here since 1935 when the Duce attacked Ethiopia.

The immense Libyan Desert gave me some answers on T.E. Lawrence. I understood what he must have found in the Saudi Arabian desert. Our raids –sometimes up to six days and nights long and sometimes 900 kms. to the interior of the territory controlled by the Nazis- gave me a perspective of the beauty of this large land of dust and sand. It's not empty, it's full of life, day and night… oh, Mrs Sylvia, I so wish you could see it!!! I have no words to describe my feelings… except my awareness of our place in the Universe is so clear.

The next time we have tea together I'll tell you about some of the lessons I found in the thick jungle of Malaysia which have expanded and filled me. I'll get through the war without loss to my mind, soul or body.

Now, returning to the chronological tale: we finally encountered the American and French armies in Algeria – the Nazis left Africa and we followed them. I read what I've written and it appears so simple and yet it was so extremely difficult.

Anyway, we jumped over to Southern Italy and they were waiting for us with open arms. We had to fight, but the Italians were fed up with the fascists, particularly the Nazis who are so cruel. We'll open our way to Rome from here. The war has not ended yet, but we now know we can defeat them. Like we defeated Rommel!!!

When I say Americans… You'll laugh, but some of our men don't like them because the Americans are so proud… I've spoken with several of them… They are very kind and innocent… and so fierce in battle!!! Among them many coloured boys, just as I saw at Dunkirk in the French Colonial army - and many young white boys; they remind me of myself during my days in Spain.

They are rich: they have food, chocolate, cigarettes, their vehicles, weapons, everything is strong and designed for this brutal war.

In Africa, when our old Canadian Chevrolet truck finally deserted us, they assigned us a new type of car, small, light, strong. Officially it's called a GP Vehicle, but the troops call it a Jeep; it runs through the desert as if it were on a cobbled street, and it's very easy to drive on any road. I'm going to buy myself one when the war ends.

I'd like this to be soon, but even once we take Rome it won't be tomorrow.

My dear lady, I must go and work now. Just after this letter I'm sending one to my mother but it will take a long time to arrive, if it ever does, so would you be so kind and send her a cable telling her I'm in one piece, and send my love to her and my sister? I'll be eternally grateful for your care and affection.

Sincerely yours,

Gordon Evans.

January, 1943

Dear Mamá,

I don't know when this letter will reach you, as you know it must first go through our censor and I don't suppose there're many who can translate the Spanish.

I imagine that this very long time without any news can't have been at all good for you, but I hope you may have taken to that old British saying, "no news, good news".

Of course I've thought about you two, but we spent a long time in the Burmese jungle, a fascinating, beautiful place but also terribly cruel. I've seen things… Do you remember the illustration of the book "Treasures of Youth" in which a young child was used to capture a crocodile on the Nile? Well, on the Asian coasts and in their great rivers lives an even larger one. I captured one that was seven metres long… Our unit ate its meat for almost 10 days!!! And we only cooked the tail (the rest was very lean and hard). Its meat is white, with a strong fish smell but its texture is similar to chicken, with more fibre.

Grandfather would have loved to have seen that monster… According to the natives it's capable of swimming thousands of kilometres to the ocean… The Brits don't believe this, they say these are lies made up by ignorant people, and that crocodiles only live in the rivers… The fact is that I was lucky, it's a very impressive beast.

I finally got onto a plane for a longer time than just a jump! Not long after we regrouped in West India, Captain Farrington received orders for our unit to take a flight. My experience up till then with planes had been brief and intense, when they trained us to jump with parachutes – I jumped over 30 times – but to travel in a plane… that's really impressive.

We boarded two Avro Yorks – which is the civilian version of the Lancaster, the plane that's floored Hitler- and we flew in a formation accompanied by two Lancasters from India to the south of Egypt. We flew for 24 hours, we only landed to load fuel in secret places in the middle of the desert. Imagine, a trip that in any other way would have taken us more than 15 days on a dangerous journey by ship!!! We were accompanied by the Lancasters because there's a Nazi mobile air unit which operates somewhere between Persia and India, and we could have been attacked; but fortunately nothing like that happened.

We flew over the desert, which I quickly discovered is not all the same, on the contrary it's an incredible palette of colours, from a loud yellow through a huge amount of shades of ocres and reds in which now and again one can see a green stain.

The noise of the motors and the movement in the air does affect you, some of the boys were sick and had some awfully bad moments but for me the trip was incredible; I'm sure that in the future people will be travelling like this all over the world!!!

I really miss your news, but as we're constantly on the move, I know that although you must be very willing, letters take an awfully long time to find their destination; I think it's probably faster and safer to send them to Mrs Sylvia and she, who's so kind, will send them on to me.

Please kiss my sister with all my love, I hope that we three can soon be together.

Your son,

Gordon.

Remedios de Escalada, August 1943

Dear son,

Here we are doing fine, waiting for winter to be over, prices have gone up and sometimes the kerosene for the heater and the stove is scarce; the world war doesn't affect our lives too much, beyond these small bothers – a lack of or the expense of basic products such as fuel, sugar, oil and flour – and only the newspapers and some street disturbances remind us that the whole planet is plunged into that horror.

Don Aurelio the greengrocer told me that last week in downtown Lomas de Zamora some St Albans students got into a fight with those from the Temperley Deutsche Schule, who had broken the shop windows of the Sufferansky opticians and painted some graffiti against Jews on the pavement; the St Albans boys got involved because the policemen who were supposed to guard the street were not in their places.

Everything is topsy turvy in our country again.

At the beginning of last June we had a coup d'etat which ousted President Castillo; you know that I would never support any form of violent seizure of power, but it was very clear that the regime installed since 1930 in itself formed a macabre expression of the shamelessness of powerful men; without this coup, this group's candidate Patrón Costas would have ended up as President… So while blood is being shed in other parts of the world, here Argentina is obliged to choose between a group of rich bandits and some gold-braided military men who attend daily mass - those who really admire the Axis and all willing to "act as guardians" to the people's rights.

Ah, if your father and grandfather were here, how indignant they would be… The years go by and I still miss them both, our conversations after Sunday lunch until tea-time and even longer…

The truth is that the new government keeps on surprising us every day with ridiculous measures; just to give you an idea: they want to substitute the "lunfardo" words in tango lyrics because they consider them rude…

As usual I've wanted to include a few pieces on Argentina, but as you see, I'm not sure they're really encouraging.

I follow the BBC news in Spanish always, and occasionally listen to the Moscow Radio report; since last February Hitler met up with the same "general" that defeated Napoleon, the Nazis will have to return the same way they came…

Isn't it all terrible? So many young men sacrificed, so many properties destroyed… If the world affairs were led by a woman, this or any other war wouldn't have lasted very long.

What I wouldn't give to have you back here with us.

Well, my son, take care and try not to run any risks, I'm expecting you back home.

Fond kisses from your mother

Josefa P. de Evans

Brindisi, January 1, 1944

Dear Mamma!

That's what the Italians say. These people are such survivors! Just like a house of cards, the structure of power that Mussolini had built since 1924 has fallen into our hands; and suddenly, not a single Fascist!!! If only the Germans were the same, all this would already have been solved… but no. They are obstinate, proud, stubborn and as soldiers, fearsome.

Adolf looked ahead, brought in the troops from the Russian rout, he drew a line on the ground and there they are, clinging to the Italian land and holding off three potent armies – four, if we count the Polish battalions- without retreating an inch. To think that when we disembarked in Sicily everything looked like it was going to end soon and successfully… I was about to think that the war would be over quickly, but it's not, the Nazis are going to drag us all over northern Europe, they're not going to surrender, they're only going to retreat when they have no other way out, when they've sacrificed many of us on their Führer's altar.

The North Americans… What strange people, what an obscene quantity of material they use! The French are in a worse condition than we are –as you must guess, they live off North American charity and our few leftovers, De Gaulle's "Free French" haven't a cent for their troops – they look at the North Americans and shake their heads rather enviously.

There're some Poles amongst us too, the only thing they want is revenge on the Nazis for what was done to them in '39; and we, the British, have brought with us people from all over the Empire: Aussies, Kiwis and the fierce Maoris; Hindus, Canadians and at least one Argentine (myself)!!!?? Did you know there are Brazilians with us as well? There's an air unit that has been talked about all over the front, so much so that they've practically wiped the Luftwaffe -which had caused us so much damage- from the sky!!!

I clearly remember grandfather's stories, which he had heard from his friend Mansilla, regarding Brazilians' courage – as well as Paraguayans' – in the Paraguayan war so I'm not surprised, but I'm glad that the North Americans are surprised: they're convinced that blacks don't have the same skill or courage as whites… I'm sure they'd love to count on Korrum and Senghor, my two corporals from India.

And it's strange that they should think like this because many of their soldiers are "boys", as they call their blacks, who have already shown their courage… And what about the French Africans, especially those from Algeria and Morocco… I don't have the best memories of them in Spain – we were so afraid when we had to confront the Riff troops… Although fortunately today they are on our side…

I've been re-reading what I wrote and asked myself what interest can you have in my soldier stories… but the fact is that I've been in these wars for so long, I don't think I remember what life is like out of a uniform…

Do I need to remind you how much grandfather loved Italy? Here in the South, after having visited Sicily and Naples, I now understand why. The Neapolitan language is understandable for anyone who speaks Spanish, while the Italians are incomprehensible to the Anglo-Saxons.

Neither the Captain nor the boys can understand the Italian spirit, and I feel so at home. They like to talk, express themselves, tell stories, they are hospitable as well as dishonest, they're used to surviving, yesterday they were total fascists, today they are fervent followers of the Allies. I feel very tender towards them, they've suffered, their lands are exhausted and they want to emigrate… Weren't they who populated our country?

It's strange how they react when they hear me speaking in Spanish, trying to sound like *Don* Aurelio… No English speaker can sound like that; they smile at me and try to be my friend; they expect the North American generosity and abundance –their food, chocolate, cigarettes, alcohol is boundless - to also overflow through us and truly, Mamma, I try and help, because if you could only see the poverty this war has caused…

So, Mamma mia, kiss my sister and trust that all this will end well.

With much love, your son

Gordon Evans

Brindisi, January, 1944

Dear *Don* Eurwen,

Your last letter arrived safely… But I could only read the first paragraphs and greetings and good wishes… Ha ha ha! I can perfectly well imagine what you wrote must have lit a fire under the censors!

At the beginning of the year I was so sure this war was about to finish soon… and all that changed so quickly.

I can understand you so well now after having seen so much since 1937… As I can't go back, I have to go forward.

I have to work really hard not to hate the Germans, as I do the Nazis. You fought against them in the last war and probably know what I feel. Monte Cassino is there and we can't get them out, not without many men dying. And it doesn't matter if they're the green devils or the armoured infantry, who are nothing more than the survivors of the Stalingrad disaster, those left by our Red partners, but what leftovers…

What makes them that way? Their food? Their drink? Something in the air? Sometimes I find myself thinking that we should act like the Romans and get rid of all the Germans on Earth, they are so tough and such fighters… Many of us respect them as much as we fear them.

We will win the day, no doubt, but Europe will be drowned in a sea of blood, much greater yet than what has already taken place.

I used to think that the issue was the Nazis, but no, after a few days at Monte Cassino, I'm not sure what to think.

As usual, there will be no news for some time. And as always, I'll request that now and again you call up Mrs Cummins, she will be very grateful to you and afterwards she will contact my mother to calm her.

Both of you have been a blessing in my life, both with wonderful hearts and powerful souls, both have been the father and mother of a lonely boy very far from his home. It doesn't matter what happens to me in the next few days till the end of the war, my heart will always be full of gratitude for you.

Your sincere friend,

Gordon

Buenos Aires, June 10, 1944

Dear son,

No bad news has arrived, so I'm supposing you're alive because I can't imagine you in any other way.

I don't know where you are since your last letter from Italy… Although Mrs Sylvia's letters arrive regularly and with much encouragement, she doesn't have any news from you either; but her optimism and trust in your strength and your fighter skills assuage my bitterness and fear.

I think the latest news of the Allied landing in France is the most positive news… Although more than once the newspapers have made mistakes regarding the end of the war, now they all agree that the Germans and their allies are in retreat. There is nothing I yearn more for than the end of the war, to have you back here with us.

Here things are happening in our own way; the military government is a cat fight, from Farrel to Rawson… the only constant voice is Colonel Perón's, who gives very pretty speeches but persecutes the communists, the socialists and anarchists as if he were Justo's son.

On the other hand, he favours syndicates without any apparent political membership, and receives them publicly.

He's the strong man in the government, accumulating positions – Vice President, War Secretary, Labour Secretary- and he gives speeches over the radio that persuade many people to support him enthusiastically.

Old Socialist friends such as Dickman have approached him… Yet he reminds me a great deal of 'Il Duce'…

They say there will be elections when the Armed Forces have "cleaned up" the country's politics… Which is the same as Uriburu said in 1930 and we saw what happened, fraud then more fraud.

Farrington and Gordon in North Africa

I don't think anything good will come out of all this… But there's very little I can do.

Fortunately, Mrs Sylvia sends me your salary punctually so we don't go through too many bad times except for those imposed by the war itself, in which we aren't participating… But it is taking our wheat, milk, meat, which have all gone up in price, as well as kerosene and even firewood.

On the other hand, all the hustle and bustle has created work… You can see it in the trams, full of people every afternoon, as are the trains… Isn't it terrible that a war brings us its benefits? Nothing good can come of this.

My son, I must stop and cook supper, I've taken advantage of your sister's siesta to write to you. I'd like to do it much more often, and I also love to receive your news.

Loving you with all my heart,

.

Paris, December 19, 1944

Dear Mamá,

I suppose you must have received the cable I asked Mrs Sylvia to send you with my news… Now I have a little more time, so I'll give you a summary of my life over the last year.

For reasons that you obviously understand, my departure from Italy couldn't include a single detail regarding our destination, as our mission was absolutely secret.

We parachuted down behind German lines into Occupied France and from there we prepared the support for last June's landing.

I'm not going to burden you with details that are of no interest to you, but I must tell you that the liaison of our mission was that French officer which you may recall I mentioned to you, the one I met at Dunkirk.

Once again a coincidence has crossed my path in the form of a person linked to my past. How many more times will this happen?

Captain Ragon, now Commander Ragon, has also been an excellent host and friend.

So our difficult mission was simplified. We fulfilled it, not without sacrifices: some good and courageous boys in our unit did not have my same luck.

The war has not ended, it's true, and as I thought, the Germans will not surrender, not without devastating their own country; the truth is that they have retreated almost entirely from France; Paris has been liberated -fortunately without loss- and the Captain, the boys and I have been rewarded with six consecutive leave days in this marvellous city. We are near London, but it is not included in our short holidays.

The war continues, in spite of our efforts and sacrifices to end it.

Ah, Maman, as the French say, if you could see this city, if you could feel the renewed happiness of these people who have lived nearly five years of the terrible dark night of occupation, the shame of a treacherous government.

People on the street smile, they hug us, they all thank us equally, there's a festive air in spite of the cold, the cafes are open until dawn –although there isn't any real coffee to drink, they manage very well with a substitute they call "chicoree". Would that be the chicory that *Don* Angel sells? And food is expensive… I think, Maman, that the French are the most optimistic people in the world. Haven't they been hungry? That's good, they say, the women are slim and prettier than ever. There's no fuel? That's not a problem, they've manufactured taxis that are actually bicycles… That's how it goes, they're the epitome of grandfather's saying, "When life gives you lemons, make lemonade…"

I can't imagine these people having passively born the Nazi occupation, how difficult it must have been for them… the Resistance tried their best and the Nazis filled up the jails and cemeteries.

Yesterday something happened to me that was incredibly moving, twice over.

In a coffee shop there was a group of soldiers in Allied uniforms but different to the French and North Americans, and my attention was caught because of the noise they were making.

I approached them and immediately recognised their accents, they were from Spain.

To my surprise, when I looked more closely at their uniforms, I saw they wore the three-coloured Republican emblem, and I felt cold shivers up my spine.

When I addressed them in Spanish they were all –eight or nine of them- silent and they looked back at me, until one of them noticed the small three-pointed star that Tony has forced me to wear on my beret –an order I'll never be able to thank him enough for; the soldier shouted out in a clear Andalusian accent: "Bloody hell, he's an International!!" And they all, every single one, hugged me like a brother, a comrade-in-arms, a friend whom you haven't seen in a long time but is never forgotten.

I cried, Mamá, and they did too, feeling no shame.

We toasted each other. Someone in the group shouted, "For those fallen in Jarama!" And we'd all shout, "Cheers!", then another "For the fallen in Madrid!" and another, "For the fallen in Belchite", "For the fallen in Teruel", and we went on naming each and every battle, in which one or another had fought.

And I say twice over because when we were going through this rite, three young men in RAF uniforms approached us timidly, also speaking in Spanish, and asked if they could join us in the toast.

And once again I felt shivers down my back, mind and soul (which weren't confused by alcohol!) because I recognised those young men had my mother's and my grandfather's accent.

Mamá, I didn't know, but there is an entire contingency of young Argentine men in the RAF, and the British community there has paid -with great effort and work- for a large number of planes…

I looked at my Spanish comrades but I didn't have to ask permission to include those brave men… They were deluged with questions, everybody wanting to know more about those volunteers who came from so far away.

It was a marvellous party in which each one talked about his far-off land, about his loved ones.

Tomorrow we will all have lunch together again, Tony wants to meet the Argentine pilots as well as the brave Spaniards.

Mother, I've written enough for today; if all goes well, as soon as I'm demobbed I will return to hug both you and my sister.

With a very full heart, I kiss you lovingly, your son

Gordon Evans

Saarbrücken, May 12, 1945

Dear *don* **Eurwen,**

I'll bet you have been celebrating the last four days, just as we have… The nightmare –at least in black and white- has come to an end.

But the end of the war has not been the end of our work and even less so, of the problems. The majority of the Germans are happy and relieved that fighting is over.

Even so, we've been obliged to be actively involved contending with the extreme fanatic Nazi elements who still believe in the war. There are snipers who now and again shoot at us.

Rumours fly around along with the news blackout and uncertainties broadcast over the radio. Everybody -we and they- go back and forth asking what's going on.

Has Hitler died? I hope so. The rumour of his suicide has started a kind of suicide epidemic among the Nazis and I must force myself to feel compassion for them.

I truly fight against those feelings. Every morning I wake up grateful to whatever keeps the Universe in one piece and me on it, and every day I go even deeper inside to find my compassion for all of us and I train and push myself to include those who until a few days ago were my enemies. Just as other boys pray, I try and keep myself conscious regarding those feelings all day. Sometimes it's not easy.

The Germans talk of a secret weapon which will be the same type as they used to bomb London, which will be launched from the Eastern countries that are not yet in Allied hands, from tiny Bavaria, the serpent's egg.

These last weeks have been the worst of all. We all knew it was over except for the Nazis.

Why did they resist so much? We're now beginning to understand, with the news regarding concentration camps all over German territory … There was one right here…

The destruction level is amazing. There's no power or drinking water in very large areas, food is scarce and most of the cities are no higher than 60 cms. It could have been worse if they had done what we found here: the water and the power plants ready to be destroyed, but they didn't get to it.

What kind of regime is capable of destroying its own country? Are they so evil that they would send their own people into the Middle Ages?

Captain Farrington is a very intelligent person, he had me thinking that from the ashes of war there would be an opportunity for capitalism, the rebuilding of Germany will be a business venture. We're not proud of this, many good people and thousands of innocent ones have been sacrificed in the name of the God of Money.

Have you still kept that brandy? I don't yet know when, but you can be sure I'll be returning to the island, and if my luck changes, I'll be able to go back home. Keep it for our toast to my freedom.

Sincerely, your friend

Gordon.

Cardiff, May 24, 1945

Dear Gordon,

We're all celebrating the news. The end of the European chapter of the war has been a source of happiness and joy; I talked to Mrs Sylvia last Monday to tell her about your last letter and she in turn was going to cable your family to let them know that you're still in one piece.

I haven't been back to London since the summer of 1942, but the newspapers and cinemas have been showing at length the consequences of the Nazi bombing.

Ever since the attack on the school in the winter of 1940 I'd been thinking about returning to Cardiff; so when the chronic lack of petrol left us out of the transport business –the public has preferred the large companies that benefitted from rationing to Glynn & Evans- I then returned to my city, in spite of the bad memories it brings.

As all the old people around me, I've been anxiously waiting for the end of this terrible war, and contrary to my custom, I joined in with the crowds' celebration.

Have we learnt our lesson? I hope so…

The news on the abominations committed by the Nazis have left everybody speechless. How could they? Those responsible must be judged by a court of judges representing humanity, and especially, the good Germans. I don't believe in generalizing about these people being evil. The first victims of the Nazi regime were, undoubtedly, the good German people who will be suffering the tragedy of the devastation for a much longer time than all that committed towards the end of May.

I'd really like to see you again soon, and also, to both dive once again into the transport and mechanical repair business.

It's very likely you'll be discharged soon, considering you've served longer and beyond normal duty.

Well, young man, just a little more effort to settle the times in which we live, and you'll still have to be careful and watch your step.

See you soon,

Your sincere friend

Eurwen Glynn

Berlin, June 1st, 1945

Dear Mrs Sylvia,

We've finally stepped into the evil nest.

I should be happy but I'm not. Nothing has been left standing except for some of the regime's main buildings. For many kilometres around the city there's not a single house to be seen.

I practice my little German as much as I can, but I don't think I'll be hired as a translator, not yet anyway!!

Most of us are satisfied with what we see. A corporal not under my supervision, Ian Donovan -who lost part of his family in the bombing of Coventry- says often how happy he is that "the 'sausages' have got what they deserved."

I think the law of retaliation (Lex Talianis) is just as evil as Nazism. As *Don* Eurwen says, "The policy of an eye for an eye will lead us to a world of the blind."

Frequently we see crowds of small children, maybe 3 years old, rummaging through our rubbish for something to eat. Most of them are orphans. General hunger is staring us in the face. Dickens would have written a huge book on the current destruction and misery in Berlin.

For now we're the guests of our Russian allies, who in this war have lost a whole country; they're feared and hated by all.

The Soviets govern very harshly, but they'll soon share power with us. Our work is still dangerous. We're in charge of searching for the mid-level SS command. The regular army has nothing to fear from our activity; the Nazis who're hidden but active have been calling on the people to "resist" the invaders (us). But the Germans are as tired as we of the war.

A friend who has been an observer in the northern region -Dresden, Hamburg and Bremen- says our blanket bombing has literally left those cities with buildings only 60 cms. high, such is the devastation.

And the death camps…

What horror we've demolished through our sacrifices…

Two days ago I had a pleasant meeting; you'll probably recall our German guest in the days previous to the war, Robbi Brecher. He's working for the high command as a translator. He still has grateful memories of you. Just as us, he's busy and on the move, we only had time for a couple of cups of tea and a few cigarettes.

Don Eurwen already let me know that you sent a cable to my loved ones in Argentina, so once again, thank you for all these years of friendship and support.

In hope of seeing you soon,

Sincerely yours,

Gordon Evans

Berlin, June 5, 1945

Dear Mamá,

I hope you can forgive me for the delay in sending you my news in a more direct way, but as from the beginning of the end of the war I've begun several letters which, because the events I'm involved in change so quickly, they became obsolete. And as I know Mrs Sylvia sent you a cable with my news, I've been postponing my son's duty until I find a sufficiently quiet time to concentrate completely on you and my sister.

We've been assured that very soon they'll give us an extensive leave to return to Great Britain, which has me hoping I might be discharged soon. There's nothing that enthuses me more than to be going home finally.

If you could see the horror that this war has brought to the Germans themselves… There's almost nothing left standing and it seems that in the days prior to surrendering they were preparing to destroy the little that had remained: water and power plants, some bridges and main highways. Imagine, Mamá, the degree of craziness of these people, leaving their own country completely destroyed.

Some of my companions don't hide how pleased they are about the devastation we found. Perhaps because I'm not English, perhaps because a long time ago I learnt the value of compassion or because grandfather's lessons are very present for me, the truth is that I couldn't help feeling sad at all I see.

I think this war was the product of a large number of factors which Nazism used to their advantage. A few days ago we detained an SS Mayor who tried to bribe us with a great amount of gold, as if all the crimes they committed could be paid off with that precious metal.

I understood then what they were, nothing more than delinquents who had jumped into power just to get rich without ever measuring the damage or atrocities they would be committing to reach their goal.

I suppose you know already about the horror of the concentration camps… The main victims of Nazism have been the Germans themselves, because the people inside those horrendous camps were German citizens. Teachers, doctors, nurses, office workers, musicians… What they did in other countries like Poland, Russia and Czechoslovakia, they first did in their own country; this horror has lasted almost thirteen years and hundreds of thousands of dead all over the planet were necessary to put an end to this. And they were no more than common bandits…

How are things in Argentina? What has been the impact of the end of the war in Europe? According to what the North Americans say, the end of the war in Asia is also near… I don't think there's been anything more anxiously wished for than the end of this damned war.

I hope my next letter will be sent to you from Great Britain, and what's more, I hope I can let you know about my expected return trip home.

Mamá, all my love to you and my sister.

From your son,

Gordon

Barnet, August 8, 1945

Dear Mamá,

We were finally given the first long furlough since the end of the war in Europe; we arrived the day before yesterday and the truth is all I've done is sleep non-stop these last two days –and for the first time since those days in Paris- in a comfortable bed, with a clean bathroom; I think I've also bathed at least five times.

Mrs Sylvia has been busy filling my stomach; the rationing going on in Britain is not felt in this house: the productive vegetable garden and the clever hands of the owner of this house have brought in an abundance of vegetables, fruit, eggs, chicken and rabbit meat. It's true that the sugar and tea have become scarce, but to my surprise, among my things there was a packet of *yerba mate* –which must be at least 5 years old- but as it was kept in a tin given to me by grandfather, it's still reasonably tasty. And you know *mate* must be sipped without sugar.

So here I am, Mamá, having scrambled eggs for breakfast, toast with raspberry jam and half a kettle of water for *mate*… Mrs Cummins doesn't quite want to sip *mate*, but I think as time goes by…

My furlough is long, two months; I have every hope that we'll be definitely discharged by the end of this period.

Mamá! Mrs Sylvia has just called me to listen to the radio, because all programmes were interrupted with the announcement that Japan has finally surrendered unconditionally, as a consequence of a new type of bomb that was dropped, capable of a level of destruction unknown until today…

This is terrible. I was tired of seeing the effect of conventional bombing, which is incredibly destructive. The only hope I have is that humanity will no longer attempt to destroy itself in this way; maybe in the future young men will not have to go through the horrors I've survived.

London is full of the scars of this war, although they're working intensely to cover them; even though English people are not very passionate –therefore, less susceptible to be vengeful- people in general are satisfied with the level of destruction in Germany.

I heard someone on the train bringing me to Enfield that we should make it disappear from the face of the Earth, including all their citizens.

Isn't it terrible that people come to think in this way? If we did this, how different would we be from the Nazis and their crimes against all the people in Europe?

I don't want to be a Nazi, I've been fighting since age 16 to remove them from power, eight years of horror and filth, pain and fear, doubt and sadness and today, in spite of all that I've lived, I've no regrets, I believe it was worth it, that my battle was fair.

But I didn't fight to become an executioner.

I hope an international tribune will be formed to dispense justice, and that in the future those that use violence, torture and crime as government instruments must be made to face the consequences of their acts.

The press is totally absorbed by the war and there's no place for news from Argentina. Would it be too much for you to send me some newspapers? I hope I can return soon and I'd like to know what has been happening in my country.

Europe is immersed in an economic crisis that will get worse as peace settles and I don't think there'll be a place for me.

Don Eurwen moved to Cardiff during the war, I suppose that within the next few days I'll go and visit him. My good friend wants us to go back into the business we tried before the war; I don't dislike the idea of being a mechanic and driving a truck, it's a good job… But I miss you two.

Mamá, I hope I can see you soon, or at least receive extensive news from you.

Affectionately, your son

Gordon Evans.

Remedios de Escalada, August 18, 1945

Dear son,

Yesterday your letter of the 8th arrived, the postman gave it to me mentioning the extraordinary speed of letters sent by airmail and how satisfied he was with the end of the war and its result.

He's a decent man, and he's been bringing our correspondence for about ten years, so when he knew you were fighting in the war in Spain he mentioned his support. Since then, every time a letter came from you he'd change his rounds in order to bring it to me first. Isn't that a kind gesture?

The news about the end of the war in Europe and in Asia has been well received by most people, although of course, there are exceptions. There have been celebrations, masses and festivities everywhere – I was invited to several of them but of course, I couldn't attend. Who would look after your sister?

I'll send you cuttings from Crítica, La Nación, La Prensa, la Vanguardia. *Don* Aurelio the grocer (who is also a comrade) and who receives newspapers to wrap up his goods, has been kind enough to separate those pages that may interest you; so the actual destiny of the papers you will be receiving was as wrapping for eggs, potatoes and onions.

My letter won't get to you as promptly as yours here because due to its volume, I'll have to send it to you by boat, but you'll be well informed.

The end of the war brought me contradictory feelings.

On the one hand, an enormous happiness knowing you're safe and sound and that you'll no longer be running risks. On the other, my horror when I saw the photos –La Nación published a supplement on the fall of Berlin and all the newspapers have published images of the Japanese cities devastated by the "atomic bomb" – there are no limits.

If this new weapon falls into the hand of people like the Nazis, what sort of future can we expect? I can't help feeling fear for the future when I think of this.

Your sister is very well, although it would be good for her to be outside in the fresh air, even on sunny winter days. She's grown a lot, but it's not difficult for me to sit her up in bed.

Do you think you'll be discharged soon? Twelve years is a long time for a mother not to see her son.

As I'm sending you many newspaper cuttings I won't make any political comments; we go from one state of siege to another, we're feeling the lack of some products, or they're expensive, such as sugar and kerosene.

Col. Perón has more and more supporters, including even among Socialists or in the Radical party; now he also appears in the gossip magazines because of a friendship there appears to be between him and a radio and film star.

Just like Mrs Sylvia, I have my small vegetable garden and some chickens, which make our life a little easier. *Don* Aurelio very kindly exchanges some eggs and vegetables for others –like potatoes, sweet potatoes and onions- which I can't grow because I don't have enough room; as you can see, we don't have any major problems.

Also someone always comes with something for me to sew so this brings in a few pesos, and added to what you send us, we aren't pressed for anything.

I do hope that as the war is over our situation will greatly improve; Argentina is a creditor of the victorious sides, so when the economies settle we will be a rich country. If there's work, everything will work out.

My son, I hope I'll be seeing you soon, an affectionate kiss, from

Your Mamá

September 18, 1945

Dear Mamá,

Firstly, thanks for the newspapers, please send *Don* Aurelio my gratitude, I've been filled up with information that otherwise I wouldn't have.

So Argentina entered the war… when it was over. And did the German submarines go to surrender over there? How strange!!!

And this Col. Perón? You had written about him before… Only now has Argentina been talked about over here -in fact, commenting on the late declaration of war - and of course, he has been mentioned.

He's the strong man in the military regime, right? Nothing very good can emerge from a military coup, but it's true that our country has been struggling for many years between democracy and the military. Isn't that why grandfather became estranged from his friend Lugones?

I think the first time I ever saw planes in the air was from grandfather's house on that Saturday we didn't go to Iberra's, and I have an unforgettable memory of how indignant grandfather was. I hardly ever saw my grandfather so angry, and then so sad.

I believe that day marks my first political recollection of the world around me. I hope sincerely that we find a way to democracy. How is it possible that a country so rich, so vast and generous can't find its way? It's not enough to point out oligarchy's vices, which undoubtedly they have… Just imagine, for the French "fair une argentine" means a rich person behaving extravagantly, and the French have this impression because of the eccentric behaviour of Argentine millionaires when they come to France; but there must be more. It's amazing that we're a virtuous people governed by a bunch of immoral men.

I can't really understand because when I left I was only a child, but I want to know, because I've always been interested in my country.

Two weeks ago Mrs Sylvia gave me (another) formidable present.

We travelled in her little MG for nine days, stopping at country houses or in small villages. We spent some marvellous, exciting days together. I sent you some postcards which you must have received by now.

First we went to Cardiff to visit *Don* Eurwen and then… Oh, Mamá, I've spent such intense and moving hours… We went to Tredegar, Meredith's village which I already knew, I don't know if you remember I visited it with Eurwen when I returned from Spain.

Dad's sisters no longer live there.

Eirin, the youngest, married a North American soldier who had been wounded in Normandy and was therefore discharged.

She went on living here until May while the young Yankee was recovering. Immediately peace was declared (four days later) they left for the U.S.A. They live in Arkansas and according to her neighbours here, they have a little boy who they called Meredith.

Siwan is single, but she became a nurse and moved to London, she works there in the Royal Navy or RAF hospital, nobody was able to tell me in which of the two or where she lives.

Bethan –who was already married and had a little boy when I first visited- lives in Edinburgh, but no-one was able to tell me exactly where either. Her husband is a mason, a trade in much demand now.

We had tea with one of Meredith's aunts, Lynn Lewis, a woman who hardly smiled and hardly spoke English. I had to bring out my Welsh –I hardly remember any Mamá!!- and in her few words of English, she told us a few stories about Papá when he was a boy.

I sang for her and the poor woman only had blessings for me. It seems I've inherited grandfather Lewis' voice. I lived all those days with a knot in my throat and teary eyes.

Like we did on that other trip with Eurwen, we then drove up to Edinburgh –which is not exactly a village- but with another destination: we went to Harry and Jack's village.

The children are big, and both look amazingly like my friends.

The eldest, Jack, is exactly like his father even in the way he speaks, he's now about 12 years old. The youngest, Harry, who's going on eleven, is the image of his uncle. Plump and red-headed, full of freckles and very shy. They're both very good pupils, and very polite. It's a shame they don't remember either their father or their uncle. Had I told you that when Harry went to war he didn't know that his wife was pregnant with their youngest? According to Maggie, it was his going away present…

What kind of craziness made us launch ourselves into the war? Harry and Jack sacrificed everything, family, work and their life to fight against Fascism, and nobody is caring for those they left behind…

Mrs Moore —who asked me to call her Maggie as my friends did- is a very pleasant woman but the years have not been good to her. Her hair is almost completely grey and she can't be much over 30 years old, although in spite of this she's still very pretty. She reminded me a great deal of you, because of how she faces the difficulties of life with a smile.

There's not much work in the clock shop —a trade they inherited from their father; clocks have become objects of luxury during these war years.

We could have done the journey in five days, but due to the rationing of fuel we had to stop and wait to recover our quota, so this allowed me to fill my eyes with the landscapes which haven't been damaged by the war.

Before this trip I went to visit what was left of the school -only the foundations and the entrance gate… The story is very interesting! It was published in a few newspapers which Mrs Cummins was kind enough to keep for me.

Fortunately no-one died as the holidays had already begun, but the teachers and pupils who were there were scared to death! Eurwen had taken his first holidays in fifteen years so he was also absent.

It was not an accident or a military target.

It was literally a personal revenge.

On August 7, 1940, in the middle of the aerial battle over England, a Heinkel 111 participating in the attack on the Barnet aerodrome (the only German plane which had managed to avoid a group of a dozen English planes), although already damaged and without the possibility of fulfilling its goal or of returning to Germany, dropped its bombs with millimetric precision on King George's School after having made the rest of the crew jump.

The following is what is so incredible: the pilot -the man responsible for the attack- was Lt Hans Rudolph Von Kassel, who had been a student at the school!!!

Von Kassel - who was the natural son of a German businessman and his English secretary- had graduated from the school the same year I was admitted.

According to what was published by one newspaper, his father took him back to Germany that same year and affiliated him to the Nazi party. After bombing the school, he went flying very low towards the sea, where the plane sank. So apparently, he died in the sea.

He must have hated the school very much to do something so terrible, don't you think?

Mamá, I hope to see you soon. Give a kiss to my sister.

Yours,

Gordon Evans

Remedios de Escalada, October 19, 1945

Dear son,

Your letter arrived on the 15th, but I haven't answered it immediately because over these last few days there has been such unrest as never before, not even during the days of September 1930 or the Vassena strike in 1918.

Perón was detained by order of the government on October 17th and sent to Martín García island, and this measure provoked an unprecedented popular movement: people came out onto the streets to claim that he be released.

The truth is I think we've all been greatly surprised by the vastness of what has taken place.

Already early in the morning shops began to close following the rumour of a revolution… Most of the workers in the railway workshops left their posts and started marching towards the city centre; there was nothing on the radio, nothing at all, and yet all one had to do was look out onto the street and see an unusual amount of humble people walking along– even along ours, which is very far from the avenue- all going in the same direction.

Yesterday's Crítica –which I bought because I believe we've lived a historical day and I kept it so you can read it when you return to us- pointed out that what I saw on the streets had happened all over greater Buenos Aires, in the west and the north.

In an attempt to stop them the bridges in Avellaneda were all raised. But it was useless, the boatmen from Maciel Island were boating the people over for free.

Don Aurelio closed his shop before midday and went with his wife, he told me yesterday. According to him, it was a peaceful party: the police always kept at a distance, watchful, at the ready to interfere, others were showing their sympathy with the cause. People had only one cry: Free Perón.

Yesterday when I went to buy the newspaper –as I don't buy it every day they don't bring it home- I managed to see the front page of La Nación, it expressed its indignation with a photo showing a multitude of people sitting on the fountain edge in the main square with their feet in the water, as if this were really serious… Imagine, a crime to wet one's feet throbbing from so much marching… only La Vanguardia showed some sympathy for the movement of the popular masses.

I don't think it's so serious if one compares it to the injustices, to the poverty which is seen so near the city centre, to the abuse against those without any money or power.

I couldn't demonstrate against them: hasn't it always been our idea that the poor and ignorant people must be uplifted, educated and taught in order for them to take charge of their own destiny? So this is what has taken place, people have taken charge, they have decided that Perón is the man who represents them.

Your grandfather and your father would have supported a popular demonstration of this size.

It's clear we have crossed a milestone, something different has begun and I don't know what it is but believe me, it can't be worse than what we have been living up to today.

For the first time since Yrigoyen –and I was just a young girl- became president, I feel that the country has a future, a destiny that will finally take place.

I can't help pointing out the very vivid impression I have had reading about the story of the sons of your friend who died in Spain; what do men who march off to war think of? Don't they think of their widows, their orphans? I know very well you have an unbreakable bond of friendship and camaraderie with them,

I sense that I too owe something to those children, right? But what need did those two good men have to march off to a war that was not theirs to fight?

I'm waiting anxiously for your return; I want you to be able to experience from the beginning what is starting to happen in our country.

With love,

Your mother

Barnet, November 6, 1945

Dear Mamá,

Yesterday I received your very happy letter, so full of enthusiasm. Do you think that Perón will be Argentina's answer? Here for the first time the newspapers and the BBC have included Argentina in their news, but they haven't been very positive; an article in the Times, very small actually, was posing the question as to whether Perón wasn't the Mussolini of South America.

Mamá, I don't have good news for you.

On the 1st of this month I was notified that tomorrow I must return to the army, I'll be on the move again.

We're being taken to India, because the end of the war has brought huge unrest in that region, which for a century has been claiming its independence. We'll be a small contingency of trained men, not an army.

They aren't expecting a war, since one of the political leaders of the Hindus is a lawyer called Gandhi – I'd already heard his name when we were there in '42 – Great Britain has kept him prisoner all these years and he's a total pacifist.

Mrs Sylvia has told me marvels about this man and his non-violent ideas, his simplicity and his skill in resolving conflicts peacefully.

At least you'll be able to continue receiving the money the Crown is paying me for my services…

As soon as I arrive I'll let you know my new address.

Feeling sad, sending you and my sister a kiss.

Gordon

Bombay, December 17, 1945

Dear Mamá,

Here we are in Hindu territory; Tony is the commander once again of the unit we were part of in Burma in 1942, so I again met up with my two corporals, Korrum and Senghor.

It appears our mission is not to fight (God willing), it'll probably be unnecessary, it'll likely be for support and above all, as custodians of the Crown's property; we still haven't been assigned a specific mission, so we're very bored in the barracks where the heat gets to everybody, including the Hindus.

There is unrest all over the country; large masses of people gather in demonstrations demanding that Great Britain withdraw.

As I told you in another letter, they have a leader whom grandfather would have loved; "Mahatma" Gandhi, whom you probably remember was quoted abundantly in an edition of Claridad magazine although I don't remember the year. Could it have been when Tagore visited our country?

He campaigns for a type of political action which in the past they've already applied here with great success: civil disobedience. They don't pay taxes, or train or bus tickets; they don't consume British products, nor do they obey the British police… I don't doubt that the promises made to the Congress Nationalist party before the war will be kept, with Attlee in government.

The Hindus are sceptical, there have been too many broken promises in the past, but Gandhi's saintly image and the strength of his moral greatness make those who are behind a violent ejection of British power to have very little or no echo at all.

The full Congress Nationalist Party was arrested during the war, Gandhi and his followers had launched a campaign for us to abandon India; there were thousands of people arrested… If they had been successful we would probably have been defeated by the Japanese.

Rumour says that they will be released at the beginning of the year; I hope this is true, because I believe that nothing conspires more against peace than men who're just being held in prison.

I must acknowledge that if I'd been a Hindu, I would have had to choose between Gandhi's earnest pacifism and the military stance of another of the Nationalist Party's leaders, Chandra Bose and his Indian National Army… My young self would have chosen Bose, my current self –after so much war- without a doubt chooses Gandhi.

It's true that Bose became an ally of the Japanese, but isn't there an old saying that "the enemy of my enemy is my friend"?

Imagine if the German masses had resisted Hitler's militarism…

The truth is that I'd like to go home, but as I can't choose my destiny, this is not so bad. If there's no war this is a good place to be, in spite of the restrictions imposed by the high command; we can't move freely about the city, we must always move in pairs and avoid certain neighbourhoods.

They're scared that an attack by some fanatic could wreck the negotiations for the country's independence.

Korrum is very enthused: his native province will be part of the new country, and his family clan's status will be raised, as they belong to the local nobility. I asked him, considering his background, why had he joined the British army and above all, why had he not applied to be an officer.

"You don't understand India, my friend… I'm a Muslim, a Hindu… As an officer I would never have prospered, because in India there's no place for Muslims… Besides, as an NCO of the British army I had much better training and combat experience than I would have had leading Indian troops."

It's clear that this good man has plans for his future!

I manage to go out, to eat at the market, to smell and taste the smells and flavours of this marvellous country; Tony has promised that we'll soon go out and visit the countryside; the cities are perturbing due to the noise and the crowds… except on the days when there are strikes, which are not frequent but on those days there's not a person in sight.

Mamá, in hopes that this will end soon so I can finally return home, your son sends you his love,

Gordon

Remedios de Escalada, January 25, 1946

Dear son,

There's a great deal of unrest here, but it's not disorderly: there'll be elections this coming February, in little more than a month, and then we'll know who is who.

Will it be the Unión Democrática? Will it be Perón? Nothing else is on people's minds. The North American ambassador is campaigning for Tamborini-Mosca and so is the Church.

This is a strange moment in Argentine history, dear son. Generals on one side and cassocks on the other… Looking back, and from what I recall, never before have they been in two separate bands… A merit of Col. Perón; I don't think he can be so bad, after all, the further away the cassocks are from power, the better for the country.

After last October 17th, there're very few that doubt the triumph will be for the "colonel of the people" as the journalists call him.

A new newspaper has been published, "El Clarín", and it supports Perón's candidacy; meanwhile "La Nación", "Crítica", "La Razón" and "La Vanguardia" with different degrees, support the Unión Democrática.

The Socialist leaders are very wrong to oppose someone who is in favour of the good of the people; even worse, the Communist Party has become part of the Unión Democrática, accusing Perón of sympathizing with the Nazis.

It's possible that a member or two of the military government are pro-Nazi, but remember the ships that left Argentina were full of food for a suffering Allied Europe, and all the German companies have been embargoed… in other words, I think those in the Unión Democrática are lying –just as they did about Yrigoyen- who was accused of every imaginable atrocity.

They are capable of any lie to stop anyone who wants to work for the people to have a place in our government.

As you can imagine, with all this going on, neither the newspapers nor the radio programmes have been saying anything about what is taking place in India. There's hardly any news about the rest of the world these days, we're so busy with our own events.

I'm interested in everything you have to tell me about India. I listen to the BBC and Moscow radio and they say such different things that I can't believe either of them.

A few days ago there was a businessman's strike protesting the implementation of an end-of-the-year bonus… Rich people's shamelessness has no limits, they protest because they have to pay workmen a little more… They are immoral, they know nothing of the suffering and needs of the poor. It's Perón who's come to correct so much injustice.

I want to know all about India, what you see and experience - your grandfather was a great admirer of Rabindranath Tagore, who besides being a great humanist and writer was a political leader who was against English dominion.

I'm sure your task there won't be easy; I don't think your spirit which is such an enemy of injustice can take up arms or become an instrument of evil and oppression.

I hope that -like up to now- you can keep your soul pure in spite of that pile of mud and manure to which destiny has seen fit to lead you.

With love, your Mother

January 2, 1946

Dear Mrs Sylvia,

I think of you very often. How long have you been away from India? I'd like to know if it has changed a great deal or, as I believe, has not changed much over the centuries. Or has it been both?

It's so mysterious to me. Almost every European I meet has a bad opinion of India. No, not of India itself and its wealth, they badmouth the Hindus, whom they call natives, mistreating them often and this makes me feel bad.

Many still think that the British should stay in power instead of the country being totally independent, even if this provokes a war. Of course, such stupid thinking is not shared by any of my army mates…

I had stopped going to the club —where I was accepted only because I was Tony's friend, his uncle is now an MP; Tony laughs at me, he says I take all this too seriously, that there won't be any war and India will soon achieve its independence.

So far, over the last five years Tony's opinion or information have never failed. He foretold the Molotov-Ribbentrop pact and how it would be broken, and the North American intervention, bringing an end to the war.

He has expressed privately to me that he admires Gandhi in the same way I do; as an officer, he can't say a word.

One of my corporals, Korrum, a Muslim Hindu, is very enthused with the creation of a new nation. I don't think it's a good idea, it'll be the source of lasting misfortunes for everybody; as Gandhi has expressed, one India is stronger than three…

Has the Red Cross finally given you information on your son? I read in the local newspaper that some weeks after the Japanese surrender, a group of British soldiers were found alive but severely hurt and ill up in the northern Burmese jungle. I hope he was among them.

With no possibility of leaving, I try to enjoy my time in this country. I must point out that it's not a tough job: everything here is a source of knowledge and experience. Early every morning I go out and find a quiet place to meditate; no Englishman is awake then and the Hindus in charge of the guard posts are respectful of the time paying attention to my soul.

I think that at the beginning they found it odd that a European should be seated in a Buddhist style, but Korrum and Senghor's support –the latter is feared by everybody- has stopped any kind of talk.

With the hope that your son will be found well, your sincere friend,

Gordon

Barnet, March 16, 1946

Dear Gordon,

I hope you forgive me for the time I took to answer your last letter, but as you guessed, John Daniel was found by the Red Cross in such a condition that he hasn't been able to talk since last October; he arrived in a hospital boat fleet from Eastern India with many other injured British soldiers and civilians the first days of December, and since then I've been totally absorbed looking after him.

He was in a horrifying condition, even though he had spent several months in a hospital; he was almost starved to death.

Now he can walk slowly and has started talking; doctors say that in some months his health will return, at least to his body… his spirit will take more time. Oh, Gordon, you should see him… he looks so wounded and broken.

He reminds me of how you looked when you came back from Spain; but you at least had a brightness in your eyes and a mumble despite your silence - but he has none of these!

Slowly he has started to eat more and has gained weight; as the Nazis did with the Jews and others, the Japanese starved their prisoners to death. John has been lucky to survive.

He was captured in Rangoon in 1942, almost at the same time you were there; a strange misfortune, my two boys in the same struggle!!!

But he's alive, and with patience and a mother's love he will heal and recover, I'm sure.

I've talked to him about you – I wrote before the war several times with your stories- and he's very pleased with the idea of having a foster brother who is a war hero, he has felt strongly the loss of his younger brother.

So my dear boy, I am totally devoted to my son. We'll keep in touch, and if God wills it, we'll have dinner all together one day.

Sincerely yours,

Sylvia

PS: Please Gordon, write to your mother as often as you can, you can't even imagine how much a mother suffers not knowing the fate of a son.

Cardiff, March 10, 1946

Dear Gordon,

Your last letter was so full of local colour and serious political information! Just as you, I really trust Mr Attlee; he's the man to solve the Indian affair.

The Empire's theft was built over the corpses of millions of good Indians, we'll never completely pay for our greedy crimes.

It's said that they'll finally grant India total independence in a post-empire framework as full members of the Commonwealth. The Indians will be free but the capitalists of London will maintain their interest and earnings.

I find my retirement life boring. I go fishing when the climate lets me; I've fully repaired the motorcycle, I think I'll ride up to Scotland next spring.

I don't know anybody here and I believe I'm too old to make new friends. I became a member of a public library and have started reading; thanks very much for your advice, books are far better than newspapers and magazines.

I've read one book a week, over these last two years; I loved Dickens, you know? I had so many prejudices about him… I also read Orwell, the book you gave me, "Homage to Catalonia"; as I couldn't find any of his books in the public library I bought another one of his about his experience as a tramp. Nice guy indeed!!!

Who has made me feel a deep thrill is Mr Conrad; he's so profoundly human!!! And Mr Cunninghame and his stories about your loved Argentina!! As he was an MP a long time, I found all his books in the public library.

Even if I dislike Mr Kipling from a political point of view, all I've read by him is motivating and moving. But if you ask me, I really prefer Mr Conrad. I will follow your advice always, you know more than I do about books.

I've spoken to Mrs Sylvia, as you asked. She's struggling with her son, who is slowly coming back to life. What a terrible experience, another victim of the Fascists.

There is some mainstream thinking in the media about creating an international court to judge war crimes. I hope so; news and stories about the killing fields are everywhere.

We, the pacifists, were wrong; war was needed to stop this large-scale criminal wave; Neville will be severely judged by history. All the mistakes made in the far past by Mr Churchill will be forgiven instead due to his role in recent years.

We the British have had the luck of having two leaders like the old bulldog and Mr Attlee; I feel lucky to be alive to see him in power.

My friend, with the hope of seeing you once again,

Sincerely yours

Eurwen Glynn

August 28, 1946

Dear Mamá,

These last days have been scary. I'm not going to write down details of the events, because with so much having taken place over the past months and particularly in these last weeks, I'd be forced to send you a book instead of a letter.

I wonder if Argentine newspapers have been reflecting, even if slightly, the deep troubles which are affecting this country.

There's been terrible bloodshed, in which we as soldiers have only had a small role; on the other hand, we're totally responsible regarding the political terms. Lord Mountbatten was negotiating India's Independence exclusively with the Indian National Congress party, while the All-India Muslim League was claiming independence for the province of Pakistan, and Dr. Jinnah refused utterly to share power with Gandhi's party, so the fighting between Muslims and non-Muslim Hindus devastated the country; the most conservative number of dead was 5,000, but there's talk of two or even three times that number.

Some Europeans – mostly those with businesses – became trapped in the fighting and were victims of the violence, but they weren't the goal: there was only one attack registered on a British company building.

Fortunately we were in charge of guarding Lord Mountbatten: our only mission has been to watch over those in charge of the Viceroy's safety, which at some point was under threat.

The main point, apparently, is India's territorial integrity; the confrontation is between the National Congress party and the Muslim League, with two diametrically opposite projects and both are prepared to resort to violence to resolve their differences.

However, the important thing is that we haven't used our weapons more than to dissuade some over-excited people who have thrown stones against the Viceroy's residence, who actually wasn't even there. Really it wasn't bad, all we did was shoot a few warning shots and everything calmed down, no-one was harmed or wounded.

It's clear that this will lead to a partition of India. I wonder why those countries who have been subjected to European imperialism cannot remain united when they become independent?

Considering these historical events has taken me clearly back to hearing grandfather's voice telling me about our independence in South America and how, every time a region threw out the Spaniards, it was the start of a civil war. The years go by and I still can't get used to the fact that neither he nor Meredith will be there when I return…

I've been really pleased to read that finally the trials against the Nazi hierarchy have begun: just as we all expected, there's an international court who's objective is to render justice to all of them and in the future, any who think of exterminating entire races will know they'll have to confront the consequences of their acts -and all of this within the framework of a true nations' congress in which no country should be absent; I believe my small contribution helped the United Nations to become the new actor in world politics, and my sacrifice and all those who died for this to happen will not have been in vain.

My dear Mamá, please kiss my sister and don't forget to keep sending me news on our country; I know that once this process ends we'll be discharged and I'll get back to you in whichever way possible.

From your loving son,

Gordon

September 16, 1947

Dear son,

Perón's triumph in the elections at the beginning of the year has ushered in a new era… full of old vices. But believe me, it's not the General's fault.

His wife does not rest: she's a hurricane of work and solidarity; she's probably the biggest sign of the changes in the air, never before did the wife of a president have such an active political role, and the oligarchy's newspapers do nothing but revile her every attitude; of course, her past as an actress has placed her in the people's enemies' hands, and they accuse her of any dishonourable action they can find.

Difficult years lie ahead, because there are many people who -preferring the injustice we've seen dominate our country so many times- want it to continue; they live from it, prosper from it and they need it to be this way in order to become wealthier - sick with lust and malice.

I'm sad to see how old friends, such as Dr. Palacios, express opinions against this change for which we've fought so many years.

Didn't they ask for agreements with all the nations in the world with no distinction between ideologies and religion? Here we are, establishing diplomatic relations with the Soviet Union after over thirty years of ignoring the Russian revolution. And the stiff-necks of society, the aristocracy with a smell of dung, protest…

And as a climax to this attitude of opening up to the world, Congress ratified the United Nations act. And those of the Alianza Libertadora Nacionalista (National Freedom Alliance) also protest, claiming that we've bowed before the Yankee imperialists… so, what are we in the end? Pro Communist or pro Yankee?

My son, I think so much complaining is a good sign, I think Perón is the man this country needs, to pick up where Yrigoyen left off –to think we criticized him so much and afterwards, when we saw the herd of pigs who took power we were so sorry- and he has what the country needs.

It's true, the cost of living is high and affects everybody, and the speculators fill their pockets by robbing us the poor, but we'll soon straighten them out; they can't say this is the result of Miranda's policies –who is criticized by all the oligarchs- because before and during the war, the price of bread, wood and kerosene went up sky high.

Anyway, my son, your sister is well; we both miss you and can't think of anything else except your return.

I want to thank you for all the postcards you send every week, it's a gesture which fills me with happiness and also, I find them very instructive; a few days ago I received a letter from Mrs Sylvia, telling me about her son's progress, who can now walk for an hour or two, and who has recovered his weight from before the war; he's not totally recovered but is well on his way; she too is very grateful for your postcards and I hope you understand that she doesn't have very much free time to write to you.

I've answered her so she can rest easy; you're very polite and I know I'm not the only one who's eternally grateful for all she's done for us.

Dear son, in the hope of seeing you soon, I send you a loving kiss

Your Mother

Karachi, August 20, 1947

Dear Mamá,

This last month has been crazy. I presume the newspapers have reflected the news over these past days, so I'm not going to overwhelm you with what you've probably already read.

I've seen my men, who are already hardened and seasoned with the war, cry at the sound of "Jai Hind" "Victoria to India" and later others shouting out, "Allahu Akbar" "God is the greatest".

On the night of the 15th after the all-day celebrations, we flew here in a DC3 together with Lord Mountbatten's Avro York, to go through the same ceremony in Pakistan.

Gandhi did not agree with what had taken place and he didn't participate in the celebrations. I see what he's seeing: an ominous and terrible ghost looming over the three new nations[6].

Mr Muhammad Ali Jinnah, Pakistan's Aga Khan in the Pakistan government and Pandit Jawaharlal Nehru in India, with Gandhi on the sidelines, should be a guarantee… but I'm afraid this is not the case, it will all end badly.

There's tension between the Muslim, Hindu and Sikh communities.

It's not just in this period, this is at least one thousand years old, and the British presence simply postponed the confrontations which are now out in the open.

To our surprise, our friend Korrum abandoned the British Army on the 17th: his clan, united by old ties to the Aga Khan, have promoted him to Colonel in the Army of the new state of Pakistan.

And he has asked His Highness for two distinguished members of the British Army to train the new army… yes, Mamá… he especially asked for Tony and myself to be instructors of the new army… and Great Britain has accepted. They will continue to pay our salaries, of course, but the new state will cover our equipment (weapons, vehicles, etc.) and their maintenance.

I'm a little tired of the militia, but this seems to be my destiny.

Please continue sending me news of my country, hardly any arrives here… although this is not strictly true: someone, knowing my origin, sent me a magazine on high society in which I finally was able to see Perón's wife's face, among other things, shaking hands with the Fascist dictator Franco and Pope Pius XII.

She's very attractive and dresses like a princess. I haven't been able to avoid asking myself who's paying for so much luxury. Is it the Argentine people? I sincerely hope not.

Another piece of news that arrived about Argentina is that Great Britain will be paying its large debt with the railway companies, this is already a fact since the end of last year. Do you know anything about this? This would be a very bad business deal for the country, according to a British businessman who has business interests in Argentina.

This man, who was part of Lord Mountbatten's retinue, and after he learnt of my origin through my good friend and boss John Anthony Farrington –the rise of his uncle as a Member of Parliament has turned him into a reference for many people- hadn't a better idea than to tell me many details about the operation in which he took part: the concession's date fell due in 1939 and due to our country's political instability, the British had ceased any investments since 1933 or 1934.

Perhaps I'm not remembering this correctly, but I think that in Barnet I have a box with letters from my father or my grandfather among which there's one, written in 1936 or 1937 mentioning there hadn't been any more purchases of new rolling stock and the existing one was to be reconditioned. Do you recall anything about this?

Also, this man –whose tongue had been loosened by alcohol- boasted that extraordinary commissions had been paid and huge investments would have been necessary for the country to have made any profit, which the British themselves were expecting to finance.

Mamá, imagine the value of the railways with an expired concession…

However, I don't take a stranger's word as the absolute truth, you know that men say many things in order to impress a soldier with as many decorations as I have, even though I may be a simple Sergeant Major.

With all my love, your son who misses you

Gordon

Remedios de Escalada, December 8, 1947

Dear son,

This is the third letter I'm writing to you without any answer, all I've received is a cable from Mrs Sylvia saying you're fine and you aren't on the battlefront.

The newspapers here have published a little about the situation in the new countries: as usual, independence occupied many pages – especially interesting was a long article in the Clarín about how British capital has destroyed India- during the first few days, but three months into the war there has only been a cable now and again.

Unfortunately they have closed the Vanguardia's workshops due to the noise; it seems the neighbours had been complaining for years and nobody listened to them; it's a shame, a newspaper with such a long record and a voice in favour of the rights of the poor, yet it hadn't been capable of respecting their neighbours.

The Embassy has not been able to give me any answer and the War Ministry has answered that your destination is a state secret… What does all this mean?

Please, Gordon, I've gone through too much over the last few years and I'm getting too old for so many displeasures.

There is so much news in the country!!!

During the next elections, we women will be voting… another move forward thanks to Perón and Evita!!!

Your father and your grandfather would be proud of this government, the first one to get busy with the really important things.

Yesterday I was told that if I go to the Foundation which is directed by Evita, they will help me with your sister and generally, with our daily life.

I'm so hopeful with the way the country is going, my son, I can't think of anything else except your return. Please, at least send me a postcard.

With all my love and a mother's concern, an affectionate kiss.

Peshawar, February 6, 1948

Dear Mamá,

Since the end of October last year everything has been really crazy. I'm not going to tell you the story because I've received your four letters all at once and I've just found out all the news in one go.

I know you must be more or less up to date with the events in which I've been indirectly involved.

The latest news, which will already be old by the time you receive this letter, is Gandhi's assassination, which has shaken us all deeply. Another victim of this craziness. How can this have happened? They assassinate a saint right in front of us and we don't do a thing?

Neither the Hindus nor the Pakistanis seem to be moved, at least not to the point of avoiding the bloodshed of this useless war for a piece of land. India is a continent, Pakistan is big territory… and they are fighting over a few thousand square kilometres, paying for this land with dead men on both sides…

How many widows? How many orphans? How many fathers and mothers burying their sons? How many must die for this to stop?

I left part of my life in the battle fields, I buried friends and illusions for the United Nations to become a reality. Where are they? Is no-one going to stop this ridiculous butchery?

February 16, 1948

Dear Mamá,

I'm going to save you all details, I hardly have enough will to pick up my pen; don't spend money on writing to me. The day before yesterday the British Crown has been good enough to give me back my life. For now I don't know my destination, I can only tell you I'll be travelling a little through India and at any of the many ports I find along the way, I'll board a ship to take me to South America. I'll send you postcards and when I can, a cable for you to know I'm OK and travelling back home.

With love,

Gordon

Edinburgh, August 7, 1948

Dear Gordon,

I've received news of you personally through Mrs Sylvia, who came by here yesterday afternoon; we had tea together, we ate plum cake, she brought us undeserved presents both for the children and for me.

At the beginning when the two boys left for the war I was very angry with them, but as time went by and having seen the difficulties caused by the Nazis, undoubtedly their sacrifice was not in vain. The only good thing in all this tragedy is that you are fine, healthy and in one piece.

Harry and Jack talked about you in their letters —which I treasure and re-read now and again- with the affection of someone of their own clan, their own family; they considered you their younger brother; Mrs Silvia brought us a photo of you in your dress uniform, at the Pakistani Independence ceremony.

The children talk of you as if you were an uncle who's on a trip, the only one of the three who survived the war in Spain, you are their live hero, and you are a good example to them.

I don't know when this letter will reach you, all of us who love you are presuming you have embarked on a long journey and I think that all us women who love you are now at peace because you're no longer in the army; Mrs Cummings will make sure that this letter reaches you.

Gordon, I have no words to thank you for all the help you have given us over all these years. You have been sending me half your salary, and Mrs Cummins confirmed that you have also been sending your mother and your sister the other half… It gives me gooseflesh to think all you've gone without all these years! I brought up two good boys, healthy in body and spirit, they were warm in winter and I fed them even when there was hardly any work. What more can I say? Thank you is a very small word but it encloses three lives.

Thank you, Gordon, you and all yours will have a roof and a hot meal while my sons and I live here or wherever we are; do all you can to be happy, you deserve to be, you have sacrificed so much for people you hardly know, for me you are the closest to St. George.

Maggie Peebles-Moore

(This letter was given to Gordon's widow, Carlos' mother, in 2008, by the youngest of the Peebles-Moore at a hostel in Teruel, at the funeral of his brother. For some unknown reason, it had never been sent. A photo of Gordon, enlarged several times, is hanging on the hostel's dining-room wall, for all visitors to see).

Cardiff, March 1, 1953

Dear Gordon,

The news of your marriage is like a spring breeze in the autumn of my life. From my window I can hardly see hills and sky. I have to imagine next spring, because against my will I'm in a room from which it's likely I'll never be able to leave.

Yes, my dear friend, my life is coming to an end.

The doctors are good and as I don't have any family around, they were frank and honest: I have a liver disease which will soon finish me off.

I'm not in very much pain, I feel a little unwell when I eat or drink. I'm still strong enough to walk, but every day I can feel my strength diminishing.

Life is not just, I've know this a long time. I survived an amazing butchery at Ypres, but I also had to survive my dearest Maggie and little Gordon.

Yes, I know, I never told you, but on that bitter day in 1919 I lost a baby which had your name.

By coincidence or not, when I saw you for the first time on that ship that brought you to my country I was a dead fish, neither your name nor your story moved me.

But when I heard you sing that summer, your voice and your way of using it melted my frozen being.

You gave me back my life. Your courage as a boy on his own in that terrible school moved me; and as did other employees of Mr Cabot's, I knew what you were going through, and your commitment to study surprised everybody, but especially me.

Yet when I heard you that day I knew then that you were not just an easy victim, and you were going to fight. So for me, your courage in not abandoning or allowing yourself to be defeated by a shameful plot of social and racial hate is a sign of the just.

Your Welsh origins is not the only reason. The education you received at home, your grandfather's work, the "*gaucho*" he made of you also counted.

No wonder Cunninghame loved your country.

I would have really liked to have saved you from the hell you have gone through in the past, at school and later, but I wouldn't have been able to stop history's savage movements. Every time you came through the windmills –Spain, Dunkirk and so many others- I have celebrated them as a personal salvation.

When I learnt of your marriage I felt as happy as if you were my true son.

I would have loved to have been there, but a person as ill as I would be a bother during such happy days. Believe me, your happiness is mine.

I'm not sending you a gift -not due to money problems because I don't have any problems. I'm not as rich as a Member of Parliament, but over the years I've invested my savings in properties which I'll not need any longer.

Some years back before entering this hospital I made arrangements for these to be at your disposal.

Knowing it would be a problem to have properties so far distant from Cardiff to Buenos Aires, I turned my small possessions into cash and opened up an account in your name at the Bank of London and South America; so attached to this letter I'm sending you all the documents so you can use it however you wish. The pound sterling is not what it used to be but it's still valuable cash.

You won't become wealthy, but it will be a good beginning for a newly-married young man.

Your friendship lit up my life, before I met you it was dark and bitter, you brought me back to the world of the living.

Gordon, I've lived my life the best way I could, I don't have very much to be sorry for and perhaps the worst is perceiving a gentle unhappiness: learn from me, enjoy what is to come.

I know you well, don't even think of coming to see me: I've left you my savings for you to begin something, buy a piece of land, become a landowner and cattleman, find your "*gaucho*" inheritance and become a legend like the Welsh in Patagonia. But please, don't spend a penny on me, because I've made all arrangements and I'll go peacefully and with all the necessary care.

When I breathe my last I'll be thinking of you, the son more than the friend who was given to me.

Sincerely yours,

Eurwen Glynn

(Found among the pages of a book that First Lieutenant Carlos Evans kept in his uniform).

Islas Malvinas, June 11, 1982

Dear Mamá,

I don't know how you'll get this letter, how it will reach you, but I don't doubt that among my enemies there'll be someone decent who'll get it to you.

The night before last we finally made contact with them; despite the darkness and cold, my men had the fortitude and courage to repel them without anyone being wounded on our side.

Yesterday morning, when it was clear to me that all is definitely lost, I ordered them to fall back. Only two of them disobeyed, for different reasons they decided to stay with me. I'm sorry for them and for their families, not so much for me.

This is not a war report, Mamá.

I just don't know how to write all I'm feeling right now.

I know I don't have to ask for your forgiveness because I know it's guaranteed.

But I need —now that I'm getting ready to face my destiny as a soldier- to explain all the years of silence.

I know they've been years of pain and bewilderment for you too.

Grandfather must have given you my love, I'm glad I called, I'm sorry you weren't there. I know you would have preferred to give me a hug, a kiss…

But Mamá, ever since that other call I made to you five years ago, it hasn't been easy for me to be a soldier, to be Argentine, to be who I am…

It's enough for me to know that Bethan is alright and safe even though she's far away, and that you and my sisters are OK and as happy as can be expected.

If Papá were alive probably none of this would have happened… But as grandfather says, history is the non-reversibility of the facts…

Since the day I spoke to you that last time I've felt ashamed.

I haven't been worthy of Papá's legacy, I haven't been worthy of the uniform I wear, or of the flag, or of Generals San Martín or Belgrano.

Yet, however…

I obeyed like a soldier, I didn't doubt, I did my duty. My country's enemies, I fought them… But I wasn't prepared for the enemies to be ourselves.

I dishonoured myself in the process.

It's not important how, the details are irrelevant. What matters is what it meant to me, and before God.

I could justify myself, say I obeyed orders, but that wouldn't be honest. I preferred, in the heat of the moment, to postpone the consequences, to go against the values with which I was educated, and I obeyed an immoral order.

I chose then, and equally what I'm doing now, all I'm going through.

I was concerned about dying then and I'm sorry.

You too have been a victim of my sin.

This is why I haven't answered your letters, why I've avoided looking into your eyes all these years.

I'm ashamed, Mamá, nothing else.

All these years living in the South has allowed me to hide, live a life on the mountainsides, in the barracks. I took refuge in my shame, I closed up.

I read your letters, many times.

I didn't answer because I didn't know how. What could I say? What could I tell you? I know of others who in these circumstances lie, but I haven't known how, I haven't had the courage to do that…

In my heart, everything has turned dark and tortuous.

I attempted to find a priest's understanding; and instead of punishing me, he congratulated me, he absolved everything without any penitence… It appears God is indulgent with the facts of war.

Mamá, this world which I believed safe and trustworthy is absolutely crazy. To respect the Constitution we turned it into dead words, to organize the country we violated the rules we ourselves set, to save it from chaos we became the chaos…

We have done things for which history will not forgive us.

I cannot forgive myself.

From the mountain I could see the station wagon standing in front of the barracks and I only came down when you'd gone.

I'm so sorry, Mamá.

I would have preferred not to make you suffer as I have done. I myself have suffered, believe me. But I can't undo what I did. None of it.

I could have had myself discharged, but I'm not sorry I didn't: in the end, this is my vocation, this is one of the possible outcomes. I face it with a curious serenity.

I'll now face the destiny of a soldier as is fitting, I'll meet Divine Mercy, I'll finally know if I'm made from the same fibre as Papá, if I'm a worthy descendant of my ancestors.

I want you to remember me as a good son, for my sisters to remember me as a good brother in spite of my errors and defects.

With all my heart, I wish you may tell your grandchildren –my sisters will fill your life with them- that once you had a son who lived dishonourably for part of his life and in the end, he was able to die honourably defending the country.

Mamá, my last thoughts will be of you, my family; Papá, wherever he is, undoubtedly will guide me along this path, as he guided me at other times in my life.

I suppose you feel as I do: I miss him since that Sunday I saw him for the last time, I miss his calm voice and his sensible and simple advice.

With all the love a man can feel for his family, I say goodbye trusting that God and our Lord Jesus Christ's mercy will be with me.

Your son,

Carlos Evans
¡Viva la Patria!

悟り

VII) SATORI

SATORI:

For Zen Buddhism, correct meditation leads you to experience freedom from suffering due to the illusion of the senses.

The four noble truths:

Existence is suffering, suffering comes from desire and ignorance, suffering can be overcome, and the way to end suffering is the octuple path.

The octuple path:

Correct understanding, correct thought, correct attitude, correct word, correct action, correct purpose, correct effort, correct concentration.

The Tiger's Path

I can smell the burning wood very sharply but I can't see the flames, although clearly the fire is ahead. The path along which we have been marching for the last three hours is directed towards some ruins.

The monsoon wind brays during the night and in the distance the black sky is crossed by lightning, illuminating everything ever more frequently, allowing us to see just for an instant the grey, velvet-like belly of the storm.

It will start to rain and will do so for days, it's important to find refuge, says Senghor.

We've been marching in the Burmese jungle for ten days and the last three have been the most terrifying, tough and intense of my whole life.

I've seen death face to face as never before.

I've been beaten, humiliated, obliged to watch the execution of three of my brave Nepalese, tied to a pole like a boar by furtive hunters and dragged through the jungle, deprived of my condition as a human being, reduced to a mere carrier of information that should be handed over like a document with a due date.

For fourteen or fifteen hours I was dragged, hanging from my arms and feet with my back just touching the ground and the undergrowth, sometimes soft but others with sharp stones and thorns.

Finally I learnt the ultimate terror, convinced that death was finally going to take over.

Not even in that dark and frozen dawn on the outskirts of Teruel did I feel so much fear nor for such a long time as yesterday. I'm not talking of physical fear that paralyzes you for a second. I mean the definitive assurance that finally everything is about to end in the worst possible way.

I imagined, during those desperate hours, the kinds of possibilities the executioner would have to torture out of me not what I know - but what they think I know. How many tools would he have? When would the actual torture begin?

I understood later that the torture had begun before, when I realized I'd fallen into a planned ambush to capture an officer or an NCO.

It could have happened to Tony, to Korrum... not to Senghor; he would have been killed or he would have killed them. I wasn't able to do this, I found I had a burning desire to live, it was like a flame.

I surrendered to save my life, without thought, guided by the egoistic desire to survive, and immediately I was horribly repentant when the Japanese officer ordered the three brave young Nepalese men -survivors of our brief combat- to line up, and with his long and sharp Samurai sword he decapitated them from behind, one by one, right in front of me.

The memory of those beautiful men who I ordered to surrender, standing and without a single gesture of fear, falling like uprooted trees, without a single cry or plea, and an instant later, the horrific surge of blood from their pumping hearts, the brief shaking of their hands or feet, their eyes in their heads open… all of this will remain in my mind for the rest of my life.

What were their dreams? And their parents, high up in the Nepal mountains, would they ever know that their good sons had died honouring their ancestors and showed a courage I don't possess?

At that moment I knew my limitations, I'd gone beyond my capacity to withstand pain, that any sort of blows from rifle butts or fists would not have broken me, but that sooner or later the skilled hands of an experienced torturer would end by breaking down any resistance, bending me with just a single phrase of their incomprehensible language.

They tied me up like a hunted animal, dragging me, and humiliating me brutally.

They beat me and I surrendered. I stupidly wanted to save my life and they killed my men.

In war's brutal logic, it didn't make sense nor was it technically possible or militarily reasonable to take four prisoners when only one is necessary.

And without any possibility of continuing, on the evening of that same day my captors camped, choosing very carefully a place that would be easily defendable, near the river that would lead me to pain and death, their backs covered by a wall of rocks some twenty metres high, apparently inaccessible.

I myself could not have chosen a better place – in appearance, impenetrable.

Naturally they didn't know that behind us Tony had sent Korrum and five other Nepalese, plus Senghor with an equal number; they didn't know that the Indian and the mixed-race Burmese could be the ray and death, the tiger and the serpent.

Korrum closed off the exit and Senghor, honouring his lineage of warriors, simply slid through the air, hanging from the cliff in the dark night with his machete and dropping from the least expected place, the wall that was supposed to protect my captors.

I saw it all, tied up and gagged as I was, unable to do anything except be a quiet accomplice. He fell from above and slid softly through the air like a spider attached to its web, jumping like a cat into a bird's nest among the men who were exhausted and sleeping, trusting in the protection afforded by the traps placed on the paths plus the four alert guards who had sealed off the place in an almost perfect lock.

My captors couldn't know that my two lethal corporals would come to my rescue.

I'll never forget the savage dance executed by my terrible saviour, the angel of death, demon of the jungle, smiling as if he were possessed, lifting his sharp knife and cutting down our enemies.

The first ones died without even waking and the last ones unable to believe what was happening.

Speedily and brutally he carried out his macabre task, always smiling, with no other sound than the sharp steel cutting into skulls, necks, bellies.

And the guards? These fell into Korrum and his Gurkhas' hands. Four against four, the fierce Japanese didn't even have time to blink as they were beheaded by the kukri knives.

So the pancake had been flipped, as we used to sing in Spain.

The officer woke up at the same time as his men were dying, and although he managed to pull out his murdering sable, he too found his limitations just as I had a few hours before: surrounded by the deadly mouths of ten Enfields .303 forcing him to choose life and drop his weapon.

Can I even judge him?

But I did.

Released from my torment –trapping my mouth, hands and feet- I encounter Senghor's light blue eyes and sadistic smile, which he shows when he's about to give rein to his brand of sadism -that brutal, provocative and edgy malice.

"He's yours, Gordon *tuan*," he whispers, wickedly and gleefully. I hesitate -than slide into those warm waters which up till then I had held back from overwhelming my soul.

I feel no pain, even though I know I'm full of bruises and cuts all over my body.

In my mind, night becomes darker.

The officer, unarmed and stripped of his air of superiority and criminally steel knife, murmurs a litany that is unintelligible to me.

"Amida nembutsu, amida nembutsu, amida nembutsu..." I appear to understand as he whispers with his eyes closed and tears streaming down his face.

Senghor walks around him, looking at him very carefully. Senghor, his hands covered in his victims' blood, wipes them on our enemy's uniform. The officer, impotent and defeated, lets him be while he continues reciting his litany.

"He's praying," I say, trying not to lose my head, forget about mercy.

Senghor is ruthless.

"No!" he exclaims, with a gleeful little laugh.

Meanwhile, Korrum and two of the soldiers drag the dead men into a pile, not before revising pockets in search of any valuable object. The Gurkhas are mercenaries and they have a right to loot.

A cigarette box, Japanese cigarettes –delicious Borneo tobacco which at some point had made the Dutch rich- a ring, knick-knacks, or a watch or perhaps a good knife made from the legendary Japanese steel, everything is acceptable except money – like us, they carry very little- photos or letters.

"He's insulting you… 'Western dog son of a bitch' is what he's repeating over and over…", and then he adds, hissing in a very low voice, so I can hardly hear him.

"Are you going to leave this dog like this? Gordon *tuan*, you saw what he did to those Nepalese… I found their bodies… They must already be food for vermin… You were there… those boys adored you, *tuan*…" and he offers me the handle of his machete, still covered in blood.

"No," I say, and I hear myself as if I'm at the end of a tunnel, numb and desensitised, blind and deaf with hate, possessed by a boiling, infinite and uncontrollable fury which I don't even want to dominate.

Against all my rules, against everything I've thought and held true all those days and horror I've lived through since 1937, I release the inner monster; and without even the need of a Dr Jekyll brew, my Mr Hyde rejects the weapon being offered.

I stand across from that man who at one point I saw as someone terrible and who I now see as very small and almost fragile, with his body still as firm as a soldier, his eyes closed and his face covered in tears.

He's very young.

"Amda menatsu," I say. I try and repeat what he says, and he first opens his eyes, infinitely surprised.

"Amida nembutsu," he says, almost about to smile, to return to life.

"Amida nembutsu," I repeat, without listening to what I'm saying.

So the Japanese man smiles, believing there will be mercy.

From the bottom of my furious being, I strike him with a precise and brutal blow to the middle of his face.

My prisoner, surprised by the violence of the blow, stumbles and bends at the waist, his right hand goes up to his nose which has been broken and spurts blood. He looks at me greatly surprised for just one second, then stands up straight again and starts repeating his litany, his mouth full of blood.

I hit him, again, again, again. Again and again, I hit him with my fists, my elbows, my feet, my knees. Again and again, meticulously applying all my knowledge of fighting and anatomy accumulated over these years at war, every fierce instruction given to me after Dunkirk.

The man is now quiet beneath the blows raining down on him; he no longer insults me, nor does he talk. At the beginning he tried to defend himself, to counterattack with some blow but it was useless.

The body to body combat techniques of the Japanese enjoy a fearsome reputation among those who don't know them, but I was trained for months in a wide range of fighting techniques and naturally, have the advantage.

I hit him and hit him again and my fury doesn't abate, my insensitivity has taken over.

He kneels and I kick him. He tries to stand and I hit him with all my strength. I find the soft spots, his guts, his testicles.

I'm deafened, desensitised.

He falls face downwards and I kick him to turn him over. I place one knee on the ground and with the edge of my hand I hit his neck, his Adam's apple and his trachea breaks with no noise.

The man goes into convulsions and I continue kicking him, until I jump onto his chest. My feet sink into his ribs which break with a dry crackling sound, like green branches in the unperturbed brush surrounding us.

In spite of it all, my enemy tries to breathe again but he cannot, and he dies. Then suddenly I collapse, my energy has gone. I have to sit down on the ground, breathing heavily and totally covered in sweat, all my muscles trembling from tension and effort.

Somebody hands me a water bottle and I pour it over my head before even thinking of what I'm doing. I haven't had any water for at least a day –prisoners are not given anything to drink- and perhaps three or four days in which I haven't eaten properly. But the only thing I can think of is to wet my face, my hands –hurt and covered in my blood as well as my victim's.

Nobody talks, nobody says anything. But Korrum's face says it all: even the fierce Nepalese are impressed by what they saw me do.

Without saying a word, Korrum hands me another water bottle -which he as a Muslim shouldn't have- and that I've baptised Daisy, full of the palm moonshine the natives make. The heat of the alcohol and the speedy drunkenness that comes over me relaxes me, it's like a blessing. I look at Senghor. His cold, feline eyes look at me with pleasure. He smiles at me.

"A beautiful job, Gordon *tuan*," he whispers and I try not to hear him.

We then march through the jungle again, we regroup, receive new orders, go out again on patrol. The war routine.

Now, before us, the possibility of fighting again. I look at Korrum.

"The footprints are of small, bare feet… women or children…" says the Hindu.

"Two grenades, Gordon *tuan*…" says Senghor.

I pat the four grenades I carry on my belts.

I look at Korrum, then at Senghor. I think. And finally, I give an order.

"Seng, behind me. Korrum, you cover Seng. You only shoot on my order..."

We walk in silence, stepping carefully, trying to guess at traps. A stick, a stone, a vine or a root, any of these can be joined to a detonator, a grenade, a trap with sharp bamboos -I know by experience, because I do this all the time.

The lightning of a while before, which took some time before the thunder, now speeds up, the breeze changes to a strong wind and the whispering of the leaves becomes a loud noise, the storm is coming closer and closer… This will cover our footsteps, but it will make the defenders more alert.

I enter the old building -made of blocks of stone- holding two grenades in my right hand, both their pins joined by a thin wire. It will need just one pull to have two live grenades.

I then see the dancing flames of a camp fire and my heart grows cold as ice. There are menacing shadows projected on a wall.

As always, time stops, slows down, a second that is as long as taking a breathful of air when coming up out of the water, just one second and then the explosion.

Without a single noise I jump to the extreme opposite end of the camp fire, I turn in the air and even before dropping I see, sitting before the fire, a bald man dressed in the unmistakable habit of the Buddhist monks, saffron and red, and behind him a small group of terrified children.

I don't shout, I roar.

"Ceasefire, ceasefire!!!" Behind me my corporals come up holding their STENs, each pointing towards a corner, and then both weapons focused on the monk and the children.

Senghor starts insulting in Burmese, English, Hindi, Pashtun, Farsi, in all the numerous languages he knows. Korrum smiles and thanks Allah.

From the depth of my memory, I use the only swear word in Spanish that Harry Moore could pronounce correctly.

"¡¡¡*CARAJO!!!*" I shout, savouring each syllable. And I shout it again, two or three more times. It's my charm, the lucky word which I've carried with me since Teruel.

Korrum smiles and tries to calm the children, some are very frightened. Senghor, on the other hand, refuses any contact with them and goes off in search of the rest of the patrol.

Already on his feet, the man smiles at me and greets me with his palms together at the height of the heart and a graceful inclination of the head and torso. The light is precarious but I can appreciate the peace on his oriental face, a quiet, calm look.

I approach him.

I give him my name.

He smiles.

He talks in English.

He introduces himself.

"I am Atisha... As you can see, these little ones with me are inoffensive, they don't represent any risk or danger to you or your men…" His voice is calm and he never stops smiling.

The tension in the air is disappearing as I look him up and down, trying to understand what I'm facing; but when I look deeply into those eyes, calm as a lake, I suddenly remember the goodness in my grandfather's expression, and I feel immediately the heat of my sudden emotion lighting up my face and eyes.

This man has something more than the same goodness in his eyes -there's something beautiful, transcendent and huge emanating from his expression, in contrast to the deep humility of his attitude and clothing.

He has shaken up my being that very instant.

Against my will I smile; I put the grenades into my backpack, I extend my hands to show myself unarmed.

"My name is Gordon Evans. Please, you can call me Gordon…" The man smiles even more and nods.

He busies himself with quieting the children, I do the same with my men. Korrum is exultant, I know he likes good actions because they are the path to Allah.

I like Korrum and his Muslim bonhomie. He's an upright soldier, efficient with just the right dose of prudence and courage, he doesn't kill to no avail nor is he unnecessarily cruel.

On the other hand, the Burmese cross-breed Senghor...

He has a huge Kali tattoo on his back, which he had tattooed in the Japanese port of Yokohama when he was 14 years old. Kali, the goddess of the three pairs of arms, Kipling's goddess and the assassin sects' goddess. The goddess of death and violence.

Korrum is a luminous man, with an easy laugh when away from the battlefront; Senghor is dark, enigmatic, ironic, scathing and cruel, provocative in everything - extremely cruel and lethal in combat, he delights in this sensually rather than as a sport.

The three of us lead a platoon of three companies, a total of 25 men under the command of Captain Anthony J. Farrington.

The stone building is the remains of an old temple which has been majestically invaded by the jungle over many centuries.

However, there are still two or three open areas; but what is more important in the rainy season, their roofs are in good condition.

I send Seng in search of the others in our unit.

The monk approaches, smiles.

"Two considerations, Mr Gordon," he pauses. "We don't have much food, but it will be enough for you and your men if you feel a plate of rice is enough to satisfy your hunger…"

His English is clear, he's an educated person.

"The other thing…" he hesitates a second, but then inhales deeply and smiles even more. "…I'm almost sure I heard you say a word in Spanish… I could be mistaken…"

I look at him, surprised.

"That's correct, yes… My father was Welsh but my mother is Argentine and I lived there until I was twelve…" Then, in doubt for a second. "Do you speak Spanish?" I ask, without hiding my surprise.

The man laughs, and his laughter is frank, catching.

"You're surprised, right?" He answers slowly, in perfect Spanish.

"It seems we have several things in common… To begin with, I'm also a half-breed… My father was Chinese and my mother from the Philippines… I was raised in Manila until I was 12; perhaps you didn't know, but before being a North American colony, the Philippines were a Spanish colony…" Then, waving his hand as if to dissolve something in the air. "… And I also lived in Spain in my youth…" He pauses, then looks at me with his beautiful, heart-warming eyes.

"That was many years ago, in another lifetime… of course in this one, but in the past…" He shakes his head. "Something that no longer exists… would it bother you to talk in Spanish? It's good for one's mind to talk in different languages, it keeps it agile and young… and Spanish is difficult to practice around here, you do understand me, right?"

It's his calmness, the tone of his voice, the intimacy born of talking a language that nobody around us can understand, maybe it's all this or maybe something else, I don't know, but that man with a carefully shorn head inspires in me a trust that up till now I'd only felt with *Don* Eurwen.

"It will be a pleasure… Although it's somewhat more than three years since I've spoken it…"

Atisha shakes his hand as if to toss away any doubt.

"That's nothing… It's probably 35 years or more since I've spoken it…" He talks slowly, searching for the words in his mind. "But you see, Mr Gordon, practice makes perfect, and it's clear you still remember your mother tongue, and you will help me to remember mine."

The wind blows harder, announcing the rain which should be there any minute.

I send my men out for as much wood as they can find because later, when the sky falls on our heads -it will rain for days, then it will stop a while and then it will rain again, this will go on for weeks- there will be nothing dry in all Burma.

I go back to talking to that man whose presence, voice or look have a calming, life-giving effect on me.

It distracts me, relaxes me.

The monk attends to the children – some of them can't be more than three years old- with patience and a compassionate smile; his similarity to my grandfather is amazing… Or is it my imagination playing a joke on me in the flickering light of the fire?

The men from the other platoons are arriving and as they do, the monk adds rice to the saucepan over the fire. On Korrum's order, a soldier approaches with several tins of different kinds of beans as well as tins of corned beef.

I order one of the boys to relieve the monk attending to the cooking.

I walk over to the entrance of the building, over which there is a big stone slab which is incredibly held up by only three columns; it shelters me from the rain but not from the violent wind which brings with it the unmistakable smell of wet earth.

With a little effort, I manage to light a Japanese cigarette, trying to drown in the nicotine my feelings from the events lived through over the last few hours.

With a soft clearing of his throat, Atisha comes up to me from behind.

"I hope I'm not intruding," he says.

I smile. The truth is, I'm grateful. I don't feel like being alone with myself…

"No, not at all," I say in English.

But I add in Spanish, "But at least we'll have food and shelter for a day or two… afterwards…"

The monk's smile widens.

"As Christians say, God will provide!!"

I smile when I hear this kind saying.

"The truth is I don't have any Christian education, any religious learning… My parents are Socialists…"

The man is calm and kind, he answers in a slightly amazed tone.

"You don't have any religious belief? You don't believe in anything?"

It is I who's amazed now because against my will, that simple question has left me absolutely perplexed. I say simple, because any of these 30 people behind us –children or soldiers- would have answered affirmatively and without a single doubt.

What do I believe in?

Do I believe in anything?

Is there anything more?

The monk doesn't wait for my answer.

"Do you think you could give me a drag of your cigarette? I know I'm being a little daring…"

I pass him the half-smoked cigarette.

He takes it.

"It's been more than thirty years since I've done this… And my heart still beats fiercely…" He puts it between his lips, inhales deeply just once while he closes his eyes in delight, and softly, he exhales the smoke at the same time as he returns the lighted cigarette to me.

He looks at me.

"Are you amazed?" He doesn't wait for my answer.

"It's good to now and again try out what we deprive ourselves from voluntarily. It tempers our will."

He looks at me while I smoke and as he does, I once again feel what I felt when I got off the horse in front of the Iberras' house, that afternoon in December when I rode for the last time, and was watched carefully by my grandfather.

I'm about to tell him this but he begins talking, without looking at me. I listen carefully. "You probably won't believe what I'm about to tell you, but you see… In Buddhism, there's no such thing as chance, nothing happens just because -everything has a cause in the Wheel of Dharma… Last night I dreamt of you."

He now has my full attention.

"You see, our daily meditation practice can sharpen our mind's perceptions, our intuition, give us a correct vision and in some cases… clairvoyance.

"In my case, this doesn't happen often and only during dreams. I don't dream as in a film or as if they were photographs. They are more like representations of Oriental plays, slow and ceremonious, full of symbols which are difficult to interpret…

"Yesterday I had a dream which didn't make sense until a while ago, when you came in through the doorway holding your weapons…

"All the images of the night before then made sense… There was a very strange dragon, not like Oriental ones, it was very different, and now I understand, it matches your medieval myths… The dragon was crying bitterly. Beneath its claws a grey dove was dying, it was praying in Japanese; and wound around the suffering dragon's back legs was a large black snake with light-blue, evil eyes that would change from light-blue turquoise to emerald green.

"I clearly felt the dragon's suffering, and I immediately recognised it as a suffering spirit sunk in Samsara but willing to come out of it… Yet what was most incredible was that the strange dragon talked to me in Spanish… He said 'instruct me on Dharma'… That's what he said…" The monk stops and looks at me.

"Do you understand?"

I sigh, flatten the cigarette butt with the toe of my boot.

"No," I say, sighing. "The truth is I don't understand a word, not only what you're saying but anything at all." I look out at the night and the noisy curtain of rain starting to hit the earth, the stones, the foliage, and resounding into the air.

"You…" I try to think of something, but I'm actually dumb, frozen and almost disarmed as I suddenly realize my absolute ignorance.

"Now that you're next to me, the dream is as clear as the rain which has yet to touch the ground… A Western soldier who speaks Spanish who without a doubt is sunk in Samsara… Aware of his suffering…"

I feel a blow to my chest as if one of the storm's flashes of lightning has hit me straight on.

I stop my sob, but I can't stop the tears rolling down my cheeks.

Then the monk, who is small and bent, leans his left hand on my shoulder, soft as a bird, and at the same time my knees begin to bend.

I've fainted before –due to hunger, due to the shock wave from a Stuka attack… I know I'm not fainting, but my body doesn't respond to my wishes, to my will, my orders -and if he weren't holding me up, I would have already fallen to the ground.

"You're lost in Samsara, sunk in it… And at the same time you're beginning to see it…"

I look at him, I don't try to understand -for the first time in years, I feel. After years of closing my feelings behind a barrier, I find I'm a sentient being.

I hear the rain for the first time.

I feel the wind against my face for the first time.

The wind brings with it the smell of the jungle and I discover a variety of scents, a spectre of flavours from the sublime to the disgusting.

And I see… What word to use here when there are no words? Is this how the blind see for the first time after recovering their sight?

A sudden weakness runs through all my muscles, as if the accumulated tension of the last days has disappeared all at once, taking with it all my strength.

I hear a single sob coming out of my mouth and then Atisha, softly but energetically like a dancer, places himself delicately on the ground facing me, the palm of his other hand against my chest with the precision of a surgeon or an assassin.

Then something extraordinary takes place.

All my anguish, pain, everything I carry with me —not just from my first day in the Spanish war but as from my birth itself- comes present and forces me to bend right over, but surprisingly it washes right through, through my body, my guts, my bones and flies away with the wind, which has gone through me as if I were hollow.

We are both still for some seconds, my impression is that time has stood still.

He looks into my eyes.

His face is my father's.

I blink.

His face is now my grandfather's.

I blink. His face changes, again and again.

"Breathe through your nose… Slowly… Fill your lungs softly… Hold the air… in… your… lungs… like that… now slowly… no, not through your nose… Take in the air through your nose… Fill your belly with air… Do you know how to swim under water? Now exhale through your mouth… slowly… good!"

Without any thought I follow his instructions, and as I do so, my senses return, although all my muscles are trembling.

I breathe, following the instructions of this unknown man who has clearly dreamt of me and the events of the previous days.

I speak with a trembling voice.

"A dragon that speaks in Spanish… My father is Welsh and the Welsh saint is St George, of the dragon… And I speak Spanish because my mother… This is unbelievable, truly…"

Atisha smiles serenely.

"Ah, you Westerners… What a great deal of damage done by Descartes with his cult regarding reason…"

"No, Descartes has nothing to do with this… Your dream… there's a mistake…"

"Now I'm the one who doesn't understand…" he says slowly. "A mistake?"

"Yes… Today I killed a Jap in a very cruel and brutal way, he was insulting me…"

He opens his eyes and shakes his head, his expression is serious.

"Ah… So you speak Japanese… You are a very educated man…"

I shake my head.

"No. No, I don't speak Japanese… But one of my men… The one with light-blue eyes…" A terrible, freezing cold feeling runs up and down my spine.

I hesitate for a second.

"Do you speak Japanese?"

He smiles, rather sadly.

"It has a Chinese root, so it's not difficult for me, when I practice a little I speak it more fluently…"

"Amida nembutsu..." I say.

He looks into my eyes and in his I see the deepest compassion. No amazement, or horror, or anger. Simple, pure compassion.

"Amida nembutsú", his voice is clear despite the wind. "… That is a prayer in Shintoism…" he says softly.

The cold spreads through my soul.

"This is exactly Samsara…" he states calmly, in a whisper.

I look at him, inwardly caved in.

"Eternal suffering in this life and in all reincarnations," he states slowly, seeking the words. "This suffering of which you are becoming aware now, exactly that, that's Samsara…"

From the depth of my frozen being an idea emerges.

"Death liberates you…"

He interrupts me, shaking his head.

"That's what it looks like, from ignorance, the not knowing about the eternal cycle of reincarnations that awaits all beings with feelings… Buddha taught us how we live and die sunk in suffering… And the path to freedom…"

"Reincarnations???" The word is not familiar to me in Spanish, only in English. The cold running through me stops a second when I recall Mrs Sylvia.

But the idea of eternally repeating this suffering just makes me feel nauseous.

"One life after another, this same suffering…" repeats Atisha, with the same expression in his eyes as my grandfather's.

"That's Samsara... A continuous rebirth as a suffering being... As a human being, as an animal, as an eager being, as a hellish being..."

My mind is a whirl of ideas, shaken by a hurricane of a variety of feelings. I light up another cigarette with the butt of the previous one.

"No... I don't understand..."

"However, it's very simple..." This man's voice is soft and he speaks slowly, almost whispering above the noise of the storm over our heads. "Everything you see, everything you feel, everything that you live is no more real than a dream... Do you recall any dream?"

I nod, taking a very pleasurable drag on the cigarette.

"Do dreams exist? However, while we are having them... and even when we just wake we have a strong feeling that what we dreamt was real, isn't that so? And where does that dream go, what happens with what we have seen, all that it has made us feel, smell, see?"

Recollecting, my mind then fills with memories, feelings, dreams.

"That's exactly what happens with what we believe is reality... everything we feel, we see, we think... Nothing, according to Buddha, is real or true, it's the great Samsara hoax."

"Are you saying that this hellish war is not real?"

"That's exactly what Samsara is, in which all sentient beings, whether human or not, are sunk... All this suffering, all this horror is taking place through the trickery of our false mind, sunk in the roots of Samsara..."

I put out the half-smoked cigarette. I breathe like this man has explained I must do, and a quiet calm -a remarkable contrast to the damp, warm windy gusts which now and again shake our parapet- moves through me with each inhalation.

Although I'm not looking directly at him, I see the monk shaking his head approvingly.

"I'm not going to say I understand, although what you're saying is clear. What you're saying is that all I've lived since my birth is not real?"

Atisha gives me a soft tap on my forearm.

"Your real mind, your true self, your true "Gordon" is behind, inside, like... Have you ever seen those little wooden Russian dolls, which are hollow and hold another smaller one inside?" The man smiles calmly when he speaks to me. I nod. In a crystal case in Mrs Sylvia's sitting room, among many objects from many different parts of Asia, I recall having seen something like he describes.

"Well, the mind is something like that... There is a real mind, authentic, true, which in all beings is watched by another, which is the one that lives sunk in the horror of Samsara. Buddha teaches that we can cut that tie to suffering..."

For a second his voice goes away, lost in the storm.

"How do we do that?" The question is out of my mouth without me even having thought about it.

"Good question!" He smiles widely, his expression illuminated. "Only three things are needed… To know the four noble truths and the octuple path, and to be spiritually open to infinite compassion towards all sentient beings, human and not human… That is Buddha's great revelation… That's the path to abandoning Samsara for good. But I warn you, it's not an easy nor a brief path. Yet in the end, with patience and infinite compassion, Nirvana awaits, absolute peace."

Peace! What a beautiful word. I haven't spoken it a single time nor thought of it since September 1939; peace, a longing that here and now seems inconceivable.

"It's not possible… There's war all over the world or almost all of it… Europe, Africa, Asia… there is no peace, it's impossible," I state bitterly.

"Peace has to begin in the mind of sentient beings for it to reach the earth…" My mind is stormy and like a film, all the violence and death, all the horror I've witnessed in the past years goes through my mind.

All this is in my mind. If I've understood correctly, Atisha is offering me a way to remove all these terrible pictures which darken my soul.

Our peaceful talk is interrupted by the sudden appearance of Tony with the rest of the unit; they had met up with the men sent by Senghor and soaking wet, they hurry into our refuge. The temple's different spaces fill with camp fires and wet, cold men; a noise which I wasn't prepared for.

Atisha goes back to attending the children. Tony has a huge smile for me; he says nothing, just shakes my hand and stares into my eyes. He's as happy as I to meet up again. He's my commanding officer but also my friend.

We concentrate on our work. I give him a summary of the events which took place since we separated five days before. Only five days! It has seemed five centuries…

We get down to work; it's important to organize everything that's happening around us; there are too many people in a small space and the enemy could be very close; we must organize lookout turns, the guards, control the small area around the temple which has become our headquarters.

There's also logistics to consider: we must feed everybody, and coordinate and prepare the small place for almost one hundred men and children to sleep.

We lack food; we're part of an army which is very orderly when retreating, together with a large civilian population that follows us through the Burmese jungle.

We sleep a while and before the sun comes up, and covered by the monsoon's downpour, Senghor and I go out in search of food; the Burmese half-caste knows this jungle, he lived in it and says he knows how to look for and find food even under the fury of the monsoon.

And so he does.

We wade into the freezing waters of the river he calls Nagh-ndra (a tributary of the Chindwin River), and he pulls out a very large fish with his hands, it's similar to the catfish I remember from my youth but as long as an arm. He uses his hand as bait and he teaches me to do the same. Covered with brief loincloths –wet clothes are a pain in the neck and one can get skin blisters – and wearing sandals which Senghor made himself from tree bark, the texture is similar to cork- we spent the morning fishing.

Standing in the water up to our waists, close to the river edge and tied with a liana rope around our waists so the current can't drag us -the rain is unending and the river keeps rising- we plunge our arm into the water, touching the vegetation at the bottom, and when we feel the fish brushing past, instead of instinctively flinching, we leave our arm hanging loosely, waiting for the fish to confuse it with a plant; and when a fish starts its sucking motion, with our free hand we grab it by the tail -although there is some fight, we usually manage to grab it tight enough and with all our strength, throw it out onto the muddy river edge.

Our fishing was very productive: we easily picked up 25 to 30 fish weighing over 5 kgs each.

Every so often, Senghor or I climb out of the water and hit the dying fish over the head so they can't drag themselves back into the water.

Just as I'm out of the water performing this task, I notice something in the river. We never stop looking downriver because that is the direction from which any Japanese boats could approach. Due to the rain, the water current is running strongly not too far from the river edge, but we can't put our faith in this; our enemies know we're retreating and will take advantage of any situation to attack. They have with them an independent Hindu army and a small and badly-armed force of Burmese volunteers which we have defeated more than once, but this does not stop them from hunting us.

My attention has been caught by what looks like a log and which against any logic, is floating against the current. I click my tongue to warn Senghor, and then the most extraordinary, incredible thing happens, something I'd never seen before.

The Burmese half-caste hardly looks to where I've pointed and then in a single, almost inhuman movement, he cuts the safety rope and jumps out of the water towards the muddy edge; and at the same time, the log changes direction and with a speed equal to a torpedo, launches itself after him.

Senghor, the toughest warrior, the most brutal and fearless soldier I've ever known, lets out a screech of terror and runs at the speed of an athlete, while behind him what I took as a tree trunk and now identify as a crocodile launches itself out of the water, a figure I've seen sometime in a drawing… But this animal emerging from the river is an antediluvian monster, speedy and huge, measuring at least 7 mts long. It speeds after Senghor, who like a cat or a monkey starts climbing the nearest tree while the beast, pushing itself by its tail, jumps up and tries to trap the man who he's taken as his prey.

Without a thought -as happens when I'm in combat- in three jumps I've reached the tree under which we had left our clothes and weapons; I pick up Senghor's rifle –in half a second I've realized that my Thompson.45 is not potent enough to stop that giant. He's already turned with a nimbleness surprising in his size and has launched himself after me.

I hang the rifle on my back and climb the wet tree trunk using arms and feet. Fortunately the foliage has plenty of branches. The crocodile jumps against the tree, shaking it badly, then it returns to Senghor's tree and does the same.

I don't hesitate. I shoot at the head and to my surprise, the .303 bullet ricochets off the animal's armour-like head. I've wasted one bullet and have four left. I target its eye, which must be the size of a horse's. From a distance of 20 to 25 mts and with this monster moving, it's almost impossible.

Then the magic of a shot takes place once more.

Time stops, I no longer hear, all I see is the target in my sight. I inhale and without thinking, wishing or anything similar, I exhale and the bullet departs.

I hit the target, but I have to repeat the shots three more times for the animal to actually stop moving.

Senghor shouts gleefully, but he takes a while to climb down from his refuge. Even dead, the animal is frightening; it must easily measure about 1 ½ mts wide and its jaw about the same, lined with teeth larger than my thumb.

All it would have needed was one snap of its jaws to cut either of us in half.

Senghor finally makes his way down and with all his strength, drives his machete into its neck behind the eyes and in front of its front legs – as thick as my thighs – in an area where the skin is a lighter colour and definitely weaker than its back, which is a dark green, almost black.

The Burmese looks at me. He's still pale.

"Gordon *tuan*, I was going to tell you not to talk to the Buddhist wizard… But after seeing this, I think you too are a very powerful spirit. You're not afraid of anything. You've killed the giant who swims in the sea… It's a miracle… Many brave men are needed to defeat it… You saw how bullets bounce off its armour…"

It's raining too much to light a cigarette. I leave him to quarter the animal and head to our refuge.

As soon as I step into the roofed area I ask for a cigarette. My hands are still trembling; I hold tight onto the tobacco and order 10 men to look for Senghor and to fetch the food. I sit on the ground across from Tony and tell him about our adventure.

That night and for the next ten nights, we have plenty of meat.

Atisha gives his ration to the children, he's satisfied with fish and rice.

Every night after our dinner, I go to the open doorway to smoke, accompanied by the monk and every time he tells me a little more of his story and a great deal about Buddhism.

Every night I learn about him and his conversion to Buddhism.

About his father, a Chinese herbalist, and his mother, from the Philippines. About the Jesuit school and Father Pedro. About the death of his mother in a cholera epidemic, and his father's, drowned in opium vapours. Orphaned at age 12, his admiration for his mentor Father Pedro, and at 16 he discovers his vocation. At 18, the Seminary in Barcelona; his ordination at age 22 and his work as a missionary in the north of China. He's horrified by his encounter with the war between the Russians and the Chinese, the extermination of his parishioners and how his habit saved his life. His years drowned in alcohol, opium and low life; his loss of faith and his rebirth in a Chinese monastery.

Every night I learned about the four noble truths and the octuple path. A little more each night, that extraordinary man opened the dark veil which had enveloped my life.

I understood that I could be in that hellish war, survive and not go out of my mind by cherishing in my heart, with infinite maternal care and compassion, all those who were taking part in it. Nothing that I learned was totally strange; in a certain way, it had been written in my grandfather's letter, which I'd lost at Dunkirk. Even in my position –or better still, above all because of my position- I could be compassionate, noble and generous.

When we said goodbye –with no attachment, hugs, or words- I understood it would not be easy. But had my life ever been easy?

We returned to the world, after marching through a jungle which had become a quagmire.

The war was still there, eager to test me.

Farewell to the Warrior

I've walked the last 50 mts without being aware of where I'm going. I got out of the car, walked up to the veranda's steps, I climbed the six well-worn marble steps up to the door without being aware I had done any of this.

Only when my gloved hand went to the door handle of the main door did I look back towards the Rambler station wagon that had brought us here. My mother, exhausted because she wanted it that way, is still sitting in the driver's seat.

My sisters and I were brought here –almost by force. She drove straight from my father's funeral at the Llavallol Cemetery to Esperanza, stopping only to load petrol and hurrying us in and out of the bathrooms.

We went past where the accident took place without even looking out of the windows.

Mamá has not cried once. At least, not in front of us.

The uniform is my shield against tears. This is what Lieutenant Prieto said to me. "*Now, cadet, you will go through a man's toughest test. You'll see death face to face, and you'll know what you're made of. You'll be seeing your father. You father was a war hero and you'll see him dead. The shield for your tears is the uniform you're wearing… Do not dishonour either of them…"*

And he left me alone, in front of a metal table holding a body beneath a pretty filthy sheet in the town's hospital. The doctor and a man in a suit –from the judge's office- and all the ceremony. The sheet is pulled aside, and yes, it's my father, Gordon Evans.

I remember nothing of the trip there or back, except for Prieto's voice, talking about faith in Our God Jesus Christ, in our country, in the sacred brotherhood of Gen. San Martín's sons, which calms me enormously.

I remember almost nothing about the wake, I hadn't slept for three days or I'd been sleeping badly, but I remember clearly the guard of honour of my Company companions, wearing their dress uniforms and giving their posthumous salute to my father the soldier.

And of course, Lieutenant Prieto, his gloved hand on my shoulder or softly pressing my elbow.

When the coffin was lowered into the ground, my Company companions, the Lieutenant and I, we all gave the military salute. We did not embrace when we said goodbye at the cemetery parking lot.

They all stood before me in line and they saluted me; it's a martial salute from the Middle Ages, when the warriors used armour and to show their respect to each other, they'd lift the visor to look into each other's eyes; and so it was. Each of my companions stood in front of me, looked into my eyes and lifted their right hand -perfectly straight with the thumb only slightly bent- to their forehead, keeping it there for maybe a second and then returning their arm to their side, at attention.

Prieto also shook my hand firmly and said in a quiet voice two or three words before letting it go, about strength and my mother and my sisters.

I was given leave until Sunday at 11:00 p.m.

Before going into the house, I see *Don* Junco approaching the car, his head down and his hat in his hand.

Don Sandaza has obviously given him the news. I know he won't talk, all he'll do is murmur a few words of condolence. My mother gets out of the car and embraces the *gaucho*, who allows it even though he's clearly ashamed.

She hasn't removed her dark glasses which completely cover her eyes, not even once since we left Llavallol. Junco picks up the bags of food which my mother bought in the town; it's likely some friends and neighbours will come by with their condolences and there won't be time to do any shopping.

My grandfather is in Rosario taking care of Uncle Carlos, he's in the hospital seriously injured; Aunt Inés said there wasn't much hope. I don't give a shit, I hope he dies. My godfather drove like a madman. I travelled with them from Banfield to San Martín that very night of the accident and I know all of this is his fault, he was so excited with his damned new car.

I enter the library; to the left side of the door there is a small, very old cabinet with a marble top and a mirror that begins at the height of my waist. I look at myself; I still have my cap on. I had put it on very low, covering my forehead down to my eyes so the peak covered them.

No tear to be seen, the pupils are light-blue, the white of my eyes is very red through lack of sleep. My blue dress uniform jacket has no crease yet; I salute myself and then, very slowly in a martial ceremony, I take off my cap, I hang it on the coat stand and still very slowly, take off my gloves and place them carefully on the marble top. I take off my belt, from which my knife hangs.

Still very slowly and looking at myself in the mirror, I unbutton the gold buttons of my jacket, one by one, then take off my jacket with the same slow movements. I must do it carefully and respectfully. I'm removing the armour against my tears.

When I hang up the jacket on the opposite side I look down at the gloves. Under them there is a series of white sheets of paper on which my Dad's pen is lying -it was a present from Mrs Cummins in England, a black Montblanc with a gold nib. On the white sheets of paper, written in dark ink, I clearly see my father's beautiful, balanced handwriting.

Montoneros supporters, 1970-1976

Several pages are covered with it. I look down. I read.

"*Esperanza, August 1975.*

I believe I haven't sat down to write anything else that isn't a letter since the good old times at King George's College, when I used to write and write, assignments for history, for literature or science... It's funny, because it's been many years since I've even remembered those days!!

To think that I used to hate that place then, and today, when recalling it, I can't avoid feeling a certain melancholy. Nothing is left of the school and I suppose that with the bombing, all that work which I was so proud of but which academically didn't give me anything, must have all disappeared.

I particularly remember a very long piece of work on boy kings... Anyway, it seems this pen is making its own way, because I really didn't want to bring back memories... Or did I?

What's true is that I wanted to reflect in writing on Argentina's political evolvement. I'm worried, very worried about the direction the events are taking us and I'm afraid, after

Perón's death at the beginning of July, everything will get much worse.

How long since I've had any thoughts regarding politics!!!

Where are our ideas born? Where do they come from? Are they born with us? Do they appear when we grow?

When I was a child, I was a Socialist. I wasn't very sure what it meant, but I knew I was a Socialist. We didn't believe in any sort of God, we didn't go to Mass on Sundays. I went to secular schools where religion was optional. I remember clearly the confirmation ceremony of some of my St Alban's companions at the Lomas de Zamora Holy Trinity Church, and the communion of a Catholic companion.

In my house, the religion was politics.

My grandfather, my father and my mother were Socialists, members of the Argentine Socialist party founded by Dr Juan B. Justo; they believed that society was not just –and I still agree with them- but with a strong public education system, just laws that guarantee equal rights and that defend the weak against powerful men's abuse, an independent justice to apply them, a good public health system and an honest State administration, social progress was inevitable.

I went as a volunteer to the Spanish civil war thinking I would defend those principles, and seen from a distance, it's clear it was imperative to stop the Francoists, as was demonstrated in the horror in which we were immediately involved afterwards; we stopped the Nazi-Fascists, but at a terrible price. On the way my political ideas suffered enormously to the point of almost dying out.

My direct experience with the Communists showed me clearly that they are no better than the Fascists, I lived through that myself. I saw good, honest people fall brutally in their hands, in a totally unjustified way; as well as the brutalities they committed after the war in Poland, Czechoslovakia –martyred first by the Nazis and after by the Communists- in Hungary and other Central European countries. I saw with my own eyes how a good man was assassinated for his religious beliefs by the Chinese Communist army…

I presented myself as a voluntary for WW2 not because I had a political idea in mind; I marched to Europe with a feeling of indignation and fury, to take revenge for all those dead since 1936, for those I knew and those I didn't.

I guess I stopped thinking in political terms –if I ever had- one afternoon in September 1937 on the outskirts of Belchite.

I was indifferent to the political commissars' work; I sang the battalion's songs together with all the revolutionary repertoire, but by then the words had no meaning, lost in the cannons' roars.

I discovered spiritual relief in the Burmese jungle, and since then all political ideas have been secondary.

I left Argentina as a child and I returned an experienced man; I left a country in which —as my grandfather said- electoral fraud was the rule and not the exception, and I returned to a country in which an ex-colonel, suspected of being Fascist, was governing.

My arrival was undoubtedly not very conventional, and in spite of all I had heard about Perón, I promised to myself I would study him without any prejudice. At the beginning my mother's letters were cautious, the Socialists began to form part of the coalition that confronted Perón, and then in the 1943 coup there were many Nazi sympathizers among the military men. There were many Nazi sympathizers in all the countries where in one way or another they had been victims of innumerable abuses in the hands of the strong nations - their most terrible manifestation has been colonialism, that atrocious form of larceny.

Fidel Castro

To be a witness of India and Pakistan's *independence* even after seeing the ferocious war which tore them apart -and which has still to be resolved between those two formidable countries- has been a gift after so much death and horror. I think shaking off the British yoke was worth it to them.

Didn't the same thing take place in our Latin America after San Martín and Bolivar's heroic feats, sparking civil wars after every independence?

Argentina didn't take part in the World War because the Brits didn't want us in the war: meat, wheat and all the other indispensable supplements travelled safely, protected by the neutrality of the Inca sun on the light blue and white flag; the North Americans, on the other hand, wanted our country to join Brazil, Colombia and other South American countries in participating in the military effort; I'm convinced that it tourned otu to be the best alternative for our country.

If the 1943 coup was led by nationalist groups with Fascist tendencies —almost the same ones who staged the coup I saw from my grandfather's terrace on September 6, 1930- the elections of 1946 were undeniably free of fraud and there was no doubt were won by Perón.

The Unión Democrática did the country a very poor favour by allowing Braden to take part in those elections.

I've often asked myself if the State Department was actually favouring Perón when they authorised Braden to take part in the campaign…

But it's also true that the whole power structure behind Rawson, Farrel and Ramírez' government was at his service. Was he not Vice President, Minister of War and Secretary of Labour and Social Security? Wasn't that how he built his power?

I returned to the country in 1949, arriving on foot from Chile and I took my time to reach Buenos Aires. It attracted and repelled me almost equally. During the years I was away both my grandfather and father had died; when I left the British Army my mother no longer received the coins with which the Empire paid my services –my poor mother, she had to share my meagre salary as a soldier with the sister and widow of my two companions in Spain, and their two little boys- and I felt ashamed. But at the same time I needed desperately to return, to try and quench the fire burning inside me.

When coming down from north to south I again crossed the landscapes which as a child my grandfather had shown me, and my soul, full of death and bitterness, started to heal with the high plateau's soft air, with the earth's varied colours, with the skies which I had forgotten were so full of stars.

Ernesto Che Guevara

Then I met up with the most humble people, and just as I had found in India, when they found me bumming around and sleeping out in the open, they never took any notice of my white skin, my light-blue eyes, my red hair. There was solidarity and friendly hands, smiles and kind gestures; physically I had the looks of a white conqueror but my clothes, my military backpack and off-the-main-road journey took me among them, and slowly their generosity opened up, and they talked to me about their hopes in that man who everybody called Perón, who would help them out of their age-old poverty.

That's how I found the second Perón of my life.

The first one I had seen very negatively –except for a newspaper in English but written by and for Hindus- through the specific filter of the written press. I had not read anything truly positive about him. The pro-communist leftists were called on to move against him –here on the democratic front the Communist Party went under Ambassador Braden's wing… and the conservative rightists complained about his pro-workers' slant.

As I said before, Mamá's letters were against him at the beginning, but afterwards she began to feel more sympathy towards the evident changes that were happening around him, and above all, the figure of Eva had captivated her.

While I headed towards Buenos Aires, each province had their own way of seeing Perón. In Jujuy and Salta the Coya people looked at him with mistrust and hope at the same time.

In Tucumán, birthplace of the great enunciator of modern Argentina, J.A. Roca, the elite as well as the rest of the higher class strongly opposed him; the middle class urbanites, disoriented, had massively followed the Unión Democrática's fantasy. The peasant people, ignorant but lucid, had understood that if the workshop or the *estancia* bosses were against him, then they had to support him.

Córdoba was another experience; the working class were more aware – although the small and middle-sized industries had benefitted from the policies followed by Perón during the war, they had been working before he arrived on the scene; the Socialist penetration and the unions that were already organized divided the working class, and they suspected that beneath the *poncho*, the colonel hid more than gifts -and that in truth he was expecting to move into the workers' movement to unify leadership. And I don't think they were wrong.

When I arrived in the city of Buenos Aires I was very impressed by the amount of people travelling in the train with the obvious intention of staying in the city, as well as by the size of the city. When I left I was 12 years old and the truth is, in spite of the time I spent there with my grandfather, I was not conscious of the size of the city – its shadow had grown but had not matured.

The hustle and bustle of the city, the traffic, the trams… I'd always believed I'd come from a provincial city, and all at once I had the impression that London wasn't that important.

It's true that everything I'd seen about Europe was still under the atrocious shadow of the war, clearly visible even in those places like Paris or Rome (which had managed to escape the bombing), but Buenos Aires, my Buenos Aires, had nothing to envy regarding any city I'd known. And that first impression never went away.

Mamá and Graciela greeted me like a prodigal son, and I lived feelings I'd hidden away and thought I'd buried in Aragón. And I saw with my own eyes how the Eva Perón Foundation had placed a sewing machine in my mother's hands, and this had literally and radically changed her working time. When I was no longer sending my soldier's salary home, my mother and my sister had remained on the edge of extreme poverty, but after receiving that gift their lives had taken a positive turn.

In addition to this, they also received a wheelchair, allowing my sister, immobilised for life, to come out of her bedroom – she could not only breathe pure air and be out in the warm spring sun, but it also completely simplified both their lives.

My heart was thankful to Perón and his wife, they had covered my back, allowing me to abandon my services to Her British Majesty and to become the master of my destiny once again.

Very much against my wishes, I was hired by the Argentine Army towards the end of 1949; through an agreement between the Allies –Perón had declared war on Germany a few weeks prior to the fall of Berlin- I was not obliged to do my military service, but the family home was small and I had no job. As an Allied soldier I could have become an officer, but the truth is that the lesser salary of an NCO was enough for my few expenses and above all, helped my mother and sister. I wasn't happy, but I was at peace; and after all, that's how I met my wife…

In the Army I found something similar to what used to take place in the Republican army: politics existed and politics were very much talked about.

But it was only one way; it was not about a debate of ideas but about an ideological recruitment in favour of President Perón; talking against him was not sensible and much less so among the non-commissioned officers.

Among the officers the acts of corruption, the perks, were a frequent part of the scene.

When a cadet of the Military School, the son of a Peronist politician, assassinated Major De La Colina and then shot himself, I personally saw how the concealment mechanisms were rolled out to avoid the name of one of Perón's men being linked to the scandal.

When Brig. Gen. Menéndez led the uprising, it was made clear to me that in spite of the intense government spying activities, not everything could be controlled. I didn't take part in that protest because then, as now, the idea of being forced by a bayonet to participate in politics disgusts me. I did what I could during that riot to avoid cadets and conscripts being involved; and although I earned some degree of hate, I know I did the correct thing – one's subordinates are what is most precious when they're one's responsibility.

It just so happens that on that 1951 morning, I was in charge of the night watch of the First Year cadets' dorm, and as no-one had contacted me to form part of the uprising –I would have refused to take part anyway- I made sure they could not get out. Before the afternoon was over, those who participated in the coup had been detained and the several cadets who had taken part were expelled.

I understood immediately that what was taking place in Argentina was not normal.

Perón used Fascist liturgy, the Fascist rhetoric and behaviour: an exasperating cult to the personality. Ships and planes, streets and avenues, parks and buildings, provinces and municipalities carried the name of the "leader" –as Franco does, as Hitler and Mussolini did- and here now, the names of Perón and Evita.

Not happy with that, he replaced the Catholic Church's private charity and other charity organizations with a system by which those needs were satisfied with state funds -but with their own stamp as *Fundación Eva Perón* (Eva Perón Foundation).

My mother was a direct beneficiary of this, and it generated a loyalty conflict in me with Perón which I was able to clear in 1955.

Also, to add to the conflict in my conscience, the noticeable presence of numerous Nazis – Belgians, Frenchmen, Yugoslavians, Hungarians and Germans- in the background of the Peronist government filled me with rejection and indignation. Perón surrounded by the frightening *Ustachas* —Yugoslavian SS- was repulsive to me, as was the presence of self-confessed Nazis such as Palevic, one of the several who visited Government House.

But I didn't take part in the 1955 coup.

The *estancia*, which had been in a complete state of abandon when I bought it towards the end of 1953, had needed all my time and effort.

My in-laws, with the exception of my father-in-law and my wife, no longer had anything to do with me because I hadn't placed my military experience in service to the civilian-military coup against Perón.

I didn't believe then and confirmed later that nothing good can emerge from a coup d'etat; I refused to take part, I refused to train in using weapons, I refused to cooperate economically; but when the first revolt in June failed, I hid in my home friends of the family who were on the run from justice.

The 1956 executions deeply affected me: Gen. J.J. Valle had an impeccable reputation within the Armed Forces; the statute of limitations, the solution which the anti-Peronist Revolution resorted to, seemed disastrous to me. My position didn't make me popular among my in-laws' social circle.

Arturo Frondizi's idea of "developmentalism" I considered novel and an improvement, integrating social justice and development, giving Argentina a place in the world; an independent diplomatic position in the Foreign Affairs San Martin Palace when facing the Cuban revolution; the North American intervention in Asia's South West and the Soviet's in Eastern Europe; these confirmed to me that at last our country was recovering its course lost in 1930.

The country, in a world attempting to recover from the delirium that had swept the '30s and '40s decades, had found a road to development that would allow it to recover a place within the community of nations from which it should never have left.

I remember my grandfather talking proudly about Yrigoyen's position on WWI regarding the North American invasion of Nicaragua -among my newspaper cuttings I have a letter from the Sandino leader published in La Nación- which my grandfather himself as well as many other Socialists had supported.

I didn't vote for Arturo Illia and I'm sorry I didn't. The military governments were inefficient, inept and brutal. Time went by and Perón was not returning.

But it was clear that Madrid was the political capital of Argentina and there was no way around it. Prescription completely deformed political reality.

The Córdoba events, the assassination of trade union leader Vandor -with no apparent link- and the permanent social conflict crushed the "Argentine Revolution"; mediocre

Gen. Onganía –whom was compared to Franco…- lasted less than a heartbeat in the Presidency; then Gen. Lanusse took a step in which he could have avoided the bragging, calling for elections with Peronism but without Perón being included.

We were all amazed to learn of the assassination of Gen. Aramburu, or almost all. I heard some Peronist pointing out that it was revenge for Valle's assassination, and I felt a cold shiver down my back. In Spain, the events of July 1936 began with killings on both sides of the two rival bands during the years previous to the war.

Executing Valle was not a minor error, it was a more than an unjust sentence, a brutal gesture but within a legal framework –the military justice code- and General Valle knew what he was facing when he set out against his fellow Army comrades.

According to the members of the Aramburu crusade, the chief of the "*Revolución Libertadora*" was in the middle of coming to an agreement with Perón in order to stop the growing political violence; and the kidnapping and subsequent assassination of the general turned into an effective means to light the spark to the hell in which we would all burn.

There is a golden rule for resolving political crimes: Who benefits from them? Who gets to kidnap a nation's general, dressed as Army officers, and considers this a service? Who benefits from assassinating him in a damp basement, covering him with lime?

The wave of crimes that followed –and they increased week after week, month after month- gives one a clear idea of the perpetrators' objective, and reminds one, to those who recall history, of the brutality that the Nazis carefully established in Germany before coming into power: indiscriminate terrorism forces the common man to tolerate any kind of outrage as long as he can go back to a peaceful life.

The Federal Court found a way to resolve the wave of crimes which were then taking place in Argentina, but their cadence and gravity filled me with concern about the future.

Nobody could foresee in 1969 that the uprising called the Cordobazo would lead to a civil war; the assassination of Aramburu was quickly cleared up; it tamely was added to the political crimes that occasionally have marked our history such as the ones against Gen. Urquiza or Senator Bordabehere.

Those of us who thought this were wrong.

The violence that took place upon the return of an old Perón should have been a warning, but not even I, with all my experience, thought that it was the beginning of something worse; on the contrary, like many others, I thought it was the death rattle, the end of a cycle of violence, that with Perón in the country everything would get better.

In the first 1973 elections I voted UCRI (Radicals) but when the May amnesty was declared and Perón's anger displaced Cámpora, I didn't hesitate: I voted for Perón and I wasn't wrong, he was the only one who could handle the increasing, daily violence… but the assassination of Rucci marked the beginning of a fierce violent period between militarised civilians and the country's Armed Forces.

I was not deceived in 1955 and neither was I deceived in 1973: I learnt in the most cruel way that peace has an immeasurable value; Perón, who can't be viewed as innocent, had encouraged this brutal ruse from his exile, so that the violence that began in 1955 and at first was quiet in the background, with no holding back then blew up as a bomb in our faces.

I confess I didn't vote for Perón for the correct reasons; but from the beginning of the 1960s, it was he who encouraged the guerrillas who had been trying to set foot in our country – the Uturuncos before the Montoneros- and it must be he who should disarm and punish those who had committed the crimes.

But Perón wasn't Peronism... what was ripped apart with the 1973 amnesty began to bleed immediately.

I keep the newspaper cuttings of each one of the murders committed since then, very carefully filed by date in a folder. They are too many: businessmen, students, professors, policemen, military men, employees. Men, women, children.

I've asked myself not once but a thousand times if Argentina really needed an armed revolution, a 360 degree turn, a new beginning.

It's true there are poverty issues –such as in Greater Rosario or in many districts of Greater Buenos Aires- but it's also true that, unlike many other places in the world, here the education is public and free, even the University itself; access to health is possible; syndicate rights are even better than many of those in the developed countries, and the trade unions are powerful; Peronist proscription is over and Perón is in power... Why is it necessary to launch into an armed combat?

It's clear this can't be separated from the confrontation between the Soviet Union block and the West led by the U.S.A. and Great Britain.

I wasn't surprised at all at the turn of events at the end of WWII.

I suffered first-hand the intolerance and ideological narrow-mindedness of the Spanish communists. Beneath their inhuman brutality I lost a brother and since then I was never again deceived: they have no qualm in betraying their best friend if they suspect a capitalist "deviation".

In the years following the war I saw supposedly educated and decent people support "Comrade" Stalin and his bloody dictatorship, and worse still, how these "fellow travelers" despised, persecuted and isolated anyone who had different ideas.

Orwell, whom I admired so much, twice suffered that informal persecution. Once when the POUM (the Spanish communist party) was dismantled and later, at the end of his life, when Stalinists around him discovered the fierceness of his prose in "Animal Farm" and "1984".

Will there be another war?

I don't think so. Instead I have the impression that all the internal conflicts of the Third World countries are, in fact, used to resolve the confrontations between the Soviets and the capitalists.

I felt empathy towards the Cuban revolution, one wanted to support any movement geared towards ending long-term dictatorships. But they've been in power for 14 years and haven't made a single move towards an open democracy; on the contrary, they've become allies with the Soviets and just like them, they've launched into a deep transformation of their society, brutally getting rid of anyone who is in opposition; this is not precisely what I consider a democratic society.

I don't believe that Socialism and Democracy should be opposed and above all, I don't believe the "dictatorship of the proletariat" is the path to progress as there can't be any progress in any dictatorship.

Also, it's clear that in Cuba and the Soviet Union the "society without classes" is directed by an elite that enjoys innumerable benefits and advantages to which the rest of the citizens have no access, and in practice they're a class above the rest.

What kind of a revolution is that?

I haven't a single doubt that with all its defects, bourgeois democracy is more adequate for human development than the Soviet communist revolution.

Perón's death just a few weeks ago, although predictable, has brought further chaos to the chaos. The stupid choice of his wife Isabelita as his successor has been the biggest mistake in history and can only be attributed to the old leader's senility.

Surrounded by a group of semi-mafia-like people -among them the grim López Rega stands out- that small and ignorant woman is not in any condition to direct even a neighbourhood club, and more chaos is just around the corner.

The government is pushing a system of illegal retaliations that can only spiral into violence, never halt it; the creation of the Triple A –Argentine Anti-Communist Alliance- and the freedom of action for the unions' gunmen has been like attempting to put out a fierce fire with buckets of fuel.

The continuous attacks on military units do not auger anything good.

Seen from a distance, I should never have accompanied Charly to join the Military School, I should never have educated him on a military life…

He has promised me that when he finishes the year he will enrol in the Faculty to study medicine, but that doesn't actually make me feel better. In the guerrilla bands there are quite a few former students from military schools. Wasn't that how they kidnapped Aramburu?

I'm afraid that my son, as happened to me in 1937, will be caught within the fierce whirlwind of a civil war which will not be long in coming, but I can't find…"

I finished reading my father's posthumous texts, and it's clear that my country is in danger -my father, with his lucid intelligence, is showing me the way.

This coming Monday I'll begin the paperwork to be accepted into the Military Academy's second year.

The Time Machine.

My grandfather stated that H.G. Wells – an author whom he admired deeply- hadn't invented anything when he wroe "The Time Machine"; my grandfather too had his own way of travelling through the centuries, of communicating with men and ideas, from the past and the future.

He said it was enough to launch a question into space from the platform of his mind and then, very calmly, run his index finger along the shelves of his huge library.

Or to review an old notebook that his great-grandfather Porrá began to write in 1776, and in it -using a particular method and written by several generations- were listed the books in a library in which the first book, dated 1695, was a Bible printed in Latin, a delicate piece of work printed on almost transparent paper and richly decorated with details in gold on its leather covers.

The Porrás who came after that ancestor so connected to Catholic practices –he had some secular position very closely related to the church's form of government- had gone on to lose their faith right up to my grandfather, who was frankly against the interference of religion in civilian life, but it did not stop him from keeping the valuable collection of sacred books, among which a translation of Calvin and another of Luther stood out. In total, the library has some thirty religious books - missals, lives of saints, books for catechism and Bibles – from different ages and with a variety of printing qualities, mostly in Latin but which also included some in Spanish, English and Portuguese, and a few in German and Italian.

This library, added to for over two centuries, is now mine, although I know it's only on loan: I must add to it and preserve it for my children and their children and also their children…

Starting from my grandfather's great-grandfather's Bible, the time machine passed from my ancestors' hands of a few copies to become one of the most important private libraries at the beginning of the XIXth century in colonial Buenos Aires, and which in its time could compete with the most celebrated libraries of that time, Father Mazie's library, Berois's and Fernández's.

Frayed and worn, it is kept between two pieces of glass and delicately framed by Maestro Porrá's father, a document in Latin signed and sealed by Pope Pious VI dated 1790, authorizing *Don* Francisco de Asís Díaz Porrá to possess –due to his proven qualities and moral Catholic virtues- books that were forbidden to the common mortals.

Therefore, it includes the main scientific, philosophical and artistic works that deeply moved the well named Age of Enlightenment and the impulse of which launched our civilization towards a continuous future whose end has yet to be written.

Included are the Diderot & D'Alembert's first encyclopaedia; Jean Condorcet's books, others by Rousseau, Voltaire, Locke, Montesquieu, Hume, Quesnay, Descartes, Espinoza, Kant, Descartes, Smith.

But it doesn't end only with the great names. There are marvellous pearls, such as the "Calendar" that covers the entire XVIII century published in Lisbon in 1748, written by one of South America's first scientists, Father Buenaventura Suarez or the "prayer against the plague" by San Vicente Ferrer, printed in 1783.

Besides books and other publications from different ages, it also has copies of numerous official documents, reproduced to celebrate the 1862 reunification, some from the May Revolution, including some from previous days, such as Mariano Moreno's "The Landowners' Representation" and a juicy economic memoir of the Viceroyalty signed by Manuel Belgrano.

Belgrano, undoubtedly the most intelligent intellectual of the May Revolution, figures numerous times in this small Alexandrian library; it contains his translation of the "Principles of Economic Science" and the first copies of the "Correo de Comercio" weekly paper.

Very tidily placed in folders in a plain leather pack are theatre programmes and handwritten invitations to social gatherings and meetings, as well as all kinds of printed texts that allow a reader to gaze into the past from a very close and exciting perspective.

No book is missing on travels around America. Those by the invader Gillespie, Parrish, Humboldt's monumental work, or Darwin's first edition, among the most notorious, the most well-known.

My ancestors have lived a most intense political and social life, which is clearly reflected in this marvellous collection of memories.

My grandfather improved this library throughout his lifetime, and before him, his father, and before him, his father; each one contributed the best pieces of work of their time, with no heed for the language –there are books in English, French, Italian, German, Ancient Greek, Latin- an extraordinary record.

Small pearls that makes one's soul rejoice, as much by their candidness as by their connection with this country's origins, of which I'm a son by choice and by right, such as Lavarden's *Sátira contra los limeños* (Satyre Against Citizens of Lima), which has comments in my great-great-grandfather's handwriting –his wife had been born in Lima- and whose opinions in verse are perhaps even better than those printed…

Together with the imposing, complete set of works by Sarmiento, there are some twenty pedagogic papers signed by my grandfather.

The Conference programme which Einstein gave in Buenos Aires together with several summaries on his theories published in the local media –the coincidence in opinions regarding the texts in La Nación and Claridad are quite remarkable- as well as a neat print of the conference's texts.

Of course all the political or literary pieces of the great local socialists are included, men whom my grandfather admired and who honoured him with their friendship: pieces by Juan B. Justo, José Ingenieros and Alfredo Palacios –almost all of them dedicated affectionately to him by the authors- as well as by Payró.

There is a long shelf containing every single book on ancient history, sometimes the authors are repeated two or three times; Pliny the Elder in Latin, in French and Spanish; Plutarch and his parallel lives, the Odyssey, Aristotle, Sophocles, Plato, Aristophanes.

No romantic is missing, Goethe in German and Spanish, but also Shelley and Byron, Swift's sharp satire and the poignant Dickens, all of them carefully aligned, in order by title, by topic, by author.

Numerous books and short stories published in Montevideo in Rosas' time also have their shelf. Mármol, Echeverría, Alberdi –one copy of his "Bases" autographed and dedicated to my grandfather moves me just by remembering it- are lined up and next to everything that has been published on Argentine history.

The history collection is amazing and includes the Jesuits Pauke and Dobrizoffer, the indescribable Mitre – glossed over by my grandfather who was particularly irritated by him- Groussac, Saldías, López, Gálvez, and other lesser known men whose names have been forgotten today; none are missing when wanting to delve into the intricate past of this heart-wrenching and dualistic country.

The shelf with historical biographies and autobiographies is complete: "Paz", written by himself, as well as Iriarte; "Rosas" written by Gálvez; "San Martín" by Mitre and by Otero; "Facundo" by Sarmiento. "Belgrano" by Mitre; "Sarmiento" by Lugones; my grandfather was so generous, he hated Mitre but all Mitre's books on history are here, and perhaps to make the detested author's important-sounding and obscure use of language stand out, my grandfather has provided comments on them with simplicity and a sense of humour.

The entertainment literature that was characteristic of the XIXth century fascinated my grandfather, and he left out none: Verne's complete collection, both in Spanish and French; the same as Duma´s father and son; all Salgari – a beautifully illustrated posthumous copy - and repeating the custom of duplicate copies, all Mark Twain in the original as well as translated; the first Spanish edition of Tarzan.

I think the collection of Argentine literature – begun by my grandfather's mother with the first copies of books by Mármol and Echeverría, the most complete you can ever dream of- up to the year my grandfather died, no obvious anthology, literary magazine or published author published between 1870 and 1937 is left out; there are autographed books by José Hernández, Eduardo Gutiérrez, Hilario Ascasubi –who when old, used to have lunch at my great- Grandmother's home; Vicente Fidel López, Juan María Gutiérrez –my grandfather was one of his pupils- Estanislao del Campo… all the books published in those brilliant years are here, within my reach.

Another of my grandfather's friends whose books are abundantly present are General Lucio N. Mansilla's, a comrade-in-arms of my grandfather's elder brother, Vicente Porrá -he'd been one of Mansilla's lieutenants- and Mansilla had taught Grandfather the art of swordplay according to French and Italian schools, and how to fight duels with pistols (two beautiful German pistols which the General had sent to be engraved with the family's crest). According to my mother, my grandfather could cut a flower's stem with them at 25 paces firing with either of his hands.

Together on one shelf – although many of them would fight each other for personal or aesthetic reasons- are all the illustrious books by Argentine authors of the first decades of the XXth century: Lugones, with whom Maestro Porrá had supper once a month until September 6th; Güiraldes, more of an Eastern religious follower; he shared a passion for everything connected to *gauchos* with Solanet, and somewhere in there are autographed books by Alfonsina Storni and Pedro Bonifacio Palacios, whom he met during his long term as an official in the Ministry of Education. Everything published by these men and women authors are there, many of them dedicated with beautiful and sensitive autographs.

Among my favourite books are Quiroga's scary brilliant writings, he's our local Poe; undoubtedly "Don Segundo Sombra"'s deep but simple spirituality moves me to tears – this tale, as an initiation book, is equal to Hesse's Damian.

Four folders full of musical scores from all ages show up my ancestors' cultural passion; my grandfather was a very good guitar player, he knew everything about our creole music; my mother was a wonderful pianist, until the old piano at home was sold after my father died.

My father also provided a small contribution.

Included are John D. Evans memoirs in an edition from the end of the 1800s, and the complete collection of "Claridad" magazine, which brings back such good memories.

And Krishnamurti, with a prologue by Victoria Ocampo; a Borges first edition; some copies of Sur, the magazine which was supposedly a counterpart to Claridad, but not to a voracious reader like my Dad, who was willing to know and to learn everything.

Konrad, Wilde, Cunninghame, Kipling, London, Bierce, Melville, all have a privileged place in that contribution.

And I have mine.

When I arrived in 1949, the living-dining room of our house in Escalada had turned into a book deposit, piles of packets tied together and wrapped carefully in the newspapers of those days, all very tightly packed from floor to ceiling.

Papá had been in charge of dismantling that powerful library as it was the only thing my mother had claimed as an inheritance, and which her sisters had given to her immediately; he had taken exactly six months to do this, working every weekend non-stop until early hours of the morning putting together those packets, all carefully organized.

Of course Mamá had not been able to go with him because she couldn't leave Cristina alone, but she used to cook and prepare his meals so that he could take them with him for lunch, tea and even supper to the big house in Barracas where three generations of Porrás had lived – he'd hardly stop to eat while he packed up all those marvellous documents.

As from the end of 1937, the living-room and the room which had been my bedroom were covered from floor to ceiling, not only the walls but also with carefully calculated shelves —one could hardly get in sideways, as long as one was thin enough- very skilfully built by good Meredith's hands, dividing up each of the rooms. This forced me, in a certain way, to join the Argentine Army - I had nowhere to sleep. In those rooms a little more than three thousand carefully packed books slept until fortune's fate, which has been so much a part of my life, allowed this —my only real treasure- to find a worthy and safe place.

When my dear *Don* Eurwen opened the doors to the future by allowing me to rescue my in-laws' bankrupt and broken down small farm, an inheritance from my mother-in-law's family, I didn't know that destiny had prepared this place for me.

It's the largest room in the house, it divides the house practically in half and originally it was a luxurious dining-room. This was the main house of the estancia "Puerta del Chaco", its papers showed that it had belonged to a Lieutenant López and been the centre of a failed provincial revolution at the time of the civil wars; and it was also where – purportedly- Garibaldi and his lover had slept during their journey through the province of Santa Fe.

On the south side are the kitchen and servants' quarters, which had been used as such until I took charge of the place; on the north side were the main rooms, three large bedrooms to which we had needed to add another bathroom next to the one which had been attached at the end of the XIXth century; it was freezing in winter but the coolest room for those stifling nights of which there are so many in the Santa Fe summers.

Organizing the 450 packets of books took me almost six years, but by the time I had finished our visitors expressed their admiration, and quite a few friends would take advantage of winter to spend some days keeping me company as well as to enjoy the original railway wood-burning stove which I placed under the window facing east, which also allows the warm winter sun to filter through, an invitation to the restful and demanding art of reading.

The organization of the collection had been imposed by my ancestors, who had also incorporated a series of folders with newspaper and magazine cuttings, as well as flyers, which covered all kinds of social, political and economic events as from the English invasions at the beginning of 1800 and ended, much to my distress, with the news on Dunkirk which my Dad had kept up to June 2 when the heart-attack interrupted his work; I know for certain that the anguish about my fate during those terrible days in 1940 began the process which ended his life.

The Nazis had not been able to kill me there, but long-distance, they had finished him.

The complete collection of "Claridad" magazine was carefully kept in folders –of which I had received extra copies all during the years at King George's College - and they remind me of my grandfather, my father, *Don* Eurwen, just by looking at the backs of the folders.

I've also made my contributions.

The complete collections of Life and Time magazines from 1939 to 1969: from the Second World War to the man on the Moon.

All works by modern, productive Argentine literature figures are here: Borges, Bioy Casares, Ocampo, Cortázar, Sábato, Arlt, Rojas, Macedonio; but I also brought in the North Americans, John Dos Passos, Hemingway, Steinbeck, Faulkner, Miller, Guinsberg; the South Americans, Martí, Zorrilla, Darío, Roa Bastos, García Márquez, Vargas Llosa, Fuentes, Benedetti, and the French: my comrade Malraux –pilot of the Republic-, the hero Saint Exupery, Sartre and Duras... once a month, my wife and I leave the children with Grandfather Rodrigué and we go up and down Corrientes Ave., diving into tons of books, seeking new emotions, new memory cartridges for our time machine.

My son does his homework on the reading table, and my daughters play around me on the floor, while I read and wait to be called to supper.

All times are now. The past which is no more except in these books –the wake of a boat in the sea- nor the future, however unpredictable, is also nestled in the ideas hidden in this written ocean.

The now is all that counts, all that is, is present here, in Charly frowning in concentration, in the seriousness with which he seeks -just as I did, as his ancestors did before- the knowledge that will allow him to journey through this life in the best way possible.

My wife is calling us to supper. We'll be back, all of us, to climb into my time machine.

浪人

VIII) RONIN

Rōnin: _____

Literally, "man wave" —a wanderer or drifter, like a wave in the sea. A rōnin was a Samurai without a Lord during the feudal period in Japan between 1185 and 1868.

On Argentina

1. Prelude

My father didn't talk to me directly about the war until my 12th birthday on November 3rd, 1968. In December of that year I would be finishing 6th grade and in a year's time exactly I would be starting my secondary school years.

Papá had stated more than once that St. Alban's College in Lomas de Zamora was a good alternative. It was a connection to his past in Argentina –he had spent all his primary schooling there- as well as the fact that it was near the Rodrigué grandparents' home. So my three sisters and I would be together again.

Almost systematically, each time he was with me and he remembered his father, he would ask me what I wished for myself in the future, what I would like to be when I was an adult; perhaps he wanted to try and awaken some sleeping vocation, or to excite my child's imagination with some possible dream.

We spent a great deal of time together because my mother moved into our grandparents' home so my sisters "could attend a good English school", as well as her working "at what she had studied", so I stayed with him on the *estancia*.

It was like a family peace treaty: I'd go to a state school in Esperanza for my primary schooling, while my sisters would attend a private school in Lomas de Zamora, the same one my mother had attended.

When I was older –much older, when my father had passed away- I understood that in some way he was trying –through me- to give back to his father what he and the circumstances had taken away from Meredith.

As every working man at the beginning of the 20th century, the most important wish my grandfather had for his son and his descendants was to achieve social progress, which meant a university career, a liberal profession.

It was not about money.

Although we weren't wealthy, the little farm –as my grandfather called it; the *"estancia"* as Uncle Carlitos called it; or home, as Papá and Mamá called it, gave us a reasonable income, as good as any lawyer or medical doctor –at least, this is what grandfather Mateo said; for Papá, much more important than to have a "good income" was to possess a university degree.

Something which he had denied himself when he'd gone off to the war in Spain.

Ever since I can remember, my answer has invariably been the same one: soldier, army, sergeant, general.

Very few times did my father ever show his deep irritation that this answer gave him. Today I understand it perfectly, but what does a young child know of war?

He used to say as part of his own experience that when children go to war or war happens around them, their childhood ends; better said, they cease being children at the first shot, at the first moment of terror.

When I stated my wish to attend Military School, my father —without losing his proverbial calm- looked at me a long moment, he shook his head a couple of times, then glanced down at his boots, locked his hands behind his back and spoke very softly to me.

"OK, Charly... I hope you'll not be disappointed, because once you head in that direction it's very difficult or even impossible to turn back... There's no way out, do you understand? I hope you never have to live through it to understand physically what I'm talking about..."

He wasn't angry —I've seldom seen him angry in my whole life- but my strong impression was that he was sad, and probably disappointed too.

This event and conversation took place unexpectedly.

The son of some friends of our family, a boy slightly older than myself, wanted to enrol in the General Espejo Military School near the city of Santa Fe, and knowing that my father had "real" military experience —as Uncle Carlitos used to say- they came to visit us at the *estancia* after my birthday with the intention of asking for my father's advice.

When the young man told us of his plans and showed us the carefully printed brochure, with beautiful coloured photographs of different scenes of the cadets' lives, I was immediately possessed by the clear vision that that's where my future lay.

I wouldn't have to wait to finish my secondary schooling —as I'd been told up till then- to form part of the Armed Forces!

I didn't understand then that it was secondary schooling with a military training. What I saw in those photos was the means to fulfil my vocation, my destiny.

Papá, as he always did, listened to the father, the mother, the young man, he studied the brochures carefully and after lunch, he invited them to go out riding with him.

When Papá needed to think carefully about something, he'd go out into the countryside; sometimes he'd drive out in the battered Jeep; others – like then- he'd mount his beautiful blue roan with his dress saddle; this had a white sheep skin over the untreated leather pads embossed with *pampas* motifs, a few nickel silver details which he had made himself with the help of *Don* Junco's expert eye, and beneath the saddle were the thick, woven red wool saddle blankets which we had brought back sometime from the province of Salta.

My father wasn't fond of giving advice but he was very good at giving it, so paradoxically, he was frequently sought out.

He understood that his words were important to those who came to seek his advice, so he never gave an immediate answer to any question, and sometimes he'd take more than a day to give his opinion.

It was a commitment he'd take on without any pleasure but with great responsibility. A horse ride, a barbecue, a ride in the canoe along the stream, a camping trip beside the river were all excuses that he made to gain some time and give a well-thought out answer, appropriate to each case.

I didn't wait, that time, for Papá to give his opinion.

Without even thinking about it -as grandfather Rodrigué used to tell me frequently, "You have two ears and one mouth, to listen twice more than you talk"- with a childish enthusiasm which I didn't even recognize, I said I wanted that same destiny, the same school, the same uniform.

This disconcerted my father to such a point that he took a whole afternoon to explain in detail his many objections to children enrolling in a military institution.

At dinner time, our guests were ready for my father's reply, and he, still alarmed by the opening I had taken advantage of, told a story in detail —something I hadn't heard him ever do before- regarding an accident that had taken place among the recruits he had trained in the Pakistan army under British orders.

Their recruitment system —typical in a nation undergoing its birth- was both voluntary and obligatory, and the recently created Pakistan Army was a mixture of young men of all ages, some obliged through some form of conscription, while others were volunteers who wanted to help create the new state.

Many of those only fourteen years old were basically motivated by the hunger that was hitting many of the country's regions.

So my father found himself training some fifty young men - yet however much they tried, they were still practically children.

With his calm voice full of inflexions punctuated with perfect silences, he told us what had happened after a shooting practice with a mortar in which they had used war munitions -that is, with explosives as well as the propellant, and not empty as was usually done in exercises.

I saw this in later life: it's common after shooting fifty or sixty charges, some grenades don't get to explode in the shooting range and this is what took place that day.

In spite of the warnings given to them and the clear obligation that they must call for the explosive experts to handle these devices if any were found, a group of very young recruits, 12 in all -the oldest 17 and the youngest had just had his 14th birthday- died or ended up severely injured after playing at passing the grenade one to the other, using one of those lethal devices as if it were a rugby ball.

"This was not a coincidence, at all. Children should be playing sports, not handling arms." This was my father talking, closing his story with the memory of the horrible impression he had of the mutilated bodies. He finished, "When the Nazis had already lost the war, they launched against us hordes of fanatical young children from the Hitler youth as cannon fodder, badly armed, badly trained, to make our push more complicated while they planned an impossible escape…" He shook his head slightly, carefully, as if wanting to remove the images he still held from that day.

"Maturity and a balance are necessary to handle anything to do with a war, and it's difficult -almost impossible- for an adolescent to be able to do this."

He ended, "Perhaps that institution, which I know nothing about, has found a way, a balance, an adequate path for the young men such as our sons to receive military instructions without any risks to them or to others. This school was founded after I'd already left for England, I don't know anyone who has attended it."

He looked at me with his kind eyes and spoke to everyone. "If I could stop my son going to a military institution, I would. But I can't: each person must follow their own destiny. I hope you can stop your son from going to that school."

I heard later that the young man had failed his entrance examination.

Our friends left that Sunday morning, fearing they had opened up a rift between my father and myself.

But they didn't know what kind of man my *viejo* was.

He loved his children, all of them, with a solid, transparent love and besides, he was a wise man. He didn't try to stop me, confront me, or make me change my mind.

Quite the opposite, he used my desire to go to military school as a way of getting close to me, to know me better, to understand what was driving me along that road.

Mamá was not a stranger to what was taking place.

I got to know, after my Dad died, that they consulted each other about everything regarding their children —my three sisters and myself- and she had suggested that if he couldn't convince me, that he should at least teach me everything he could to make me the best cadet possible.

Whenever there was any conflict – there were very few, but still, they existed- between my Dad and myself- Mamá was the mediator between us.

My mother's arguments are always very simple, always convincing. She was capable of selling him the moon because he loved her blindly.

Also, my mother has a chilling optimism, which allows her to confront any situation calmly and with a positive attitude; she's capable of finding the good side to meteorites raining down onto the planet, to a cloud of locusts invading the fields or to a visit by Uncle Carlitos and his friends.

This was how my Dad, who had initially rejected my idea of going to the military school, took me to visit the Liceo General San Martín, an hour's ride from my grandparents' house in Banfield.

So it was that that summer, before beginning 7th grade, the last year at primary school and at the end of which I'd have to sit for the entrance exam, that Papá began to tell me –in his deep, melodious voice- about his war experiences.

These weren't heroic tales in which he was the protagonist: they were about other men's acts of courage, about the sacrifices and self-denials of those who had fallen, the pain of losing friends and companions, the fear of one's own death.

When I did learn of his courage and how effective he had been as a soldier, it didn't come straight from him; it was because I had the fortune of meeting some of his comrades. From him all I heard was about the evil, horror and fear that a soldier lives through; sometimes, in spite of himself, a soft glow of pride appeared when he told of his companions' feats.

Only with the passage of time and the circumstances of my life in which I became involved because of my own choice, did I understand my father's reasons when he told me his war stories.

He tried desperately to keep me away from a fate which he personally knew was a terrible one, with the crude knowledge of someone who had lived and survived many long years of horror in the most terrible wars that had torn apart the first half of the 20th century.

Let me be clear. Papá didn't give in to my desire as an acquiescent, passive parent. He introduced all kinds of obstacles, all kinds of reasonable and rational arguments to avoid my entering the Liceo.

My *Viejo* was clear since the first day he heard my idea.

War was an extraordinary situation, killing so many people, ruining many more people's lives and from which no-one returned unscathed – it brought nothing good or healthy.

But I'd inherited his stubbornness, and to each statement, to each story I'd find a positive side, which pointed to my Rodrigué inheritance. There was one argument my Dad couldn't refute: he had survived, and he was still a good man.

This is how he changed from being in frank opposition to critical cooperation during which he didn't spare me any of the horrors he had seen and experienced during his war years.

In the winter holidays of July 1969 we went on our first visit to the Liceo.

To my father's surprise, the Liceo's Deputy Director was Col. Llogri, who had been one of his students at the military academy in 1951. The colonel remembered my father perfectly and they greeted each other first with a military salute and then with a firm handshake.

The smiles they exchanged augured a good beginning to our visit.

Papá didn't have good memories of his time in the Argentine Armed Forces.

The soldiers' uniforms, their badges and weapons reminded him too much of those he had fought against in Europe.

Party politics – Peronists and anti-Peronists - and Menéndez' failed coup in 1951 had definitely pushed him out of the Army.

But he kept good memories of the cadets and conscripts with whom he had forged a bond of likeability and respect.

I learnt much later that Llogri had managed to stay in the Military Academy – after the September 28th trouble – thanks to my father, who had locked the bedroom doors of the Year II cadets and stopped them from taking part in what turned into the failed revolt.

Other cadets who had shown support to the revolt had been inexorably expelled, regardless of their academic marks.

As we were doing the rounds of the Liceo, the colonel recalled my father as his NCO trainer with affection and gratitude, because he had none of the unpleasant manners or Prussian-style violence, and possessed notable leadership skills.

Llogri immediately understood my father's qualms and to my surprise, he shared them. He then went on to describe the Liceo's objectives: to train independent young men, self-disciplined, trained intellectually to study and physically to achieve a harmonious development; and he emphasized that although they were well instructed in a military style, it was not their intention to incorporate them to the Armed Forces but to retain them as reserve officers.

He also said the magic words that my father needed to hear.

"Sergeant Evans, the Liceo was created to form reserve officers with the best academic education possible; the boys spend five years with military discipline and the statistics show that few cadets from this or other military schools in the country then enrol in the Military Academy. The Liceo is a cemetery for early military vocations. There are more lawyers, medical doctors, engineers and accountants among those graduating from the Liceos than from other schools. I myself attended this same school between 1944 and 1949 and from my class -24 of us graduated- only two of us continued on to the Military Academy… And my companion left to become a priest… Which is almost worse than to become a soldier, right?" They both smile at the joke.

Later, as we returned home, Papá spoke calmly to me.

"You know what, Charly? It took me a while to remember him but I clearly recall now the young man who's now a colonel. He was efficient, serious about his work, no bad moods or ill manners. He's a good leader, and is neither a political nor religious fanatic…

Perhaps it's not such a bad idea for you to be trained under the influence of a man like himself…" he said agreeably as we got into the pick-up.

Today I can understand that Papá didn't want me to get involved with a morass of ideas, which like a virus had adhered to military structures since the 1930s decade, and which he had personally fought against everywhere he'd been in the world since his youth.

But the providential meeting with Llogri had cleared many of his doubts, and hope had returned that at least I might fulfill Meredith and grandfather Porrá's dream.

"Will you be a doctor? A lawyer? Or perhaps a professor?" He used to say, with a certain joy in his voice. "I mean, after being a soldier…"

And I, stubborn as a mule, would answer that after being a soldier, I'd be a soldier again. And my father would laugh, but he wasn't being sarcastic or mocking me, not at all.

He was happy because he knew that nobody, after being a soldier, wants to continue being one for the rest of their life. He knew that in the current modern days the military castes had been swept out, that he wasn't a Samurai and my destiny wasn't to follow in his footsteps.

The following Friday he went to pick me up at school as soon as I finished classes and we drove to my grandparents' home.

Although we'd travel every weekend, we generally started out on our journey after tea-time in order to arrive just after dinner, unless there was a special event and then we'd leave after midday.

This time he came in the pick-up to school and we had lunch on the way.

I didn't know it then, but my father had decided that if I was going to be a cadet in the Liceo, I'd be the best on all levels.

We arrived at my grandparents' shortly after tea-time and I spent the rest of the afternoon playing with my sisters; next morning he woke me just after sunrise and without having breakfast, drove over to Grandmother Pepa's, and she gave me coffee with milk and sweet biscuits.

Although I asked where we were going, Papá only smiled and said, "You'll see."

Going to Buenos Aires for me always meant something fun like a party, holidays, happiness.

My life at the age of 12 or 13 was strictly set geographically in a line which joined -without too many stops- Esperanza with Banfield; although I knew by heart and in the correct order all the signs along the highways we travelled on: "*San Carlos Centro*", "*San Jerónimo Norte*", "*Gobernador Gálvez*", "*Serodino*", "*Timbues*", "*Carcarañá*", "*Roldán*", "*Funes*", "*Pérez*", "*Empalme Villa Constitución*", "*San Nicolás*", "*Ramallo*" and the numbers of the corresponding highways: "*Nacional 9*", "*Provincial 10*", "*Provincial 6*"; we never stopped except for what was strictly necessary in some service stations, almost always at those of the Automóvil Club Argentino.

So entering the city that Papá carefully drove through on each trip made that particular one a special journey.

We drove over a very high bridge, a huge metallic structure which can move the main middle span for the passage of large ships coming up the river's brown but very calm waters; and except for its size, colours and forms the area is not too different from the port of Santa Fe, which was my point of reference regarding cities.

But everything else was absolutely impressive. From that high bridge we could see before us an endless horizon of tall buildings which seemed to have no end, an image which only lasted a moment because after that we were devoured by the world around us.

The traffic, which was a little lighter because it was a Saturday, seemed confused and noisy. We drove along a large avenue lined with tall platforms in the middle, in which policemen in blue uniforms with white sleeves directed the traffic with exaggerated hand signals, together with the bright red, yellow and green traffic lights.

Our mysterious destination – Papá had not told me a word about where we were going- was revealed after some 30 blocks.

We parked the pick-up on an incline –Lavalle St- and walked very quickly up half a block. Then we went into a shop which to my astonishment had a medieval armour guarding the front door.

In the shop window there was an exhibition of unimaginable amounts and kinds of weapons. For hunting, for sport, hand guns or rifles, knives, weapons for smokeless gunpowder, attacking rifles, vintage, new, used… Pedro Worms & Sons filled my eyes and I stood in silence by my father.

At home in the estancia there was a semi-automatic Browning 12/70 shotgun; a *palanquero* (lever rifle) .44 magnum calibre; and a .45 pistol which Papá kept in good working order –he'd clean them periodically- and every so often –not in any regular way, sometimes some friend would come with a box of bullets - they'd shoot at tins or bottles placed on the ground around one of the Australian tanks in one of the fields or paddocks.

But the weapons were never loaded, and kept under lock and key in a cupboard; only the .45 pistol was kept in a cloth holster but always out of sight, either in the pick-up's glove box or inside the bedside table.

Papá would sometimes let me go with him when he'd practice shooting or when he cleaned the guns.

I used to like to gather the shells from the ground and smell their acrid, sharp smell that was still there even a few days later.

My father was very strict regarding one's behaviour when there were weapons around: the rules were clear and there was not a single reason to break them.

They were divided into two types: those that applied when the weapons were loaded, and those that applied whether the weapons were loaded or not.

Weapons must never point at people, always into the air or down to the ground. The automatic weapons must never be handled or passed over to anyone else when loaded.

The finger must never be on the trigger, always on the trigger guard.

When they're not being used, one must be completely sure that no bullet is left in the chamber.

The weapons that are put away and not to be used immediately must be emptied of bullets.

Basically I had incorporated this strictly applied code, I can't really remember when it was given to me but I'd simply always known it.

I didn't use any of these weapons to shoot with, my father considered they were too heavy and potent for a boy of 11 or 12 years old.

On the other hand, for my personal use I had a powerful compressed air rifle, it was a BSA calibre 5.5 and I used to spend all afternoon shooting while out riding, my targets were cactuses, tins, and now and again hares and partridges.

The weapon rules were just as valid for my own rifle.

We weren't fanatics about hunting or weapons but as in all *campo* properties in Argentina, it was normal for one or two weapons to be kept at home mainly for safety and as a defense.

Yes, we used to hunt but not as a sport —my *Viejo* said killing shouldn't be considered a sport — we needed to be clear in learning how to live from Nature.

Once or twice a year we used to go upriver in the canoe with our weapons, our fishing gear, a little rice, and we'd eat only what we hunted and fished; we didn't even take matches -Papá could light a fire from anything he found at hand, rubbing together sticks, branches, stones, canes.

Papá was very brief and concise in the armoury.

He bought an automatic Garrand Springfield .303 rifle and plenty of cartridges for the latter and for each of the weapons at home. Later, when I was at the Liceo and had to show my shooting skills, I realized that with that rifle he had taught me to shoot with a very potent automatic weapon, learning how to hold my shoulder steady with the recoil and not let that be an issue, allowing me to concentrate on what was important: to hit the target.

Fill my lungs with air through my nose, aim, softly let out the air through the mouth and let the shot surprise me...

Today, taking into account the events that took place later in our country, it seems extraordinary yet at that time it was enough to go to a police station with one's I.D. as well as the invoice for the weapon for the police to emit a permit for carrying and owning a gun.

All the *campo* grocery stores sold weapons and bullets for hunting - .22, .32, .38 and the various shotgun cartridges —and it wasn't difficult to also find the .45 calibre cartridge, which was used mainly by the provincial police, as well as for the many Winchesters and "*palanqueros*" —the Winchester with a lever- which were very common in Argentina's Northern provinces.

The shop employee wrapped up the weapon and ammunition in a long -not very tall- wooden box, painted green and with rope handles, and later I would learn this was the standard box for carrying long weapons. As there was close to 30 kgs. between the weapon and the ammunition, due to their weight I couldn't carry it, so we were helped by the armoury employee.

In a way, that day was the farewell to my childhood.

Papá took me to lunch at a *pizzería* on Corrientes Ave —he left the pick-up with our purchases in a car park just 50 mts. from the restaurant — and when we were at the table we had a conversation which at that time I didn't believe to be very important, but later, when I was in the Liceo, at the Military Academy and as an Army officer, it would be fundamental in my life.

"Charly, tell me, what do you think is the most important aspect in an army?" he asked, looking me in the eye.

I started to talk about the uniforms, flag, weapons.

Papá let me talk and when I had exhausted everything in my child's imagination, he shook his head with that affectionate smile that appeared when he was going to talk about something important.

"No, Charly. There is something that is the core for any army. That's discipline. Perhaps starting with the Romans and very probably the Egyptians and the Greeks, there's no army if there isn't any discipline…" That conversation that I listened to as a devotee became a monologue, a speech without any pomposity or loquacious words and which would mark my whole life.

"Listen… When you enrol in the army you do it with and because of an idea -independence, freedom, democracy, your country- and that idea remains in your mind for just a few hours, perhaps a few days. It doesn't matter which idea took you to enrol in the organized Armed Forces, it's the first thing they're going to take away from you. Because an Armed Force is an organization created with the objective of resolving and managing in the most efficient way possible the most horrifying catastrophe ever generated by man: War. Your ideas then are not very important, all that matters is the efficient way each one of those who are under fire will behave, and everything be resolved the quickest way possible with the least amount of victims on your side or on the enemy's… Charly… Nature is never so brutal or takes such a long time at it as our species… I've seen such things, Charly… Horrible things and on such a scale that it makes earthquakes, hurricanes, volcanoes erupting and floods seem kinder… I hope you never have to go through the door into the hell which is war…

"The truth is that to be able to manage this catastrophe efficiently, only one thing is needed: vertical discipline, obedience without a single hesitation right up to the moment of sacrificing oneself. Later on in the battlefield you will learn about shades –I hope you never have to go through that school- and the subtleties. But first you need to learn to obey. Right is right, left is left… There is no "later" or "I'm going"… What do you say to me in the morning before going to school?"

It makes me smile, and I hang my head.

"Please, just a little longer…" He laughs and nods.

He then turns serious.

"That's not discipline, it's the opposite. I hear other fathers asking for discipline in school, but that's because I think they don't know. They've gone through military service, they've been instructed on how to be soldiers, but they haven't understood that everything they went through during that long time when in service to their country, it was to teach them discipline. There are military men who don't understand the importance of discipline, as there are writers who don't understand grammar; yes, they apply it, but they don't understand what it's for. That's what happened to the Nazis.

"It's not about manufacturing robots that don't think or obey without saying a word. Many times I've seen sergeants arguing with their lieutenant and majors with their colonels. But a well-understood discipline makes an intelligent person understand an idiot, that an idiot act with clarity and that the group be more intelligent than both… Discipline is to know and obey the rules, nothing more than that…"

Papá talked with a pleasant and melodious voice, I loved to listen to him because everything he talked about or said was interesting.

"So, my dear Charly, you're going to start living in a different way with me. We're going to do the following… Firstly, it will only be one hour a day. You will have to obey my orders, no matter how stupid, absurd or humiliating you consider the order – to start with, only an hour. After that, we'll see… Secondly, we must begin with your physical exercises. Another hour? Yes… One hour a day of daily exercises is good for a young boy your age…"

Papá was not talking like a machine gun; on the contrary, he spoke calmly, slowly and with pauses. All this speech came out between silences, and he would ask me my opinion or my ideas.

At that time I would have done anything to become a soldier, so I accepted all his ideas without a thought - they were nothing more than a programme to prepare me physically, intellectually and spiritually to enrol in the army.

Therefore my whole life was to change as from that moment.

Up till then I went to school in the morning, Papá took me and then picked me up very punctually, we'd have lunch together in the kitchen and after that I was free to do whatever I wished. It was a privilege I had earned as from my first years in grade school, because my marks had always been good and it was obvious that in seventh grade I would be the flag bearer.

I generously used that time by riding and helping *Don* Junco and the peons with the cattle, or boating in the canoe, or walking through the forest with my air rifle. In that way I got to know our land called "*La Puerta del Chaco*"- every corner, every clump of trees, every field and every branch of the stream.

Officially, all that was over.

Papá had every afternoon of each day planned - after lunch, every hour and every second with some type of activity. Today I think he was trying to dissuade me from my project, but I can't be sure because the results were conclusive.

Once a week, Papá took out the weapons and instructed me on how to use them. Shooting with them was not how I started, though. For at least two months, all I did was clean them and take them completely apart; only when I was capable to doing this blindfolded did my shooting instructions begin.

I learnt the terrible shooting power of an automatic rifle such as the Garrand; the impressive impact of the .45 pistol and the shotgun; I saw my father's extraordinary shooting skills and I discovered that I too had inherited that gift.

The following year I enrolled in the Military School with the second best average marks, a position which I resolved the following year by becoming top of my class; I kept that position throughout fifth year and continued with it into the Military Academy.

All that year with Papá was my preparation for what would turn into the rest of my life.

After lunch I slept a 45-minute *siesta* and then we'd become ensconced in the library; Papá had got hold of the Liceo's examination programme –maths, Spanish language and grammar, literature, Argentine and universal history- he studied it all and then deployed all his intellectual skills, setting up a study system which was divided into parts and very methodical at first, but became more demanding and unpredictable as time went by.

Every day, for 15 or 20 minutes, he would ask me alternately about all the subjects in the programme, both what we had studied that day as well as anything in the past.

Today I can see the old teacher who had taught him had left a surprising heir.

Very soon it became clear at school that my work at home had become very deep and intense.

My teachers immediately noticed my father's efforts; they treated me very affectionately and would chat with me, very differently than with any of my school companions; at some point they said I needn't even go to school and should just take my exams at the end of the year; but my father considered that to be the flag bearer was a great honour which I had earned through all my efforts.

After the academic work we spent more than an hour with physical exercises. As all children in the countryside, I led an active and physically demanding life, although I didn't practice any sport systematically.

I took part in football games played at school; although I wasn't very interested in this game, I didn't mind being kicked –that is, if they dared, they knew me well enough to know I was quick to retaliate with my fists- so they often chose me to play in one of the competing teams.

My *Viejo* took my physical condition to the level of a top sportsman.

He made me work with my body to achieve greater resistance, flexibility and strength in each part. Legs, trunk, arms, head, step by step he'd work me to a point where it seemed I could go no further, and then I would reach a new point, a new achievement: more Kgs in heavier weights, more knots in the climbing rope, the number of press-ups and squats, amount of times trotting around the garden, etc.

Before six months had passed I could squat, jump, walk on my hands, carry half my weight in a backpack, run for considerable distances or climb walls and ropes with an ease which even today I find astounding - and I know it was the result of the intelligent training my father set for me.

Twice a week I supposedly had three complete hours to myself; but Papá had organized things in such a way that those hours I had to dedicate to tidying clothes, and cleaning and tidying up my room completely. Sometimes he himself would deliberately mess up my room and oblige me to put everything away again.

I very quickly understood how the system worked because it's very simple. You obey and everything works perfectly.

On Fridays we'd sit together at tea-time and together evaluate how our work had gone that week. I think that what happened one week in October showed me what discipline meant to my father -that week I had complained more, I hadn't completed my homework and I hadn't paid enough attention to cleaning and tidying my room.

After all, I was only a twelve-year old boy…

The fact is that that particular Friday, without even getting angry, Papá asked me two things.

"Do you really want to go straight ahead right through to the end and enrol in the Liceo, or would you prefer to abandon that idea now? It's your decision. If you wish to continue to the end and become a cadet, think up a punishment which you think is directly related to violating the rules which you yourself helped me set…"

That weekend I didn't travel to Buenos Aires.

For the first time in my life I stayed alone at home with a severe warning to Junco and Herminia, the cook: I was punished and was not to ride, nor was my room to be tidied nor was anyone to cook for me. Both of them stayed away from the house: I had to cook for myself, clean and tidy everything on my own…

This is how the idea was made clear to me: if you are in the system you must comply with all the rules.

2. Allegro ma non troppo

"Prieto has been assassinated!!!"

The shout, almost a scream, ran through the Liceo like a damp, sticky wave; the commotion spread like flames in a dry field, especially taking hold in the fifth year cadets, those who best got to know First Lt. Carlos Alberto Prieto because he was our instructor the first years.

I'm disturbed and don't know what to think.

The officers on duty shout out orders.

The initial chaos ends almost immediately. We quickly become organized. I trot to my section of first year cadets —we're all looking at each other, uneasy, not understanding what is going on.

In just a few minutes, the whole Liceo is formed up in the main courtyard.

Col. Llogri stands in front of us. He is serious, very pale, his jaw clamped together and his eyes shiny.

Llogri had been Prieto's instructor when the latter had been a cadet at the Liceo, and often we'd seen those two men treating each other with affectionate respect.

Llogri doesn't shout. He speaks strongly. His voice resounds across the courtyard. We are completely silent. The order comes across clearly: "Atten-shun". The sound of all heels hitting the ground at the same time echoes for a second.

"Cadets! I have the sad duty of informing you that at dawn this morning, when First Lt Carlos Alberto Prieto was leaving his home to come to the Liceo, he was ambushed by an unknown number of subversives and despite the Lieutenant's heroic resistance, they achieved their criminal objective… The law will see to capturing these assassins!

"He fell just as he lived: with a patriot's courage… Those who did not know him have men next to them who have witnessed his exceptional goodness and his Christian values. Do not weep for him; remember him with respect and above all, see him as an example!!! Don't be disturbed or scandalized, don't claim revenge: you are the youngest members of an institution which will be rescuing the country from chaos, reflect on this. ¡VIVA LA PATRIA! (LONG LIVE ARGENTINA!)"

The sound in the courtyard responds as a single voice.

-¡VIVA LA PATRIA!

While I watch over the cadets under my charge, I try to sort out my thoughts, but especially my feelings.

Prieto.

"Smooth" Prieto.

First Lt Prieto.

The man who had accompanied me at the saddest and most difficult time in my life just one year ago had been cruelly assassinated.

This episode was not totally unprecedented.

Papá had a folder in which he had rigorously kept newspaper cuttings on the endless-seeming deaths and which were a scourge in the country since the 1970s.

The folder had two tabs: subversives, and military men & civilians (syndicate officials, public officials, businessmen, etc.)

I had continued with his work. Every weekend –which I alternated between Banfield and Esperanza- I went through the three newspapers which had the most information –Clarín, La Nación and Crónica- which they kept for me at Tano Molinario's petrol service station, my last stop before arriving home.

I now had to add to the list the name of a man whom I had respected as a person and as an army officer.

I shared the indignation I felt with my class companions and I was tempted to subscribe to "Chancho" Páez's opinion, who was calling for a slow and painful death for the assassins; instead, I kept busy calming down my young cadets who were as upset as small fish in a frying pan.

Of course they were scared; how could they not be, if a man as brave and upright as Prieto had been killed in cold blood? He wasn't the only one, either; during those years we had seen how officers from all the armed forces, all ranks and in all kinds of circumstances were killed with a determination and methodically right out in the open on public streets.

They had assassinated Major Viola together with his daughters; Admiral Quijada when he was taking his purchases out of his car; Col. Larrabure after a long and cruel captivity; Gen. Gaý and his wife… Lt. Ibarzábal, executed inside a caravan… The list was long, Prieto was just one more.

The boys from First Year's third company, my cadets, were not expressing their fear – on the contrary: they had launched into a verbal competition on how they would react to subversives, they wanted to show how ready and able they were to fight.

Fortunately, with very good judgement, the cadets of First, Second and Third Year were not allowed at the Liceo's exterior guard posts.

Several times the guards in the armoured casemates had had very brief exchanges with passing cars, from which came hails of bullets against the Liceo.

Some twenty days after my father's funeral, this had been my baptism of fire. At first I had felt an atrocious fear but very quickly, as if my father had whispered in my heart, I found my commanding voice; I shouted out my orders to the soldiers who were already shooting, and as the bullets hit our post, I'd called headquarters with the information on what was taking place.

I was mentioned in the daily report and was given a special free day as a reward.

At that moment I realized that everything I had learnt at the Liceo, in addition to my father's extraordinary training, had all served me well…

After the line-up broke apart I had to calm the youngsters, being careful to put them in their place without humiliating them, allowing them to show their anger but making sure they realized they were little more than inexperienced fledglings…

The next day Prieto's wake was held at the Liceo's chapel; he had been placed in an open coffin despite having received several shots in the face. The family had agreed to this: there was no shame in his wounds, they were clean but on view.

For the last twelve hours –from midnight to midday- I formed part of the guard of honour in the funeral chapel.

I hadn't cried at my father's funeral most likely because my mother remained as calm as a Spartan, or because Prieto's attentive and firm presence had helped me withhold my pain.

But I wasn't able to avoid the warm, salty tears running down my cheeks when I saw Prieto's mother, father, his sisters and above all, his pregnant wife, who had all broken down when having to view the terrible spectacle of that good man's body, torn apart by bullets.

Nobody said anything to me because we were all equally angry, equally in pain.

That weekend I argued for the first time with my sister Bethan; there was only eleven months between us and we had always been inseparable, during our childhood as well as through our young teenage years. Then when we were just over 15 years old, she took an immense step: while she was in her 3rd year of secondary school she studied and sat for all the fourth and fifth year exams; so by the time I was in my last year at the Liceo, at 17 years old she was already in her first year of medical school.

My Rodrigué grandfather was happy that someone in the family was following the career which he loved so much and which had brought him so much satisfaction, and he helped her with any resources at hand; our Uncle Carlos was still in hospital, battling between life and death, and if he survived he would still be suffering from brain damage; he would no longer be able to practice as a doctor.

Bethan, who had also inherited my father's intelligence and Mamá's mettle, took advantage of every opportunity to learn; before even completing her secondary schooling (as she had finished ahead of time), she spent all her free time with our grandfather.

After the accident, just as I had been occupied with Papá, she had accompanied our grandfather, going back and forth with him to Rosario –where Carlos was in hospital- and she had helped with the management of the Clinic together with our aunts Inés –in charge of the dentistry area- and Neneca, who was head of the physiotherapy department.

It was not a trivial argument.

Prieto and my indignation were central to this scene.

She had argued, "…not only men in the Armed Forces die… heads of syndicates, students, professors, catechists are also murdered… Not only the ERP (People's Revolutionary Army) and Montoneros are assassins… So is the government, with the Triple A…"

Bethan used part of her scarce free time cooperating with a group of catechists who spread the word from the Gospels in Banfield's poorest areas; since Papá's death she had also started to bring home all kinds of pamphlets against Isabelita's government.

They were guided by a priest from the Palotino order who showed sympathy towards the liberation gospel, which considered the live Christ more like a revolutionary rather than the son of God, and whose death had been an example for the world; a few weeks before the anniversary of Papá's death, the assassination of Father Mugica had sent her into a weeping crisis; she had attended his wake in the shanty town and together with a big crowd she had marched in the funeral procession.

Perón's death the year before had personally marked us all.

Papá had accompanied Grandmother Pepa and Aunt Cristina to pay their condolences; I'd worn my uniform twice for the same reason, once with my companions from the Liceo, and another time with my father, my invalid aunt and my Peronist Grandmother; after all, the dead man was President of the country.

His death and the events prior to it had divided the country into two, and the Liceo was not far-removed.

A few –very few- were really sad; others felt that the end of an era had finally come: only the "old man" could have ended the stateless subversion at its root.

Nobody was telling us what the true political situation was.

My father had left that posthumous text in which he clearly pointed out the internal conflicts to which we were being pushed, not so much by external conditions as much as by the irrevocable division there was within Peronism itself.

My sister and I argued hotly, holding antagonistic positions.

Subversives manifest the profound aggressiveness capitalism exercises over the poor, it's just an extreme contradiction to an already immoral system, she said.

Subversion is nothing but a band of mercenary assassins who want the country to be assimilated into an atheist and Soviet communist world, I said.

When our voices began to rise, Mamá –who hardly ever raised hers, she used the same system as Papá, she'd talk so quietly that you were forced to approach her to understand what she was saying- shook us with a shout that was almost a shriek: "Enough", she said.

And she sent each of us to our room, as if we were children.

My sister and I, just like a metaphor of the country, never spoke to each other again except for polite family greetings - we didn't exchange any more ideas, or make comments on any books, something we had done all our lives.

3.- Allegro cantabile

My father had his 50th birthday celebration on July 9th, 1971. Of all the fantastic holidays that I had experienced in my short life, those are the ones I think of as the best of all.

Papá had travelled to Buenos Aires especially to take part in the Liceo's celebration of Independence Day, the line-up and traditional chocolate for officers, parents and cadets; Mamá had excused herself because of commitments to my sisters and their hockey. We had the weekend to ourselves.

After the ceremony, we returned to the estancia straight from the Liceo: the sacred winter holidays always began with my father's birthday, which we'd celebrate with a few friends and members of our family, with cuts of lamb or calf carefully grilled for many hours by *Don* Junco's skilled hands.

After that we'd leave on one of our trips that had provided me with so many memories.

Except that this year there wouldn't be any trip, but Papá didn't know this.

Mamá, with her usual bonhomie, had promised to arrive very early on Sunday morning, bringing Grandmother Pepa, Cristina and my sisters, loaded with cakes and sweet desserts which my Grandmother was such an expert at cooking.

Actually, Mamá had prepared everything to give Papá a gift that would leave all of us unforgettable memories.

My mother, my sisters and I had all planned months ahead for our surprise to be absolutely effective; Mamá had spent hours writing letters and planning every detail of that surprise.

It hadn't been difficult for me on Saturday morning to convince my father to go out in the canoe for a "little trip", which sometimes when we had time could last several days; I asked him to share this trip as a reward because my name and high marks had been mentioned at the ceremony on the Friday morning, and I knew that he must be proud of my performance at the Liceo.

We never took much with us: a backpack with a little rice, dry fruit, lentils, some fishing lines and a shotgun with four or five cartridges; it had rained heavily the previous days and the river was quite high, so we cheated and used the motor to go upriver towards the west, looking for the woods where we used to camp on the northern river edge. We only carried a small tent, warm coats and one change of clothes.

We knew we had to be back by Sunday midday, not any exact time as Junco knew how to grill the meat so it was always perfect for whenever people arrived.

On Sunday morning I did everything to make our manoeuvres as slow and time-consuming as possible, I had to give Mamá time to arrive with the surprise when we sat down at the table.

We had many accomplices, in different parts of the world. Grandmother Pepa had actively participated in the execution and planning of this party which was to be unforgettable.

That Sunday Papá scolded me several times for my apparent clumsiness: I dropped an oar which took me some time to get back; I choked the motor, which forced us to row; I took a long time to pick up a couple of ducks which I'd shot in spite of Papá's protests, reminding him that Grandmother Pepa loved *Doña* Herminã's duck cooked in an orange sauce.

We arrived well after midday and Papá was not surprised to see that there was an unknown car amongst the others: Mama's station-wagon, Sandaza's Ford, grandfather's Kaiser Carabela and Uncle Carlitos' Fizzore sports car.

It was only when we approached the grill where the meat was cooking that he realized there was something odd taking place: the unmistakable sound of bagpipes and standing in front of him, in uniform, were three of his war comrades.

In order: Captain Farrington; Corporal Wes Mosteland; soldier Ian Mac Allister. The fourth was Sergeant Major Jimmy Taylor, wearing his classic kilt and playing the bagpipes - he had actually not been a companion in his unit but they had trained together at the army command school after Dunkirk and very surprisingly, they had met up again at a party at the Lomas de Zamora Club.

As long as I live, I'll never forget the look on my father's face.

I know that many thoughts went through his mind in just a few second, the time it took him to stand at attention before his comrades, salute them and then embrace each one.

They had all lived through many years since they'd last seen each other; Farrington, a little older than my father, his head full of grey hair; Mosteland wore his hair long like a hippie, tied in a ponytail; and Mac Allister was completely bald.

Later they showed us photos that had been taken at different times and one could clearly appreciate the differences; they had also brought letters and notes from other men in the unit who had not been able to travel for the long and expensive journey.

Mamá, together with Grandmother Pepa and Jimmy, had plotted out this plan a year before; they had contacted Farrington, who frequently met up with Mac Allister and at least once a year with other men in their unit; and with Mosteland, who lived in California and was working as a stuntman in Hollywood – he had been found with much patience by Jimmy, who used to exchange letters with many of his old war comrades. All of them had pitched in to buy Mac Allister's ticket, as he was always having trouble keeping a job. Papá had his fiftieth birthday surrounded by those men with whom he had spent the best and worst years of his life.

They spent two weeks at home and I was their mascot, the warrior puppy to whom they talked unceasingly about his father's feats.

It's not that my father hadn't talked to me about the war; on the contrary, I knew about these men's courage, and that my father loved them like brothers, admired them as classic heroes, but he'd never told me about his role as a protagonist - he was simply a witness or sometimes, just had a secondary role.

Mamá, always a very good judge and possessing the patience of a Penelope, spent three days with us and then, with the excuse of driving back Grandmother Pepa and Aunt Cristina, she bundled my sisters into the station wagon and didn't return till the day before I was due to leave: the old warriors would spend one more week together, on their own.

Today, many years later, I perfectly understand the love between my parents, built over the years with patience and a great deal of mutual trust.

Jimmy Taylor, my grandfather and Uncle Carlitos left the evening of the following day.

The days spent with these men were rich and very instructive. I saw my father in a different light, which made me admire and respect him even more than before.

Every day was like a party, a celebration of being alive, but also remembering gratefully those who with their sacrifice had allowed them to continue living.

In just a few days, my speaking in English went from correct to perfectly fluent.

In spite of July's cold weather, we toured the property on foot, on horseback, in the jeep.

We fished catfish, which we cooked right there on the river edge; we grilled a lamb in the middle of the southern woods - and I heard the stories which my father would never have told me.

Farrington was very likeable, Mosteland grumpy and Mac Allister seemed to have a serious alcohol problem. None of his friends reprimanded him: they looked after him, they bathed him when necessary, they covered him with warm blankets so he wouldn't feel cold and they listened to him when, after a long speech insulting them, he broke down into a weeping fit.

Afterwards, when he had fallen asleep, they told me that towards the end of the war, in a town in the area of Sarre during the hard winter of 1944-45, he had been the only survivor of the twelve members of his platoon in an attack on a fortification full of SS soldiers; one by one, he had picked up each dead companion and had never stopped firing at the enemy, using the arms and ammunition of the fallen men until the North American tanks arrived – this division took another twelve hours to overcome the Nazi resistance.

Released from the British Army immediately after the end of the war, this man was never the same person after that day, and his life had been a long series of failures at jobs, in relationships, socially.

Farrington had met up with him by chance eight or nine years previously, and had taken care of him ever since.

Mosteland, who was Australian, had been with my father and Farrington in the Pakistan army, in which he'd enrolled after the end of the war in India; he had wandered around the post-colonial Asian lands, covering his expenses with the sale of a property he'd inherited from his father in Australia.

Some years later he had acted as an advisor to the Southern Vietnamese army during the first years of the North American intervention, but after a period there he'd realized that sooner or later the war was not going to end well. He emigrated to the United States in 1962, he'd wandered around with hippies in a long party that lasted for years until in 1966 he'd met a Mexican girl who worked as a maid in a Hollywood producer's home - and at a party he'd tried to beat up the producer after this man had made a pass at the girl. After having –instead- beaten up five bodyguards and left them out of action, the producer had offered him a job as a stuntman.

He'd married the Mexican girl in 1968 and he had two children, they were expecting a third and he said they were planning on 12…

Farrington had abandoned the army almost immediately after my father. For former soldiers there were many opportunities and good jobs, with high salaries and many benefits. In 1949 he'd been hired by Rover, the English car manufacturer, and he planned to retire in 1974 to dedicate himself fully to his passion: fly fishing.

He had got married immediately after arriving back in England with to a Scottish woman who he'd met at work –his boss's secretary- and they had one son who was born in 1953, on the same day as my parents' wedding day.

Baptised with the same name as his father, he had not accompanied him on the trip because he had just enrolled in the British Army's Academy for officers.

Every day there was a new tale, a profound and disturbing story that was told to me alternately –to my father's faked anger- by each of these brave men who knew him so well.

Farrington told me how he had met my father - dirty, thin and in rags after the defeat of the Spanish Republic; and at the same time he recalled the terrible days at Dunkirk when my father had shot down a Stuka that had killed one of his aggressive schoolmates together with all his platoon.

I'll never forget their sad voices when they both said, almost simultaneously, "Derek Jones… Poor bastard…"

As for Mosteland, when we were sitting in front of lovely lighted fire in our fireplace at home, he told me how father, together with a mixed-race Burmese, had captured a gigantic marine crocodile somewhere in the Burmese jungle. "You play rugby, right? That cursed animal was about 25 yards long!!! It fed not only all our unit but a pile of youngsters who were wandering around there with a…" Farrington interrupted him with a short, "That's enough Wes…" It was enough seeing my father's saddened, dismal expression on his face to understand that that story did not bring back good memories.

On the other hand, another afternoon when Papá, Junco and I were trying to get the "gringos" to drink *mate*, my father laughed happily when Farrington told him something about which my father had absolutely no knowledge.

Farrington knew Papá's history in all the smallest details; we, his family, could envisage only the little he had told us.

We knew about Mrs Cummins not so much from him but through Grandmother Pepa, who had a photo of this woman, already an old lady sitting like someone from a noble family, surrounded by her eldest son, his Hindu wife and three small children.

We knew that the eldest child was called Gordon after Papá, and that Grandmother Pepa, my father and Mrs Cummins had written to each other until Mrs Cummins died shortly after my birth.

In 1952, Papá had asked Farrington to travel to Scotland to visit the relatives of his two dead companions from the Spanish War – we hardly knew anything about that period in his life- and Farrington had found that the two young boys to whom Papá used to send part of his salary from the British Army –until he left active service- were students and boarders at a very good school in Edinburgh.

The captain continued to show interest in the development of those two young men towards whom he knew Papá felt the kind of debt which is never documented.

Some years later, once this good Mrs Cummins had died, Papá's former boss learnt, by chance, what had taken place: the lawyer who managed Farrington's inheritance from his paternal uncle, the former Ministry of War official who had exercised a certain influence in both their lives, was also handling Mrs Cummins affairs in Great Britain.

The lawyer had talked about having to sell a property in Barnet, and Farrington happened to remark, with no vested intention, that he had visited that town several times.

This is how he learnt that he and Mrs Sylvia shared the same lawyer; it awakened his curiosity because of the coincidence, so he asked for whom was the money from that sale intended; and the lawyer, an old friend of the family, very indiscreetly told him that the object of that sale was to guarantee a university education for two Spanish War orphans, sons of a dead soldier in the British battalion.

Farrington did not need to see the papers to understand what that extraordinary woman's posthumous deed had been.

Papá laughed, his eyes teary, praising life's mysterious ways, eternally grateful for that gesture that without a doubt completed a debt he felt he had with those boys.

The eldest had graduated as a medical doctor in 1964 and the youngest, as a history professor in 1966.

That marvellous winter I understood how the horrendous war had forged the historical, perpetual friendships that continued even after death.

I returned to the Liceo and never told a soul about those holidays - because the only one who could have understood them, "Pelado" Vittoriosso, was no longer at the Liceo. He was a fifth year cadet whom had built a relationship of confidence and friendship with me when I was no longer an inexperienced newbie and with whom I could have shared those terrible stories - but he'd left the Liceo to wander the wide world in search of his own destiny.

Papá's friends left, leaving behind a photo album that would never even remotely reflect what those beautiful winter days had been.

4.- Adagio fortíssimo

My whole world imploded in mid-1977.

Before that, I graduated from the Liceo with the top marks of my year class called "Uspallata" –in honour of Gen. San Martín's mountain pass- as well as the top marks of the whole Liceo, flag bearer and first in the daily order of merit: In the five years at the Liceo I had only been penalised five times, three of them for collective sanctions.

I went straight into the Military Academy's second year, in the same month the Armed Forces defeated Isabel Perón and focused on taking over public office: We closed the Congress and all political parties, forbade all public activity – strengthening the state of siege that the Congress had approved due to the growing internal violence, and in which the Peronist Party held the majority- and we enacted an incredibly tough "paralegal" code that overrode all laws the country had drawn up over the years.

It was the most forewarned coup d'etat in history. Months before, in mid-1975, there were many voices claiming that someone had to put some order into the crumbling state of affairs to which Perón's widow had taken the country's government – she had been placed there as Vice President by Perón himself in a display of nepotism, considering she hadn't any political experience.

The whole year in which my father died –just a few months after the President's death- had shown unprecedented disturbances, and the following year an Executive order for the Armed Forces to "wipe out" the guerrillas in the province of Tucumán had led to a river of blood: every day, news of death and destruction.

In December, a few days before Christmas, a violent attack by the irregular troops - in an unprecedented demonstration of force in different parts of the city- ended in a resounding defeat: we crushed them.

For me, the ultimate outrage had been Prieto's assassination, but everyone had outrages: in the northern province of Tucumán a fire had been lit, and in the guerrillas' minds, this would set fire to the whole country.

Since Perón's death, not a month had gone by without some kind of battle or a bomb going off in some part of the country; in the provinces of Formosa, Tucumán, Catamarca, Corrientes.

Almost every day assassinations were committed in plain daylight.

The victims were always military men, policemen, businessmen, CEOs of important companies, trade unionists, university professors; according to their executioners, "enemies of the people".

I was caught unsurprised on the day of the coup d'etat - they were my first days at the Military Academy, where the day's announcement was taken almost as old news.

Shouts of happiness and of "*viva la patria*" were heard, hugs abounded in a festive atmosphere, and I wasn't totally removed - although in my ears I could hear the phrase written by my father and repeated unceasingly: "Nothing good can come from a coup d'etat."

Chile had been the first to lead by defeating Allende, a communist –I clearly remember my father pointing out then that his was a legitimate government and his assassination was a vulgar crime covered up as a suicide- and soon other countries in the region would follow.

Now we were getting ready to eradicate the "red disease" as the chaplain used to call it, without the inconveniences of bureaucratic hindrances invented by civilians and which only served to benefit the enemy.

I was too young and innocent to understand that the process of national reorganization would fill the country with clandestine jails and common graves and that, in my father's wise words, nothing good would come from it.

The guerrilla organizations publicly spoke of their satisfaction regarding the coup, believing that this would only deepen the system's contradictions until the people as a whole would rise up -and follow them, the guerrilla groups- as saviours.

On the coup d'etat's first anniversary, I was the star of the ceremony taking place in the Military Academy's parade ground: Best marks in the Academy's full divisions of four years, top marks in the military subjects, champion marksman with a pistol and rifle, first in the hand-to-hand combat techniques. These were all added to my "service files" from the Liceo, which is how I was converted into the Argentine prototype soldier.

In an unprecedented measure, six cadets from fourth year and I, from third year, were all promoted on that day to the rank of Second Lieutenant and incorporated to active service, ipso facto, as full officers.

The academic jump was solved in a very simple way: we would have two opportunities to sit for the examinations of the missing subjects with a self-study programme, and once we completed these we would graduate with a technician's degree in "military sciences".

As an extra prize, I also received the province of Tucumán as my destination, where since 1975 the operation "Independencia" had been underway, in which the army was openly fighting units of the ERP and Montoneros rural guerrilla groups.

Finally, my destiny was right there within my reach.

And as I learnt almost immediately, to my misfortune.

Before leaving for Tucumán, I spent the previous weekend divided between my grandfather Mateo's house, with my mother and my sisters, and a lightning trip to the estancia. I wanted to ride with my godfather Junco in order to quieten my thoughts.

Junco had started working with Papá immediately after he finished his military service; he was 22 years old then but according to my father's description, he had the seriousness and calm of an older man.

Sandaza had brought him to the estancia as soon as he learnt that Mamá was pregnant (with me), and that she would no longer be able to work side by side with my father - at every opportunity since then, Junco expressed his gratitude for the introduction.

Junco was born son, grandson and great-grandson of *gauchos*… His eyes were slanted, there was no doubt that his skin, the colour of earth, was directly connected to his native Indian ancestors; he was an Indian in his virtues, a character of few words and reserved as a *gaucho*.

He worked with his Welsh boss for a salary, but as the months went by an unbreakable friendship emerged which pointed to the virtues of both men; yes, Papá paid him a salary. But Junco – to me *Don* Junco- was much more than an employee. He was my father's adopted brother and treated as such.

At the beginning, as was usual, they used to speak to each other with the formal "*usted*" (a formal "you") and the *gaucho* used to call him "*patrón*" (boss) when he spoke to him.

The property was a ruin; Uncle Carlos had been through it like a plague, he had left a manager who had sold even the wire fences; to make the property productive, Papá had worked from dawn till dusk, no days off, unceasingly.

When Junco began working with him, Papá told him that he could not pay overtime, as was included in the statutes covering a peon's work and which had been enforced by Perón - so Junco had the weekends off.

Besides, completely opposite to the custom throughout the Argentine countryside properties, he indicated to Junco that he could bring his horses to feed in any of the unused fields on the *estancia*.

So for the first month Papá continued with his work routine, while Junco went off to the town of Esperanza with the money my father handed him every Friday at the end of each week.

During the second or third month that Junco had begun working as my father's employee, Papá found him putting up the fence posts which he himself had been planning to set up on that Saturday morning.

Papá asked him what he was doing, and the man answered, with a smile, that he was resting. Papá thought Junco was pulling his leg, so a little on the defensive he told Junco that he didn't have the money to pay him the double wages that would have been his due according to the law for working on a Saturday.

So Junco then looked him straight in the eye, and spoke in his very calm voice, "Look, *Don* Evans, before working for you I had other bosses, some were dishonest, others were like Sandaza, men of their word… I never saw any of them working more than I, up till now… You let me bring my horses here as was done in my grandfather's time… I'm going to work by your side, equally, as was done at that time… I'll rest when you rest and eat when you eat… I don't know how to do it any other way… I can't go off to the town's bar thinking that a *gringo* works more than I do… Money isn't everything…"

From that day on, Papá and Junco were inseparable, and together they made that small property into a model farm - what a farm dedicated to agriculture should look like on a small scale.

Junco used to tame horses a different way and he won over my father immediately. Junco didn't hit the horses, or tie them up or was violent towards them in any way.

Probably because of his own life of pain and suffering, my father had a different view about things, because he loved animals –all animals– a great deal and he was always aware of making sure they were well treated, he didn't tolerate any kind of cruelty or bad treatment.

Whenever we hunted or fished and the animal was butchered –chicken or lamb, pig or calf- Papá would ask for forgiveness and he'd talk to the animal to comfort it in its process of dying.

When my father saw how Junco used to spend weeks stroking a young horse, whispering into its ears old words that he'd learnt from his grandfather, Papá chose that man as his brother.

This was mutual, because Junco made it his habit to apologise to the animals he had to kill, talking to them softly and gently in order to accompany them during their dying process.

Going absolutely against mother's side of the family and their prejudices –basically my Grandmother and my Uncle Carlitos- he asked Junco to be my godfather and this was, perhaps, the best gift in my whole life.

Just as his grandfather had taught him, Papá did everything possible for the creole virtues to form under my skin and reach into my soul with no words, just with gestures, with looks. All of this I learnt in the most natural way, my hands grew in the hollow of the hardened palms of my godfather's hands.

My father and Junco appreciated and respected each other as if they'd been comrades-at-arms.

As soon as he was able, my father made sure Junco bought himself a small house in town. He had a wife and two children but they had separated and she –an embittered woman- made sure to take everything he earned.

At each cattle auction, Papá would separate a few calves and very slowly he had helped Junco to set up a dairy farm managed by his brother-in-law; Junco was hopeless with money matters: as long as he had enough for his daily rations, he cared very little for anything else. He was a *gaucho* in his virtues and his defects, if you can call being disinterested a defect.

He was very good with horses, but as far as women went….

Mamá had adopted him in the same way as Papá, and she supported my father when they made Junco my godfather.

Papá had a blue roan that was a luxury –he never failed: people wanted to buy it from my father at every single auction- Junco had tamed him especially for my father. On the other hand, for my sixth birthday, Junco had given me a black horse with a white star on its forehead, and I'm still riding him; and my grandfather Rodrigué –an admirer of all creole things and a great reader of literature on the art of horse riding – has never failed to praise him all the years he's been with me.

Junco was an expert at all *gaucho* skills: he platted his reins; he made or assembled bridles, saddles and *recados*; he was very good at shoeing horses; and he knew every blade of grass on the Estancia Puerta del Chaco.

My father and he were mutual admirers, and sometimes at cattle auctions they'd team up in informal exhibitions competing with other *gaucho*s to lasso, brand or separate tough steers - they were an unbeatable pair.

They knew each other well and could predict, with mathematical precision, the movements of the other man. They would each take charge of one or two hundred heads of cattle because they could guess what the other one would do.

He took deeply to heart Papá's death, I know. He said little, but he became more protective of my mother and my sisters, and he began treating me like a man.

I would not be who I am without Junco in my life.

That is why, before leaving on my first assignment as a soldier, I went riding for a while with my godfather.

It's not that Junco was a great talker; on the contrary. He was quiet, and appeared not to be very expressive in serious matters; he was kind and fun at times when we relaxed.

I say he appeared to be, because the truth is Junco was very sharp and sensitive when required to be regarding serious or grave matters.

We rode that day, we counted cattle and we herded animals from one field to another, as if it were an ordinary day. At midday *mate* time –just as in the summer the day is cut in two with a long siesta in order to avoid being under a burning sun, in winter, to take advantage of a short day, only a short break with *mate* and some bread are shared in order not to interrupt work- and it was then I gave him the news of my destination.

He said nothing.

But at the time of my departure, when daylight was fading, he said something that I didn't understand then; it was only after months had gone by that it became crystal clear to me.

"Be careful, son… It's not clear… Your father never grew tired of saying, evil is everywhere… There are no good sides, bad men abound… Terrorists as well as soldiers…"

Next morning at dawn I arrived at the city of Tucumán, my destination.

They were very busy days; if entering the Liceo and the Military Academy had been an impact for me, entering a barracks wearing the Argentine Army uniform was like entering Heaven.

Everything began badly.

The chief of the Unit to which I'd been assigned welcomed me personally, but it was not a good interview.

Col. Soriano, just as Col. Llogri, had been trained at the Military Academy by my father, but he did not have the best memories of him as Col. Llogri had.

Neither did he hold back in pointing this out to me.

"Did you know your father was a "red", or in the best of cases, a Peronist..? … He stopped my companions and myself from participating in the Menéndez coup in 1951… If your father hadn't intervened…"

"My colonel, my father fought…"

I tried to defend my father but he cut me short. "Do you intend to be a long time in the Argentine Army?... You'd better get used to not arguing with your superior… Don't make me show you up in front of all the battalion for what you are, an inexperienced fledgling… Get out of my sight, present yourself to your officer, I'm placing you under arrest for five days."

That bad start was an omen of what would follow.

I took charge of my platoon after complying with my days of arrest; it wasn't bad. Dead hours locked up in my own room with nothing to do except look at the ceiling; I wrote to all my family - to each of my sisters, my mother, my grandparents, my aunts, to my grandmother Pepa and my aunt Cristina – and to some of my Liceo companions, to Sandaza… I exercised just as I did when I entered the Liceo; I read the Bible and the military code, and Clausewitz… locked up for 120 hours, 7,200 minutes, 432,000 seconds.

Of course, from that first day my name was mud in the mouth of all the regiment, and even soldiers in the lowest ranks gossiped about me.

My life there would not be easy.

A section of two platoons was placed under my command, each one formed by a Corporal and five conscripts; and we immediately entered into a war routine established since 1975 in the province, and which after the coup had grown with General Bossi as Governor.

The city was under martial law, but this was not noticeable during the day, if one omitted the military controls on the roads and in public transport; it was at night, when only official cars were on the road that the full weight of our presence could be felt. Immediately they broadcast what had been achieved: our actions were almost finished; out in the bush and woods – in the Famaillá area- we held dominion, and in the city we had them cornered and had almost destroyed their full operative capacity.

The subversives were on the defensive. In other provinces such as Catamarca, Buenos Aires and Santa Fe they were still fighting with their criminal and evasive methods.

But here in Tucumán the orders of the expired Peronist government had been almost totally complied with: we had destroyed all subversive actions.

My work and my men's - under the orders of First Lieutenant Sandoval Dash, in charge of four platoons and supervised by Captain Molina- was routine work: we controlled cars on the highways; the buses on the outskirts of the city; we set up controls outside the entrances into the poor neighbourhoods, asked for documents; we frisked people in search of hidden weapons and we arrested anyone suspicious: young men with a beard or long hair, with no distinction of social classes - we already knew that the guerrillas were sons of both the rich and the poor.

Sometimes we worked as a support group when in an area of the capital or of the suburbs there was an operation to search for and destroy the subversives' hideouts.

I did nothing beyond obeying and giving orders - setting ourselves up in combat positions, covering each other, searching for an invisible enemy who was hidden among the inhabitants and could be anyone.

On Friday October 28th, 1977 we received night orders; almost no different to other days except we would not be taking all the conscripts: most of them had received their normal weekend passes.

As always I sat in the cabin of the Mercedes truck which was at the end of the column headed by Captain Molina's Jeep.

I remember the day and the date because that night my whole world fell apart. Corporal Nazareno -a man from Corrientes and as dry as the Sahara Desert- was driving the truck and did not speak a word in the whole long hour we travelled south along the national route; then after 40 more minutes on very bad earth roads he did nothing but complain about the state of these roads.

Nazareno deeply despised me, as did all the other NCO's of the regiment. Soriano was very aware of this.

Col. Soriano was not a chief who was particularly appreciated, but on the other hand he was feared and respected; the NCO's showed a kind of worshipful fear together with respect and blind obedience which had accompanied Soriano since he was a First Lieutenant.

Soriano was verbally aggressive, he was always ready with a sharp, ironic remark, he was quick to punish and deliberately unjust with those who did not fall under his good graces; however, he was respected for the personal courage he had shown during the "Independence operation".

In the forest he had personally been at the head of columns who went in masked into the bush, and he had fought against enemy patrols three or four times. In the city he led the raids facing subversive bullets. He lived in the barracks and never used civilian clothes.

In the city he moved around in a green Ford Falcon accompanied by an escort of two identical cars with five men in each.

We knew he was married, but his wife and children lived in Buenos Aires. Soriano had a mistress, and the first time a Corporal happened to mention that she was a prisoner I did not believe him; I thought it was one of those jokes they tell the newly arrived just to laugh at them - I never said or asked anybody about anything.

But it was the truth.

As the weeks and on duty periods went by, I saw a woman who left the office and the Colonel's bedroom and was driven under guard to a place outside the city. As time went by and thanks to an NCO's indiscretion, I learned that it was where the guerrillas or those who cooperated with them were detained

I was not liked by the Colonel nor did he trust me; I knew that from the first day. There was no-one in the barracks who knew me from my life before, nobody who could report on my military conditions or my loyalty to the Army, to the government, to the country.

I had the institution's backing, I had my Second Lieutenant's dispatch and my service record from the Liceo and the Academy… But there in the barracks in Tucumán, they were worth nothing.

There was nothing official, nobody said, "Second Lieutenant Evans, we have this issue…"

My peers – we were at least a dozen Second Lieutenants, I was the most recently graduated - shared lunch or supper with me and talked trivialities; my superiors –even those closest, such as First Lieutenants – never failed to punish me for all kinds of offenses or defects – the condition of my uniform, real or imaginary offenses by my subordinates, the state of health of the company under my charge, or the sanitary conditions of their rooms or bathrooms- depriving me of my leaves and writing them into my file like gobs of spit on something they do not like.

I didn't mind; when I left the barracks I could always visit Dr Máximo Seleme in the city, he was an old acquaintance of my grandfather's to whom I'd paid my respects at the first opportunity; otherwise, I'd take advantage of each arrest to write to my mother, my sisters, my grandparents.

I was where I wanted to be, I was a soldier in my country's army and I didn't care about anything else. I did suffer, it's true, because at the Liceo and at the Military Academy I had enjoyed my chiefs' favour and friendliness, but the suffering was not much more than what I'd felt in my former life - on the contrary, I had never been popular among my companions.

Nobody was clear, nobody was explaining what the problem was.

That Friday I learnt everything, all at once.

5.- Intermezzo corale

My hand sticks to the rock.

My forearm is joined to my hand by the wrist, and by the elbow, to the arm.

My shoulder joins my body, trunk, neck, legs and my hand sticking to the rock.

And like a magical act, my left –unskilled- hand lifts my body until it allows my other hand to take hold of a jutting rock.

The air is thin and cold.

I'm perspiring in spite of the low temperature, which will not change until I move away from the mountain's shadow side.

My body is now a delicate and precise clock's mechanism working almost automatically.

I don't think and I move.

I think as a movement, I'm a thinking movement, I'm a thought that moves.

I AM.

One foot burrows into a hollow, the other hangs in the air.

Below, two or three hundred metres of emptiness: just razor sharp rock. My body turns when needed. I'm not using a safety rope, I don't need or want it.

I'm precise as a surgeon or a sniper.

I look at the irregular wall of rock, full of hollows and sticking out rocks, and hardly plan my climb: I'm following my instinct, my heart on fire.

The flight of the condors doesn't distract me, I'll enjoy them when I reach the top.

While I'm on the mountain I'm infernally free.

I don't think of or remember anything: the cold and the risks force me to focus on the here and now, with no past or future.

I know this will change when I sit on the rock where this wall ends – just one step further upwards, to my destination today – when I take a sip of caña which I carry in a flask -and then pour out the rest as an offering to the Pachamama; a habit I took from an NCO -from the province of Jujuy- who couldn't live anywhere else than the Patagonia.

Unlike others, I know how I got here.

I finally sit on the overhang to which I've headed periodically since the summer of 1978, when we almost went to war with Chile; I had just arrived from my private hell, and hardly knew what this new planet was I was exploring.

I can see the narrow, dangerous pass which, after a two to three days march, leads to the thick, southernmost jungle covering the Chilean side of the Andes.

I can't smoke, the wind devours my cigarettes.

Instead I kiss the flask, take a long draught and throw out the rest into the empty air and it dissolves in the wind. I throw away the half-smoked cigarette behind me - it too disappears, swallowed up by the mountains.

"For Pachamama…" I murmur.

I know that unavoidably the memory will return… I allow it.

While I wait for its onslaught, I melt into the glorious landscape of the infinite sky, infinite mountains, infinite clouds…

I don't want to remember, but neither do I want to forget that fateful Friday in which –in one fell swoop- I lost my humanity, my family, my friends, and I became dead inside, a ghost living amongst live people.

The trucks were in a circle, their headlights illuminating a line of men and women dressed in rags, their arms tied behind their backs; there are many, perhaps twenty, I don't count them.

A few of the ragged-looking people are digging a pit with picks and shovels, it must be about three by five metres long and two metres deep.

Sandoval tells me they are prisoners, guerrillas, terrorists.

There is a deep silence and the prisoners' faces reflect their terror. Some of them have been visibly beaten, their bodies marked with dry and bleeding wounds and bruises.

Soriano has me called by a corporal who acts as his bodyguard, his trusted man and valet.

"How are you, Evans?" He speaks ironically.

Against all custom, rules and regulations, he is playing me for a fool with his tone, he's provoking, using the familiar "*tu*" in Spanish – no mention of my rank.

"Ready for your orders, Colonel," I speak firmly, at attention while I salute him.

"Let's see what you're made of, little English boy…" he whispers.

"Your father was a Commie, he was in the Republican army, and he cooperated with the English enemy to bring about the Reich's fall…" He laughs.

"An apple never falls far from the tree…" He looks me up and down and doesn't hide his contempt. He's sitting on the hood of the green Falcon. Beside him is Corporal Vélez, who went looking for me - he glances at Soriano with his hang-dog face.

"I have a surprise… I've kept it especially for you…" says Soriano, while with his head he signals to me to turn around.

I turn my body 180 degrees and my blood, my body, freezes.

In front of me, standing in pain and with great difficulty, is Vittoriosso. His hands tied behind his back, dressed in rags that at some time were a workman's shirt and combat *bombachas*, in bare feet, his body impressively disfigured by beatings, cuts and bruises of all colours, exuding a recognisable smell of urine and excrement.

"*Pelado*" Vittoriosso.

Braggart Vittoriosso.

Humberto Vittoriosso stands before me - the fifth year cadet from the 1970 "Federales" graduates promotion.

His left eye -the only one he can open- lights up and his swollen mouth, in which clearly there are teeth missing, makes a kind of grimace which could be interpreted as a smile.

He barely nods, and looks me straight in the eye.

The two NCO's guarding him, one on each side, hit him with wooden batons.

"Keep your head down, you bastard…" says one of them.

Soriano interrupts him.

"No… No, corporal, let them greet each other, they know each other, a little bird told me…"

Vittoriosso was what was called my "sponsor" at the Liceo.

One of the customs linking one generation of cadets with the next was for graduates to take charge of instructing the younger ones. It's an honour for the fifth year cadets to take care of the inexperienced fledglings, to help them to graduate from earth-bound bipeds to gallant cadets.

It's an initiation process, sometimes rough and a little cruel, but it serves those who don't fit in, those who have been forced to enter the Liceo to be able to leave without being expelled.

From the first day I showed my mettle, the strength of my vocation, my deep wish to be there.

My physical training was superior to many of the fifth year cadets. They could make me dance to their tune, pull me out of bed at any time, make me run around the main courtyard in briefs carrying my bedding on my shoulders, but I never hung my head or asked for compassion as did the rest of the boys in my company.

Vittoriosso was not our company chief at first.

The first one was the "Negro" Velázquez, who lasted only three weeks at his post: he challenged an NCO whom he had heard praise Perón to fight "without stripes" in the bathroom, and the officer on duty that day had found them in a fistfight.

Fighting "without stripes" is as old a tradition as any army, but it was also a tradition that if you are discovered, your career is over. Velázquez was expelled that same week.

Vittoriosso was different from all others in the Liceo.

His Italian great-grandfather had arrived in the country sent by the Italian King Humberto I; he had joined the Argentine Army as a Lieutenant Colonel and had trained a whole generation of military engineers.

During Gen. Roca's presidency, Vittoriosso had participated actively in the topographical survey of the Patagonian provinces and had worked at delimiting several cities in the southern Buenos Aires province.

Vittoriosso's grandfather had participated -and died very young- in the Parque revolution together with members of the Radical party, and his father had been an officer during the 1943 revolution.

Pelado Vittoriosso was the youngest of a dozen brothers and sisters, and the only one who had claimed the family's military tradition. He had hardly known his father, who had died an old man when his youngest was three or four years old.

They were a scandalously wealthy family.

When we became friends, he had told me that according to a family tradition, their forefather was one of Cesar Borgia's "*condottieri*" – Borgia being the well-known son of Pope Alexander VI and on whom Niccolo Machiavelli had based his book "The Prince".

The Vittoriosso clan claimed the rare honour of having an ancestor who at the beginning of the XVI century had been assassinated by Borgia during a dinner celebrating peace.

The "*condottieri*", commanders of the different armies Borgia led in his attempt to unify Italy to remove it from French and Spanish influence – the most powerful countries at that time – had all revolted at the same time, claiming their unpaid salaries.

Borgia came to an agreement with them and promised not to take revenge.

Of course, he was a shameless liar.

He invited all his old comrades-in-arms to a dinner to celebrate their truce, they were to attend without any weapons; and as Borgia appeared alone, unarmed and without any guards, the condottieri believed him – except for that Vittoriosso ancestor, who at that time had to be carried on a stretcher due to some wound or illness… He kept repeating as if in a delirium, "don't believe him, don't believe him, I'm his teacher, he's going to have us all killed…"

Borgia accompanied them into an enormous room where they found a long table full of delicious food -he offered them their seats, and when the wine was served he took a sip from every wineskin to show that the drink was not poisoned; he then discreetly left the room through a small door hidden in a wall, after which a mob of men armed with daggers, knives and swords entered and massacred every single commander and their men, including the prostrate ancestor who was not so delirious.

Pelado loved telling this story once he had accepted you into his intimate circle of friends.

He was charismatic, the leader of his company, a top student in all subjects, an accomplished sportsman – he was not only an outstanding rugby player as wing for the Liceo's team, he also stood out in complex Olympic disciplines such as the triathlon, in the military pentathlon and in martial arts – yet he was discreet and almost humble.

He was named "Pelado" (Baldy) because his blond hair disappeared when he was closely-cropped.

At first we were not friends.

He was a good superior, considerate with the weaker boys, just in his punishments and above all, he protected us from other abusive cadets such as "Assassin" Gándara, "Tarzan" Bollini or "Billiken" García, who used to take pleasure in tormenting any fledgling that crossed their paths.

They used to meddle with all those in First Year, except for Vittoriosso's company.

Later, when we became friends, he told me that he hadn't approached me because I didn't need help.

I had entered the Liceo as if I'd arrived at the Promised Land, my dream had come true and in my view nothing appeared serious or horrible.

I already knew how to make a bed in three different ways; how to put together a backpack impeccably; organize my cupboard just as was set in the rules; polish my shoes; and once uniforms were handed out, how to polish buttons and buckles.

I had gone through all these things at home with my father and I performed adequately as from the first day. I was not even bothered when the company chief used to point me out as an example – it earned dislike from my peers – or that fifth year cadets would compete to try to break me.

"*Pelado*" took care of the other cadets and left me to take care of myself, although he always had an eye cocked to avoid any possible abusive attempt against me.

My seriousness and focus to do as I was told had called his attention.

On the other hand, after he took charge of the company, I saw him as a leader who I could follow and admire.

When the cadets in Third Year pledged allegiance to the flag, *Pelado* approached me and stated, "Congratulations, Cadet Evans, your Company is outstanding and you stand out amongst them… You have marched with poise…"

I felt rewarded. *Pelado*, whom we all admired as a model cadet, was talking to me after the ceremony.

"Thank you my Fifth Year cadet!" I said, standing at attention.

He smiled.

"At ease, cadet, your efforts to leave behind being a fledgling is very clear…" And then, to my surprise, he spoke frankly.

"You have a future here at the Liceo, Cadet Evans… You have earned my respect these past months… You deserve my trust as I see the visible efforts you have made…"

My heart jumped with happiness, I know I blushed as red as a tomato, but this helped me to stop my feelings from getting away. I stood at attention, saluted him and I spoke, trying to hide my emotions, "Thank you, my Fifth Year cadet! I will be worthy of it!"

"OK, at ease, cadet… Carlos, you can call me Humberto… privately, of course…"

That was an informal gift that happened between the older cadets and the newer ones.

Most of the Fifth Year cadets – happy to finish their military training days – used that custom to approach the cadets who had older sisters… but this was not *Pelado*'s case.

My sisters – even Bethan, who was already very beautiful – were very young for men of eighteen, and besides, this was not *Pelado*'s style, he was a true gentleman.

He came home for supper several times, he spent one week on our farm and above all, he met my father, who immediately acknowledged him as a positive leader.

A certain bond was forged between them which allowed my father to honour him with some stories of the Spanish war and above all, what Pelado was most interested in, the war against the Nazis.

It appears this ran in the family: Vittoriosso's father had been pro-Allies and when he was about to leave the Army, the GOU (*Grupo Unido de Oficiales* – United Officers' Group, a nationalist secret society within the Argentine Army) took over the Argentine government.

Vittoriosso's confrontation with the cadets who privately showed off their sympathy for Nazism was clear and direct: I had seen him severely rebuke a Fourth Year cadet who had insulted a Jewish First Year cadet, and later he had challenged anyone who defended the Third Reich's colours to a fight "without stripes".

He was the Liceo's martial arts champion.

Vittoriosso was my friend throughout my First Year. Then as often happens in intergenerational friendships, we had slowly stopped seeing each other, although we always exchanged end-of-the-year cards and he attended my father's funeral.

Now there he was, across from me, swollen and deformed, covered in old and new blows.

"Here's a gift for you, Second Lieutenant Evans…" says Soriano.

"Execute the prisoner," he barks out.

Pelado looks at me from his only half-open eye, his tongue licks his red, swollen lips and he barely nods his head.

"Are you a coward or deaf, you fledgling? I gave you an order…" roars Soriano.

Then he repeats, "Execute the prisoner, shoot him in the back,", and he shouts, "He's a traitor to the country… He wore our Army uniform, he dishonoured it by adoring the Red flag… SHOOT THIS TRAITOR IN THE BACK!!!

I don't know what happened, or why I obeyed.

Everything happened at the same time, like in a rite or a macabre dance.

Pelado started twisting, trying to untie his hands. I heard him say clearly, "Not in the back, not in the back… I'm not a coward, I don't deserve to die by an execution in the back…"

 I hardly remember anything else.

They hit him on the back of the legs with the batons several times, forcing him to his knees and ended up pushing him to the ground.

I don't remember cocking the gun, nor having placed myself at his back, but I know he was shouting in spite of the gag over his mouth while he tried to turn over.

"Not in the back… Not in the back…"

I don't know if I took aim or not.

I don't remember the first shot either but now if I close my eyes, I still see the percussion cap clearly as it traces an arc in slow motion and how the bullet left a red-black hole in the middle of his back, and hear how he roared like a wounded animal, vomiting blood from his gagged mouth, trying to stand up, to turn around, not to avoid my shots, not at all, he wanted me to shoot him face on, and I can't remember shooting twice more until he stopped moving.

I don't remember when I returned my gun to its holster, against all my rules loaded and with a bullet in the chamber, but I clearly remember Soriano's breath smelling of wine and *salame*, approaching me provocatively until he had brushed against my ear and whispered joyfully, "Good, very good… I'll be inviting you when we fuck your little leftist sister, the little red must have a lovely, tight little pussy…"

I remember the warm wave that went through me, filling up to my eyes… And when it was about to explode in my head, I clearly heard my father's beautiful, deep voice, which I never again heard so clearly. "Cool it."

"Cool it."

"Cool it."

I remained quiet, cold, while pistol and rifle shots went off, I heard the screams of horror and pain, the sound of the rest of the prisoners being executed. I remember it all, except how or who carried off *Pelado*'s body.

My whole being wanted desperately to get out of there, and my survival instinct clearly said: The only way to manage and come out unharmed was to be as calm and quiet as a Patagonian lake.

I had to call home.

I had to save my sister.

For this to happen, I must act with the same calm serenity which was how all those present were acting in that savage, brutal ritual, and not allow the horror around me to show on my face.

I had been trained to be a soldier, not an executioner.

My family had to be defended, as clearly it had been threatened.

I didn't care about Prieto's assassination, nor all the brutal and savage things performed by the ERP or the Montoneros.

Papá had said this to me the time I had celebrated, not long before his death, the execution of a supposed terrorist. "You don't fight cannibals by eating them, Charly… You don't remove Nazis from a country by killing them all…" he said, and I hadn't understood.

Now I did.

Was my sister a terrorist? Could she have gone that far?

I decided, as we returned by the same road, that I didn't care -I didn't care if they killed me either, but firstly I had to save my sister.

I thought… And thought.

I decided my course of action the very moment we arrived back at the barracks.

I didn't sleep. At 5:30 a.m. I dressed in civilian clothes —there was an order that we should do this if we wanted to go out alone- and at 6:30 a.m. I asked at the guard room for my weekend pass, hoping Soriano hadn't cancelled it.

Once out on the street, I took a "safe" taxi —driven by a policeman- and I had him drive me to Independencia square. I walked for two hours through deserted streets, paying attention to see if I had been followed, and not wanting to come across some squad which would force me to reveal my position.

A little before 9 a.m. I rang Dr Seleme's doorbell, and he welcomed me like a family member.

He immediately asked me if there was something wrong, if I felt well, that I didn't look it. Just as my grandfather, he was a doctor through and through and he could detect sickness just by looking at a patient.

I was sick from fear, revulsion, shame.

He immediately left me alone with the telephone.

On the fourth ring, at the other end I heard my mother's clear, sing-song voice.

"Son! What a lovely surprise… You can't imagine all I have to tell you…"

I interrupt her. I didn't say hello, nor I love you, nor I miss you – not a word to waste.

I cut her short coldly, brutally, cruelly.

"Mamá… Be quiet and listen to me… Listen to everything I'm going to tell you, I'm not going to repeat it, I'm not going to call you again… I'm not asking, I'm ordering you, you understand… You must…"

She interrupts me, alarmed.

"What's happened, Charly love?"

I almost shout.

"I said to listen to me and not to interrupt… This is life or death and I don't have time to explain, I don't know if they have tapped the telephone… Get Bethan out of the country right now, right away, immediately… Don't ask me how or when… You hang up and you leave home in the truck, don't go in the station wagon, they probably know that vehicle… Stay at the estancia for four or five days… Ask Sandaza for help, he's trustworthy and he will know how to do this, cross to Corrientes in the canoe and when you're there get hold of a vehicle and drive to Brazil… Avoid any controls, you got it? Mamá, this is life or death… You do as I tell you right now…"

My mother's voice has broken, she's on the edge of tears.

"What are you saying… What are you saying…" she repeats, like a litany.

"Shit, Mamá, don't make me repeat it all again… Did you understand what I said? Don't ask me why, or how, nothing… Bethan could be in grave danger, if she stays in Argentina I can't do anything, I'm nobody, please understand… I can also be killed if they suspect that I helped her or had some information…"

Something I say calms my mother completely, she suddenly sounds as always, serene and controlled.

"Alright… alright… I've understood… When will I see you? When are you coming home? Please, I… I… please," she says in a soft voice, so sad.

"I don't know. I don't know… Do what I've told you, please… please… Give Bethan a kiss from me, tell her I love her so much… Take care of her, take care all of you… Please."

Mamá is still talking when I hang up.

I have a knot in my throat, my eyes are full of tears, I dry them with my grey coat sleeves.

Seleme protests kindly as I leave the house, insisting I stay for lunch. I lie shamelessly: I have an official duty.

I took another taxi all the way to the town of Monteros and spent all my salary getting drunk in a whorehouse, the unwritten rule for the winners in all wars.

I try to forget.

With cheap brandy I do.

While on the mountain I forget.

When I come down from the mountain now, I've left a lot of bad memories behind.

Every time I descend, for two or three days I don't have a single drink, I sleep soundly. And later, relentlessly, my memories return.

When I've left the mountains behind, and I'm back in the town and have the barracks in view, I pull out the German binoculars my father's English friends brought him for his fiftieth birthday. I look carefully at the Regiment's gate.

I know it's not the time of year, that my youngest sister is still in secondary school; classes have begun, that it's impossible the Rambler Classic should be parked in front of the barracks - but just in case, I still look around very carefully.

Since that Saturday morning of my call I never saw my mother again, I didn't speak to her, nor did I write.

At the first chance, Soriano had managed to get rid of me; he didn't dismiss me but suggested I wasn't fit for service in the army and sent me back to Buenos Aires.

To my surprise, Llogri was in the Army's Personnel department. I didn't need to tell him much. He and Soriano knew each other well, they disliked each other intensely and without hypocrisy. Llogri felt responsible for what I had gone through, clearly he knew everything that had taken place.

Thanks to Llogri I'm here in a mountain regiment, lost in the Patagonia. I lead a simple life, the rules are clear. Mountains are not forgiving of mistakes.

I learnt from scratch and made new colleagues.

Nobody cared about my daily quarter bottle of cheap peach brandy -seven bottles a month- which the conscripts in my company used to throw into the garbage pile.

On the mountain we're brothers; we're links in a chain, at the head of which there isn't always an officer or the man who's been there the longest —but there's the most experienced, who has climbed most times, the calmest, the most trustworthy.

I became the best soldiers' instructor Colonel Echazú ever had, and that's all the old man needed to know. He had graduated before Soriano and Llogri and had survived several purges, he was from the generation before Gen. Bussi. All Echazú hoped for was that none of those in his same promotion become a general, in order for him to retire having completed his total years of service and thus enjoy a full salary.

He was a reserved man, with no ambition other than retiring, and he made my life easy.

A group of us would go up into the mountains five or six times a year; I'd actually go up twice that amount because I'd climb in winter as well as in summer.

At the beginning my companions and superiors would say I was crazy to climb the mountains on my own; but very soon when they saw how I had progressed in the group climbs, they were no longer concerned.

I go to Buenos Aires once a year, with no fixed date or any routine, avoiding the holiday months and Banfield. I go up to Esperanza, I work a little on the *estancia*, I ride with Junco and I go by to greet Sandaza only when I'm leaving.

Since then my mother writes me a letter once a month. I read them and keep them neatly in an old wooden box which has a map of Argentina clearly engraved on its cover. I took it from the farm, carefully removing its contents and placing them in one of the many folders in the large library at home.

It was where my father had placed the keepsakes of his lifetime, letters which he had received throughout his travels around the world.

I don't answer my mother.

Every summer shortly after New Year she arrives at the wheel of her Rambler Classic station-wagon, she sets up a tent by the stream at the entrance to the town and camps there with my younger sisters.

The first time I saw the car parked at the barracks gate I left through the back, and was reprimanded very mildly by Echazú in his characteristic fashion.

Now I leave earlier.

Mamá has repeated the ritual every year over the last five years.

She wrote 60 letters, five Christmas cards, five New Year cards, five birthday cards. Never a reproach, never a question about my absence or my silence.

Every letter exhibited her fierce optimism, full of news about the family, my sisters, about Bethan working as a nurse in Brazil, about Siwan and her talent as a tennis player, about Eirin and her musical talent, about my grandfather and his new hobby, military models…

Memories of a life I once had.

Memories that disappear when I climb the mountains.

I wrote to my grandfather once, shortly after arriving at this destination, when I heard about Uncle Carlos' death, after he had been in a coma for three years.

Sure of my mother's absence, I enter the barracks and realize there is an unusual party-like atmosphere.

It appears that at dawn today, a special naval infantry unit has recovered the Islas Malvinas/Falkland Islands.

6.- Finale molto fortissimo

I kick my black horse so it will cut off a young steer from the herd to be vaccinated. I've cut off twenty but Junco has beaten me, he's already cut off thirty seven.

We haven't spoken the whole day, it hasn't been necessary.

From La Quiaca in the north to Ushuaia in the south, from Mendoza in the west to Misiones in the east, thirty million some Argentines know that little over a week ago Argentina has recovered sovereignty over the Malvinas/Falklands Islands, illegally appropriated by the English Crown in 1833.

I arrived at the *estancia* yesterday evening and we've been working with the cattle since early in the morning: tomorrow the vet is coming to vaccinate and castrate, and the animals must be clean and ready.

As we've completed more than half the work, we stop to share a *mate*.

Junco starts a fire with some thistles and dry branches, and takes water from the stream to heat it in the kettle blackened by smoke. We share the *mate* in silence.

After three or four rounds, my godfather finally breaks the silence.

"It's good then, isn't it… they were stolen…" He looks at me, waiting for my reaction.

"That's what it seems… Now we'll have to hold up when they hit back…"

"Yeah, we'll have to hold up, as usual… Will you be going there?"

"Yep… They're sending me to talk to the islanders, because I speak English…"

"Yeah, you speak it very well… You were very small when you used to talk to your father's friends from the war… Will they come and fight?" He becomes serious.

I smile.

"No, I don't think so, they're older men… Besides, I don't think there'll be a war… We're the U.S.A's allies in Central America and the British are their allies in Europe … I imagine we'll end up negotiating…"

"I hope so… There's so much to do in Argentina before looking for trouble in some far-off land…"

Surprised, I look at him.

"You don't agree we should recover territory occupied by a foreign country?"

"Look, son, I'm not gonna argue with you or anyone… The military –I'm sorry but I've gotta say this- have no idea how to govern… Look what's happened to the price of cattle, of milk… everything's worth less and less… And there's many more people who are poor… Nobody has enough money… I'm lucky, you and your family have been more than generous to me… But I see and hear what the neighbours say… Why are they so concerned about two pieces of rock in the sea when the Patagonia is empty, right?... Very close to us here in the town of Charata and to the north, there are so many hungry children… Islands? Yeah… When there ain't no more peons with no work, or peasant woman with hungry kids…"

Junco surprises me. He always does. His simple *gaucho* appearance always makes me forget that this man spent years beside my father, they were like brothers; he talks in a simple way, but his reasoning, his way of thinking things out is intelligent and complex.

I hear my father's voice in his reasoning.

"You may be right, *padrino*… But it's what's happening now and tomorrow I'm leaving for the islands."

Junco says nothing. We get back to work until sundown.

He takes me back to Santa Fe in the broken-down Jeep that Papá bought before I was born; we take more than an hour for the fifty-odd kilometres, and arrive at the airport when night is falling.

All I'm taking with me is my soldier's regulation bag and I'm wearing my uniform again with my higher rank insignias; finally, after an expected delay, I was promoted to First Lieutenant less than four days ago.

Junco does not go in with me, I say goodbye to him at the waiting room entrance.

At the LADE airline company counter Sandaza and his friend, Notary Public Fortunato Del Sastre are waiting for me; I hug my family's old and dear friend, who once again is helping me out.

I sign the papers that make Junco owner of my part of the farm.

Sandaza's eyes are full of tears.

He holds my hand very tight and looks me in the eye.

"Go and see your mother…" he murmurs, smiling kindly.

I don't answer, I just shake my head.

I don't sleep on the brief flight which will leave me in Aeroparque, the Buenos Aires city airport.

I think briefly about destiny, about luck, about how events in life start weaving the net in which we move -we form part of it and we're not even aware.

The Liceo's director ends his career in the Army's personnel department; from there he rescues me from Colonel Soriano's claws and saves me physically, mentally and spiritually when he places me under Colonel Echazú.

And what's more, he provides me with a new passion, a new religion, a new aim in my life, because in that mountain unit I discover my love for climbing.

And now, after handing me my First Lieutenant dispatch –in the barracks they used to call me "the eternal Second Lieutenant" because my promotion had taken so long- a new destination and position: "Public Relations Officer".

And a promise.

"When all this ends –which I hope will be soon- we will resolve your sister's situation… There's nothing against her, I can assure you… However, you did well in sending her out of the country… These savages do what they want and they don't hold themselves accountable to anyone…" states Llogri.

He talks to me in the familiar "tú", affectionately, and above all, reveals to me that within the apparently monolithic "National Reorganization Process", there is subterranean, dangerous dissent, alternative paths.

Gen. Galtieri divides the waters, not all of the high ranking officers think that filling the islands with soldiers, such as we're doing, is a good idea. "It's our guarantee that there won't be a war, it'll force them to send thousands of soldiers," say the government supporters. Llogri is frank and direct: "So stupid, if it comes to war they'll send 3,000 men and they'll annihilate us. We won't be able to hold them back, not even for ten days. We have to negotiate now, we have to convince the civilian population that we're their best option and then get out and leave a symbolic garrison, together with another with U.N. peace troops and English troops… They'll never be able to remove us from there… You're important there, your English will help us with the islanders…"

The LADE Twin Otter lands at Aeroparque.

I have to wait several hours for my next flight: it leaves at 04:30 a.m. with a stopover in Comodoro Rivadavia, then on to Puerto Argentino (Stanley). The airport is invaded by soldiers carrying their full equipment: all ranks and everybody with an air of enthusiasm and nervousness.

I hesitate for a while. I then pull out some coins and stand by a queue of conscripts who are waiting in front of a large, orange public telephone box. They stand at attention, salute me and let me go to the front of the queue.

I dial the number for my grandfather's house. It's 10:30 p.m., Mamá must be in bed reading, it's a habit she's always kept.

He picks up. His quiet voice lights up when he recognizes mine.

"Charly! What a surprise… Such a long time… We miss you so much," he says, and I can hear the old doctor hiding a sob.

My heart burns and my blood has turned cold…

In spite of the noise around me from the soldiers' excited and constant murmuring, I hear him and I feel my chest tighten into a knot.

"Are you OK, grandfather?... I'm fine… My promotion came through…" I tell him, trying to cheer him up.

"We're all very well, your sisters have grown so much… You should come and visit us… Are you in Buenos Aires… Your mother left this afternoon for the farm…"

I sigh. Sandaza…

"Yes, grandfather, I'm at Aeroparque, I'm leaving shortly… For the islands…" I close my eyes when I think of the lie I've just told him…

"Son!" He sighs deeply as he speaks. "I know it's your job… But please, take care of yourself…"

I tell him not to worry, nothing will happen, it'll only be a few weeks and then the United Nations will intervene, they won't let a war happen between Allied countries.

"Yes, yes… But you can see how everyone is acting… And that drunkard's bragging… This is not going to end well… I'm praying as I haven't done in years… I hadn't prayed since your Grandmother died… I hope this craziness ends without loss of life… We've already lost too much…"

"Grandfather, remember how the business with Chile was resolved, very likely the Pope will intervene again, it'll be OK, don't worry… I must go, grandfather, there are so many people waiting to use the phone… Kiss my sisters for me, my aunts… My mother… When I get back we can have lunch together, like before, I promise you, Grandfather, I swear this in Papá's memory…"

I can hear the old man's sobs at the other end, and I have to force myself not to let my tears fall.

I take advantage of a small post-office –opened up especially for soldiers to be able to send their goodbye letters- and I write to Grandmother Pepa. I'm not going to call her, I know that by this time she has been in bed asleep, some hours ago.

We board the plane by hierarchy.

I'm given a seat in the middle of the plane above the wings, at a window on the left-hand side. Beside me is a staff sergeant and a sergeant occupying the other seats. They're from Mercedes, province of Corrientes.

After our formal greetings, there are no more exchanges: we belong to different castes, we'll only be in communication if we're under the same commander, in the same unit.

I tighten my seat belt and look out of the window. On my side I can see the avenue, the river, some boats in the river channels and then the dark sky – and very far off, lights from the city of Colonia, in Uruguay.

I'm tired, they have been five intense days since I left my barracks at the foot of the Andes; I travelled by plane, in a jeep, I rode on horseback all day, I talked to my grandfather. I pull down my cap's peak and fall asleep.

I dream with Papá, eating a barbecue with "*Baldy*" Vittoriosso. They look at me, laugh at me. It's the first dream I've remembered in five years.

I wake up when the plane is taxiing along the runway in Comodoro Rivadavia. I've missed the sunrise over the sea. We don't have a long wait, it's just a technical stopover. We take off again, and as the flight hours become less, the atmosphere on board becomes silent, almost mystical.

When the Captain announces that in a few minutes we'll be able to see the islands, we go against the orders of staying in our seats and we all stand up and sing the national anthem. When we sit down the "*Viva la Patria*" can be heard throughout the plane.

As soon as the plane has stopped taxiing along the runway there is another bout of "Long live…" and we embrace, for a minute abandoning the military order's rigid difference of castes. On the Malvinas (Falklands) ground, I return to my position as an officer and my seat companions, as NCOs.

All hopes for a peaceful settlement regarding the Malvinas (Falklands) issue have disappeared since the end of April; I don't read newspapers nor do I listen to the radio, but I know what's going on, because everything is more or less public, everybody talks to each other, and although I don't talk much, I listen to it all.

At the United Nations, the Argentine delegation was swept aside due to the clearly joint Anglo-North American foreign affairs policies.

The Yanks have unsuccessfully tried to convince the Armed Forces' government to retreat from the islands surrendering all conditions; in a speech made from the balcony at Government House, Gen. Galtieri shouted to thousands of Argentines gathered below, carrying light-blue and white flags and wearing rosettes with the national colours, "If they want to come, let them come… We will give them battle!"

And Perón's *plaza* boomed with a single voiced, "Argentina!"… The whole country was on fire with patriotism and military zeal.

We saw it over TV, in the confiscated offices of the FIC Co. (Falkland Islands Company).

We were a small group of 8 or 9 Second Lieutenants —among them two from the Liceo and several university graduates on commission- as well as a few First Lieutenants, who were working as translators or participating in recruitment activities among the 1,800 Kelpers, the native citizens of the Islands.

None of our group had ever experienced being under fire.

My fighting experience compared to my father's was laughable: our time in Tucumán had been something like spending one busy summer night.

However, I know enough to understand that a combat such as we've never seen before will come upon us - mortal and dangerous fighting which will change us all forever.

We received our instructions from a Captain in Intelligence and we had a script which we had to follow regardless. Our objective was to push local people's opinion in our favour.

From the first day I knew that my work was a monumental stupidity, condemned to be a most absurd failure.

We were there to recover Argentine land that had been usurped by a foreign power. Convince them regarding what?

We hadn't hesitated to slaughter subversive action by killing them all, the fighters as well as the support lines with hardly any discrimination; we had assassinated close to ten thousand fellow citizens with no mercy, we had buried them in unmarked graves, we had thrown them from planes; and we were being sentimental regarding 1,800 second-class citizens from the dregs of the British Empire, offering them constitutional rights which we denied our own on the Continent.

It was clear that those who were directing all of this were a bunch of louts, not even capable of understanding that the British would never accept negotiating under pressure; while Puerto Argentino (Stanley) was filling up with troops, the British were sending a naval operations force and some three thousand Royal Marines.

And there are all these rumours that Russia is going to become our ally, that the Peruvians are sending us bombers, that Kaddafi is giving us missiles…

And that the Montoneros are in support and that ERP cells are working in undercover operations.

Inexplicably, radio stations, television channels and newspapers joined in with the success-oriented reports which the Military Junta was broadcasting regarding the Malvinas operation.

I slowly began to be aware that this situation was only going to worsen: my companions were talking about the situation along the same lines as Gen. Galtieri, and I knew that several were fervently looking forward to a real war.

The Kelpers were mostly enemies rather than friends: they were British in both their characters and education, they wouldn't be easily defeated.

Just a few cooperated with us.

They had to, because Argentina, "the Continent" as they call it, means good and cheaper schools with an English education; a large and modern British Hospital; and a small but well-connected Anglo community; they receive fresh vegetables and fruit from the Continent, and cylinder gas; the metal airstrip -on which war planes were now landing- had been built for passenger planes operated by LADE, with regular flights to and from Comodoro Rivadavia.

Most were "loyal" to the Crown, and yet they weren't full British subjects: they were connected to the Falklands Islands Company (FIC) and were so considered by the British Foreign Office.

They didn't like us. They knew what we had done to the guerrillas, as everything had been reported by those exiled in Europe, and at first they were afraid of us.

But Gen. Menéndez, the military governor, as well as Gen. García, chief of the T.O.M. (Teatro de Operaciones Malvinas, the so-called Malvinas Operation) had guaranteed the fulfilment of the national constitution throughout the Malvinas Islands (Falklands) territory.

They stopped fearing us. On the other hand, they then started hating us when the governor began changing the habits and customs.

Towards the end of April I started to loath my work, when the Southern Atlantic cold began in earnest.

By chance, my path crossed with Megan Fraser's.

I had met her at my sister Bethan's fifteenth birthday party; her father managed an F.I.C. farm and thanks to the '60s agreements between the U.K. and Argentina, she was a student at Barker's College with my sister.

She hadn't changed much, at least her face. Perhaps she was slightly plumper, and she was wearing a long kilt and a big goose-down jacket.

Meg and I had danced that night and we had kissed passionately in the Banfield house gazebo.

We met up two or three more times, we went to the cinema, and then as happens at that time in life, we lost interest in each other. I think that at that time, too, I started going out with one of my class companion's sisters.

Since then I hadn't thought of her again.

Megan looks me straight in the eye. She has recognized me.

I smile as I approach, I pull off my right-hand glove as I come up to her when imperceptibly something makes me stop.

She's not smiling. She looks straight at me and doesn't smile.

My smile is frozen and I've stopped -in front of her, but not close enough for our hands to touch.

I lick my lips, my mouth is suddenly and inexplicably dry.

She talks.

"You're Charly Evans?" She speaks in Spanish.

Then, "Shame on you, Charly… Shame on the memory of your Dad!!! You're a damn Nazi!"

And unhesitatingly, she spits in my face and continues walking on.

I stand there for a few seconds - then with the back of my gloved hand I wipe Megan's spit off my face.

This had taken place and as yet the war hadn't even started.

But then the month of May came round, and everything got worse.

They sunk the Belgrano.

The weather got colder, and what's more, every day cannon blasts fell, they were totally unpredictable. It might be sunny, no wind, and suddenly the air would be filled with explosions and screams.

I started my rounds to try and find some form of alcohol and I discovered a black market. Everything was obtainable with money: Governor Menéndez imposed the Argentine peso and naturally there were those who wanted to make a profit.

June was approaching, dense and cold, when quite by chance I had another surprise when visiting the airport, which had already been bombed. I meet up with Fernando Ruiz Vidal, a corvette lieutenant wearing a navy pilot's uniform.

He was a Liceo companion, he played wing in the Liceo Naval's rugby team; he was one year ahead of me and had been my arch-rival on the field.

But I liked him -during the third halves of each game we used to share a hamburger or a hot dog and a Coke and we'd chat. He was courageous and very fast, we'd often cross in our games but we never attempted to attack each other. We found our technical draw very funny, and we'd formed a mutual respect.

Our paths had crossed in several parties at one or the other Liceo, but we weren't friends, we couldn't be, we were both among the best in each of our teams, we were rivals, the Army and the Navy.

I knew other people in that crazy place -which Puerto Argentino had become- but no-one whom I knew from that time.

We shook hands with pleasure, we told each other our stories.

At the beginning we didn't trust each other; but afterwards, as the hours went by and with the agony of having little or nothing to do, we began to be frank.

We laughed at the things which we saw were beginning to be more and more absurd, and we burnt up with each bombing.

Unlike me, he had been in contact with the enemy three times, he flew a Naval Air Force subsonic plane; this had been totally destroyed in the bombing of the morning before.

A victim of the misunderstandings between the Forces, which could be felt everywhere, the plane had been left on the runway –the Air Force personnel were very busy attending to their own planes- and the plane had been destroyed by artillery.

The following days we wandered around, waiting for a supposed British invasion of Puerto Argentino, so we were carrying rifles. Sometimes we talked as if we were alone, sometimes we told each other stories about the Liceo.

I did not tell him about Vittoriosso.

Another day I went to pick him up at his cabin at the airport and found he'd been arrested: incredibly, the Navy had lost his file, they had no idea who he was, they not only couldn't assign him a new plane, they'd restricted his movements to the small airport building until they could solve this issue.

In my whole life, I don't recall having ever seen anyone so indignant as that man. War is absurd always, but all of us there were living the worst comedy of errors.

I said goodbye as best I could.

War was burning all around me and I was doing nothing except walking back and forth carrying useless papers.

I went to the personnel office and sent a cable to Colonel Llogri requesting to be assigned a position with military responsibility.

Contrary to my low expectations, I received an almost immediate answer to the request.

A replacement was needed at a front line position some 40 kms from the city, at the other end of the island, and my assignment was at combat level.

My new commander is Colonel Soriano.

In a brief flight following the island's landscape —at a height of no more than 8 or 9 mts so as to avoid the radars on British ships surrounding the islands- the Huey helicopter pilot Lieutenant Anaya leaves me some 100 mts from the command post, on which I see a tattered light blue and white flag blowing fiercely in the wind.

I see a few half-buried tents completely camouflaged by the peat and the scarce vegetation in the area. It is intensely cold and during the night everything freezes up.

At the commander's tent I give in my papers to Corporal Vélez, Soriano's lapdog. Soriano leans out of the tent.

"No Evans, you can't come in to my headquarters… You'll leave a trashy smell… The corporal will give you your instructions. If I see you around here again for any reason, I'll have you shot as a deserter, do you get it, you asshole?"

Varela gives me the coordinates, and I march for three long hours over the hills and peat bogs, sometimes I sink up to my ankles - a very difficult walk, sometimes easier, sometimes worse.

I arrive at my post: it's a mobile radar station, surrounded by a series of fox holes in which a group of soldiers are lying, looking very glum. The radar has not worked as from the first attacks.

During the bombings at the beginning of June the machine gun had been destroyed, and the First Lieutenant in charge of the platoon had been seriously wounded in the attack; since then First Sergeant Escobar led the platoon the best way he could.

Which wasn't too well.

He was crude and stern, his training came from a tightly closed, top-down approach in an army which had not taken part in any conventional conflict in 112 years: five generations of soldiers who had never even heard the sound of a cannon.

And the constant cannon fire which has been going on has weakened nearly everybody. Escobar is at the end of his tethers.

As I approach the awning which has been precariously set up on the radar's northern side, I immediately come upon a soldier staked to the ground.

Escobar looks at me, with a mixture of relief and contempt.

"He stole a sheep, and our superiors told us that sheep must not be touched…"

"Untie that man immediately…" I look at the soldiers, all of them freezing cold in summer uniforms, hungry because all they eat are very small portions of rations lacking in calories.

"Where is the evidence?"

Escobar looks at me.

"The sheep, Sergeant…"

He points towards the back.

"See if you can make a stew to give to the troops… They need it."

The wind and the cold are constant; there are few sunny days, and soon every day is grey, and the nights get longer.

Every day I make the men of the two sections -forming the small unit under my leadership- do physical exercises; we improve the defences, placing them in a better position, we move the fox-holes to higher ground.

No further than a half-hour's march there is an abandoned house where we find some metal sheets; other men must have sacked the place because the roof's beams are on view and almost all insulation material is gone.

We take what we need, sheets of metal, wood to make fires; I order them to catch as many sheep as they can, it's cold and the meat will not go bad.

We organize our kitchen in a hole, and we make a pipe we brought from the house into a kind of chimney which practically hides the smoke completely. Every day, in spite of the cannon fire which sometimes falls near our area, we have one hot meal.

The days go by; we hear the news on a Tonomac radio confiscated from a soldier, and we only use it for one hour a day to save the battery. We celebrate our May 25th holiday beneath a cold drizzle and cannon fire.

At night, Radio Nacional news reports on a fierce air battle; this we know because we hear the turbines as they fly over us; we sing out "Viva la patria"; we sing the national anthem; one or two pray for victory.

The sacrifice hasn't been enough.

They have disembarked somewhere and as May ends one night beneath an intense storm of sleet, we fire and are fired at, the contact was as brief as it was intense; we shot two ammunition clips each. In the morning all we find are cartridges everywhere, they didn't even leave the clips.

They were just testing how strong our defences were, how sharp our weapons.

Once again the tense calm, if you can call artillery attacks calm, the calm of Harriers flying over; the helicopters almost don't make it, somewhere Soriano's anti-aircraft defence has stopped them.

The snow is falling, and now and again, bombs fall and explode.

Some read the Bible; I try Shakespeare, a book my father gave me at the same time as my first year uniform for the Liceo: Henry V. I also have Papá's war diary, which sometimes is as clear as a Bible, other times as cryptic as a puzzle.

And while Radio Nacional reports on our successes, we grow colder and colder in spite of our sheep stews. The cold is a relentless enemy, at least a quarter of the men have trench foot problems - their boots have frozen as well as their toes, and it's harder and harder to generate heat for their feet.

My thoughts —kept to myself- tell me we're not going to survive up to our Flag Day on June 20th; and on the night of June 11th we hear on Radio Colonia that Gen. Galtieri and Gen. Menéndez have quarrelled, that the war is lost, and Puerto Argentino (Stanley) is about to fall in a matter of days.

Before the sun comes up, I order Escobar to lead the company - to take them as far as Puerto Argentino (Stanley), and if he encounters any English soldiers he must surrender. And just as this man had obeyed me every day, he says he won't go, he's not going to lead anyone: First Corporal Bernardo can take the men, and he's going to stay to defend the position – and I'm so tired I don't argue.

Romero, a soldier from the province of Entre Ríos, who is a quick talker with an ubiquitous disposition —the one I'd found punished severely for having killed a sheep – also abandons the company in retreat and chooses to stay with us.

When I asked him why, he said that his father was a strong peasant, just as he was, and before leaving for the Malvinas (Falklands) he had killed two people out of jealousy; so it would be better to be dead than jailed, in addition to dying for the country.

I couldn't argue.

Who am I to judge him?

Here we are, the three of us in fox holes separated by quite a few metres, with plenty of ammunition and two clips for each FN FAL covering a useless radar from the beginning of the war. As night falls, there follows a calm and mysteriously windless period, and at grey and purple sunrise, we saw the red berets.

I don't know who shouted first, but I bit my teeth and I started shooting wildly, using up all the cartridges I had left.

I don't know who the last to shout was. I remember it all, and I don't know if I shouted like the others, Long Live Argentina – *Viva la Patria*.

¡Viva!

To the Malvinas-Falklands fallen

EPILOGUES

I

Lieutenant… Tony… it's over. The man is dead."

"Yes, I know, Ron, but I know him… I knew him…"

"Tony, that's what you said, his father and yours knew each other…"

"No, no, what I mean is… I'll show you. I have a photo in my wallet. From the '70s, I don't remember if it was 1970 or '71, I was in the army and that's why I couldn't travel with my father… But look at this photo, the man on the left is my Dad, and in the middle, there's the boy…"

"I see… I'm sorry, Tony. I told you, he was on the wrong side of the road."

"Really? Was he? You don't have any qualms about this? Was he really on the wrong side? So wrong that he gave his life for what he believed in…"

"Just as four of ours did: Raleigh, Macey, Ferguson, Kringbert. And eight wounded: Romney, Adams, Connelly, Taft, Bates, Thomas and Lowry – he's very bad… And Harris…

"I know, Ron… But… What is this all about? To save a Conservative government that doesn't want to lose the next elections?"

"Come on, Tony, don't lose your head now. Don't break down in front of the men. This shit isn't over yet, they need you in one piece. We already know this is all related to politics."

"No, Ronnie, this isn't about politics, it's about good, brave boys killing other good, brave boys."

"Come on, mate, that's a great thought but those ideas here can drive you crazy. It's not worth it, don't go there."

"I won't Ron, I'm OK, but I don't like this. I knew that boy, his father was like a brother to my father, like you and me…"

"I understand… But we can't do anything more now, and we must start moving on."

"Do you have those stress pills you told me about? I could do with some now…"

"Yes…

"Give me one…"

"Sure, chief…"

"I must write to our boys' families…"

"Don't worry about that, the government will do it."

"I know, but I must do it as well. My father also used to do that for every man he lost… It's a way to…"

"But… You're taking his things?"

"Yes. I have to find a way of getting them to his family."

"I understand, but you're crazy. All this shit will be over soon. It's already gone on way too long."

"You're right, Ron, a stinky, shitty game. I'd also be happier unemployed… Let's go, we have to move…"

II

The bar on the top floor of the Sheraton Hotel in Buenos Aires is identical to all the others he's seen around the world, whether in Asia, Europe or in North America – it's not full, but neither is it empty. The colour of the curtains and chair covers varies, but the style and design of the furniture is the same, as well as the employees' uniforms and the signs' and menus' print.

Most of the clients sitting at the tables are hotel guests, but the sophisticated style and air conditioning also attracts the local –somewhat snobbish- public, eyeing the tourists who are beginning to visit Buenos Aires, attracted by the democratic Spring that little more than two years ago had begun with Raúl Alfonsín's government. The city is boiling in January's summer heat, but it's also due to people's effervescence, trying to rebuild the country after seven almost incomprehensible years -as well as people starting to become more aware of the torrent of atrocities that are coming out publicly into the light.

He's walked around the city, and when they ask him where he's from, at the beginning he used to say Canada, which is what was recommended when he applied for his passport. This was how he spent the first two weeks. He slowly realized then that everything he'd been told about Argentines was not exactly true. They were much more complex than what he'd heard.

The very friends in London who tried to dissuade him from this trip begged him never to reveal that he was a veteran from the Falklands (Malvinas) war. They were South Americans, fierce, bloody dangerous cannibals.

Instead, he'd met up with warm, friendly, vociferous, curious people and extraordinarily concerned about how he experienced them; everywhere they asked him to give his opinion about them, to discuss and exchange ideas. The taxi drivers and the waiters in the bars, people on the street and the girls in the *plazas*.

He timidly began to say he was English and he found that instead of attacking him they invited him to a cup of coffee, to chat, discuss, to explain. He had come invited by an NGO organizing meetings between soldiers who had fought on opposite sides –all his friends in London had suggested a psychiatrist if he was suffering from war trauma – and he had found that the NGO's initiative had been healing.

He had taken part in a meeting with professional soldiers –officers and NCOs – and had been moved to tears with the stories of those who had been his enemies. At the beginning he had felt an enormous tension –different to the fear when entering into combat, it was more like anxiety when jumping with a parachute- but as he listened to the veterans, even with his own difficulty of just beginning to understand Spanish, he had felt deeply moved.

At the back of the auditorium where the meeting was being held, a man about forty years old was sitting alone, in the completely empty last row of seats. The man had covered his face with both hands, his shoulders bent over his lap. He was clearly crying quietly.

He stood up suddenly from his place at the table while somebody was talking – his untimely move interrupted the speech as he approached this perfect stranger.

He placed his hand on the man's shoulder.

The man sprung up, as if his seat had ejected him. The silence in the room went deeper than when the speakers had been talking.

For a second, fear ran through the room that the two men would get into a fight.

He never took his hand from the man's shoulder. He looked into his eyes and clearly could see his tears.

He then spoke, in his stilted Spanish, "I really am so sorry." He didn't know why he had to speak, it was so far from his usual custom, and never thinking of the possible consequences, he opened up his arms as wide as he could. For a fraction of a second his whole being wondered what he was doing – then the big, strong man responded with exactly the same gesture back.

As he embraced the man, he felt the same way he had felt on June 14th, 1982, when he and his men had hugged as they stood on the esplanade in the port of Stanley, capital of the Falklands or better said, "Les Melvinas" as he'd started to call them out of respect for his hosts. He had embraced Ronnie Ferguson, the medical assistant, Andrew Kelly his sergeant, and then all the men in his unit. It wasn't because of the victory. It was because they were alive.

Now, in an embrace with this total stranger he felt he was hugging a comrade-in-arms, a man whose virtues he understood, a feeling which his friends, family or neighbours could never even fathom. His own eyes filled with tears because their feelings were the same.

After that meeting he also attended several private lunches and he always encountered warmth and respect.

While on the street he had been invited to a centre for veterans that was just starting to be organized. The Argentine officers suggested he not accept the invitation because there was a great deal of resentment still around.

He didn't follow their advice. He hadn't followed any advice when he was told not to come to Argentina. Among the veterans who were conscripts –so different to his subordinates, who were professional soldiers- these men were recruits obliged to form part of the army. He felt a little fear when he saw many with dark faces, some had very long hair and were wearing some pieces of clothing from uniforms. He heard some shouts and perhaps an insult.

They then allowed him to speak. He had learned Spanish after the war and although normally he found it difficult to speak, at that moment he was able to pronounce words completely, clearly, intensely. He had not come to flatter anybody. He simply wanted to acknowledge the courage they had shown in combat in a hostile environment and against an enemy that was technically superior; and tell them that as a professional soldier he hoped to never have to face such a brave enemy again, just so willing not to accept defeat. That he had felt a great deal of fear and had lost good and brave men fighting against good and brave young men.

He was not speaking in the name of anyone except his own, and he would not have been able to live in peace if he hadn't come to show his true and sincere respect to each and every one of them.

He looked at the thirty-odd young men in the audience who couldn't be more than twenty-two or twenty-three years old, and he saw they were all almost as moved as he was – he understood then that what he was doing was correct, and what had been torn inside was beginning to heal.

Nobody clapped, but the thirty or forty-odd young men approached one by one and shook his hand.

As he sat there in the bar, after five months of not having touched a drop of alcohol he felt tempted to ask for a glass of whisky.

He had begun drinking in Stanley (Puerto Argentino), almost a bottle of the Irish distilled whisky daily; two years had gone by and he had only stopped drinking when he began planning this trip.

He was now about to face the worst moment. In a way, he was back at the battlefield, to return something he'd brought from there in the hope of recovering his peace of mind.

The woman entered the bar with an energetic, firm step. She was so beautiful that he wished she was not the person he was expecting to see. She had dressed carefully, with a simple grey suit that highlighted her white skin and extraordinary green eyes that looked like emeralds because of her red hair neatly combed back into a pony tail.

He felt a cold shiver down his back when the young woman went up to the bar and very discreetly talked to the barman. The latter pointed him out to her.

He stood up and extended his hand to shake hers. She barely touched it, then she sat in the chair across from him.

Neither of them knew what to say to the other.

She knew who he was.

Should he offer her a drink?

They remained in silence for a few seconds, uneasy.

He then pulled out a brown paper envelope from a black briefcase he had placed on another chair, and from inside the envelope he took out a book - its covers clearly showed its age.

The woman's face then relaxes with a smile, both moved and sad.

"That book was my Dad's… And before that, my Dad's grandfather's…" she says, her finger tips brushing over the book's beautiful leather covers.

"I know… *Es un libro, antiguo, más de cien años…* This book must be over one hundred years old… You must excuse my bad Spanish…" And he doesn't know what else to say. I'm so sorry?

The silence between them deepens. He feels like swallowing a great big dose of whisky, but he holds back.

She can't or doesn't want to stop looking at the book's cover. It's clear she's also uncomfortable, that she doesn't know how to react to the man across from her, whom she too finds both elegant and attractive.

"My father inherited it from his grandfather… It's printed in Spain in 1877… I think the translation is very bad…"

"Shakespeare's "Henry V" – *Es un texto muy difícil,* a very difficult text! My favourite…"

He then plunges his hand back into the envelope.

The metal name-tags drop onto the table with a brief, sharp clink.

She stares at them at first with horror – but when she places her hand on them, her expression changes into a sad, emotional smile.

"He was my older brother… by just eleven months… He was very good to me, we were such friends… until… he asked my mother to send me out of the country. I hated him for that. Today I know that he probably saved my life. Do you understand?"

He nods. "Your brother was a brave man. *Sí, mucho coraje…* I don't have… I didn't have *el coraje de ver a tu madre…* see your mother."

When she closes her hand over the army name-tags, tears start running slowly down her cheeks.

She wants to ask. She wants to know. She then looks into the darkest, ocean-depth gaze of the Englishman's blue eyes across from her and understands completely. She sees the pain of this man who was once her brother's enemy and grasps perfectly that he's going beyond his courage, and rather than doing this he'd prefer to be jumping over the enemy's trenches.

"I… my Dad… *Mi padre y tu padre*… A whirlwind of thoughts run through his mind. He tries to find in English or Spanish the best words to explain what he'd like to say, but one after the other, the words slip away.

"I know, my Dad loved your Dad… When I was small your Dad came to my house," she says.

He opens his eyes and shakes his head. He stutters, then opens his wallet and shows her the tattered photograph he keeps there.

As he looks at the photo, he realizes that every person in that image is now dead. She realizes this at the same time.

With her index finger she gently strokes the photograph.

"Were you… there… at the time..? Were you with…? She shakes her hands, trying to exorcize the words: dying, death, combat, fighting.

He can say no more than what he's said. All the speeches he had thought up about the death of that brave Samurai had vanished from his mind as if a divine wind had blown through him. What kind of honour can you mention to a mother who waits, a sister who fears, a daughter who suffers? Courage? Sense of duty? Patriotism?

"*Tu hermano es*… Your brother is… was… *Fue un patriota*… A brave patriot."

"He was my only brother…" She is sobbing with a dignity which sears through him to the core of his soul.

He knows he cannot say more than what he's already said. Yet he goes beyond himself and speaks again.

"*Yo estuve ahí, con él*… I was there with him, until the end… *Hasta el último*… Until his last breath…"

"Did he suffer?"

"No… *Durmió*… He went to sleep… No pain… *Lo siento*… I'm so sorry, I was responsible…"

She interrupts him.

"No," she says, and repeats, "No."

She shakes her head emphatically.

"He was killed by a drunken general… A corrupt organization, with a killer's mentality… The greed, the need for power of a government convinced it would be governing forever…" And she repeats several times, "No, no, no…"

Finally, he takes out a small diary, with red leather covers, from which hangs a small magnifying glass.

She then starts sobbing for a second, she covers her face with one hand, while with the other she picks up the old diary and places it on the book.

"Thank you," she whispers. "For my mother this is like bringing his ashes home."

He finally feels then that his soul is free, that it will be possible to heal, that his debt on the battlefield is now paid.

She picks up all the objects and puts them away in the brown paper envelope, shakes his hand in silence and leaves.

He sits down again, rejects the temptation of asking for a tumbler of whisky, and convinces himself that the dead soldier has secured the best side of the bargain.

POST SCRIPTUM

Once the process of writing the novel had ended, it wasn't easy for me to let go of each of the protagonists' destinies.

Over the course of two years and in a very personal way, I was joined to the Evans family and the people who were connected to the development of each of the characters' stories.

I felt the need to scrutinize the life of each a little more, to know that finally the novel was finished. The story has its own life and it was very difficult for me to disengage myself from them, but of course I was obliged to end the story. In order to scare away the ghosts that hovered around, I researched a little more regarding the secondary characters who had had an important role in the lives of Gordon and Carlos Evans.

For example, the Iberra brothers abandoned their mythical corner store at the end of 1947; Rafael, *Maestro* Porrá's friend, died victim of a robbery in which he tried to defend himself using a knife. Two years later, the youngest brother, Mario, opened a passenger hotel in La Plata, capital of the province of Buenos Aires, a few blocks from the railway station. He died on his property of a heart attack on the evening of the start of the 1955 revolution.

Captain Farrington and Gordon Evans had no more contact with nor did they hear anything further regarding French officer François Ragon, with whom they fought in the north of France at the end of WWII.

At the end of the war the French government called upon him to halt the revolt in Algiers; fiercely unhappy with the actions of De Gaulle's followers, he requested his leave from active service but it was denied three times. At the end of 1952 he immigrated to Senegal, where he worked as a school teacher until he retired in 1968. He had two children – Max and Marie- and lived a long life surrounded by affectionate neighbours.

Korrum, Gordon's Pakistani subordinate who became a Colonel at Pakistan's independence, was promoted eventually to a General in the Army. He was hanged in 1970 for remaining loyal to the government of Ali Butho, a member of his clan.

Senghor, the other NCO who served under Gordon's orders in Asia, deserted the British Army a few days before India's Independence was declared. Some years later, with another name, he was revealed as the strong man in Burma (today Myanmar's) intelligence service; he died in 1989 in a questionable plane accident.

Mrs Cummins returned to India together with her eldest son in 1948, despite all the warnings regarding the dangers of an independent India.

Mr Cummins Jr., after his long recovery from the effects of his time as a prisoner of the Imperial Japanese army, managed to recover two trucks of the forty he had at the beginning of the war, and he returned to the transport business. With the financial support firstly of his mother and then of his father-in-law —he married the daughter of a rich businessman (the head of an ancient clan) from Rajajistan- in a few years he became one of the most important transport businessmen in all South East Asia.

Mrs Sylvia, as a wedding present for Gordon and Mariana, sent them a full set of cutlery —silver as well as another for daily use- manufactured by an extraordinary Hindu silversmith, a beautiful set which still lies in some dining-room cabinet drawer at the estancia "La Puerta del Chaco".

Harry Moore and Margaret Peebles' two sons grew and were educated under Mrs Cummins' secret protection. Jack, the eldest, graduated as a medical doctor at the beginning of the 1960s; a few years later he immigrated to Belize, where he lived and prospered until his sudden death when visiting his brother. Harry, the youngest, after his mother's death in 1962, sold the family's properties and went to live in Teruel, Spain. There he opened an inn, and after Franco's fall in the mid-'70s the inn became a gathering place for the international battalion survivors. Jack Moore's burial took place in Teruel, agreed upon with his Belize family.

Tony Farrington heard of his friend Gordon Evans' death through a brief letter from his widow; they continued exchanging Christmas and end-of-the-year cards until his death in 1981, from lung cancer.

Lieutenant Tony Farrington Jr. left the British Army in 1983. He visited Argentina three times -1984, when he met Bethan Evans; in 1988; and the last time was in 1992, when diplomatic relations had been re-established. He came with the intention of meeting with Malvinas war veterans, with some of whom a true friendship was born. In 1995 he was hired by the United Nations as an expert deminer and he worked in the international organization until his retirement in 2015.

Dr Manuel Rodrigué never recovered from his grandson's death in the Malvinas (Falklands) conflict; his state-of-mind was already weakened after the deaths of his son and his son-in-law -he never recovered and died in 1982.

Josefa Porrá de Evans, Grandmother Pepa, died two years later; Mariana Rodrigué de Evans took over her sister-in-law Cristina's care. She boarded her at a small mental health home run by the *Don* Orione institution in Claypole, and provided for all her physical and affectionate needs, visiting her regularly every week until Cristina's death in 2003.

Bethan Evans finally graduated as a medical doctor in 1991, and since then she works with the Medecins Sans Frontieres; after having spent more than 25 years working in the most dangerous war zones of the world, she became a consultant for the European Union in all humanitarian matters; she did not see Tony Farrington Jr. again. She stayed single, although she did adopt three Cameroon orphans who today are teenagers.

Carlos Evans' two younger sisters, Siwan and Eirin got married almost at the same time -1985- and had two children each. Siwan immigrated to the U.S.A. in 2001, Eirin moved to San Martín de los Andes, province of Neuquén, in 2003.

Mariana Rodrigué Evans did not visit her son's grave until 2007. Coincidentally or not, two weeks later Lieutenant Farrington Jr. also visited the cemetery on the same mission.

Arturo E. García Mendez

GLOSSARY

Chapter II, V, VIII

Alpargatas:	Rope-soled, flat canvas espadrilles.
Asado	Barbecue; any meat cooked on a grill over charcoal or wood.
Bombachas	Baggy work trousers, used by all who ride/work on horseback daily
Campo	Can refer to the countryside, or a property in the Argentine countryside, the alternative name for a farm or estancia.
Dulce de leche	A very sweet jam made from beaten milk and sugar, used on desserts or as a spread.
Estancia	Large farm in Argentine countryside; equivalent to an estate or ranch in the U.S.A.
Gaucho	Name for the Argentine countryside man who works on the estancias, usually an expert cattleman and horse-tamer; more than just a farm worker. Descended from original natives and often a Spaniard half-breed.
Grapa	Grappa, a colourless brandy distilled from fermented grape pulp.
Gringo	Name for a British or American "foreigner", equivalent to "Yankee".
Mate	It's the given name for the herbal infusion sucked from a gourd through a metal straw. The herb is called "yerba", and the gourd itself is the "mate", but informally the infusion is called "mate" as well. It is a shared drink, after pouring hot water into the gourd over the yerba it is passed from person to person; also taken individually. Any time of the day or night.
Padrino	Godfather
Pampas	Plains

Pampero	Strong westerly winds, coming from the pampas
Pizzería	Pizza shop
Poncho	Warm garment placed over the head covering most of the body, no sleeves
Puchero	Stew
Pulpería	Grocery in the countryside, also acting as a bar serving alcohol
Recado	A saddle used in Argentina, with trappings and no saddle tree, just joined by laced up leather thongs
Retruco	A call in the game of cards called "truco"
Siesta	Afternoon nap
Sudestada	Strong southeast winds bringing a storm
Sulky	Small, lightweight one-horse cart
Truco	Popular card game, with Spanish ads
Viejo	Informal name for father: "old man"

INDEX

ACKNOWLEDGEMENTS — *4*

I) SEPPUKU — *8*

II) BUSHIDO — *22*

III) HAGAKURE — *46*

IV) KATANA — *80*

V) GEISHA — *142*

VI) HAIKU — *166;*

VII) SATORI — *232*

VIII) RONIN — *268*

EPILOGUES — *324*

POST SCRIPTUM — *332*

GLOSSARY — *336*

Arturo Emilio García Méndez

I was born in the city of **Lomas de Zamora, Buenos Aires province**, on November 12, 1959.

Due to my father's work, a few days after I was born we moved to the city of Santa Fe; this was a Paradise for me, a friendly and kind world and I still consider it my childhood home town, and as *Borges* expressed, my first "**fatherland**" (Patria).

Leaving it was a painful experience. Cement streets are not always better than earth ones...

We moved to the city of **Adrogué, Buenos Aires province**, in 1966.

My primary education was at a school around the corner from home. I learnt to read very quickly and I remember the brands of cars prior to that. To read was a magical discovery, my entry into the world, my second birth of the many others that would come in the future. I got through secondary school ingloriously; I tried for an architect degree but fortunately for that art, I left before the first year had gone by.

I failed in an attempt to enter either the Argentine Navy or Army Schools.

Between the ages of 15 to 28 I travelled a great deal: first in **Argentina**, later I lived in **France**, in **Spain** and spent long periods in **Germany**.

I like films and ethnic music.

I've been writing since my teen years.

I began my career in journalism in the oldest newspaper in the European continent, "**El Diario de Barcelona de Avysos y Noticias**": Between 1981 and 1988 I became a reporter, with a mixed amount of luck; I participated in important projects such as the mythical women's magazine *Emanuelle*, directed by *Oskar Blotta* ("**Satiricón**" editor) and other lesser ones, such as the **Eroticón** and **La Cotorra** magazines.

Between 1989 and 2000 I worked in advertising, also with mixed fortune; in a small agency such as "*Brecher&Brecher*"; medium-sized such as *Publimén* and large ones, like *Atacama Publicidad Exterior*, which introduced mural publicity on a large scale in Argentina.

I worked as a copywriter, staff writer and I learnt computer design; I also designed and organized all the corporate communications and publicity for a multinational mortgage company.

The 2001 financial tornado in Argentina caught me at the startup of an outdoor advertising Company: I had the honour of going bankrupt together with **J.O. Pereyra**. I suffered the upheaval together with millions of other Argentines.

I spent ten years of my life reading nothing else but **Argentine** history, without writing a single word for a longer period, over 12 years.

In 1997 I became a father, the most important and best thing for me in my whole life.

When I was going through my worst period and I thought I had ruined everything, when I had no more hope and the way I lived only put me to shame, Gordon Evans whispered his whole story in just a few seconds. I started to write in longhand, because I had no computer, no electric light or water; I submerged myself in that story and for two years I wrote non-stop for several hours a day. From the moment I picked up my pencil and placed the point on the first 3 x 5 card my life began its healing process, slowly but surely and one after another, miracles took place. The hazardous first author's edition was financed by friends I thought I'd lost; the second edition was published by a small but prestigious publishing house; more friends helped me finance part of its translation and I then had the unconditional support of its translator, *Catherine Kirby*.

Nothing would have been possible without my family's steadfast help, my daughter's support and my clan's and my friends' safety network. The only thing I'm truly sorry about is not being able to share these days with my father, who didn't always agree with my choices yet was always ready to help me out.

After finishing "**A Samurai Destiny**" I published a small book of poems, "**De un silencio a otro**" ("From One Silence to Another") (ISBN 9781731236074) in which I expressed 30 years of poetic experiences/practice.

I am currently working on two novels, a book of short stories, I am gathering more poems for another book and eventually, an autobiography.

Made in the USA
Columbia, SC
17 February 2023